LEGENDS

THE MEN ON THE FLYING TRAPEZE

H.J. "Walt" Walter

Legends
Copyright © 2022 by H.J. "Walt" Walter

ISBN
978-1-958122-02-0 (Paperback)
978-1-958122-03-7 (Hardcover)
978-1-958122-01-3 (eBook)

Table of Contents

Acknowledgments

To my wife Dolores, for always being there when I needed guidance. For being so patient when things went wrong. For always supporting what I was doing no matter how much time it required writing alone in my study.

To a dear friend, Edie Fleeman, for helping in editing my book and making welcome suggestions to improve its content.

1

"The Beginning"

Flomaton, Alabama, November 20th, 1929

It was still the middle of the night when the Georgia/Florida train came to a stop in the railyards of Flomaton, Alabama. The old number 65 steam engine had been making about 22 miles per hour after Bob Fitzwater boarded in Atlanta, Georgia. Bob had been traveling on trains since he left pre-aviation screening some three days earlier, at Hampton, Virginia. Lieutenant Junior Grade Robert Fitzwater, U.S. Navy, had been ordered to report to the Commanding Officer, Naval Air Station, Pensacola, Florida, by November 23rd for duty involving flying to begin his new career to become a Naval Aviator and earning his wings of gold.

There was a lot of shaking, starting, and stopping while his Pullman berthing car was being decoupled from its present train and attached to its new engine. The porter told him there would be a two-hour delay while waiting for a train from New Orleans, Louisiana, to arrive with cars attached also going to Pensacola, Florida.

Bob tried to go back to sleep, but it was useless. He was now wide awake, so he just laid there deep in thought of what lay ahead when he reached his new base. After two hours, the starting and stopping began again and he felt the train lurch forward and begin to gain speed. As dawn approached, he arose, took a shower, dressed in his dress blue uniform, and made his way to the diner car.

They were serving breakfast, which he ordered along with a cup of coffee. As he was sipping his coffee while waiting for his breakfast, a young man entered the dining car who immediately caught his attention. He was attired in a naval officer's uniform with the rank of Ensign. He appeared to be looking for a place to sit. Bob waved and motioned for him to join him at his table.

As he approached, he extended his hand and introduced himself, "Hi, I'm Ensign Paul Day," he said.

They shook hands, "I'm Bob Fitzwater. Come join me and have a seat. I just ordered breakfast."

Paul took a seat opposite Bob "I'm on my way to Pensacola to start flight training," Paul said.

"That's a coincidence, I am too," Bob said. "And where might you be coming from?"

"That's a long story, Bob. I was stationed on the USS Lexington. We just returned from the Canal Zone where we participated in the latest fleet exercise and then I was sent to San Diego, California, for pre-aviation screening. I've been traveling across the country from the West Coast for a week now. Where are you coming from?" he asked.

"I was stationed on the USS Omaha out of Norfolk then went to Hampton, Virginia, for my pre-aviation screening. I've been on the train for only three days. It looks like we might be in the same training squadron. By the way, where are you from originally?" Bob asked.

"I was born and raised in Sault Ste. Marie. What class were you in at the academy? My class was '26," Paul said.

"Graduated class of '25, spent the first three years on the USS West Virginia then went to the Omaha," Bob said. "I'm originally from Bemidji, Minnesota."

"I went directly to the Lexington at Fore River Shipbuilding Company at Quincy, Massachusetts. In 1928 we were transferred to the West Coast at San Pedro, California, which is part of Los Angeles," Paul said.

"Sounds like we've had similar experiences, Paul. I guess I will go to my berth and pack my ditty bag and get ready to change trains."

Paul said, "I'll see you at the terminal, Bob. I guess we have to catch the Pensacola and Fort Barrancas Railroad out to the base. I understand it dates from 1870. It is an eight-mile line connecting Pensacola with Fort Barrancas which is on the edge of the Naval Air Station."

"See you then," Bob said.

Another hour of sand and pine trees passed before the train pulled into the station at Pensacola. There were only three tracks and one led to the base. Bob exited the train and walked over to the track for the Pensacola and Fort Barrancas Railroad. There he saw Paul and walked over and took a seat on the bench with him.

"Train's running a little late, Bob. I asked the Purser and he said it would be a half-hour before the train would arrive, so it appears we have some time to kill."

It was quite warm for a November day in the panhandle of Florida. The temperature was up to 75° and it was only 11:00 a.m. The humidity was low which made the situation bearable.

It was a Wednesday and the number of people waiting for the train was small. Only a few people were waiting on the platform to catch the train to the base.

Paul looked at Bob and said, "I'm thirsty. Wonder if we could get a soda or glass of water?"

Bob responded, "Let me go into the terminal and see what I can find, Paul. What would you prefer, a soft drink or water?"

"If you can get a soda, I would like a root beer," Paul said.

"Okay, I'll be back in a couple of minutes," Bob said.

As Bob walked into the terminal, he took in everything around him. He was a little surprised at how isolated this part of Florida seemed to be. There were no direct roads connecting it with other large cities and no airline service into their airport. The base was 8 miles from town and roads to it were unimproved. He was surprised by the number of pine trees he had seen on this trip. He had expected to see more palm trees.

He arrived in the terminal and spotted the food vendor where he purchased two bottles of root beer and went back down the platform to where Paul was sitting. There was a roof over the platform, which at least kept them out of the sun.

Handing the bottle to Paul, "Here ya' go, Paul. It's almost a little cold but anyway it's wet."

Paul took it from Bob. "Thanks, Bob," he said.

They sat quietly drinking their root beer and taking in their surroundings.

The train pulled in from the base and off-loaded its passengers and cargo. The conductor stuck his head out of one of the car stairs, "All 'board," he yelled out to the people waiting on the platform.

Paul and Bob grabbed their small travel bags and climbed aboard. There were only two passenger cars, so they took seats in the rear car. The baggage personnel loaded the baggage and cargo.

The train lurched forward and started its eight-mile trip to the naval base.

On arrival at the base, it came to a stop amongst a few buildings. There was no terminal, only a small platform for passengers to load and unload. The two naval officers picked up their travel bags and walked down the three stairs of the car onto the platform. There was a small building and a bulletin board next to the loading platform. Paul spied a base map on the bulletin board and they walked over to look at it. They figured it might give them some information on where to go to check into their new command and where the Bachelor Officers Quarters (BOQ) might be. It was of no help, so they turned to find another source of information. Bob saw a Shore-Patrol Petty Officer standing at the end of the platform. They walked over, and after exchanging hand salutes, they asked directions to the base personnel office. After receiving directions, they retrieved their luggage and began their trek to the personnel office.

On arrival in the personnel office, they presented their orders, and after some time, were given a check-in sheet and directions to the BOQ. Their paperwork contained a small map of the base and after locating the BOQ (Building 16), they walked over and checked in at the main desk. The steward's mate assigned them adjoining rooms with a shared bathroom.

They discussed their check-in and decided it was an all-day affair, so they put it off until the next day. They sat in Bob's room and chatted a little bit. It was still early afternoon and the officer's Mess was a closed Mess of which one had to be a member to eat so they found the main office where they joined the Mess. They spent the remainder of the afternoon lounging around, mostly talking about their upcoming adventure.

The two of them had dinner in the officer's Mess and afterward spent some time in the main lobby area just outside the dining room. The area was fitted with large lounge chairs, couches, and coffee tables, a place where they could get comfortable. They met a few other officers undergoing flight training and they spent the evening finding out more about what was in store for them. Two of the officers they met were still in ground school while a couple of others were halfway through their basic training. They asked many questions during the conversations.

Next morning

The next morning, after breakfast, they put on the uniform of the day, dress blues, and began their base check-in. It was a long extended process. They started at the post office filling out their locator card so mail could be forwarded to the BOQ. Next was the chapel, security, and several other offices. Before lunch, they finally reached the pre-flight school. The class assignment was class 47-29. Instruction would begin on Monday morning at 0800. The final stop was the executive officer's office where they met the Executive Officer, Lieutenant Commander Al Smith, who then took them into the commanding officer's office where they met the Commanding Officer, Commander Ed Barkley. Lieutenant Commander Smith had been Commanding Officer of Fighter Squadron Ten and had flown off USS Lexington while Commander Barkley was a seaplane pilot who had been stationed in Panama at Naval Station Coco Solo in the Canal Zone. Both were experienced Naval Aviators with more than 3000 hours of flight time.

The Commanding Officer welcomed them and made them feel comfortable. He told them this would be a long hard process where usually only 30% of those entering completed the curriculum and earned their wings. The Commanding Officer was one of the first naval officers to earn his wings as was the Executive Officer. After discussing their hometowns with them for a few minutes, the Commanding Officer rose, as did everyone else, and they were excused.

They still had to turn in their check-in sheet to Officer Personnel before their check-in would be complete. They were walking across the unpaved parking lot when out of the blue and going at a high rate of speed, a 1924 Alfa Romeo RM sports car skided its tires and spun into a parking space, just missing the two of them by a mere few feet.

Bob's a little pissed and cries out, "Hey sailor where are you goin' in such a hell-of-a-hurry?"

A young Ensign stepped out of the car. He stood about 6' tall with short blonde hair, "Sorry, Sir, I am running a little late and need to check in before they close for the day." He put on his hard hat and saluted, "I'm Walt, Walt Pellman. I'm sorry I upset you, Sir."

Bob returned his salute and stuck out his hand, "I'm Bob Fitzwater and this is my friend Paul Day. Your apology is accepted," and in a semijoking tone said, "and don't let it happen again."

"Thanks, Bob, I'll probably see you around. I'm checking in to flight school to become a Naval Aviator."

"Yeah, you probably will see us around. We're just finishing checking-in to the base for flight school," Bob advised.

Paul liked this brash young Ensign. "We're in rooms 115 and 117 at the Q. Ask for a room near ours as we'll probably be in the same preflight class."

"Okay, will do," Walt said.

The three of them entered the building. Paul and Bob turned in their sheets while Walt gave the Yeoman his orders and officer's record to begin his check-in procedure.

Bob and Paul left and began the long walk back to the BOQ.

When Walt arrived at the BOQ, he checked in with the desk and was assigned room 116, just across the hall from Bob and Paul. He also joined the Mess and was placed on the approved list so he could eat his meals there.

Dinnertime was approaching and he knocked on Paul's door and asked, "You guys ready for some chow?"

Paul and Bob joined Walt as they walked down for dinner. They had donned their civilian clothes, and as it turned out, were all dressed practically the same. Each had on a white shirt and tie with gray slacks and a navy blue sport jacket. It was customary to dine in the Mess with a coat and tie.

Walt broke the ice, "You guys look spiffy tonight. Must have shopped at my tailor shop."

As it turned out they had all purchased their outfits at the base PX before they departed for Pensacola.

Over dinner, they grilled Walt on the usual, where was his last duty station, his hometown, naval academy class, and other family facts.

Seems Walt was academy class of '27 and had been assigned as First Lieutenant on the USS Mississippi, homeported in San Pedro. Walt had also taken his pre-aviation screening in San Diego, California. Walt indicated he had reported back to his ship for three months after screening to complete a Caribbean Cruise before his relief reported aboard. Paul and Walt began to compare notes on Los Angeles since they were both stationed in San Pedro at the same time although on different ships.

Walt was originally from Newport, Rhode Island, and his father was President of Socony Oil Company. His upbringing was quite different from Bob and Paul's as he had been a member of the socially wealthy elite when he went to the Naval Academy. He was used to being catered to during his entire life, but that was about to change.

After dinner, the three of them adjourned to the BOQ bar, which they had recently discovered, and sat down for an after-dinner libation. Since alcohol was prohibited, they had lemonade instead. The sea stories were hot and heavy with each man trying to outdo the other in telling his tall tale. They met other flight students who were in various stages of the flight program on the base. Many questions were asked and answered, but none gave them the true feel of what was in store for them. They would have to experience it personally before they could put words and thoughts to flying a Navy airplane.

Walt would need to finish his check-in during his spare time and pre-flight classes started early Monday morning.

Monday Morning

Morning broke clear and warm for a late November day. After breakfast, the three young naval officers walked briskly over to the school's command building to start their pre-flight classes. On the way, they rubbernecked at the Boeing NBs and Curtis N-9s flying over the base. They were ready to fly but that would have to wait. The ground school would be at least twelve weeks and plenty to learn.

When they arrived, they discovered there would be eight students including them in their class. Turns out Bob Fitzwater was the senior student by date of rank and was designated the class leader. They all checked in with the administration office and were directed to Room 104 after completing all the paperwork.

Upon entering Room 104, they took their seats on the tiered seating. The classroom was set up for 20 students. It almost felt vacant with only eight of them in attendance. Within ten minutes, their two main instructors entered. Bob called everyone to attention. Lieutenant Russell stood at the podium and told the class to be seated. He introduced himself and in turn introduced Chief Petty Officer Bryan Hurtsliff. Turned out Lieutenant Russell was from the Hamptons on Long Island, New York, while Chief Hurtsliff was from Hope, Arkansas.

Lieutenant Russell went through an outline of the curriculum which consisted of aircraft nomenclature, aerodynamics, aircraft engines, aerial navigation, meteorology, and Morse code. The students were told they would need to be able to read code at ten words per minute, which turned out to be a formidable task. In addition PT classes would be required three times per week.

After the formal introductions, the class took a coffee break, and upon reassembling, Chief Hurtsliff took to the podium.

Using an easel and large hand-lettered posters, he began their indoctrination into aircraft nomenclature. In their prescreening before they came to Pensacola, all the students had been tested on what parts made up an aircraft however now they got into definitions of gross weight, empty weight, cruising radius, and how engines operated. They would be flying the Boeing NB-1. Chief Hurtsliff indicated that this aircraft might have one of two different engines. Some were equipped with the Lawrence J1 radial engine while others were equipped with war surplus V-8 engines. Power for both was in the 200-horsepower range which gave them a maximum speed of 100 miles per hour and a service ceiling of 10,200'. They would have practical work on tearing down an engine as the course progressed so they could see how it was constructed and operated. All engines were furnished with a direct current generator which supplied six volts to the electrical system of the aircraft. All aircraft were being retrofitted with cockpit lighting for night flying as the Bureau of Aeronautics had mandated each pilot have ten hours of night flying before graduation.

The students were warned about spinning this aircraft as some of the earlier aircraft would not spin, but those which would be most times unable to recover from a spin. Paul whispered to Walt, "remind me not to attempt that maneuver."

Lunchtime was approaching, and after they finished the nomenclature class, they broke for lunch. The students all walked back to the BOQ and entered the officer's Mess. It was a single menu and they were quickly served a soup and sandwich. There was no time for relaxing as they were quickly back to begin the afternoon classes consisting of meteorology and copying Morse code. After class was over, they wandered back to the BOQ.

The three of them decided to stop in for a lemonade before dinner. They sat in the corner, and after they were served, Bob spoke up. "Well, what did you think of our first day back to school?" he said.

"I'm having trouble understanding Chief Hurtsliff," Walt said. "He doesn't speak my kind of English."

"He probably doesn't understand your New England English either, Walt," Paul observed. "You'll just have to muddle through it."

"I'll depend on you guys to take good notes to get me through," Walt responded. "Getting through the code test is going to be tough though. I'm getting all those dashes and dots mixed up right now."

"You'll have plenty of time to master that. We have twelve weeks and I hear you can work overtime after we start flying to pass the test," Bob said.

"From what I gathered it looks like the NB-1 will be a snap to fly except for the stupid spin characteristics of the plane," Paul observed.

"I'm not worried about flying right now," Bob chimed in. "I'm concerned about getting through pre-flight. Are you guys about ready for dinner?"

Both Walt and Paul indicated they were ready, so they finished their drinks and walked over to the Mess dining room. After dinner, they sat down in the lobby and engaged in more conversation with other flight students. Of course, the conversation centered around flying and the United States Navy. Walt had heard from his family and asked the others if they had heard about the stock market crash. None of the others had so Walt described what was occurring and how it was affecting his family. He said his father had predicted a tough financial time for a lot of families soon.

Paul was sometimes the center of the discussion in that his tour on the USS Lexington was of great interest to all, as many of the students longed to be a carrier pilot. Paul was great at storytelling, usually narrating tales about the landings and take-offs. Soon discussion centered around the Landing Signal Officer.

Paul had done his research and related how Commander Willing became known as the first LSO. As Executive Officer of USS Langley, Commander Willing studied carrier landings by having them filmed with a hand-held movie camera. He next got into the habit of standing on the flight deck platform on the aft port side of the ship. The pilots became used to him standing there as they lost sight of the deck when their engine blocked it out when they were on short final. Soon the pilots and Commander Willing developed some standard signals designed to help them improve their approach and landing. Paul related that it was said Commander Willing first used a couple of sailor's white hats in each hand to signal pilots. Next were a couple of solid round paddles for signaling. That proved difficult because the wind was constantly trying to blow the paddles out of his hand, so a smart engineman developed a round wire paddle with cloth strips stretched across to let the air blow through the paddles. Paul indicated these were paddles still in use on the Lexington.

A few questions centered around the arresting gear which Paul had not studied very well, but told the questioners that it was electrically operated with hydraulic sheaves to help stop the aircraft as the wire was pulled out. That seemed to answer all the questions, but Paul was still responding well into the evening. He became quite popular and was considered the carrier expert by most flight students.

2

"A CLOSE ENCOUNTER"

Pensacola, Florida

Bob, Paul, and Walt struggled through the pre-flight subjects during the next few weeks, but were mastering them as time went on. Walt particularly enjoyed the hands-on aircraft engine sessions. Tearing down an engine fascinated him and he thrived at soaking up the knowledge learned from this particular activity. Bob seemed to enjoy the sessions in the code room, copying dots and dashes at a high rate of speed. Meanwhile, Paul liked the class in meteorology and felt it to be his most challenging subject.

They had been at it for almost four weeks and Christmas was approaching. Both Bob and Paul had talked to their families, wishing them a Merry Christmas and telling them they would not make it home for the holidays. They discussed what each was planning for the holidays. It was agreed by all of them that it was too much of a trip to go home for the holidays as it would entail four to five days each way to reach their homes and they would have only nine days off anyway.

A trip to New Orleans seemed to be their best plan. They decided to stay at the Roosevelt Hotel. Walt said he would contact his father and ask him to get them a reservation. The plan was to stay seven days beginning on the 26th of December and returning to Pensacola on January 2nd.

The last day of classes was noon on the 24th so the three naval officers just relaxed that afternoon and helped Walt get his car in shape for the trip to New Orleans.

Walt took care of all the engine needs including changing the oil while Paul and Bob cleaned the interior and finally cleaned and waxed the exterior. When they finished, the black 1924 Alfa Romeo RM sports car sparkled like a brand-new car.

Dinner in the Mess was relatively quiet as many of the officers had already departed for their Christmas leave. Christmas day was even quieter as the Mess was even more vacant. During the day Walt suggested a short trip out to Corry Station to look at the F-4B fighters currently being used as advanced trainers.

After lunch, the three of them piled into the Alfa Romeo and headed off to Corry Station. It was only an eight-mile drive and soon they were out on the flight line climbing into the cockpit of one of the F-4Bs. These were the first F-4Bs produced for the U.S. Navy. They were fabric covered with a 500 horsepower Pratt and Whitney engine and one centermounted .30 caliber (7.62mm) machine gun just in front of the cockpit. It was a lot of fun just sitting in the cockpit imagining flying the airplane and then landing on a carrier. They were all hoping that it would happen one day and soon.

After leaving Corry Field they ventured into downtown Pensacola to see what the town looked like. It was beginning to look like a Navy town and much advertising in the store windows was directed towards attracting Navy men in to buy their products. The town was mostly deserted as the streets were fairly empty of people and cars, and even the trolleys were sparsely occupied. The few restaurants in town were closed for the holiday. After an hour of cruising around, Walt headed back to the base but not before stopping to fill up the gas tank with fuel. They were pretty much ready to depart for New Orleans in the morning.

Back on base, it was approaching dinnertime so they went into the BOQ and dressed for dinner. The Mess put on a great feast for the few officers who were still there and they all walked away having eaten too much. The Mess provided cigars for after dinner so these naval officers went into the front sitting room, lit up their cigars, sat down, and relaxed. The evening's discussion centered around their upcoming trip.

They all lamented about having to miss Christmas with their families but it was soon forgotten as they contemplated their trip to Louisiana. During the discussion, Walt had gone back to his room and retrieved the road maps showing the route to New Orleans. He laid them on the coffee table so all three of them could study them. Their route would take them mostly on Federal Highway 90 through southwest Florida into Mobile, Alabama, then into Gulfport and Bay St. Louis, Mississippi, and finally into New Orleans. They figured the trip to take them at least seven hours so they planned to leave by 7 o'clock Central Standard Time, which would put them in New Orleans by 4.

It was getting late into the evening and each had some packing left to do so they walked back to their rooms, wishing each other a "Merry Christmas", and settled in for the night.

Pensacola, Florida

The three young naval officers were up early, had breakfast, and packed Walt's car for the trip to New Orleans. It was close to 8 as they drove out the main gate of the naval air station. Walt was at the wheel with Bob in the copilot's seat doing the navigation while Paul was in the back seat struggling to get comfortable amongst the luggage. He would do most of the kibitzing during the trip.

They traveled out past Corry Station then onto a country road and finally reached Federal Highway 90. In about an hour they crossed the Chattahoochee River and entered the city of Mobile, Alabama. It was a quiet port city on the Gulf of Mexico. The streets were tree-lined with beautiful live oaks and majestic mansions. However, as they proceeded downtown, the city took on more of a working-class venue with warehouses and small businesses. Many were obviously out of business since the Wall Street market crash on October 29th. They noticed a lot of people standing in lines looking for work and some just for food. Many were just loitering on street-corners as there was little work for anyone.

Paul remarked that they sure were lucky to be in the Navy and having a vocation ensuring a roof over their heads and a place to eat. Shortly they were out of Mobile and headed for Biloxi, Mississippi. It was approaching 10 o'clock and time for a pee. Walt spied a gas station so he pulled in and asked the attendant to "fill-er-up." Meanwhile, each, in turn, used the head (bathroom for civilians). Bob purchased three Nehi sodas, which the gas station owner had on ice in an old tub.

Walt also had the attendant check the engine oil. He reported to Walt that it was just a little low but not even a quart so no oil was added. Walt's engine was one of Alfa Romeo's racing engines and the tolerances of the parts were much more precise resulting in very little leakage of oil and small burning of oil. After finishing their sodas, they once again piled into the car and continued on their way to New Orleans.

After passing Gulfport, they soon entered Louisiana, and about 1:30 p.m., they passed the city limits of New Orleans. Bob had the city map in his lap and he and Paul were searching for street signs so Bob could direct them to the Roosevelt Hotel. Ah, Roosevelt Way was spotted and Walt pulled up to the entrance of the hotel.

They were quickly swarmed over by bellhops looking to take care of their luggage and valet service wanting to park the car. Walt turned over the keys, tipped the valet service, and walked into the lobby with Bob and Paul in tow. The lobby was magnificent. It was finished off in dark oak paneling, beautiful glass chandeliers, thick carpets, and some of the most gorgeous furniture the three of them had ever seen. They proceeded over to the check-in counter where Walt identified himself, which seemed to cause the staff to want to do everything in their power to serve him and his two friends. They were given a suite on the sixth floor with two bedrooms, a bathroom, and a connecting sitting room. The sitting room was more like the lobby area of the BOQ. It was spacious and well fitted with modern up-to-date furniture. It also was equipped with a telephone, which was a luxury none of them had ever experienced. The room faced to the southwest, giving them a beautiful view of Canal Street, Bourbon Street, and the Mississippi River. On the table were a complimentary fruit basket and some cheese and crackers.

The Bellhop delivered the luggage and put it in the appropriate bedrooms for each of them. Walt provided a tip for the Bellhop and ordered a pitcher of iced tea. He would have preferred a beer, but prohibition was still in effect so tea would have to do.

Somebody turned on the radio and AM station WWL came alive with Jazz from Benny Berrigan. He was followed by some of the other greats of the day including Red McKenzie and guitarist Eddie Condon and featuring a young drummer named Gene Krupa. There were other recordings by musicians from the Chicago jazz scene such as Bix Beiderbecke, these recordings being examples of Chicago-style jazz. The station played such numbers as "China Boy", "Sugar", "Nobody's Sweetheart", and "Liza".

During a break in the music, the station advertised the upcoming broadcast that evening featuring Duke Ellington would be coming to the audience from the Blue Room of the Roosevelt Hotel. Paul piped up and said, "Sounds like the place to go after dinner tonight. What ya say, guys?"

Walt and Bob nodded in agreement.

The tea arrived and the three dug into the cheese and crackers and some of the fruit basket.

Discussion about where to go to dinner was the centerpiece of their interaction. The three of them decided on Antoine's, a quaint French restaurant on St. Louis Street. Time was approaching 7:00 p.m. and they had decided on a late supper. There was a lot of banter on whether they should try to find a speakeasy and imbibe in a few alcoholic drinks. Bob pointed out that being arrested in a speakeasy might affect their careers and was it worth it. Walt said it probably was since he had already been in some and tasted alcohol. Bob and Paul had been drinking since they joined the Navy and thought it was a great idea.

They dressed for dinner, wearing their usual white shirt and tie along with gray slacks and their blue blazer. Antoine's was close by so they walked. They arrived at Antoine's about 8:00 p.m. and were told a table would be available in about 45 minutes. The waiter directed them to the ladies' room and said he would find them when their table was ready. At Antoine's, a door in the ladies' room directed one to a secret bar called the Mystery Room, where it was no mystery what went into one's coffee cup.

Upon entering the Mystery Room, they found a place at a table off in a corner where Paul had spied an exit door. He figured if the place were raided they had a good chance of making it out without being arrested. Since Bob and Paul didn't know much about alcoholic drinks, Walt suggested they start with a Rum and Coke drink as that is what he had while on vacation with his family in the Caribbean. The waiter brought them each a drink and they paid cash as requested.

The place was jumping. A small band was blaring out jazz while a bunch of flappers was hitting the dance floor and "cutting a rug." The room was smoke-filled as most of the men were puffing on cigarettes or cigars. For the three of them, it was exciting as they had never experienced anything like this before.

Time passed quickly and finally, the maitre-d' found them and directed them to their dining table. Antoine's lived up to their reputation. The table was set with a very clean and pressed white tablecloth along with white linen napkins for each place setting. English silverware was used for the place settings while old English silver accessories were used for the salt, pepper, and sugar bowl. The busboy filled their glasses, one with water and the other iced tea, using a sterling silver pitcher. The waiter brought the butter served in a silver butter dish probably imported from England and manufactured before 1875. All in all, it was an elegant beginning. The three men were given a menu, which was encased in a leather binding.

Paul spoke up, "Damn, do you see the prices on this menu?"

Walt responded. "Don't worry about that, Paul. I didn't tell you guys but my old man said he would foot the bill and treat us to a well- earned vacation, so don't hold back. Order what you like."

"That's mighty nice of him," Bob said.

"I think I'll get seafood," Walt said. "Haven't had much of that since I left California."

"I'm in for the steak, I guess," Paul added.

The waiter returned to their table, "Gentleman, are you ready to order?" he asked. Turning to Bob, "What would you like for an appetizer, Sir?"

"Let's start with some French onion soup followed by a shrimp cocktail," Bob said.

"And for your main course?" the waiter asked.

"I'll have the 8-ounce fillet mignon, medium rare with the bearnaise sauce, mashed potatoes, and steamed okra," Bob said.

"Sir, a salad comes with the dinner. What's your choice?"

"I'll have the Betty salad," Bob responded.

Next was Paul. "I'll have the 10 ounce New York steak, rare, with hash browns and corn."

"Would you like an appetizer, Sir?" the waiter asked.

"Yeah, start me off with a bowl of clam chowder and a shrimp cocktail," Paul said.

"And for your salad?" the waiter queried.

"Make it a tossed salad with oil and vinegar," Paul said.

Walt was last to order. He chose the shrimp cocktail and French onion soup for starters followed by the main course of sea bass along with fried okra, coleslaw, and French fries. For a salad, he chose the house salad with French dressing.

The waiter thanked them for their orders, and as soon as he left the table, another waiter brought them some cornbread, sweet pickles, cheese bits, and bread and butter pickles.

The soup course was quickly served followed by shrimp cocktails all around. The three of them were getting into the meal. The main course was served and once again they indulged themselves in dining splendor.

There was little conversation during dinner as each was enjoying eating, leaving little time for talking.

There was a small discussion concerning a couple of lovely ladies in the room, but was quickly dismissed when their parents were spotted with them. None of these fledgling Naval Aviators were currently dating a specific lady and were free to play the field.

They finished their dinner off with a dessert of New York cheesecake and a cup of Cajun coffee.

Paul spoke first, "Why don't we go back to the Mystery room for a nightcap before we hit the midnight show at the Blue Room?" he mused.

"Sounds like a plan," Bob said.

The waiter brought the check and Walt opened his wallet, took out some bills, and paid the check.

"Are ya sure we can't contribute?" Bob asked.

"Nah, the old man sent me enough to take care of things," Walt responded.

The three of them headed off to the Mystery Room for a nightcap before they returned to the Roosevelt Hotel for the midnight show. They went through the ladies' room and the back door and entered the Mystery Room. As they entered, Paul spotted an empty table and directed Walt and Bob in that direction. They sat down and ordered a drink. Next to them was a table of three young ladies about their ages. Walt engaged them in conversation and found they were visiting from Kansas. Within a few minutes, he invited them to pull up their chairs at Walt's table.

Walt proceeded to introduce everyone.

"Hey, guys, I want you to meet Jo, Jane, and Zimmy. Ladies, this is Bob and he's Paul. They all engaged in the conversation, but soon Bob was paired with Jo, Paul with Jane, and Walt with Zimmy. The jazz band was still playing and soon the ladies had their guys up and dancing the Charleston. They were having such a great time that they missed the midnight show at the Roosevelt Hotel. As the evening slipped by, it was time to say goodnight so the guys walked the ladies back to their hotel. It was just down the street from the Roosevelt. Being the gentlemen that they were, they invited the ladies to brunch at 11:00 a.m. at the Roosevelt.

As they walked back to the hotel, the conversation was very animated. The three men had a great time and looked forward to more encounters with these beautiful women from Kansas.

The next morning the three naval officers were in the lobby well before 11:00 a.m. in anticipation of their meeting the ladies for breakfast. Shortly after 11 o'clock in walked Jo, Jane, and Zimmy. They were stunning in their long dresses, high heeled shoes.

Walt made it a point to tell Zimmy she was looking classy in her attire. He grasped her hand and led the group into the dining room for brunch. Once seated, the interaction was extensive and the chatter among all parties was fast and furious. The waiter interrupted in a loud voice asking if they would like to order. Walt took charge and ordered everything on the brunch menu and directed it be served family-style. That way they could pick and choose what each wished to eat and not be restricted by individual ordering.

The six of them were seated at a huge table and a couple of waiters set the breakfast dishes on the table. There was everything from oatmeal to pancakes to Belgian waffles and omelets.

During breakfast, there was much giggling, laughing, and lots of good conversation. They all hit it off well and brunch lasted into the afternoon.

The guys and ladies spent the next few days doing things together and visiting all the tourist sights. There was little time for getting to know the ladies more personally as they stuck together and never allowed the guys to be with them separately. They just decided to enjoy each other's company and settled for a short relationship as the ladies would be going back to Kansas the day after New Year's.

During the week, they visited Pat O'Brian's club and restaurant. It was a great experience as O'Brian's had a new young piano player who was known by only one name, Mercedes. She could play any song that was written in the 20th century, a phenomenal talent.

For New Year's Eve, Walt made plans for the six of them for the Blue Room of the Roosevelt Hotel. They were featuring Count Basie and his orchestra and a young trumpet player, Louis Armstrong.

There was much anticipation of the evening to come. The three naval officers had brought their evening dress uniforms in preparation for New Year in New Orleans. That meant soft shirts with French cuffs with cuff links, button studs, a white vest, white suspenders, a bow tie, and black shoes topped off by navy blue pants and dinner dress blue jacket. It was the Navy's answer to a civilian tuxedo.

Time was approaching 8:30 p.m. and they were meeting the ladies at 9 o'clock. They took the elevator to the lobby and decided to sit while they waited. The ladies were generally a few minutes late so they expected them to walk in about 9:10 p.m. At the appointed hour, the ladies walked into the lobby. Their entrance was certainly a showstopper. The three of them were stunning in their formal evening gowns and the guys greeted them with great anticipation. Each was presented a corsage that was pinned to the upper right shoulder of the dress. The corsages were all roses, with Zimmy's red, Jo's white, and Jane's blue. Each girl was offered a left arm to latch onto as they walked toward the elevator. As they exited the elevator, there was a photographer who asked if they would like their pictures taken. They all opted for an individual couple's picture as well as a group picture. The photographer said she would print two pictures of each couple and six group pictures so each could have one.

The maitre-d' met them at the door and seated them in the center of the room next to the dance floor. Since dinner was on Walt's old man, they ordered the best in the house. The ladies selected the lobster tail as that was almost unheard of in Kansas. The guys selected the fillet mignon. Walt had previously given the waiter a fifty-dollar bill for a bottle of wine. It was brought out in a coffee server and poured into their coffee cups to help disguise what was being served. Bob observed that prohibition sure was a pain in the ass.

There was a local band playing for background music and dancing. There wasn't much cross-table conversation as each couple was engaged in their own. Walt had expressed to Bob and Paul that he thought he could fall for Zimmy given half a chance, but he realized this was a passing fancy as the ladies would be going back to Kansas in two days and the guys would be returning to Pensacola to continue their flight training. Paul and Bob had also agreed with Walt so the relationships remained platonic.

After dinner, dancing was on the agenda and the couples danced almost every dance. Around 11:00 p.m., Count Basie and his band took the stage and began their show. Louis Armstrong performed a few numbers while Jan Ingraham sang a few of the songs. In between those performances, dancing was the order of the day.

As midnight approached, coffee cups were refilled and, on the stroke of midnight, Count Basie's band played Auld Lang Syne. Confetti and balloons were released from the ceiling and a toast by Jane to the new year was hoisted with a long lingering kiss given by the ladies to the guys.

The couples were enjoying each other's company and so they danced into the wee hours of the morning. By 6:00 a.m., they were exhausted and the band finally played "Goodnight Ladies." This was the cue that the evening was over. Paul suggested a little breakfast before they took the ladies back to their hotel and said their final goodbyes.

They boarded the elevator and headed for the restaurant on the first floor. On arrival, they were greeted and seated at a table near the windows. They ordered a small breakfast of eggs and bacon while still carrying on their animated conversations. Around 7:00 a.m., the sun broke over the eastern horizon and showed through the windows. After breakfast, Bob went up to their room and retrieved their uniform hats. They could not go outside without them as that would put them out of uniform and their training would not let them do that. The ladies latched onto their guy's hands and they walked a couple of blocks to their hotel hand in hand. When they arrived in the lobby, Bob, Paul and Walt continued their conversations with their dates. Each couple drifted off into separate corners of the lobby. Walt and Zimmy had real feelings for each other and they were wrapped tightly around each other, embraced in a long lingering kiss. Paul and Bob were likewise engaged. None of them wanted it to end, but eventually, the guys kissed the ladies goodbye with promises to write to each other.

Walking back to the hotel, they were all in a great mood discussing their great evening with the ladies. Upon reaching their suite, everyone collapsed in bed and were quickly overcome by sheer exhaustion.

After some eight hours of sound sleep, Bob was the first to awake driven by the urge to empty his bladder. He tiptoed into the bathroom so as not to wake Paul and Walt. However, when he finished, he flushed the toilet, which was loud enough to wake his friends.

While standing in the middle of their sitting room, Paul spoke first, "Hey Bob, what the hell are you doing up so early and making all that noise?"

"Yeah, Bob, I could have slept another five hours," Walt added.

"Well, nature called and I couldn't lay in bed any longer so I took action," Bob responded.

"All right, you're forgiven. What the hell time is it anyway?" Paul asked.

"I see the mantle clock over there says it's almost five o'clock. Looks like we slept about eight hours," Walt said.

After each took his turn in the bathroom, the conversation continued.

"What say, how about we order room service? I don't feel like getting dressed and going down to the dining room," Walt interjected.

Bob chimed in, "That sounds like a great idea. Remind me to thank your old man when I get to meet him, Walt."

"Yeah, me too," Paul said.

"Well, here's the menu. Look it over and we'll order," Walt said.

The three of them studied the menu. Finally, Walt spoke up, "How about we order the cold cuts and fruit bowl? I don't feel like a big meal or heavy food."

"Sounds like a plan," Bob answered.

Walt picked up the phone and called room service. About twenty minutes later there was a knock on the door and Paul invited the room service waiter into the room. The waiter wheeled in the cart with the cold cuts platter along with the fruit bowl and some hot tea.

Walt signed the check. Along with the cold cuts were some Ritz crackers, sliced bread, and a few condiments, mustard, catsup, and mayonnaise. The three of them dug into the food while Bob then poured each a cup of tea.

With the conversation bolstered mainly by their experience with the ladies, it continued well into the evening.

Finally, Paul stated the obvious, "We better get packing, guys. We are going to need to leave early tomorrow for Pensacola."

"Yeah, you're right, Paul," Bob observed, "Tuesday will be back to class for us."

Walt chimed in, "Believe it or not, I'm looking forward to doing just that. The sooner I finish ground school, the sooner I get in a cockpit."

Paul responded, "I like that plan, Walt. Can't wait to strap on that baby and pour the coal to it. I get goosebumps just thinking about flying."

The three of them finished their packing and settled back down jawing about their New Orleans experience and the ladies.

3

"FLIGHT AT LAST"

New Orleans, Louisiana

The next morning, they climbed into Walt's car and headed for Pensacola. Everything went smoothly and late in the day they were pulling into the parking lot of the BOQ at Naval Air Station Pensacola.

Tuesday morning they were all up early, had breakfast in the Mess, and were off to class in the preflight building. They had finished their powerplants class and were now studying basic airframes and aerodynamics. Navigation and weather were still taking a couple of hours a day as was copying Morse code in the code room. Paul was having a little difficulty with code while Walt and Bob breezed through and were up to eight words a minute. The goal was to reach ten words a minute and then be tested.

They studied the nomenclature of the NB-1 aircraft and the aerodynamics associated with it. Walt was impressed with the powerplant. It was a Lawrence J-1 model producing 200 horsepower resulting in a top speed of 100 miles per hour. It was a two-cockpit, equal-span biplane of conventional configuration with interchangeable wheeled and float undercarriage. The pilot and instructor sat in tandem, open cockpits with the student in the forward cockpit and the instructor in the rear.

Bob and Walt finally passed the code test, Bob at 12 words per minute and Walt at 15. As the weeks passed they were now down to studying navigation and weather. Since it was being applied to aviation, it was determined that weather would now be known as Aerology. The three of them had little trouble with navigation as each had been exposed to it aboard ship during their tours.

Social life for these naval officers was boring. There were speakeasies in town and in the county of Escambia, but as naval officers, if they were caught in a police raid in a speakeasy, their careers would be over, so they decided not to frequent these dens of iniquity. To cater to their young naval officers, the commanding officer of the Naval Air Station allowed the students from the Gulf Park College for Women to attend dances at the officer's club each Friday evening. Bob, Paul, and Walt loved these dances as it was one way of relaxing after a hard week and the ladies were mostly gorgeous and interesting.

Classes let out at 4:00 p.m. and the guys walked back to the BOQ. They relaxed in Bob's room for about an hour, drinking iced tea and munching on chips. After dressing in their grey slacks, shirt and tie, and blue blazers, they wandered down to dinner in the Mess. The conversation centered around the upcoming dance that evening. It was difficult to score with these women as they were bused in on a school-owned bus and left directly for school after the dance was over. These were high-class women usually from wealthy families with great upbringing. Their manners were impeccable as that was what the college was noted for. After graduation, when these women returned to their homes, many would be welcomed into their local social circles.

There was a lot of smooching off in the corners but nothing ever came of it as the dances were well monitored and getting a girl alone was an impossibility.

Pre-flight was ending as they all had been in class now for eleven weeks. After classes in week twelve, a small reception was held in the officer's lounge, catered by the commanding officer, after which an informal graduation ceremony was held where the Commanding Officer awarded graduation certificates and a class picture was taken. On Friday, Bob, Paul and Walt reported to the personnel office and received their squadron assignment for the basic flight phase of training. All three of them were assigned to Training Squadron VN-1D8 located in Hangar 3 at the airfield. They took their check-out/in sheets and completed the items except for the squadron training department. They would do that on Monday morning.

Monday morning rolled around and the three of them checked in with the training department of Training Squadron VN-1D8. Here they received a syllabus manual as well as an aircraft handbook with standard operating procedures. Between the two books, it was all they needed to study for the flights through their solo flight. They were each assigned a flight instructor with whom they spent the rest of the day discussing what would be required for flight A1 and what to study in the manuals. Their instructors each gave them a copy of the aircraft open book test which would need to be completed before flying flight A1. The next two days were spent completing the open book test and having it graded by their instructor. Each of them was debriefed by their instructor and any missed questions were covered as to the correct answer. During this time, they were scheduled for an area indoctrination lecture and approach and landing procedures for home field.

Walt's instructor, Lieutenant (JG) Tom Woolcock, was a "plow back." He had graduated from flight training about four months earlier and was brought back as an instructor. Plow backs were the best Naval Aviators in their class and were there to maintain the graduation of high-quality aviators for the fleet.

It was the middle of March and the temperatures were already starting to warm from the winter season. Flying clothes for this time of year were a warm sweater over the uniform shirt and tie, heavy pants similar to riding pants, and Wellington boots. All pilots were issued a lambskin leather flying jacket and a leather helmet. Walt met Tom on the Hangar deck where they went by the parachute loft and each drew a chute for the flight. They proceeded out to the flight line with Tom quizzing Walt on the procedures and maneuvers to be flown on flight A1. They were assigned aircraft #6, an NB-1. When they arrived at the aircraft, they put their parachutes on the lower wing and proceeded to pre-flight the aircraft. As they walked around the aircraft, Tom asked Walt what he was looking at and what was the normal condition it should be in. Pre-flight lasted a little longer than normal, but when it was finished, they donned their parachutes and Walt climbed into the front cockpit with Tom in the rear. After fastening their seat belts and shoulder harnesses, Tom spoke to Walt through the Gosport and asked if he was ready to start the engine. Walt gave Tom the thumbs-up signal and Tom told Walt to start the engine. Walt gave the lineman the engine start signal. Fuel was turned on to feed the engine. The lineman took a position in front and pulled the propellor through three revolutions. He stopped on the starboard side and shouted "contact." Walt turned on the magneto switch and responded "contact." The lineman pulled down on the prop blade but nothing happened. He repositioned the prop and pulled it through once again. This time the engine back-fired and then roared to life. Within a few seconds, it settled down and began to run smoothly. The rpm settled at 800 and oil pressure rose to 60 pounds per square inch. Walt monitored the cylinder head temperature and it began to rise. He held the brakes on the rudder pedals and gave the lineman the signal to pull the chocks. Once completed, the lineman took his place forward and to the port of the aircraft. Walt signaled he was ready to taxi. The lineman motioned him forward and saluted when Walt was clear to taxi on his own. Walt turned the aircraft facing toward the control tower. He received a green light which cleared him to taxi for takeoff. Tom was talking to him all the time, giving him directions on where to go and how to taxi. The wind was out of the southwest and so takeoff direction would be heading 235°. With the large radial engine, taxiing required s-turns in order to see where the aircraft was going. Walt reached the end of the takeoff runway, and while holding short, turned his aircraft into the wind for his engine run-up. The cylinder head temperature was within limits and oil pressure was steady. The battery voltage was steady at 6 volts and the compass was reading 240°. Walt pushed the throttle forward and the RPMs inched up and settled at 1500 RPMs. This was the magneto check rpm so Walt selected the right mag and noted a 20 rpm drop. He went back to the both position and rpm recovered to 1500 RPMs. He then selected left mag and again the rpm dropped 25 RPMs. He returned the switch to the both position and RPMs recovered once again. He then brought the throttle back until the rpm stabilized at 800 RPM. Walt then signaled for Tom to read aloud the takeoff checklist. As Tom read the checklist, Walt performed the item and gave Tom a thumbs-up. He set the altimeter at 10', then checked the controls for complete freedom of movement and operation with the shoulder harness locked as the last item on the list. He then turned the aircraft facing the runway and taxied up short, observing the tower for a light. The tower responded with a green light, and after checking for any landing aircraft, Walt taxied out onto the runway and held the brakes, checking the heading as 235°. He advanced the throttle and released the brakes. The aircraft lurched forward and rolled down the runway. Tom applied a little rudder to keep the aircraft headed straight down the runway. Within 600 feet they were airborne and Walt was on his way.

Airborne over Florida

After getting airborne, they turned right out of the traffic pattern over Pensacola Bay and headed northwest. They leveled the plane when they reached 3500'. On reaching a cruising speed of 90 knots Walt reduced power on the engine to 1800 rpm. Crossing a point north and west of Corry Station, they were in their operating area and could begin maneuvers.

Tom took control of the airplane and demonstrated slow flight and stalled the aircraft and recovery. He then accelerated back to 90 knots and turned the aircraft back over to Walt. It was now his turn to stall the aircraft and perform slow flight. He lined up on the property lines heading north, reduced the power to idle, and held the nose slightly above the horizon. He retrimmed the aircraft down to 50 knots then held back pressure on the stick. At 46 knots the aircraft shuddered and stalled. The nose fell through the horizon and Walt added power to the engine and gently raised the nose back to the horizon. The aircraft lost 800 feet in the stall before it once again began to fly. He accelerated to 75 knots and reduced the power. After retrimming, Tom talked him into slow flight. He reduced the power and decelerated to 50 knots, adding power to maintain altitude and speed. His next maneuver was a 20° angle of bank turning 360° then reversing direction and banking 20° for 360°, ending up on the original heading. Next was practicing climbing and descending at 50 knots. Walt was then directed to accelerate to 80 knots and head for Site 6 where they would practice a few landings.

Procedures for traffic pattern entry directed aircraft to enter an imaginary circle one-half mile from the center of Site 6 at a 45° angle and at an altitude of 800' in a counter-clockwise direction. Site 6 had no designated runways but was just a grass field and landing would be into the wind. There was a windsock located in the southwest corner of the site and sometimes the ground personnel would start a fire in a pit located there. Walt determined the wind to be out of the northwest. He was turning in the landing circle, and as he approached the downwind area, he descended to 600' and turned into the wind over the landing area. There were two aircraft on the downwind leg for landing so Walt set up and turned 180° taking interval on the second aircraft for landing. He slowed the aircraft, completed the landing checklist, and prepared for landing. The approach speed would be 60 knots with a landing speed of 50 knots. As he passed abeam the intended landing point, he reduced power on the engine, applied carburetor heat, and began a descending turn ending in a rollout, wings level over the end of the runway. Touchdown was on all the wheels and tail skag.

Walt added power and the aircraft accelerated. Take-off was normal and he accelerated to climb speed completing the touch-and-go landing. He observed the position of the downwind aircraft and took interval on that aircraft for another touch and go landing. After completing six touch and goes, Tom directed Walt to head for home. Walt climbed to 1500 feet and headed southeast for NAS Pensacola. He entered the traffic circle and descended to 800 feet, turning southeast on the downwind for the landing runway. He slowed the aircraft to 60 knots and observed a green light from the tower clearing him for landing. Upon passing the end of the runway he commenced a left turn descending. He rolled out over the end of the runway at 50 knots, landed in the first hundred feet of runway, and taxied back to the parking area next to the hanger and shut down the aircraft.

As Walt exited the aircraft, he had a big smile on his face. Tom, his instructor, asked him what he was smiling about. Walt said, "That was one hell of a flight, Tom. I really enjoyed it."

Tom responded, "I'm glad you enjoyed it. We still have a lot of work to do. Let's go back to the Ready Room and debrief the flight. As they entered the hanger, they turned in their parachutes at the loft and proceeded to the ready-room.

Tom started the debriefing. He asked Walt if he had any questions about the flight. Walt said he had no questions so Tom began. "On your takeoff roll, you were a little lax in putting in left rudder because of the torque of the engine. Don't forget your aerodynamics where this slipstream from the prop puts pressure on your vertical tail. That's why you need to add rudder to keep yourself straight on the runway."

"When you reach altitude, be a little smoother in pushing the nose over into a level flight. That just takes a little practice and we have 11 more flights before solo so you have plenty of time to learn that."

"Your stalls were pretty good as were your landing procedures. On your turns, don't forget back pressure on the stick to maintain altitude. Do you have any questions?"

"No, Tom," Walt answered. "I understand what you are saying and what I need to practice on A2"Okay. We'll, see you tomorrow. Have a good night," Tom said.

Tom left the Ready Room while Walt stayed to study his operating procedures. Within a short time, Bob and Paul with their instructors entered to debrief their flight. Walt got up and got a cup of coffee after Paul and Bob were finished debriefing.

The three of them sat in the ready-room for quite a while discussing their first flight. It was quite animated with all kinds of hand gestures mimicking each of their various flight maneuvers, proving once again that pilots can't talk flying without using their hands. Paul seemed most excited about stalling the aircraft, describing his stalled aircraft as an uncontrollable limp dishcloth as his aircraft went nearly wings vertical when it stalled then fell off some 1500' before recovery. It was more violent than what Bob and Walt had experienced.

Bob was all excited about his flight, in that his engine had backfired a few times in the landing pattern. His exact words were, "That SOB farted about six times. Thought we might have to dead stick it into some field."

Walt responded, "Yeah, Bob, all you were worried about was missing supper.

Paul chimed in, "Nah, he was concerned about not sleeping on white sheets tonight and also maybe having to walk a few miles to get home."

"I not so sure we shouldn't check Bob's skivvies for stains," Walt said.

"You two guys can go piss up a rope," Bob interjected.

Paul and Walt just smiled at each other as they felt they had achieved their goal in their needling of Bob.

"Come on you two," Paul said. "Let's get cleaned up and go to dinner."

Bob chuckled, "I'm convinced. Let's get going."

Paul and Walt could see Bob was over his little snit and was taking their kidding in fine fashion. All of them realized this was going to be a long-term friendship. They went to their lockers in the Hangar where they stowed their flight helmets, white scarves, and leather flight jackets, then headed off to the BOQ.

Next Day, NAS Pensacola, Florida

The day started early for the three fledging Aviators. Walt and Paul had an 8:30 a.m. launch for flight A2, while Bob had a 9:00 a.m. launch.

Walt met Tom in the ready-room at 7:30 a.m. for his pre-flight briefing. The briefing included all the maneuvers they would conduct during this flight. Tom introduced steep and coordinated turns for this flight. When he finished his briefing, Walt proceeded to the plane to preflight the aircraft. On his way to the plane, he stopped at the parachute loft and checked out his chute. As he reached his plane, he observed Tom step onto the ramp proceeding towards the aircraft. He began his preflight and was soon joined by Tom who observed his actions. He was remembering all the items Tom had directed him to check during the preflight. The amount of oil on the engine was a judgment call and something he needed to learn. He determined this engine was normal. He checked both wheels to determine the condition of the brakes and examined the condition of the fabric for tears and tension. He also checked the condition of the tail skag. Tom also pointed out the condition of the wing tension cables. After the walk- around, Walt bounced his observations and judgment on the condition of the aircraft at Tom. Tom responded he was correct except they should ask the maintenance department to check the tension of the cables on the port wing as they seemed to be a little loose. Tom showed Walt what he was talking about.

The two of them manned the aircraft with Walt in the front cockpit and Tom in the rear. The wind today was out of the southwest so Walt taxied to the east end of the airfield and held short of the runway. He turned into the wind, set the brakes, and proceeded with the engine runup. He checked both magnetos and the RPM loss was within tolerance. He reduced power and completed the take-off checklist. After locking his seat belt, he turned the plane directly at the tower which was the signal to the tower personnel that he was ready for take-off. The tower gave him a green light and cleared him for take-off. He taxied into position, held his brakes, and began to add power for take-off. He released the brakes and began his roll while adding power to the max for take-off. He raised the tail to takeoff attitude, lifted off at 50 knots, and accelerated to climb speed of 75 knots. He made a right turn out of the pattern and continued his climb to 3500 feet. After passing west of Corry Station, they entered the practice area.

Once again Walt went through yesterday's maneuvers, shallow turns, and slow flight. Tom took control of the aircraft and showed Walt steep turns. These were done at a 45° angle of bank. Tom introduced the use of the needle/ball instrument. One needle width was a standard rate turn while a steep turn was two needle widths. A standard rate turn was a turn of 180° completed in one minute. Tom stressed the need for increased back pressure of the control stick because of loss of lift on the wings usually causing loss of altitude. A perfect steep turn was done with no loss of altitude. Tom turned control of the plane back to Walt where he practiced steep turns which consisted of 360° in one direction followed by a reversal and a 360° turn in the other direction. Tom explained the need for mastering the use of the rudder to make coordinated turns where the ball in the instrument remained centered at all times.

After Walt had done a series of four steep turn series, Tom directed Walt to enter the turn to the left and raise the nose about 25° above the horizon and hold it there. He coached Walt and told him to expect a stall. Sure, enough the plane stalled to the right, wings leveled and nose fell through. Recovery required power back to idle, stick forward, nose down, and as soon as airspeed had been gained, power on, nose on the horizon and accelerate to cruise speed.

Next Tom coached Walt through a steep turn stall to the right. He cautioned him that this stall would be quite different. As far as Walt was concerned, it sure as hell was different. When the plane stalled, it flipped over to the right on its back, upside down. Recovery was quite different. The nose fell through, so it was reduce power to idle, using the ailerons, roll the aircraft right side up, pull the nose back to level flight, and add power to gain airspeed to cruise speed.

Level stalls were then practiced and Tom asked Walt to proceed to Site 6. Walt admitted he did not have the slightest notion where Site 6 was from his present position. Tom chastised him for not having location awareness and stressed the importance of it at all times. He reoriented Walt, and pointing out significant landmarks and then directing him on how to find 6. They proceeded to 6 and entered traffic. Walt made six pretty good touch-and-go landings, after which Tom directed him to "take them home."

Once back in the Ready Room and during the debriefing, Tom indicated the flight was highly satisfactory, but he gave Walt a below average for position awareness. He once again reviewed coordinated turns and stall recovery.

Paul had already been debriefed so they had a cup of coffee and waited for Bob. In a few minutes, Bob and his instructor returned and debriefed his flight.

Walt asked Paul and Bob if they had done any steep turn stalls. Before they could answer, he described how the steep turn stall to the right had flipped the plane on its back. It was the first time Walt had been upside-down in a plane. He was excited and animated in his description and said what a great feeling that was. They were all excited about their experience and were looking forward to tomorrow's flight.

4

"One Step Forward"

More of the Same

In the days that followed, repetition of all maneuvers was stressed with marked improvement. Two flights per day became the norm with the only new maneuver being steep turns at 60° banking. All three students completed flight A7. The next flight in the syllabus was A8, a progress check to see how each was proceeding in their ability at becoming a Naval Aviator. Walt was scheduled up first. It was a hot and muggy Florida afternoon, and the air was quite turbulent.

Walt met his check-pilot in the Ready Room where his check-pilot laid out how the flight would proceed. He indicated that he would not offer instruction during the flight and gave Walt the list of maneuvers to accomplish and in what sequence.

Walt proceeded to the parachute loft, checked out his parachute, then to the plane which he preflighted, then climbed into the front cockpit and awaited his check-pilot.

His check-pilot soon arrived, climbed into the rear cockpit, and gave Walt the signal to start his engine. He did so and began his taxi toward the take-off end of the duty runway. His instructor, Tom, had briefed him on what to expect of his check-pilot so he had meticulously studied his procedures until he could recite them in his sleep. He reached the end of the runway, turned his aircraft into the wind, and conducted his engine runup. Both magnetos checked within limits and his prop operated smoothly. Carburetor heat was normal, so he reduced power to flight idle and got a signal from the check-pilot that he was ready for takeoff. Walt turned the aircraft directly at the tower, got a green light for takeoff. He taxied into position on the runway, held the brakes, and began to add takeoff power. He released the brakes and began his takeoff roll. As he passed 40 knots, he raised the tail and set takeoff attitude. At 50 knots, he lifted off, and accelerated to 70 knots, and began his climb. He passed 500', turned out of traffic, and proceeded northwest to the operating area. After passing Corry Station, he leveled off at 3500'.

His first maneuver was a straight-ahead stall. He completed that and went right into a steep turn stall to the left followed by a steep turn stall to the right. He felt great exhilaration when it flipped over on its back. After recovery he climbed back to 3500' and demonstrated slow-flight for his check-pilot. Next came a standard rate turn followed by a series of steep turns at 45 and60 degrees of bank. He nailed the 60° banked turn and didn't lose a foot of altitude. He then proceeded to Site 6, entered traffic, and made 5 of the most beautiful touch-and-go landings he had ever performed. He departed the pattern and proceeded directly to NAS Pensacola where he executed another perfect landing. After landing he taxied to the flightline where he was parked by the Plane Captain. After shutdown, he and the check-pilot walked slowly towards the Hangar. For the first time since they had manned the aircraft, the check-pilot spoke. "I'll fill out the yellow sheet in maintenance," he said, "You can go to the Ready Room. I'll meet you there."

"Roger that, Sir," Walt responded.

Walt reached the Ready Room and poured himself a glassof iced tea, tooka seat, and waited for hischeck-pilot.

Pretty soon his check-pilot appeared and took a seat across the table for his debriefing.

He began, "Ensign Pellman, I must say you handled that plane like you owned it. That was by farone of the best progress checks I have ever been on. The only criticism I have is on your 60° steep turns. Be a little smoother of theuse of your rudder on the reversal. Remember, you need to ease out of it as you reduce your angle of bank and feed it in smoothly as you increase your angle of bank in the other direction. I think you are ready for flight A9. Good luck," he said as he rose and stretched out his hand to congratulate Walt.

Paul and Bob had just departed on their progress flight so Walt decided he would go back to the BOQ. When he reached his room he was so hot and sweaty he jumped in the cold shower and cooled off. He slipped on a pair of shorts then stretched out of the bed to relax. He had drifted off in sleep, and before you knew it, he was awakened by the slamming of a door acrossthe hall anda loud yell from Bob who had entered his room through the hallway between their rooms.

"What's withyou two guys?" Walt asked.

As Bob started to answer, Paul came in from across the hall.

"I had one hell-of-a shitty flight," Bob offered. "Not as bad as Paul though, right Paul?" he added.

"Yeah, mine was so bad I got a down for the flight. Had to see the training officer before I left the Hangar. He gave me two extra flights and a recheck. How was your flight, Walt?" he asked.

Walt not wanting to make either of them feel bad said, "My checkpilot said some of my maneuvers needed a little work, but my landings were good. I managed to get a satisfactory grade."

Paul was still wound up from the flight. "My landings were satisfactory, but my flight maneuvers need a lot of work, according to my check-pilot," Paul said

"Well, let's let it rest for a while and after dinner, we can discuss your flight and see what you need to concentrate on to improve," Walt said.

"Sounds good to me," Paul responded. Bob nodded in agreement.

They decided to change into dinner dress and go have some grub. In about 30 minutes all three were dressed and ready for dinner. They walked down the hall toward the dining room. Dinner turned out to be a light summer offering of shrimp cocktail followed by cold cuts and macaroni salad with watermelon for dessert. The drink was iced tea served southern style: "Sweet."

After dinner, they walked out into the lounge area and turned on the big floor model radio. Lowell Thomas was just coming on the air. His main story centered around how bad the depression was becoming. In '29 Wall Street had the big crash, but now it was starting to affect the whole population of the United States. More and more people were out of work and trying to find a job to put food on their dinner table.

The three young naval officers all declared they sure were happy to be in the Navy as getting a job on the outside might be a problem. Paul stated the obvious, that it wasn't affecting them a whole lot since the surrounding area was almost all agricultural and fishing. The main industry was the pulp mill in Flomaton, Alabama, just north of Pensacola making paper pulp from the multitude of pines in the area.

Lowell Thomas went off the air and a half-hour later "Amos and Andy" came on. It was turning out to be one of the most popular comedy shows on the radio. They listened to the show, laughed at the hilarious jokes, and just relaxed after a hard day flying.

Finally, Walt asked Paul about his flight today.

"What did you have difficulty with today, Paul?" he asked.

"Just sloppy on altitude control, slow flight, and steep turns," Paul said. "Stalls and landings were good. Positional awareness was also okay," he added.

"We can work on those things if you want to," Walt said.

"Right now?" Paul queried.

"Yeah, right now," Walt responded. "Okay, let's give it a try, if you think it will help."

"Alright, Paul, let's start with steep turns. Close your eyes and visualize yourself in the cockpit, in cruise, at altitude," Walt said. "Put your right hand on the stick and start your sequence. Verbalize what you are doing."

"Okay, I am starting my 45° angle turn to the right. My angle of bank is increasing and I am adding right rudder. Now applying back pressure on the stick, starting to lose a little altitude, more back pressure on the stick, still losing altitude."

Walt interrupted, "Roll out wings level Paul, and reset your altitude. Are you reset?"

"Yeah," Paul said.

Walt started to speak, "Okay, Paul, this time I am going to talk you through the turn. Coordinate all three axes as you start. Start a little back pressure on the stick, right aileron, and right rudder. Keep increasing back pressure as you increase aileron and rudder. When you reach 45° angle of bank, neutralize your aileron and keep applying back pressure until the nose refuses to drop. Now check your geographical markers and fence lines. When you are approaching 360° of turn, lead it by about 30° and now slowly apply left aileron. As your angle of bank lessens, ease up on right rudder and back pressure on the stick. When you reach wings level, the rudder should be neutral as should be your back pressure with your nose on the horizon. Now continue your left aileron, add back pressure on the stick and feed in left rudder as your angle of bank increases. As you approach 45°, neutralize your ailerons and continue your turn, until you are approaching your original heading. Now start to ease out of the turn coordinate your controls until your wings level on your original heading."

"Hey that was cool, Walt. I could really see my turns and required coordination of my controls."

"Okay, Paul, I think you have the idea. Just practice your maneuvers on your own whenever you feel like it and I know things will improve."

"I think I got the idea, Walt. I see Bob is asleep over there. He has his eyes closed."

Bob chimed in, "I was visualizing a hot chick at the beach in her bathing suit while you guys were flying planes." What Bob was really doing was visualizing the steep turn maneuver as Walt was coaching Paul through it. He just didn't want them to know it.

That reminded Walt, "Hey, guys, I need to write a letter," so he excused himself. Of course, that brought out the barbs and banter.

"What are you doing Walt," Bob asked, "going sweet on your honey from "Wichita?""

Paul added, "Nah, he's never met a girl who would give him the time of day."

"Okay, lover boys, see you in the morning," Walt retorted.

Solo at Last

The flights now came hot and heavy as the three flight students continued through A-stage of their basic training. Paul had his two extra flights and got outstanding grades on his recheck. A couple of training days had been lost due to weather. Summer in Florida always brought thunderstorms and they had their share for a couple of days.

Walt and Bob were scheduled for their A-12 flight check on the same day. Paul was only on A-9 with his having to fly an extra three flights.

Walt met his check-pilot, briefed the flight, and proceeded out to the aircraft after checking out his parachute. He was already strapped in when his check-pilot arrived. He started his engine and proceeded as usual after take-off out to the operating area. He performed all the required maneuvers and was directed to Site 6 where he made four touch-and-go landings. On the fifth approach, the check-pilot told him to make this landing a full stop. Walt touched down beautifully came to a stop, turned off the runway, and parallel taxied back to the take-off area. The instructor told him to set the brakes. Walt was startled when the check-pilot appeared on the port wing and leaned into his cockpit.

"Make three touch and go landings and then a full stop to pick me up. I'll be waiting right here," he stated.

"Roger that, Sir," Walt answered.

His heart increased a few beats as he realized he was going to be alone in this aircraft. His mind raced, but in the end, this is what he had been working for since flight A-1.

He checked for traffic, and no one was on approach, so he taxied onto the landing area, added power, and roared off into the wild blue. He took interval on the downwind traffic and fell in behind him. As he came off the 180, he reduced power and put on carburetor heat. He slowed to 50 knots, and as he lined up with landing area heading, rolling wings level, he flared for touchdown. The aircraft stalled and touched down softly. Walt turned off carb heat and added power smoothly accelerating to take-off speed. He made two more touch-and-go landings. On the next pass, he made a full stop, and cleared the landing area, and taxied back to the takeoff area. Two check-pilots were waiting and he suddenly realized that Bob was probably in the other plane doing touch and go landings.

The check pilot got strapped in and signaled Walt he was cleared for takeoff. After take-off, he turned left out of traffic and headed directly for NAS Pensacola. Upon reaching Pensacola he observed traffic and entered a normal traffic pattern. At the 180 he checked the Tower for landing approval. The tower gave him a green light clearing him for landing. He completed his landing checklist, and slowed to 50 knots. Over the threshold of the landing area, he flared the airplane and stalled, touching down smoothly. After taxing back to the flight line, he was directed to his parking space by his Plane Captain. He shut down the aircraft and climbed out to be greeted by his check pilot who was already standing on the ramp. They walked together towards the hanger with the check pilot telling Walt what a great job he had done. He said he especially liked his landings. They then turned in their parachutes to the paraloft and proceeded to the Ready Room for debriefing.

The Check pilot debriefed the flight and gave Walt above averages for most of his maneuvers. The check pilot left, while Walt remained and got himself a cup of coffee. While waiting, Paul and his instructor entered the Ready Room and debriefed the flight. After Paul's instructor departed, Paul came over and sat with Walt while both waited for Bob and his check pilot to return.

"How did your flight go?" Walt asked Paul.

"Things are going a lot smoother," Paul responded. "I have two more flights before my check flight on A12."

It wasn't long before Bob and his check pilot entered the Ready Room. Their debriefing went quickly and smoothly and soon Bob joined Paul and Walt at their table with a cup of coffee. The three of them were animated with discussion of their flights just completed. Bob and Walt were ecstatic having just completed their first solo flight. They described what it was like to be up in aircraft by themselves and depending on their skill to get the aircraft safely down. Suddenly, both looked up at Paul who is standing over them with his survival knife in his hand.

"What the hell are you doing, Paul?" Walt asked.

"I'm starting a new custom in naval aviation," Paul said. You guys are both going to lose your tie as I'm going to cut half of it off."

Paul proceeded to each of his friends and severed half of their tie. They were all laughing heartily when another instructor walked in.

"What the hell is going on in here?" the instructor asked.

"Ensign Day has just started a new custom, Sir," Bob answered.

"And just what would that be Lieutenant?" the instructor asked.

"He decided when a student first solos he should lose half his tie, so he cut ours off with his survival knife, Sir."

"That sounds like something worth repeating," he stated. "I'm going to make note of that and pass the word to the other instructors in the squadron."

"Yes Sir, thank you, Sir," all three said in unison.

It was Friday and the three of them sat there trying to figure out what to do for the weekend. They had been spending almost every weekend at the officer's beach on the base. Finally, they decided to venture out and see how things were at Gulf Beach.

They stowed their flight gear in their lockers and proceeded to walk back to the BOQ, still discussing the upcoming weekend.

Monday Morning

Today was going to be a busy day for the three officers. Walt and Bob had two flights scheduled while Paul had only an early morning flight. They all had breakfast together and soon after departed the BOQ for the Hangar. Upon arrival, they all changed into their flight uniform and settled down in the Ready Room. After a short wait, Bob and Walt's instructors arrived briefed them on what to practice, and sent them off to man their aircraft. After receiving their aircraft assignments, they proceeded to the flight line to preflight and man the aircraft. In a short time, they were airborne for Site 8 Able. Here they would practice their landings and takeoffs. After six touch-and-goes, Walt left the pattern to practice his stall series. He climbed to 4000' and proceeded through his stalls. After he completed them, it was time to return to base. He headed southeast towards NAS Pensacola, descended to 1500', spotted the double bridge over the inlet west of the base, and turned into the landing circle at 1000', and looked for his pattern entry point. He descended to 800'. The wind was westnorthwest so as he passed the downwind end of the landing area, he turned west-northwest to parallel the landing traffic pattern. He spotted the last aircraft, which was downwind for landing, and turned and took interval on that aircraft. He completed his landing checklist, and as he passed abeam the landing point, he began his 180° turn descending for landing. He reduced his speed to 50 knots and rolled out of his turn directly over the end of the runway, flared his aircraft, and stalled just as he touched down. He taxied back to the flight line, parked the aircraft, and upon reaching the Hangar, turned in his parachute. He signed in the aircraft with maintenance and proceeded to the Ready Room.

In short order, Bob showed up. After changing uniforms they had a quick lunch at the BOQ. They did a lot of talking with their hands telling each other how they had performed their maneuvers. After arriving back at the Hangar, they changed into their flying uniform and sat down awaiting their instructor.

This phase of training was designated precision flying. Its goal was to teach the student how to be more exact in their flying with very close tolerance maneuvers. This included flying precise altitudes and exact airspeeds, smooth transitions during maneuvers, and placing the aircraft on an exact spot when landing. As the student progressed, tolerances shrank to very small numbers.

After manning the aircraft and takeoff, Walt and his instructor were proceeding out to the practice area. He was instructed to perform his stall series with minimum loss of attitude. During his steep turn stall to the right, the aircraft snapped over on its back and began an inverted spin. This was a new situation for Walt and he was momentarily disoriented. He quickly recognized a spin to the right, applied left rudder, and lowered the nose. As the spinning stopped, he rolled the aircraft right side up, returned his rudder to neutral, applied back pressure on the stick to stop the loss of altitude, and added power simultaneously. His loss of altitude was only 800'. His instructor's only comment was "Nice job, Ensign."

Walt climbed back to his working altitude and completed his stall series. He then performed slow flight. After completion of this maneuver, his instructor directed him to descend to 1500' and proceed to Site 8A for landing practice. During the briefing for the flight, Walt's instructor had described the introduction of a new maneuver. It was practicing a dead stick landing. This involved simulating the loss of an engine and then making an engine-out landing on a grass strip or airfield.

Walt was instructed to descend at 65 knots at 500 feet per minute, and upon reaching 1500', cruise at 80 knots until joining traffic at Site 8A. He departed 5000', reduced power and slowed to 65 knots, and descent at 500 feet per minute. After descending about 1000', he finally settled down and got everything steadied out. As he approached 1500', he added power to accelerate to 80 knots and leveled the aircraft at his assigned altitude. While he was heading to 8A, he observed smoke on the surface indicating wind out of the northwest. He was currently heading south-southeast so he figured he would need to join the traffic pattern west of 8A and circle counterclockwise until he could descend to traffic circle altitude heading northwest. As he joined the traffic circle, his instructor cut engine power indicating loss of the engine. Walt immediately began to slow to 60 knots and trim the aircraft. He was passing abeam the intended landing point on the field, heading 180° opposite the landing direction. He was still at 1500' so he turned past the abeam point and began a descending turn towards the landing point. As he was approaching final heading, his instructor showed him how to "skid" the aircraft by applying left ailerons and right rudder while maintaining proper airspeed. They lost altitude very quickly, and as they cleared the boundary fence, returned the aircraft to balanced flight with wings level and neutral rudder. Speed was just a little fast and they landed a little long. On touchdown, Walt placed carburetor heat off and smoothly added power for a touch-and-go landing.

As they got airborne, Walt's instructor directed him to take interval on traffic but to turn downwind 30° short of the previous heading. This time they would land 30° off the previous landing heading. This was to practice landing when the wind was not blowing directly down the duty runway, a "cross-wind" landing in effect. As they approached the abeam landing position, the instructor coached Walt through the procedures. First was a little more increased angle of bank because the wind would blow the aircraft closer to the landing area in the first 90° of turn. After passing the 90, decreasing angle of bank was required so as not to overshoot the runway heading. This required keeping the windward wing down and applying right rudder in the left turn to keep the aircraft headed straight down the runway. Touchdown was slightly different than normal with the windward wheel touching down first in the stall then the downwind wheel. Walt was instructed to keep the aileron applied into the wind so the wind would not lift the wing until lift was lost completely. Touchdown was beautiful and Walt slowed the aircraft until he could taxi back to the "into the wind" landing area and join normal traffic.

The duo made three more crosswind landings as well as one more dead stick landing before proceeding back to base. Approach and landing were normal. After parking the aircraft, they proceeded to the Ready Room for debriefing. During the debrief, Walt was commended for his progress in his precision maneuvers and received high marks for his handling of the inverted spin. He was encouraged to pay more attention to his assigned speed and altitude. When asked for comments or questions, he stated that this sure was a flight crammed with new stuff and his mind was on overload at the moment. His instructor reminded him that practice makes perfect and would get easier the more he practiced the maneuvers. He reminded Walt he was not to practice dead stick landings on solo flights. With the briefing complete, Walt's instructor departed.

Bob and his instructor entered the Ready Room and debriefed the flight. When they were finished, Bob changed into his uniform and he and Walt walked back to the BOQ. They were very animated and described their flights to each other. Walt's inverted, flat spin was the topic that took up most of the discussion. All Bob could say was he hoped that never happened to him.

That evening at dinner, the whole table of officers were keenly aware of Walt's inverted spin and the discussion was hot and heavy on the subject. After dinner, Walt excused himself and went back to his room. He took pen in hand and wrote a letter to Zimmy. He apologized for not answering her last letter sooner. He told her about his experiences with his training, what was happening in the local area and about the weather. He closed telling her he really missed her and hoped they could get together soon, really soon. He placed the letter in an envelope, and sealed it, then placed a stamp on it for mailing. Before retiring for the night, he reviewed his flight procedures for his upcoming flight the next day.

5

"Plan for Relaxation"

Progress in flight

The three intrepid student pilots were now progressing quickly through the flight syllabus. Paul had soloed once while Bob and Walt had logged four solo flights. They had been introduced to a new landing field called Silverhill. It was located over the state line in Alabama and was designated for solo flights only. It was about a fifteen-minute flight from NAS Pensacola. On his last flight to Silverhill, Walt had discovered the watermelon patch next to the runway and had come up with a sinister plan. He decided they needed a way to have a drinking party at the beach without being obvious. So, he planned to steal a watermelon and get some White Lightin' to sweeten the melon.

He proposed his plan to Bob and Paul who were more than eager to participate. He set his plan in motion the next day. He talked with Moses, the groundskeeper at the BOQ, and asked him if he knew anyone who could supply him with a bottle of White Lightin'. Moses said he could get him a bottle, but it was going to cost him a "buck." Walt figured a dollar for that was well worth it so he gave Moses a dollar. The next day Moses showed up a pint glass Mason jar filled with a clear liquid. Walt met him out behind the BOQ and picked it up. Now all he had to do was furnish the watermelon. His solo flight was scheduled for late that afternoon and he figured this would be a great time to do it. On his flight, he rushed through his maneuvers and then proceeded to Silverhill. He made a series of full-stop landings, and while taxiing back for take-off, he cased the watermelon field to make sure it was clear. On his last full-stop and while taxiing back for takeoff, he stopped the aircraft about 25 yards from the melon patch. He set the brakes and left the engine running, then jumped out and ran over where he picked a large green watermelon and carried it back to the aircraft. Once there he stowed it in the back seat and secured it with the lap belt and shoulder harness, then climbed back in the front seat and continued his taxi for takeoff. While flying back to base, he was trying to figure out how to get the melon to his car which he had driven to the hangar for just that purpose. He arrived back at the flight line after 5 o'clock. Almost everyone had departed the area so he parked the plane and left his flight jacket and gear in the backseat covering the melon. He told the Plane Captain he would be back shortly to pick up his gear and to just leave it in the back seat. He walked back to the hangar, checked in his airplane with maintenance, and proceeded to his car. Then he drove out on the flight line, parked next to the plane, and retrieved his gear and the watermelon. Just as he was about to get into his car he heard this deep, stern voice behind him say, "What's going on here, Ensign Pellman?"

It was the Squadron Duty Officer. Walt froze in his tracks, almost lost his car keys, and responded, "Just retrieving my gear, sir. I had forgotten and left it in the airplane."

"Well, get your car off the flight-line ASAP before the old man sees it and asks questions," the Duty Officer said.

"Yes sir. I'm on my way now," Walt said.

Walt got in his car and drove off toward the BOQ. *"Boy that was a close call,"* he thought.

He arrived at the BOQ and carried the watermelon, disguised in his flight gear, into his room. Bob and Paul were there in seconds asking whether he was successful or not. He went to his closet and brought out the melon, displaying it with pride.

"What happens next?" they asked.

"We need to get a bottle of grape juice from a grocery store. Then we can cut a plug and mix the white lightin' and grape juice in the melon. Once we do that we will put the plug back in and let it stand for a week. Then we'll be ready to party," Walt said.

"Right now, let me get cleaned up and we'll go to dinner."

After dinner the three of them sat around out on the veranda and plotted their next move.

Walt started the conversation, "I have an early afternoon solo, so after I get back I'll make a run off the base, stop at that grocery store in Warrenton and get us a bottle of grape juice."

Paul piped up, "My flights at the same time as yours Walt so wait for me and we can go together."

"Hey, that sounds like a great idea. I'd appreciate your company," Walt responded.

With that, their conversation slipped back to discussing their flight progress and beautiful women.

"By the way, Walt, have you heard from Zimmy lately?" Bob asked.

"Yeah, I had a letter a couple of days ago. She applied with American Airways to be a flight stewardess on that new model transport airplane. It's a Ford 4-AT-E Tri-motor. It's the one powered by three 300-hp (225-kW) Wright J-6-9 Whirlwind nine-cylinder radial piston engines. One of the requirements is she has to be a registered nurse. She has an interview in Wichita in about a week."

"Damn, that sounds like a great deal," Paul said.

"That must be some airplane to fly with those three 300 horsepower engines," Bob observed.

"It probably flies like a piece of shit," Walt said. "I was reading about it and it only cruises at only 90 miles per hour. Its take-off weight is a little over 10,000 pounds. It also carries 14 passengers plus a stewardess with two pilots. I don't think that's for me. I like the single-engine, single, or two-seaters, fighters preferred. Who the hell wants to be a babysitter to a bunch of civilians?"

"You're right, Walt. Fighters are the way to go for military pilots," Bob said. I think I'm off to bed. I have an early flight and then a very late afternoon flight. Probably see you guys at breakfast."

Bob wandered off to his room while Paul and Walt remained on the veranda talking flying for another couple of hours.

Next Day

Bob was up early, had breakfast, and headed off to the hangar. Walt and Paul made it to breakfast just before 9:00 a.m. as the dining room was about to close. After breakfast, they headed off to the day's activities with their first flight at 11:00 a.m.

They made it back in time for lunch at the BOQ and then were off for their early afternoon flight. After completing the flight, they met in the locker room, changed into their uniforms, and headed out to Walt's car. The trip out to the grocery store was pleasant. The summer weather was hot, but not too muggy and the wind was blowing some 5 to 10 miles per hour, making it feel a little cooler. Upon arrival at the store, they asked the proprietor if he had any grape juice. He directed them to where they could find it and within a minute they had a 12oz bottle in hand, ready to check out. It cost all of $.35. After paying were back on the road to the base.

Upon arriving at Walt's BOQ room they ran into Bob who had been waiting for them for about a half-hour. Bob and Paul sat down in Walt's room while Walt retrieved the watermelon from his closet.

He set it on his desk and balanced it with a couple of rolled-up towels he had retrieved from his bathroom.

"How are you going to cut the plug?" Paul asked.

"I'll show you guys. I have done this before," Walt responded.

He reached in his pants pocket and pulled out his jack-knife with its five-inch blade. He opened the blade and jabbed it into the center of the melon. He cut a two-inch angled circle through the rind. Then he got the bottle cork-screw he had borrowed from the civilian who ran the beverage room in the BOQ and inserted it in the center of the plug he had just cut in the rind. He twisted the plug with the corkscrew and then pulled up on it. The plug popped out just as clean as could be.

"That was as beautiful a job as I have ever seen," said Bob.

Walt sat down and said, "Now it's your turn, guys, to mix the brew. Pour in the grape juice first and then the White Lightin'."

Bob and Paul proceeded to follow Walt's directions. After they had finished pouring in the white lightin', Walt very carefully put the plug back in. He then took a piece of tape he had obtained from the squadron maintenance chief and placed it over the plug to cover the edge of the plug all around.

"Okay," Walt instructed, "Now you need to roll it back and forth to mix it well within the melon."

After they had rolled it for about five minutes, Walt directed them to place it back in his closet and support it with the towels as he had before on the desk.

"Good job, guys," Walt observed, "Now all we need to do is roll it about every other day to mix it really well."

"When is it going to be ready to drink?" Paul asked.

"Should be ready on Saturday," Walt responded.

"Geeez, I can hardly wait for the weekend," Bob chortled.

Saturday Morning

They all woke with great anticipation. It was going to be a fun day. They had only a handful of drinks since prohibition started and most were on their trip to New Orleans during their New Year's leave.

After breakfast, they put on their bathing suits and headed off in Walt's car for the "Officers Beach" on the base. Paul was charged with caring for the watermelon. He looked silly sitting in the back seat with that big watermelon on his lap covered by a large bath towel. On arriving the three of them walked down to the beach, found a quiet place, and set up on their bath towels from the BOQ. They all stretched out and proceeded to observe the arrival of some of the young ladies now home from college on their summer break.

Soon it was too hot to continue to lay on the beach so they took to the water of Pensacola Bay to cool off a little. Paul got into a conversation with a couple of the ladies while Bob and Walt went back to their towels. Soon Paul and the young ladies came back to where they all were gathered.

Paul introduced the ladies, "This is Susan and this is Karen," Paul said as he pointed to each of the girls. "This is Walt and he's Bob," he continued.

They each acknowledged one another with a "Hi."

The ladies questioned them about the watermelon, and finally they confessed that it was loaded with Panther Piss, and were asked whether they would like to share some. The ladies were sharp enough to catch the meaning of the contents and said they were interested.

The guys had brought some glasses from the BOQ, so Walt pulled the plug and they tilted the melon until the contents began to flow. They put a small amount into each one's glass and stood in a circle while they tasted it. They all decided it was smooth, especially with the grape juice, so each had a little more.

Walt returned the plug to the melon while they all sat down on the towels and got better acquainted. Turns out one lady was the Admiral's daughter while the other was the base commander's daughter. They were both students in their junior year at Bryn Mawr College.

Later in the day, the five of them finished pouring the last of the Panther Piss. Walt pulled out his trusty knife and cut the watermelon into slices for them to eat. There was still plenty of juice in the melon and everyone had a good buzz on when they had finished eating the melon. They decided a frolic in the water would take an edge off the buzz so off they all went into the water. It was getting on into the afternoon and everyone felt they had enough sun, so the guys bade farewell and drove back to the BOQ. When they arrived, everybody was so beat they collapsed into their respective beds and each took a long afternoon nap.

Paul was the first to awaken. He was hungover but very hungry. He woke Bob and Walt and they decided it was still possible to make supper. They dressed casually as dinner was a picnic type, which was being served on the patio outside the back of the BOQ. They made it before the serving line was closed. Dinner was hot dogs on a bun served with homemade pork and beans. There was also pecan pie for dessert. It turned out to be a great way to finish the day. As dusk fell they sat around drinking iced tea and enjoying the company.

Acrobatics

The three intrepid fledgling aviators passed their precision flight checks and moved into the final phase of basic training. This next phase involved acrobatics. The maneuvers were all in their infancy and instructors were learning as they went along.

Walt was the first to be scheduled for his C-1 flight. He met his instructor in the student Ready Room. His instructor was Lance Fuller, one of the first pilots to fly off the USS Saratoga. The pair briefed for flight and soon they were airborne. After reaching the L4 training area, Lance had Walt perform some of the precision maneuvers. Having completed those maneuvers satisfactorily, Lance took over the aircraft and demonstrated the barrel roll. He described to Walt the requirement to line up the aircraft on a road. Most roads were either north-south or east-west because the country was divided up by sections and property lines were mainly aligned with the four main points of the compass.

Lance aligned on a north-south road. WWhile describingwhat he was doing and what was required, he pulled up the nose of the aircraft, maintaining positive G-force and commencing a smooth left roll, increasing the angle of bank. The first checkpoint was 45° nose up and 45° angle of bank. Lance continued describing how he needed to look over his shoulder and pick up the east-west road which would be 90° from the start of the maneuver. Upon reaching this point, the key was to be wings parallel to the horizon, but inverted and lined up with the east-west roads. Continuing the maneuver, Lance maintained positive G-force, but began to decrease the angle of bank until reaching wings level with the horizon and back on the original north-south heading at the starting altitude. This was the ultimate ever-changing balanced flight maneuver. It put together all the previously developed skills and helped the student hone his flying skills.

It was now Walt's turn. Lance gave him the aircraft and Walt shook the stick left and right indicating he had control of the aircraft. He set his altitude exactly at 5000' and lined up on the north-south roads. As he commenced his barrel-roll, he started the nose up while initiating increasing angle of bank to the left. Soon he felt Lance on the stick telling him to raise the nose some more. He reached the 90° inverted position, but saw he was about 30° off the east-west heading. He continued around and while keeping positive pressure on the nose, shallowed his bank until he was wings level and altitude stable. He found he was still off heading about 30° and low on altitude, having leveled off at 4800'.

Lance suggested he try another barrel roll to the right. This one turned out to be a little easier, because as the aircraft slowed, it tried to slew to the right even more. As Walt rolled out on the original heading, Lance commented that it was a little better but needed a lot of work.

Lance took control of the aircraft and demonstrated the loop. This required accelerating to fast cruise then pulling the nose up with a steady 2G pullup, relaxing to zero Gs at the top of the loop, inverted. Then starting down the backside, increasing the G-forces to 2Gs and leveling off at the original altitude. This seemed to be a relatively simple maneuver. Lance turned the aircraft over to Walt and talked him through a loop. It was fairly successful and so they tried another. Walt admitted to himself this was sure fun.

The next maneuver for the day was the Immelmann turn. It consisted of half loop followed by starting down the backside, then rolling the aircraft right-side-up and pulling the nose up to level the aircraft. This maneuver was designed to teach the student unbalanced flight, which was needed to keep the aircraft on heading when rolling the aircraft while maintaining original heading.

Walt took control of the aircraft and did two consecutive Im- melmann turns, ending up on the original heading. Lance's only comment was they were pretty good. He took control and demonstrated the last aerobatic maneuver. This was the toughest one of all, the aileron roll. It consisted of raising the nose about 20° above the horizon then, with the use of ailerons, rolling the aircraft 360° until wings level rightside-up, all the while maintaining the same heading. This required using the rudder to maintain heading. Once again Walt took control and practiced a couple of aileron rolls. Lance's assessment was all the aerobatic maneuvers would need plenty of practice to master.

Walt went through another series and afterward headed for Pensacola. Once back in the Ready Room and after debriefing, he sat back and decided he was quite tired from pulling all those Gs and his body ached. He concluded that this phase of training was going to take some getting used to.

Fall Approaches

The first of October had come and gone, and the three intrepid airmen had been at this training for some 10 months. Each of them had completed all their aerobatic flights including their final check ride. Walt's basic training final grade average was a whopping 3.98 while Paul and Bob had to settle for a 3.79. This put the three of them in a good position to decide what kind of advanced training they desired. When they appeared before the Training Officer, he asked each of them if they desired fighters or seaplanes for advanced training. Each, in turn, requested fighters and were issued orders to report to Corry Field the following Monday to begin advanced training.

The three of them were ecstatic about their new assignment. They gathered their flight gear from the hangar and bid farewell to NAS Pensacola.

On Sunday they packed Walt's car with all their worldly goods and headed off to Corry Field. When they arrived, they checked in to the newly constructed BOQ. Once again, they managed to get rooms near one another. They agreed this was going to be one hell-ova-hoot.

Monday Morning

They were all up early and itching to get started. After breakfast, they walked over to the administrative offices and presented their orders to the Officer Personnel Officer. The Chief Yeoman made the endorsements and issued them a check-in sheet for the base. They were assigned to Training Squadron 2 to fly the Stearman NS-1. After making the rounds of the usual check-in places, they found themselves in Hangar 6 and checking into TSQ 2. The Yeoman completed their check-in and ushered them into the Executive Officer's office. Lieutenant Commander Wilberforce welcomed them into the fold and briefed them on the idiosyncrasies of Corry Field. He also told them the Commanding Officer usually had visitations scheduled on Sunday afternoons and that they should check with the Admin Officer to confirm a time to make their call. He also told them to come back on Tuesday morning to see the Commanding Officer because he was presently out flying and wouldn't be back in his office today.

Their next check-in place was the Training Office. Here they left their flight logbooks and talked with the training officer. Their first phase of training would be formation flying and they were assigned to flight section C-26. Besides the three of them, Lieutenant Junior Grade Jack Wilson joined them as a flight of four. Before they could fly, however, ground school and PT was once again in their daily program.

On Tuesday morning, bright and early, they found themselves outside the Skipper's office. The Skipper's Yeoman quickly ushered them into Lieutenant Commander Osborn's office. As they entered, the Skipper arose from his desk and welcomed them.

He began, "Gentlemen, it's a pleasure to have you aboard. We are here to help you in every way possible to complete this phase of training and assist you in achieving your wings of gold. In order to get here, you needed to prove you deserve it. This you have done or you wouldn't be here. Make the most of it, because if you don't get it here, the Fleet will not be so forgiving. Now each of you give me a short bio of your service up to now."

Bob, Paul, and Walt, in order, gave the Skipper a short bio. He was impressed with Paul's tour aboard USS Lexington and asked a few questions. He indicated he had served on board USS Saratoga and had gained much knowledge of Naval Aviation from that tour. The Skipper stood, shook each man's hand, and wished them well in their training.

As they departed the Skipper's office, Paul offered, "The old man seems like a great guy."

"Yeah, he does," Walt said. "Should be a good tour working for him."

"I'll buy that," Bob said.

They had lunch and reported to the ground school building for the start of their classes. The first week was aircraft construction and systems. Chief Petty Officer Roth began the class describing aircraft construction. "Gentlemen," he began, "the NS-1 is built using traditional construction techniques. The fuselage is a steel tube truss design with formers and longerons to define the aerodynamic shape. Wings are of traditional construction with wood ribs and covered by fabric, silk to be exact. The ailerons are of a tapered design with corrugated aluminum covering. The engine is a Wright J5 Whirlwind nine-cylinder air-cooled radial engine 250 horsepower."

He then brought up a line drawing on his easel. He continued using his pointer. "The length of the NS-1 is 24 feet, 9 inches, wingspan 32 feet, and height 2 feet. It seats a crew of two."

Chief Roth then described the cockpit configuration. He described each instrument, knob, switch, and handle.

"Gentlemen," he stated, "you will be tested on this nomenclature. Know each item because the test will be blindfolded and you will need to touch each one."

After the class had a ten-minute break, they came back into the classroom and Chief Roth started his lesson once again.

"Let's now talk about the powerplant on this aircraft. It is a Wright nine-cylinder radial engine rated at 250 horsepower. It is quite different from the in-line engine on your previous flown aircraft."

The chief had a cutaway engine and he droned on for two hours describing each part and its function within the engine.

Chief Roth ceased his lesson and told the class to take a lunch break and to be back at 1300.

At 1300 the class returned, took their seats, and Chief Roth continued where he had left off. He asked if there were any questions on anything he had covered previously.

There were a few questions that were answered quickly and the Chief once again began.

"Our next area of discussion is the performance factors for this aircraft," he said.

He put up another chart on his easel.

"Engine is uncowled. Maximum speed is 108 knots and a cruising speed of 83 knots. With the current fuel capacity, its range is 368 nautical miles and a service ceiling of 13,200 feet."

The class was dismissed and Walt, Paul, and Bob walked back to the BOQ.

Paul broke the silence. "Well, that was a very brief indoctrination into the NS-1."

"Yeah, I felt like I was driving a fast car," Walt responded.

"Hell, I could have learned that much just reading the flight handbook," Bob noted. "Did you guys check the schedule for tomorrow by chance?"

"It looks like a navigation class," Walt said. "It's listed here as maneuvering board navigation, whatever the heck that is."

"Shouldn't be too difficult," Paul said. "I had some navigation training on the Lexington and it was about like we had at the Academy except we actually navigated the ship."

"How the heck are we going to plot on a chart in the cockpit while flying the airplane?" Bob mused.

"I guess we'll find out tomorrow," Walt said. "By the way, we should check with the old man's Yeoman to see when we should make our call on the Skipper. We need to get that done as soon as possible."

"Hey, Buddy, that sounds like a great idea," Bob offered

They arrived at their quarters, changed clothes, had dinner, and settled down afterward for a long discussion on what they had learned that day in ground school. It was a good technique to solidify what they had been taught that day about the NS-1.

Wednesday Morning

By 7:30 a.m. the three of them were off early on their way to ground school. They arrived early enough to grab a cup of Java before settling down in the navigation classroom, waiting for the class to start.

Lieutenant Junior Grade Kit Carson entered and the class stood at attention.

"Be seated, gentlemen," he directed. "My name is Kit Carson and I will be your instructor for this phase of your training. I have flown off Lexington with VF-1 and am well versed with maneuvering board navigation. If you will reach into your desk you will find a maneuvering board which will be the basis for this course. Please do not remove it from the classroom as we have only sufficient boards to use in class. So, let's get started."

Lieutenant (JG) Carson began by describing the board and the circular slide rule attached to the lower right side of the board. It had been simplified with a fixed log ruler on the outward circle, calibrated in nautical miles, and a movable inner circle calibrated in time. Soon they would learn how to manipulate this simple calculator.

The board itself consisted of a clear plastic cover with a circular compass rose printed on its face. Mounted at the center under the plastic was a circular disc with circles representing 10 nm each and squares representing every 60 nm.

Once Lieutenant (JG) Carson had explained the nomenclature of the board, he began to explain how to use it.

The class lasted most of the morning, and as he was finishing his lecture, he explained to the class that there would be four more morning sessions. After answering all the questions, he dismissed the class.

As Bob, Paul and Walt left the classroom, Bob checked his ground school schedule.

Bob commented, "When we finish this class, we have 10 sessions of Aerology followed by a test in copying Morse code. I guess they want us to keep up our proficiency of 10 words per minute."

"That's a bummer," Paul said. "I sure hoped we were finished with that."

"You know you love that stuff, Paul. It keeps you off the street, at night," Walt answered.

"In your dreams, old friend," Paul replied.

"Well, at least we get to fly a half-day for a while anyway," Bob interjected.

"Yeah, I was looking at some of the formation flying stuff last night and it's fairly easy and straightforward, but I guess it will take a lot of practice," Walt offered.

"So, what's on the schedule for this afternoon, besides PT?" Paul asked.

"We have to meet with our instructor at 1330. A Lieutenant (JG) Ted Carter. I hear he's a real badass," Bob said.

"He has that reputation only because he is a perfectionist. He believes Navy pilots should be the best and exhibit it in their flying at all times," Walt said. "so let's just show him we are the best."

"Okay, okay, Mister perfection, we'll do it your way. Practice makes perfect," Paul said.

As they were headed out the door for the BOQ, Walt said he was going by the Commanding Officer's office to check with Skipper's Yeoman on when they could make a call on the Skipper.

He caught up with them at the BOQ. They were already seated for lunch.

"How'd you make out." Paul asked Walt as he was taking his seat at the table.

"We have an appointment on Sunday at 1400 with the old man and his wife at their quarters," Walt responded.

"I guess we'll have to break out our Sunday go to meetin' clothes," Bob offered.

"That's the plan, old Buddy," Walt said.

They finished lunch and were off to Hangar six to meet Lieutenant (JG) Carter.

6

"New Friends"

Formation Flying

The trio of student aviators entered the Hangar and were met by the fourth member of their flight, Lieutenant (JG) Jack Wilson. After greetings all around they wandered down to the student-Ready Room. It wasn't quite 1330 so they sat down at one of the briefing tables awaiting the arrival of Lieutenant (JG) Carter.

As Lieutenant (JG) Carter approached their table, they were pretty sure it was him, even though they had never met, and all stood up at attention.

"At ease, be seated," Ted said. "I'm Lieutenant (JG) Ted Carter. I am going to be your lead instructor for this phase of your training. How about each of you telling me about your background."

Bob started. "I'm Lieutenant (JG) Bob Fitzwater. I'm originally from St. Paul, Minnesota. Graduated from the Naval Academy class of '25. Spent 2 years on the USS West Virginia then the USS Omaha."

"That's great, Lieutenant. Great to have you aboard," Ted responded. "And Mister Day, what's your story?"

Paul began, "I was born and raised in Sault Ste. Marie, Michigan. Graduated Naval Academy class of '26. Served 3 years on the USS Lexington and finally came to Pensacola for flight training. I'm single and looking. That's about it, Sir."

"Wow, Mister Day, I envy you having served on the Lex. I hope to hear more of your experiences on the Lex as we progress through training," Ted said.

Ted looked to Walt and asked, "What's your story, Ensign Pell- man?"

"Sir, I grew up in Newport, Rhode Island, graduated Naval Academy class of '27, rowed varsity crew. Spent 2 years on the USS Mississippi out of San Pedro, California."

"Sounds good, Mister Pellman. Glad to have you as a student." Then turning to Lieutenant (JG) Wilson, Ted asked, "What's your story, Lieutenant Wilson?"

"Sir, I'm originally from Fredericksburg, Texas. Graduated Naval Academy class of '25. I served on the tender Gannet (AM-41). She was a minesweeper and was assigned to the task force with USS Langley (CV- 1). That's where I became interested in naval aviation," Jack said.

"That's interesting," Ted noted. "Did you know the Nimitz family in Fredericksburg? Commander Nimitz was our Chief of Staff in Pearl Harbor when I was stationed there and he was from Fredericksburg."

"Yes, Sir, I heard of the Nimitz family growing up. Commander Nimitz' old man has a hotel in Fredericksburg," Jack added.

"Well, that's interesting. Anyway, gentlemen, now that we are acquainted, let's get down to the syllabus.

"The formation flying syllabus will be 13 flights. Your first four flights will be a two-plane formation and the remaining nine flights will be four planes. I will be your primary instructor and will be assisted by Lieutenant (JG) John Burtt, Lieutenant (JG) Paul Eubanks, and 2nd LT Jerry Elliott. You will meet them before your first flight."

Ted continued. "We have adapted formation flying to what you will be doing in the fleet. First of all, when we return to the field we will perform a new maneuver. It is called the "break." You will come straight towards the runway on runway heading. As you approach the runway, the tower should give you a green or red light. If you receive a red light, you will continue up the runway for 30 seconds and then make a wide left turn and proceed downwind on the reverse heading of the runway for another run into the break. When you pass abeam of the landing point you will make another left turn and enter the break. Assuming you receive a green light, you will check for other aircraft already downwind for landing. Taking a 30-second interval on that traffic, the leader will blow a kiss," that brought chuckles from all the students. Ted demonstrated touching his hand to his lips and then extending his hand towards his wingman, "and break left at 45° angle of bank while slowing to approach landing speed. Each wingman will in turn break at a 10-second interval on the aircraft ahead using the same technique to get in position downwind for landing. Normal procedures from there to landing. Any questions to this point?"

"Blowing a kiss, sir. Are you sure that's what we should call it?" Paul asked.

"Gentlemen, it is what it is," Ted said.

Ted continued. "The only part of formation flying we will discuss today is the actual position of each aircraft. The remainder of the maneuvers will be briefed for each flight."

For this part, Ted grabbed a couple of aircraft models. He placed the two aircraft in position while describing their relationship. "Normal formation is called an echelon. We always form up in right echelon, 10 feet nose to tail, 10 feet wingtip to wingtip, and 10 feet step-up. In turns, you will always maintain this position. Overall it is called the parade position."

Walt raised his hand. "Sir do we take off in this position? If not, how do we get to the correct position?"

Ted answered. "Great question. Takeoff will be individually, then proceeding out to a predesignated rendezvous point and then form up in formation. Let's concentrate on that for now. Later on, we will modify that and adapt our procedures to the fleet methods."

Ted continued. "Now we may also fly in left echelon. So how are we going to change from right to left? First, the leader will give the hand signal to change to left echelon. That signal is a clenched fist, arm bent to a 90° angle, raised and lowered twice in a pumping motion."

Ted demonstrated then continued. "The wingman will drop down to 10 feet stepdown, then slide over to the left side while maintaining 10 feet nose to tail, stop the slide at 10 feet wingtip to wingtip, and then move back up to a 10-foot step up."

He moved the model airplanes to show the maneuver and said, "It will all become very clear when you perform this maneuver."

Ted opened the discussion for questions. All four students chimed in with them and after another half-hour, all questions were answered.

"Gentlemen, this concludes our training session for today. I will see you tomorrow afternoon for your first flight. Check the schedule board for time and aircraft assignment."

Ted left and they all sat and discussed the contents of the lecture for a few minutes.

Finally, Paul said, "Well let's go down to scheduling and see what's in store for tomorrow."

When they arrived at scheduling they checked the chalkboard. Bob was scheduled to fly with Paul while Walt was scheduled to fly with Jack. Their flights were at 1330. Bob and Paul had Ted Carter and John Burtt as instructors while Walt and Jack had Paul Eubanks and Jerry Elliott as instructors.

"Well, we have our assignments for tomorrow. Not much more we can do here. Since it's early, why don't we go over to the beach at NAS for a couple of hours," Walt said.

There didn't seem like much enthusiasm for that.

Bob said, "I think I need to study my maneuvering board lesson one more time. That stuff is confusing, to say the least, after that I have a PT assignment."

"Yeah, I'm going over to the coderoom and brush up on my code copying, I need to keep up my 10 words per minute since we have a monthly check-up coming soon." Paul offered. "What are you going to do, Jack?"

"I think I'll go with you, Paul. I need to brush up on my code copying," Jack answered.

Walt interjected, "Okay, you guys. If you're all going to becandy asses and be studious, I'm going over to NAS and play some golf."

Walt walked over to his car, jumped in, and sped off for mainside Pensacola and a game of golf. He had played very little since arriving at flight training and it would be a good diversion for him. It was only eight miles and soon he was pulling through the main gate. The course was just about 500 yards from the gate and he swung into the parking lot just outside the clubhouse. He had a change of clothes with him and he went into the locker room to change. He put on a brown golf shirt, matching browncolored pants, and a visor on his head. He went over to the golf shop and rented a pair of shoes and a set of clubs. He purchased a dozen balls and a bag of golf tees. He sat down to change his shoes and wait for some playing partners as the starter told him a threesome would be coming in a couple of minutes and he could make it a foursome.

The threesome soon arrived and the starter asked them if Walt could join their party. They agreed and he was introduced by the starter as the fourth player. Walt walked over and introduced himself to the other players.

He extended his hand to each of them, "I'm Ensign Walt Pell- man," he said.

Turned out his playing partners were Rear Admiral William McMillin, Head of the Bureau of Aeronautics. Founder of Naval Aviation; Lieutenant Commander Charles E. Rosendahl, Senior Lighter-Than-Air expert; and Captain Frederick J. Horne, Commanding Officer, USS Saratoga.

What's your handicap, Mister Pellman?" The Admiral asked.

"About 10, Sir," He responded. "Although I haven't played in quite a while, Sir. I have been quite busy learning how to become a Naval Aviator."

"That's okay, Son. We all have been very busy with our responsibilities, so we're all in the same boat. Just a little rusty when it comes to golf. Let's just go out and have a great game and enjoy ourselves," The Admiral said.

The three players nodded in agreement.

"We can tee off in order of seniority, and after that, low score can tee off first on the next hole. Is that agreeable with everyone?" Admiral McMillin offered.

Fred Horne spoke for everyone. "Sounds good, Admiral."

Admiral McMillin stepped up to the tee and hit the ball about 280 yards straight down the fairway. Fred Horne was next and he drove his ball almost as far but just slightly left. Max Rosenthal was next and his ball was shorter than the other two and on the left edge of the fairway. Walt was last and he thought to himself *"just hit it straight."* His shot was straight down the fairway at about 260 yards. He hadn't hit it as hard as he knew he could just so he could keep it straight. Walt figured this was not a competition, just enjoy the afternoon and don't make a fool of himself.

Each of them parred the first hole so the tee-off order remained the same. By the fourth hole, Walt had the honors as he had parred the third hole while the others had bogeyed it.

That's the way the afternoon went. They were finally reaching the 18th hole and Walt was +9 over par, Admiral McMillin was +13, Captain Horne +16, and Lieutenant Commander Rosenthal was +17. On the final hole, they all shot even par and everyone seemed happy about their score. While walking the fairways, there was a lot of naval aviation business discussed and Walt had just listened mostly, absorbing what was being discussed. Some of it he didn't understand but it was an enjoyable afternoon. While they were putting up their clubs, Admiral McMillin spoke to Walt.

"Ensign Pellman, why don't you join us in the clubhouse for a cool drink?" he said.

"Yes Sir, that would be fine," Walt answered.

Walt turned in his clubs and shoes and walked into the clubhouse. The other three officers were already seated and Walt joined them.

The waiter came and took their order. The choice was coffee, iced tea, or lemonade. Walt opted for the lemonade.

After ordering, Captain Horne offered, "Sure wish this prohibition was over. I would like a nice glass of scotch and water for a change."

"I hear some rumblings in Washington that congress may try to pass a repeal to the amendment soon but it is going to be tough," Admiral McMillin observed.

"Whenever we deploy to Guantanamo Bay, Cuba or the Canal Zone we can get drinks in the O'club," Rosenthal said.

"Yeah, that's one of the perks for a deployment," Horne offered.

Turning to Walt, Admiral McMillin asked, "Mr. Pellman, you were saying your father is into oil. Just what does he do?"

"Sir, he's the CEO of Socony Oil Company," Walt answered.

"And how long has he been with that company?" The Admiral asked.

"I'm not sure, Sir, but I think about 25 years. I know it used to be part of Standard Oil which of course was dismantled by the Supreme Court under the Sherman Anti-trust Act," Walt said.

"Yes, I remember that. We had to change our contract for aviation gasoline and shipboard fuel oil because of that," The Admiral said.

The four finished their drinks, and as they were getting ready to leave, Admiral McMillin turned to Walt, "Mister Pellman, we are having dinner tonight at the Commanding Officer quarters. How about joining us?"

"That would be wonderful Sir. What time should I be there and what is the dress for dinner?" Walt asked.

"I think about 1930 will be fine and civilian dinner dress is in order."

"Yes, Sir, I'll be there," Walt said.

Walt went back into the locker room, changed back into his uniform, jumped into his car, and proceeded back to Corry Field. When he arrived at the BOQ he ran into Bob.

"Hey, Buddy, how was your golf game?" he asked.

Walt replied. "Had a great time and met some great officers. I have to change clothes right now as I have an invitation to dinner over at main- side."

Walt had about an hour to shower, change clothes and get back over to mainside to be on time for dinner. He decided he could tell the guys later with whom he had played golf.

"Who are you having dinner with?" Bob inquired.

"Just the guys I played golf with this afternoon," Walt replied.

"Well, have a great dinner," Bob responded.

"Will do, old friend," Walt said.

Walt quickly got to his room, took a shower, and dressed in his civilian dinner dress outfit, which of course was a white shirt, tie, gray pants, and blue blazer.

Within 30 minutes he was off to Mainside Pensacola and Captain McDonald's quarters. He arrived with 5 minutes to spare. This was going to be some night to remember.

Dinner Glorified

Walt knocked on the front door and waited. He was greeted by Mrs. Susan McDonald, the Commanding Officer's wife.

"Good evening, Mister Pellman. We've been expecting you. Come in please," she said.

She extended her hand. "A great pleasure to meet you," Walt said.

As she stepped back to close the door, a beautiful young lady appeared from the open entrance to the living room. Susan turned, "I'd like you to meet my daughter Karen," she said.

"I believe we met the other day at the beach. Hello again, Karen," Walt said.

He was taken in once again by this beautiful woman, but before he could engage her in conversation, Susan said, "The men are all in the drawing-room talking aviation and I expect you would like to join them?"

Walt joked but was somewhat serious, "With two beautiful women to talk with, I might just stay out here," he quipped.

They both blushed. "Let me show you to the drawing-room," Susan said.

She led him down the hallway to the back of the house and into the drawing-room.

All those in the room turned as she entered, "Gentlemen, our guest Ensign Pellman has arrived."

Captain McDonald stepped over, "Thanks, Susan. Mister Pellman come join us," he said.

Walt joined the group. "Good evening, Admiral," he said as he shook Admiral McMillin's hand.

"Good evening, Mister Pellman. I'm pleased that you could join us, the Admiral said.

The others in the room welcomed Walt and shook his hand. A servant with a tray of drinks appeared and offered one to Walt. He took it and sipped a little. He was shocked, it was Cuban rum with coca-cola and a slice of lime in it. He found out later that Captain Horne had acquired it in Panama and had brought it from the west Coast when he came for the conference.

The conversation went back to what they had been discussing before Walt arrived, the status of naval aviation and the introduction and future improvements planned in the Lighter-Than-Air community. Admiral McMillin was very keen on the two new dirigibles ZPS4 and ZPS5. He described how they were soon to be launched and commissioned. Lieutenant Commander Rosendahl offered the fact that the trapeze off the USS Los Angeles, which had been tested for aircraft recovery while in flight, was being adapted for use on the ZPS4 and ZPS5.

They also inquired of Walt about his aviation training and when he expected to graduate and earn his wings. He told them his expected wing pinning ceremony would be about March 1st, 1931. They all seemed quite interested in his progress and were glad to hear about the quality of training he had received thus far.

Walt listened intently to the conversation about the trapeze and its test program. Finally, he could no longer remain quiet and decided he needed to add to the conversation.

"Admiral, may I add my two cents to the discussion?" Walt asked. "Of course. Have at it." Admiral McMillin replied.

"Well Sir, from my engineering background and my limited study of aerodynamics I believe there will be difficulty with aircraft handling and safety issues on the trapeze once the dirigibles become operational for testing. Let me explain further. Once the airship slows its forward speed below the stall speed of the aircraft which is hooked up to the trapeze, it will probably start to flop from side to side due to turbulence generated by the airship's engines. From what I heard described here tonight, there could be a safety issue with damage to the aircraft and possible injury to the recovery crew on the airship. Perhaps a couple of stabilizing struts could be attached to the aircraft's wings to lock it in place before slowing the airship. I'm not sure how this could be done at this point, but theoretically I could see the need for such a modification and procedure."

"That's quite an analysis, Mr. Pellman," Lieutenant Commander Rosenthal observed.

"Yes, Sir," Walt responded. "It's all theoretical of course, Sir. I would need to study the drawings and read the reports of the pilots doing the hookups on the Los Angeles to confirm whether I am on the right track or not."

"He brings up a good point, doesn't he," Admiral McMillin observed. "I hadn't seen any procedures and findings on that particular test in the reports sent to me. We are doing that test, aren't we, Chuck?"

Lieutenant Commander Rosenthal responded, "Sir, I don't think we have that procedure written into our testing at this point."

"Perhaps we should consider it then," the Admiral quipped.

Thinking to himself, Admiral McMillin was impressed by this young naval officer and he filed it away for future consideration.

The discussion continued for another few minutes and was interrupted by Susan McDonald, "Gentlemen, I believe we are ready to sit down for dinner. Will you please join me in the dining room?"

Susan offered her arm to Admiral McMillin, as he was the senior officer. The Admiral placed her arm in his right arm and she escorted all of them into the dining room. Captain McDonald stood behind his chair at the head of the table since he was the host and Susan took the seat at the foot of the table. Admiral McMillin took his seat on Captain McDonald's right and then all the others present took their seats. Walt was seated on the left next to Susan as he was the junior officer present.

Susan signaled the household staff to begin serving dinner. They started off with a crab soup followed by a shrimp cocktail. The main course was prime rib with baked potato and asparagus. Finally, they reached the dessert which turned out to be New York Cheesecake. Red wine was served throughout the dinner along with southern iced tea.

The conversation during dinner centered mostly on how the country was doing in this great recession and how it was going to affect naval acquisitions and operations. Walt mostly listened and had a nice conversation with Susan about how she was enjoying her daily living in Pensacola.

Dinner being over, Susan said, "Gentlemen, why don't you adjourn to the Florida room and I will have some libations served up there."

They all stood and first thanked Susan for the great dinner and then went into the Florida room. Captain McDonald offered them cigars, which they all lit up. The Florida room was a great place to smoke as it was a screened-in porch on the rear of the quarters which overlooked Pensacola Bay. Shortly one of the servants appeared carrying a tray of after dinner drinks. Tonight, it would be Kahlua, a great coffee liqueur.

The discussion once again turned to the development of the dirigibles. Admiral McMillin offered the progress of the construction and estimated completion date. Admiral McMillin was also interested in what was happening with the USS Saratoga and asked Captain Horne what he was seeing in the way of furthering the role of naval aviation.

Captain Horne seemed to savor the opportunity to discuss the Saratoga, especially with the boss.

He began, "Well, Admiral we are still analyzing the results of Fleet Problem IX. I believe we can prove that the aircraft carrier can be a single effective striking force. We are working on developing a coordinated attack on land targets using our aircraft in the most effective way against enemy targets.

"On a much smaller scale, we are developing standard Landing Signal Officer signals, which we will send up for your approval as soon as we have decided on them for promulgation to all carrier commands. As you are aware, things are changing rapidly with the introduction of aircraft with flaps and retractable landing gear. We need to add those signals to our resume. We are also going to add a platform for the LSO to work from. It will extend over the aft, port catwalk on the edge of the flight deck.

"The final immediate thing we are doing is adding night quals to our flight schedule since there is now an order in place for each pilot to have 20 hours of night flying and 20 night landings."

"Sounds like you have a full plate, Fred." the Admiral observed. "By the way, Fred, we are thinking about giving you a Marine Scouting squadron.

Should happen beginning January next year. They will be flying the SU-3. It has a 600-horsepower engine and cruises at 145 knots. I think you'll like its radius of action which should be around 250 nautical miles. Should give you a great scouting area."

"That sounds great, Admiral, I look forward to having them on board," Fred answered.

Walt interrupted the conversation, "Sir, I would like to excuse myself as I have ground school and an early flight tomorrow. Captain McDonald, I appreciate spending the evening with everyone, Sir. It was a great learning experience."

"It was a pleasure, Ensign. Glad to have you as a guest. Good luck with your training," he said.

With that Walt headed for the door. As he passed the living room he spied Susan so he stuck his head in the door, "Mrs. McDonald, thanks for the wonderful evening and dinner. Please pass my best wishes to Karen."

"Oh, you're leaving so soon," Susan said. "You're welcome. I hope you had a great evening."

"Yes, Ma'am, "Walt responded. "It was a once in a lifetime experience for an Ensign. Goodnight Ma'am."

His drive back to Corry Station took about 20 minutes and soon he was in his bed trying to get to sleep. It had been an eye-opening experience. Just to meet Admiral McMillin, Captain Horne, and Lieutenant Commander Rosenthal, all giants in naval aviation, was a once-in-a-life- time happening.

7

"Recreation Time"

Next Morning

Walt was up early, showered and shaved, put on his summer dress uniform, and headed off to breakfast by 7:30 a.m. Soon Bob and Paul showed up.

"How was your dinner last night, old Buddy?" they asked.

Walt had decided not to disclose who he had dinner with because he knew he would take a lot of badgering and all the usual friendly naval aviation harassment. Trying not to show too much enthusiasm he answered, "It was okay, I guess. Not a big deal. Just a couple of out-of-town guys I met on the golf course."

Trying to change the subject he interjected, "Did you guys review the formation procedures for the flight today?"

"Yeah, Paul and I walked through the procedures step by step. I think we got it down pretty good," Bob said.

That misdirection seemed to lower the temperature and the need to continue the inquiry into Walt's foray the night before. The conversation about flight F1 took over and highlighted their breakfast interface. The three of them finished breakfast and took off walking over to ground school and their first class. It would be more maneuvering board problems to solve and would take a lot of concentration. Another class had been added for their second meeting of the morning, more aerology. It appeared that aerology was going to be center stage for a while, and as their instructor said, "You can't get too much of this stuff as your life may depend upon your knowledge of the weather."

The morning went quickly, and after a light lunch, they were at the Hangar preparing for their afternoon flight.

Ted Carter entered the Ready Room with his sidekick John Burtt and met Bob and Paul to begin briefing for their flight. They were followed into the room by Paul Eubanks and Jerry Elliott who came over and introduced themselves to Walt and Jack. Turns out Paul is a former fighter jock from VF-1, the Tophatters, off the Lexington. Jerry described his background as a torpedo pilot having served in VT-4, also flying off the Lexington.

The briefing proceeded with Paul Eubanks taking the lead instructor. He described each maneuver they would perform and how they would proceed. Their rendezvous point would be a left circle at 3000' over the Highway 90 Perdido River Bridge. The bridge was directly 10 miles west of the runways at Corry Station with Highway 90 running east-west just south of the base perimeter.

Briefing complete, Walt and Jack were dispatched to the flight line to preflight the planes. They checked out their parachutes and proceeded to the aircraft. Just as Walt finished, Paul arrived. "Well Ensign Pellman how does she look?" Paul asked.

"She looks in great shape, Sir," Walt answered. "I think the brakes should be checked after we return. Looks like excessive wear."

"Now how in the hell can you determine that?" Paul inquired.

Walt directed Paul over to the port wheel. "If you look at the area of the brake shoe and the spokes, there is brake dust all over them," Walt pointed out. "I believe that shows excessive use of the brakes on the previous flight."

"Looks like you are correct, Mister Pellman. We'll write it up for maintenance when we get back," Paul said. "Let's get aboard and get this thing underway."

The Plane Captain assisted both of them in getting strapped in and took his position on the starboard side of the plane in front of the propeller. After completing all required checklists, Walt gave the Plane Captain a thumbs up and a circling motion with his right arm extended upwards and two fingers only. This was the signal to start the engine. Walt put the mixture in full rich, cracked the throttle off the rear stop. The Plane Captain turned over the propeller by hand, two complete revolutions. This was to prime the engine with fuel. The Plane Captain gave Walt the hold brakes signal and called out "contact."

Walt responded "contact," while he held the brakes and turned on the magneto switch. The Plane Captain grasped a prop blade and quickly pulled down on it. The engine coughed and he did it a second time. This time the engine roared to life and stabilized at 800 RPM. Walt gave the signal to pull the chocks, which the Plane Captain accomplished, then he signaled Walt to taxi forward, saluted, and sent them on their way. Walt had checked the wind direction, which was almost out of due west, so he proceeded east to the takeoff end of runway 26. He cheeked the control tower and received a green light to continue taxiing. Upon reaching the eastern field boundary, he turned into the wind and ran the engine up to 1600 rpm while holding the brakes. He then switched the magneto switch to left while checking the RPM loss, then right to do the same and returning the switch to both magnetos. Both magnetos checked okay. Walt completed his takeoff checklist and pulled up short of the takeoff runway, turning his aircraft towards the tower looking for a green light. Within 30 seconds he received a green light, signaling he was cleared for takeoff. He checked the approach to the runway for traffic before taxiing onto the runway for takeoff. Once on the runway, Walt added power for takeoff and within 600' was airborne. He set climb speed and power while climbing straight ahead to 3000' where he leveled off at cruise speed. As he did, he was approaching the Perdido Bay Bridge. Paul signaled him he had the airplane.

Paul started a wide circle around the bridge while waiting for Jerry and Jack to appear. Soon they joined the circle, and since they were going to lead the formation, Paul began demonstrating how to "join up."

Paul increased his angle of bank and began intercepting Jerry. As Paul began closing on Jerry, he shallowed his angle of bank and kept his closure angle at approximately 30° and steady. Soon he matched Jerry's angle of bank and zero closure speed in a left echelon position of 10' noseto-tail with a 10' stepdown. As quickly as he was stabilized, he slid under Jerry with a minimum change of angle of bank and then stabilized in right echelon maintaining 10 feet of stepdown. Once stabilized, he moved up to his final parade position of 10' nose-to-tail and 10' step-up.

He indicated to Walt to take the aircraft, which he did. They proceeded in a northwest direction while Walt practiced the parade position, which consisted of maintaining his nose-to-tail and step-up interval.

For the next 30 minutes, Walt practiced changing echelon from right to left and left back to right, also carrier breakups and rendezvous.

The team changed the lead as Walt and Jerry began to repeat all maneuvers so Jack could get the same experience Walt had just gone through. After another 30 minutes of drills, Jerry indicated to Walt to return to base.

Walt turned southeast and headed for Pensacola. The wind was still out of the west-southwest, and it was time to practice the new approach and landing procedure. He circled counterclockwise keeping the landing field off his left-wing. When he passed abeam the landing end of the runway, he descended to 1000' and began a tighter turn heading straight up the runway. Passing the landing point, he scanned for other traffic on the downwind leg that were already set up in the landing sequence. When he saw no further traffic in the downwind, he gave his wingman the break signal by blowing him a kiss and put the aircraft in a forty-five-degree angle of bank, reduced power on the engine, and descended to 800'. As he approached a heading 180° from landing runway heading, he rolled out and leveled the aircraft at 800'. Passing abeam the landing point of the runway, he began a shallow descending turn. His goal was to roll out on runway heading over the end of the runway at 10' and proceed to land the aircraft in the first 50' of the runway.

Turns out he was extremely successful and made a perfect landing. As he slowed the aircraft, he turned off the runway and proceeded to the parking area near the Hangar. After parking and shutdown, he and Paul proceeded to the Ready Room for debriefing.

They waited for Jerry and Jack to arrive before beginning debriefing. Minor points were discussed, and questions answered. Paul and Jerry departed just as Ted, John, Bob, and Paul arrived. Their debrief was short and sweet, and Ted and Paul departed.

The four flight students sat for a while and discussed their experiences on F1. The admin Yeoman entered the briefing room looking for Ensign Pellman. He handed Walt a memo stating that he was required to be in the Commanding Officer's office at 1000 tomorrow morning.

"What do you guys suppose that's all about?" Walt said. "Probably some public relations thing," Paul responded.

"Well, I'm not going to worry about it," Walt said.

With that having been said, they picked up their gear and headed for the BOQ.

Next Morning

Walt was up early. Despite saying he was not going to worry about meeting with the Commanding Officer, he had a fitful sleep doing just that. He just could not figure out why the Commanding Officer wanted to meet with him. He went to breakfast and afterward sat in the lobby of the BOQ reading the morning paper. It would be a long wait until 1000.

Time passed slowly, and as the clock approached 0930, he walked over to the full-length mirror in the lobby and checked his dress blue uniform to make sure everything was neat and in order. He checked his hat to make sure the white cover was pristine, and the gold band looked good. Of course, it was but it was just a nervous reaction.

Finally, it was time to go, and he proceeded to the admin building and the Commanding Officer's office. As he entered the Commanding Officer's office he was greeted by the Commanding Officer's Yeoman.

"Good morning, Ensign Pellman. The Commanding Officer will be with you in just a few minutes. Please have a seat while you are waiting."

"Thanks, Petty Officer Stillman. Do you know what the Old Man wants to see me about?" Walt asked.

"The Skipper will brief you when you see him," Yeoman Stillman answered.

A few minutes later, the Executive Officer, Lieutenant Commander Wilberforce entered the waiting room. Walt stood and snapped to attention.

"Good morning, Mister Pellman," the Executive Officer observed.

"Good morning, Sir," Walt replied.

"The Commanding Officer is waiting for you, Sir." Yeoman Stillman offered.

As Walt and the Executive Officer were about to enter the Commanding Officer's office, a photographer from the public relations office entered the waiting room and joined them. The Executive Officer knocked on the Commanding Officer's door, opened it and entered with Walt and the photographer in tow.

"Good morning, Skipper," he said. "I guess we're all here."

Lieutenant Commander Osborn rose from behind his desk and came around to greet the Executive Officer and Walt. The Yeoman had followed them into the office, and at that point, handed the Skipper a folder. The Skipper opened it, read it, and handed it to the Executive Officer.

"Will you do the honors?" Lieutenant Commander Osborn asked.

The Executive Officer opened the folder and began. "Attention to orders. Having the utmost trust and confidence in Ensign Walter John Pellman, the President of the United States takes great pleasure in appointing Ensign Walter John Pellman, United States Navy, to the rank of Lieutenant Junior Grade in the United States Navy, effective September 1st, in the year of our Lord One Thousand Nine Hundred Thirty. Signed Herbert Clark Hoover, President of the United States."

The Executive Officer handed the folder to the Yeoman who then placed it on a table then asked Ensign Pellman to sign the papers. Walt sat down and signed the papers, then stood at attention. The Commanding Officer and Executive Officer both congratulated him and directed the photographer to take a picture of the three of them. When they finished the Commanding Officer turned and said to Walt, "Mister Pellman, you're out of uniform."

Walt answered, "Yes, Sir, I will remedy that in a couple of hours."

Lieutenant Commander Osborn responded, "Well done, Mr. Pellman. We're finished here. Dismissed."

Lieutenant Junior Grade Pellman left the Commanding Officer's office and went back to work.

Walt had walked back to the BOQ for lunch. Bob and Paul showed up and their first question was, "What happened at the Commanding Officers office?" they asked.

Walt had a big smile on his face, "You are now talking to Lieutenant (JG) Pellman so show alittle respect."

Bob's face lit up like a kid with chocolate candy. Paul had a slightly dejected look on his face.

"Hey, Buddy, congratulations. That's really great. You deserved that promotion," they said. Paul was somewhat bewildered. "My promotion should have also come through," Paul added.

Bob and Walt were somewhat distraught, suddenly realizing how disappointed Paul must feel.

Bob then made a suggestion. "Hey, Paul, you need to go over to officer personnel. Once in a while the bureau screws up and misses somebody who really has been selected."

Walt backed up Bob and seconded his suggestion. "Yeah, personnel can send a message and ask the question, did they did miss you on the promotion."

"Okay, I'll go over this afternoon and inquire," Paul said.

Walt then told them the complete story of what happened and how. He indicated to them how shocked he was and how proud because of the way it played out.

When he finished, he just said, "So let's go to lunch."

Flight progress

Formation flights F2 through F6 were more of F1 except for the introduction of the fleet parade position. This position was being used for the runway break-up for landing, so it was not new, but was introduced when flying away from home base also. All flights were now solo with the introduction of four-plane formation. On flight F8 a new formation tactic was introduced. The instructors called it free cruise. In turns, instead of maintaining wing position, the planes matched the angle of bank to the leader and allowed the plane to slip into a position underneath the plane ahead of it information. It in effect was a vertical formation with only 10' nose to tail with each plane being directly below the other. This type of formation allowed steeper angles of bank but easier for wingmen to maintain position.

The four intrepid fledgling aviators breezed through the formation syllabus and on F13 all received good grades for their check flight. Their final formation flight was a scouting formation with four planes abreast, spaced at 200 feet in a straight line.

Their next phase of training was night flying. They were all required to log 20 hours at night and 20 landings. Their first two flights involved takeoff, climb to their assigned altitude, and circling the field until signaled down to complete 5 landings.

Monday they were all scheduled for the first of their night flights. After a leisurely day, they reported to the Hangar. Scheduled takeoff time was 1830. They changed into their flying uniform and headed for the briefing room. The instructor briefed them on night procedures and gave them each an assigned altitude for circling the field until signaled down for their 5 landings. They were also briefed on emergency procedures. Caution was advised to be aware of propeller vertigo. This usually occurred when the sun was low in the sky shining through the prop. The constant motion of the prop flashing the sun cyclically resulted in vertigo.

Walt and Bob were assigned to circle the field at 3500' while Paul was assigned to 2500'. Higher altitudes were given earlier takeoff times.

The students manned their aircraft and started engines. At that time, fog formed over the field resulting in zero visibility. They had all been briefed on this possibility, and when it happened, their Plane Captains were advised by the instructor that flying was canceled for the night. They shut down the engines and secured the aircraft.

On reporting back to the briefing room, the instructor advised that they would be scheduled again for tomorrow. It was a letdown as the students were keyed up all day in anticipation. However, they all took it in stride and secured for the night.

The next night the process was repeated, and the weather was beautiful. Bob and Walt took off first and climbed to their assigned altitude of 3500'. Paul followed to his assigned altitude of 2500'. It was twilight at takeoff and after a half-hour, it was completely dark. The lights from the city were visible in the distance but the countryside was generally dark. Most farmhouses were without electricity and used kerosene lamps for light. There were a few lights on the base and the runway was now lit with kerosene-powered lamps. There was no visible horizon, but the stars were brighter than these pilots had ever seen. As a result, it required a constant scan inside the cockpit to maintain altitude. After 30 minutes of cruising at altitude, the tower flashed a green light for those planes cruising at 2500' to descend into the landing pattern. This signaled those cruising at 3500' to start their clock timer. Standard operating procedures called for a ten-minute respite then a descent to 2500'.

On the green light, Paul descended to 800' and entered the lefthand traffic pattern. As he passed abeam the landing point on the runway, he began his 180° descending turn for his first touch-and-go landing.

As Paul was completing his fourth touch and go landing, the tower signaled the green light to those circling at 2500' to descend to the traffic pattern and begin their landings.

Paul made his fifth landing which was a full stop, after which he taxied back to the ramp and parked his aircraft. Bob and Walt finished their five landings and also parked their aircraft. They returned to the Ready Room and were debriefed by their instructor, who had been observing their landings at the end of the runway. They were animated and a little excited at having experienced their first night flight. The conversation was hot and heavy all the way back to the BOQ.

The second night flight was a repeat of the first. All went well and was completed with great enthusiasm.

The next two flights were a triangular cross-country to the west of Corry Station and returning to base for 3 landings. Flights five and six were extended cross-country flights consisting of four legs and return to base.

Since they were flying only at night, they had plenty of leisure time. Paul had acquired a 19' Lightning class sailboat which he kept moored at NAS Pensacola marina. Walt had some hours sailing when he lived in Newport, Rhode Island, so he guided Paul and Bob in the intricacies of sailing. They all enjoyed their time sailing on Pensacola Bay as it was a great time to relax and get away from their flying routine. It made them more focused when they did their night flying.

Thanksgiving rolled around and they dined at the BOQ dining room. Dinner was a little sparser this year than in previous years. The Great Depression was affecting all aspects of their life in the Navy and dinner was one of them. After dinner, they settled in the lounge and lit up cigars, which were furnished courtesy of the U.S. Navy. The conversation centered around finishing their night flying and what was next. Christmas crept into the conversation and each of them had a strong opinion on what they should do during their time off. Paul thought they should go back to New Orleans and invite the ladies from last year. Walt nixed that idea. Zimmy was going to have to work through the holidays, flying the milk run from Chicago to Wichita. Jo and Jane likewise had to work during the holidays as the hospital was short of staff. As nurses, they were pulling a 12-hour shift, four days a week. Bob opted for a trip to Cypress Gardens in central Florida. He had heard they had a terrific water show and the gardens themselves were a great site. Paul and Walt both gave Bob the Naval Aviation treatment. They thought that was too much of a choirboy activity. Finally, Walt came up with a suggestion. Why didn't he get the old man to send the company Ford Trimotor down to Pensacola to pick them up and bring them back to Newport for the holidays? The house had plenty of room for them and they could take a side trip to Lake Placid for a little skiing. Walt was sure the old man would go for it and there would also be plenty of parties for them to attend during the holidays.

They all agreed that would be a blast, if Walt could pull it off. He said he would talk to the old man in the next week.

They had nothing scheduled for the weekend, so they spent most of the time on Paul's sailboat. Most of the ladies they had met over the summer were back at college so female companionship was at a minimum.

The remainder of the night flights were a snap. They all passed with flying colors and were now officially advanced flight students. All they had left before receiving their wings was gunnery, instrument flying. and carrier quals.

Walt had contacted his old man and he had agreed to send the Trimotor to pick them up on the 20th of December. With Christmas falling on a Thursday this year, they were given two full weeks of leave. They wouldn't need to be back until the 4th of January. This would give them 16 days off from flight training.

They all had dinner at the Mess that evening and after they went back to their rooms, Paul came over to Bob's room.

"Hey, Buddy we need to do something for Walt's parents when we go up to Newport," Paul said

"Yeah, we should but what do you get for people who have everything?" Bob asked.

"I just figured it out," Paul said. "I can get some special tea for Mrs. Pellman and Walt said his old man likes Cuban cigars. so why don't you run down some Cubans for his old man?"

"Alright," Bob said. "I can do that."

Having settled what, they would get as a gift for the Pellmans then planned on how to accomplish it. Paul would contact his Chinese friend in San Pedro and Bob would scout out the tobacco shop in Pensacola for the cigars.

Next Day

Once again ground school was required before they could begin their instrument flying. Instrument flying was in its infancy, and they soon learned that all they had to fly instruments with were the needle ball and compass. An artificial horizon was in the testing stage, but not ready for general use in flight training. The radio range had been developed, but the Navy did not have any equipment in the training aircraft to utilize this technology. As a result, the instrument syllabus consisted of only 6 flights. Since it was approaching the middle of the month, the Squadron Training Officer decided starting instrument flying with Christmas holidays coming up so quickly would require too many extra refreshers, Walt, Paul and Bob were told they would start flying after they returned from the holiday leave.

For the next week, all they had to do was report in for morning muster and then they had the rest of the day off. On Monday Bob asked Walt if he could borrow his car to run an errand in Pensacola. Walt threw him the keys and told him to drive carefully. Bob drove into Pensacola and visited the Tobacco shop on Palafox Street. He bought 4 boxes of the finest Cuban cigars they had in the shop. They even gift-wrapped them in a Christmas paper. He drove back to the base and stowed them in his room. At dinner, he returned Walt's keys and thanked him for the use of his car.

Later in the week, Paul received a large package at the Post Office. When he picked it up, he recognized the return address as his friend in San Pedro. California. He knew it was the tea, so he went by the Base Exchange and stopped at the gift-wrapping desk. They Christmas wrapped the tea for him, and he took it back to his BOQ room.

They spent the next week on Paul's sailboat sailing Pensacola Bay. Most days for lunch, they pulled into a fish camp, and after beaching the sailboat, gorged on fresh seafood. The days were still mild and warm, and they enjoyed relaxing in the sun.

On the 19th the three intrepid naval officers decided they would stay on base and get packed for the trip to Rhode Island. It was wintertime and Rhode Island was bound to be cold and snowy, so they packed appropriately. Walt's dad had indicated the plane would be in Pensacola on the 19th, and they should be at the airport by 6:30 a.m. ready for departure on the 20th. The flight would take some twelve hours, so it was going to be a long day. Later that day they packed Walt's car in preparation for an early departure.

After a leisurely dinner, they settled down in the comfort of Bob's room and talked about their upcoming adventure.

Next Morning 20 December

The three men were all up and about at 4:00 a.m. After a shower, shave and getting dressed, they were ready to depart about 5:00 a.m. It would take them about 45 minutes to drive to the Pensacola airport, which was located on the northeast end of the city. The officer's Mess wasn't open this early and there were no restaurants for breakfast, so they had to do without. At 5:46 a.m. they pulled into the parking area at the airport. The Trimotor was parked on the ramp just outside the Fixed Base Operator's Hangar. They grabbed their luggage, and walked onto the ramp, and set it down under the wing of the aircraft. The two pilots came out of the Hangar and greeted them.

"Good morning, gentlemen," one of them said as he extended his hand. "I'm Eric Olson and this is my co-pilot Darius Young."

Walt shook his hand. "I'm Walt Pellman." Pointing to Paul and Bob, "and this is Paul Day and that's Bob Fitzwater."

Erie responded, "A pleasure to meet you all. Let's get your luggage aboard and get this show on the road. It's going to be a long day."

While picking up their luggage, Paul asked, "How long a flight is it going to be?"

"Probably be a 14-hour day," Eric responded. "We have planned fuel stops in Columbia, South Carolina, and Philadelphia, Pennsylvania. Then if the winds hold, we should be okay. We can stow the luggage in the luggage compartment in the rear of the plane," he said as they stepped up into the aircraft.

Darius remained outside the aircraft, and just as they boarded the aircraft, a small panel truck pulled onto the ramp. It stopped next to Darius, and he pointed at the aircraft. The driver retrieved a couple of boxes and a gallon jug. They followed Darius to the aircraft and placed the boxes and jug inside the access door.

"That's our meals for the day," Eric said. "Should be some warm egg and bacon sandwiches and hot coffee once you get settled. We should be airborne in just a few minutes."

Darius pulled the landing gear locking pins, and climbed aboard and made his way to the cockpit. Paul and Bob were surprised at how plush the cabin was furnished. The cabin floor was carpeted. There were a couple of leather-covered chairs and couches, and a dining area with a table and four chairs.

They all settled into the chairs and soon there was a roar of one engine, then another, and then a third. The aircraft began to move and quickly they were on the runway and rolling for takeoff. The pilots climbed on course to 1500' and were headed for Atlanta. Once at altitude, they reduced rpm on all three engines and leaned the mixtures for cruise setting. They were now cruising at 110 miles per hour.

The noise within the cabin was somewhat muted by insulation that had been installed all around. Walt dug into one of the boxes until he found the egg sandwiches.

"How about a sandwich, you guys?" he said to Paul and Bob.

"Sounds like a winner," Paul said.

Walt offered one each to them. He took an additional two out of the box and headed for the cockpit.

Upon reaching the cockpit, he spoke to the pilots. "Hey, I brought you each a sandwich," he offered. "You want a cup of coffee?" he asked.

Darius answered, "Yes, thanks, Mr. Pellman," he said.

"Just tell me where the coffee cups are and I'll get you guys a cup," Walt said.

Eric spoke up, "There are cups in the cupboard just behind the dining table."

"Got it," Walt replied.

He went back into the cabin to get the pilot's coffee.

8

"Meeting the Family"

Enroute Newport

They had been traveling 13 hours already and were just now crossing Long Island Sound. The outside air temperature had fallen from a balmy 68°F in Pensacola to 20°F at altitude. They had been flying in the dark for about an hour and a half with not many lights visible and plenty of snow on the ground making it difficult to navigate. Fortunately, the Trimotor was equipped with the new radio range receiver so the pilots had some sort of navigation.

Soon they approached New London, Connecticut. There were quite a few lights along with the new-fangled street lights. The pilots turned east and began following the coastline towards Rhode Island. In short order, they were crossing Narragansett Bay and ahead could see the lights of Newport. When they were over the city, the pilots turned northeast following State Road 114. They would soon be approaching the airport, a small grass strip of about 3500' just past the three lakes and southwest of Portsmouth. At the last stop, in Philadelphia, Eric had called the airfield and gave them an approximate arrival time. As they crossed the lakes, the pilots spied the airport dead ahead. The airport operator had lit kerosene flare pots lining the runway to give the pilots some reference of the location of the airport. Eric set the plane down soft and smooth, then rolled to a stop. He taxied back to the Hangar area, parked, and shut down the engines. Darius was quick to come back into the cabin and open the rear boarding door. There to greet them was a black Pierce-Arrow Town Car and a chauffeur. Before deplaning, Bob, Paul and Walt had broken out their winter flight jackets to guard against the cold. Each had only one piece of luggage and handed it to the chauffeur, who then stored it in the trunk of the Town Car.

Eric had come back to the cabin and Walt thanked him for a great flight and wished him a Merry Christmas. He did the same with Darius, as did Paul and Bob.

The three of them climbed into the Town Car and were off to Newport.

"Damn, it sure is one cold son-of-a-gun," Bob acknowledged.

"Yeah, didn't know how much I appreciated the warm temperatures in Pensacola," Paul countered.

"Jeez, you guys have been here only five minutes and you can't stand the weather," Walt observed. "Wait 'till it really gets cold."

Paul reminded them he was from one of the colder places in the United States, Sault Ste. Marie, Michigan. Bob was no slouch either as he hailed from St Paul, Minnesota.

The trip took about 20 minutes and ended with them driving up a circular driveway on Bellevue Avenue, arriving at the biggest mansion Bob and Paul had ever seen. As they exited the car under the porte-cochere they were greeted by Walt's mom and dad.

Mr. Benjamin Pellman was a tall man in his early fifties, with slightly gray hair, fair-skinned, and in fairly good shape. He was dressed in a white shirt with a cravat, herringbone wool slacks, and a dark gray smoking jacket. Mrs. Lucy Pellman was a tall, thin blonde-haired lady in her late forties, wearing a full-length, sweeping woolen brown dress covered by a brown wool, long-sleeved jacket, and brown leather pumps. She was wearing a gold necklace, matching gold earrings, and a gold watch.

After a few hugs, Walt turned and said, "Mom and Dad, I would like you to meet my two best friends." He pointed at Bob, "This is Bob Fitzwater and the other dude is Paul Day."

They both shook Walt's dad's hand. "A pleasure to meet you, Sir." And Bob delicately gripping Mrs. Pellman's extended hand kissed it lightly and said, "A great pleasure to meet you, Ma'am."

Paul did likewise, "Great to meet you, Ma'am and thank you for allowing us to spend some time with you during this upcoming holiday season."

"We are pleased that you made the trip up to see us," Lucy said.

"Come on in out of the cold. The staff will take care of the luggage," Ben said. "Let's go into the study and have a warm drink."

"That sounds great to me," Bob said.

Ben asked, "Walt, have you and your friends had dinner?"

"Yes Sir," he responded. "We had something to eat on the plane."
"Well, if you need anything, just ask," Ben said

Turning to the butler, "Jason, please bring us each a hot buttered rum."

They all sat down in the large overstuffed chairs in the study and the conversation turned into a question and answer session, the Pellman's asking and the three of them answering. It mostly centered around what they were doing in Pensacola.

The butler quickly served the drinks and they were savored by everyone.

Bob was first to address the subject. "Sir," he said, "that is the finest drink I have had in a couple of years. Last holiday season, all we had was homemade bourbon and white lightning."

"Oh, that's right. You fellows spent that time in New Orleans. Not much legal booze there right now," Ben said.

"Yes, Sir," Paul said. "We had a great time and by the way, Sir. Thank you for sponsoring us."

"My pleasure, Paul. I figured you fellows needed a break. It was the least I could do since you managed to keep Walt out of trouble."

"Not sure we did a good job, Sir, but we try to do our best. Sometimes Walt does his own thing and we can't get him under control," Bob added.

The conversation lasted well into the evening. Finally, after a couple of hot buttered rum was washed down, Lucy said.

"I suspect you boys may be tired and wish to go to bed."

Bob answered, "Ma'am, the company has been great, but you are correct it has been a long day and I am having trouble staying awake. Perhaps it is time to retire."

"I thought so," she said. Turning to the butler, "Jason would you show our guests their rooms and, Son, your room is ready for you. The staff gave it the once over earlier today."

"Thanks, mom," Walt said. He stepped over and kissed her on the cheek. "See you in the morning, Dad."

Walt joined Paul and Bob as they followed Jason up the staircase to the second floor and their rooms.

"See you guys at breakfast," Walt said. "No need to get up early, so sleep as late as you like."

"That sounds like a great idea Walt," Bob reiterated. "See you in the morning."

"Goodnight, guys," Paul said as he entered his room.

Bob and Paul were wide-eyed as they entered their rooms. There was a fireplace in each room with a fire already burning in it which gave the room a warm glow as well as heat. The staff had banked the fire so it would burn slowly during the night and not go out. The bed was huge with a feather mattress and plenty of covers to keep warm. Both Bob and Paul were quick to change into their P's and settle into bed and sleep.

It was after nine o'clock before everyone was up and around. The fires had been tended to during the night without waking anyone so the rooms were warm and cozy upon waking. Bob was the first to get out of bed as he had a great urge to find the bathroom. As he swung his feet out, he touched the floor, and low and behold, there was a pair of fuzzy slippers which he put on. Next to the bed over a clothes rack, he found a warm housecoat which he slipped on. He quickly found the bathroom then proceeded to open the door connecting to the adjacent bedroom which Paul occupied.

"Hey, Buddy," he whispered. "You going to sleep all day?"

Paul rolled over, rubbed his eyes, "Yeah, I'm going to sleep all day. This bed is so comfortable I'm having breakfast in bed."

"Well I'm going down for breakfast," Bob said. "What do you think of this place?"

"Holy shit, Bob, if I could live like this I might even consider getting a civilian job."

"You'd give up flying and the Navy for this kind of life?" Bob asked.

"Well, maybe for a week or so." As they both laughed. It was obvious that the two of them were committed to the Navy life and becoming Naval Aviators, as was Walt.

"Okay, I decided to go down for breakfast," Paul said.

"Alright, Buddy, I'm going to get cleaned up and get dressed. Holler when you're ready," Bob offered.

"You got it," Paul said.

They took turns using the bathroom and getting cleaned up and shaved. About that time, Jason knocked on the bedroom door and entered the room.

"Good morning, Sir," he said. "I hope you slept well. If you need clothes to wear, the closet is stocked with your size clothes." Paul stuck his head out of the bathroom. "Good morning, Mr. Day, Your closet as well is stocked with your size clothes, if you should need them."

"Thanks, Jason, I'll take a look," Paul said.

"Is there anything I can get for either of you?" Jason asked.

"Nah, we're good to go," Bob said.

"If you need anything laundered, just place it on the bed and the staff will take care of it, Sir," Jason noted.

"Roger that," Paul said.

The two of them searched the closets and came up with appropriate attire for the temperature expected. A warm shirt, wool pants, and a wool sweater were what each selected to wear.

They walked downstairs and into the dining room where Lucy and Walt were already seated.

"Good morning, Mrs. Pellman," they both offered.

"Come sit with us and have some breakfast," Lucy said.

"Did you guys sleep well?" Walt asked.

"Slept like a baby," Bob said.

"Yeah, me too," Paul added.

"What would you like for breakfast?" Lucy asked. "We have most anything I think you'd like."

Jason was standing just inside the door waiting as Lucy turned to him and signaled for him to approach.

"Just tell Jason what you would like." She said.

Paul spoke first. "Jason, how about a couple of biscuits of shredded wheat and a glass of orange juice."

"Will that be all Sir?" he asked.

"I think so," Paul said.

Bob's turn was next, "I'll have a couple of eggs scrambled with 3 slices of bacon and some wheat toast."

Jason left the room, placed the order, returned with a coffee server. He turned over the cups, and poured Paul and Bob a cup of coffee.

"Ma'am, would you or Master Walt like another cup?" he asked.

"No, thank you," she said. "Son, do you want another cup?" "Yes, I'll have one more cup, Jason. Thanks."

Jason poured the coffee then retreated to the kitchen to retrieve Paul and Bob's breakfast.

Paul's shredded wheat was placed in front of him. It had been covered with hot water, drained, and then buttered. It was steaming hot. Bob's eggs were just right, cooked with milk and soft but not watery. They both dug in and devoured it as they hadn't had a decent meal since dinner two days earlier.

Since it was Sunday, the three of them decided to just stay around the house and just relax. Walt's dad had gone into the office early, but was expected home for a late lunch so they sat in his drawing room and planned what they should do after Christmas.

Newport, Rhode Island

Walt opened the conversation, "I think we should go up to Lake Placid and do some skiing. Christmas is on Friday, which we could spend here with the family, then leave on Saturday. That would give us Sunday, Monday, and Tuesday at Lake Placid. Then we could drive back on Wednesday so we're here for New Year's Eve and New Year's Day. I expect we will need to fly back to Pensacola on Sunday so we're ready to fly on Monday the 4th. What do you guys think?"

Bob chimed in, "That sounds like a great plan, Walt. How are we going to implement it?"

Before Walt answered, he asked Paul his opinion on the proposal.

"I'm in. I can handle that schedule. What about ski clothes and reservations?" Paul asked.

"I will talk with Pop and Mom and see what they can do for us. I am sure they can get it done," Walt said.

Having settled on their plans for after Christmas, they still had four days ahead of them before Christmas to fill their schedule.

"Have you guys ever been to Boston?" Walt asked.

Neither Paul nor Bob indicated they had.

"So how about we take the train into Boston one day and see if there is a hockey game," Walt said. "They have a professional hockey team, the "Boston Bruins," which are pretty good. We can also see if the USS Constitution is open for visitors."

"I wouldn't mind seeing that old ship," Paul quipped. "I'd like to see what shipboard duty was like back in the day."

"Yeah, that sounds like a good plan, guys," Bob said.

With their plans kind of settled, they went back to relaxing and enjoying the day.

The *New York Times* newspaper was delivered to the house around noon. It was put on the train out of New York City during the night, distributed and delivered locally by their agents.

Jason brought it into the drawing-room for them to read. Bob took the sports section while Paul grabbed the front page. That left Walt with the business section.

Walt was very intrigued as the cover page story related to the construction of the dirigible ZPS4 and subsequent plans for the launch. Construction of the Hangar in which to build it began in the spring of 1929 and by October the first ring of the fuselage had been brought to the Hangar in Akron, Ohio, from Goodyear Plant Number #3. The U.S. Navy and the Goodyear-Zeppelin Company were planning a huge celebration for the christening. There was currently a search for naming the hugedirigible. The writer supposed that it would be christened sometime in late July or early August time frame. It was reported that Lieutenant Commander Charles E. Rosendahl had been selected as the commanding officer. He was one of the officers Walt had played golf with back in Pensacola, Florida. Walt was intrigued by the story as that had been the center of discussion at the dinner at Captain McDonald's quarters in Pensacola.

Walt didn't think any more about the ZPS4 story and moved on to see how the economy and stock market were doing on recovering from the "Black Friday" Wall Street crash of October 1929.

Bob chimed in with a story from the sports section concerning the dominance of the Boston Bruins Hockey team in the current professional hockey league. They were on a winning streak having won consecutive games against the New York Rangers, Ottawa Capitals, Detroit Red Wings, and the Chicago Black Hawks. The Boston fans had been packing the arena despite the hard economic times. Bob wondered if tickets would be available with that kind of rabid fan base. Walt assured Bob that if tickets were available, his dad's administrative assistant would find them.

Paul reported he had been reading a long story about the Soviet Union, that the Central Executive Committee of the Soviet Union had published a decree forbidding workers to change jobs without government permission. Also, the Soviet government forcibly closed the Japanese- Korean bank in

Vladivostok and seized its assets, accusing the bank of violating the Soviet money trading rules. And finally, Vyacheslav Molotov became Chairman of the Council of People's Commissars of the Soviet Union, replacing Alexei Roky.

The three of them got into a long discussion of the communist ruling class as they all had studied the subject while at the Naval Academy. The discussion lasted for over an hour and was of great interest to all of them.

The mood was broken by Ben, as he entered the room.

"I see you found the *New York Times*," he said. "Hope you found things interesting. Sorry, I had to go to the office for a few minutes this morning, but we had some difficulty out at an oil field in Oklahoma and it needed my attention. You boys about ready for some lunch?"

At that point, Lucy entered the room.

"I thought I heard you, Ben," she said. "Glad you're back. I was about to have Jason rustle up some lunch. I was thinking something along the lines of a roast beef sandwich and a fruit cup. How's that sound?"

They all agreed that the menu would be great.

"I'll also have some nice hot tea to go along with that, if everyone wishes."

Walt answered for the group. "Mom, that sounds just fine. It will be a change from all that Navy coffee we have been drinking. Maybe it will teach us a little more sophistication."

"Okay, I'll get Jason started. Give him a couple of minutes then mosey back to the dining room."

They all nodded in agreement and sat down for a few minutes of discussion on what to do that afternoon. They all agreed they didn't want to get dressed up and leave the house so it was decided they would stay in and play pool for a while, maybe read a book or just visit with the Pellmans.

Jason stepped into the room and announced lunch was served.

The conversation during lunch concerned their plans for the remainder of their stay. Ben told them they could ride into the office with him the next morning and he would introduce them to Marilyn, his administrative assistant. They could present their plans to her and she would see to it that they had all the proper arrangements made.

Monday Morning, Newport, Rhode Island

Everyone was up early and down for breakfast before 7:00 a.m. since Ben wanted to be in the office before 8:00 a.m. After breakfast, they said goodbye to Lucy and hopped into the Pierce-Arrow Town Car. Edward was their chauffer today and it was a short 15-minute drive to Ben's office.

When they arrived, Marilyn was already at her desk, just outside Ben's office. As they approached the desk, she stood to greet them.

Ben spoke, "Marilyn, I would like you to meet my Son Walt and his two friends. This is Paul Day and Bob Fitzwater."

"I'm pleased to meet the three of you," Marilyn said as she extended her hand and shook each of theirs.

"I am glad to finally meet you too, Marilyn," Walt said.

Bob and Paul also greeted her in like fashion.

She was a gorgeous woman, 5'-8" tall, curly blond hair, very fair skin, and beautiful facial features. She was dressed in a high collar white blouse, a full-length black wool skirt, and a black, high necked, full sleeved jacket.

"Marilyn, the boys here have some plans for the next week and I would like you to please help them arrange the details if at all possible," Ben said. "Meanwhile I am going to see what's happening in the world of oil this morning. Come into the visitor's lounge while you're waiting to hear about your plans."

Ben went into his office and Marilyn started the conversation.

"Now tell me what we need to do for you?" she asked.

They all sat down around her desk and Walt began to lay out their plan.

"Marilyn, we would like to go to Lake Placid for some skiing on Saturday the 26th and return on Wednesday to 30th. We will need transportation there and back and some ski clothes while there. I expect we can rent ski equipment at Lake Placid. Our other trip would be to Boston for a day trip and a Boston Bruins hockey game, if you can get tickets. I think either the 22nd or 23rd are the two dates we wanted to go. We were planning on taking the train if possible. That's our entire plan. What do you think?" Walt asked.

"That all sounds doable," she said. "Bruins tickets might not be available, depends on whether there will be a game on the dates you wish to attend, but we can work on it if available. I will need your jacket and pants sizes for the ski trip."

She handed Walt a pencil and pad of paper. "Write down your sizes and then go relax in the visitor's lounge and give me some time to work on the details."

They all complied with her request, and when finished, Paul handed back the pad and pencil. They moved into the visitor's lounge and relaxed. In about an hour Marilyn walked into the lounge. The three men stood and greeted her.

"Okay, here are the details of your trip to Lake Placid. I have arranged for one of our company cars, a Cadillac V-16, to pick you up at the Pellman's the morning of the 26th at 7:00 am. Edward Langret will be your chauffeur and you should arrive sometime around 6:00 pm at the Lake Placid Club. You will have a suite with two bedrooms and a sitting room as well as a bathroom. You are scheduled to depart on the 30th at about 8:00 am and arrive in Newport around 7:00 pm. When you arrive in Lake Placid, your ski clothes should be available in your room. Now, do you have any questions?" Marilyn said.

"Will the car be available while we're there?" Bob asked.

"Yes, Edward will give you the phone number where he will be staying, if you need transportation. However, I don't see a need for that since all Shoppes and restaurants are all within walking distance of the Lake Placid Club."

"That's great," Paul replied.

"And what about the Boston trip?" Walt asked.

"I was just getting to that, Sir," Marilyn said. "I'm afraid those plans will need to be altered or adjusted. The Bruins are on an out-of-town tour 'till after Christmas so no games are scheduled this week."

"What do you guys think?" Walt asked. "Do you still want to go see the USS Constitution?" We could make it a leisurely day. Late morning train, lunch in Boston, then the tour and catch a late afternoon train back."

Paul spoke, "That sounds like a good plan, Walt. Why don't we just do that and have a relaxing time."

Bob seconded Paul's suggestion.

Turning to Marilyn, Walt said. "Well, I guess it's settled, Marilyn. Thanks for making all the arrangements for us. We sincerely appreciate all the help."

"You're welcome. That's what I do for your dad all the time," she said.

"Great, I think we'll wander around town and then have lunch," Walt said. "If you could please tell my dad we'll be back after lunch, that would be great."

"Certainly, Mr. Pellman. I will let him know you'll be back after lunch."

The three of them left the office and headed toward the wharves. They wanted to see the fishing boats and processing plants which are a large portion of Newport's industrial activity. Unfortunately, the activity along the wharves was extremely limited since the fishing boats went out early and usually returned around 3:00 pm when the fish processing plant swung into action. They went back up Monroe Street and visited a few shops then stopped at the White Horse Tavern for lunch. They all opted for a seafood lunch. After finishing lunch, they decided to visit the Naval War College, which was an easy walk. The college was located on Coasters Harbor Island in Narragansett Bay, which was just a short walk from where they had eaten lunch.

The original building was renamed the "Naval War College Museum" with the other two buildings named Luce Hall and Mahan Hall respectively. They enjoyed their visit and had a chance to see some of the museum artifacts.

Time was approaching 2:30 pm so they walked back to Walt's dad's office. Things were buzzing now with about 15 employees of the company busy in their offices.

They once again stopped in Marilyn's office where she greeted them and asked if they were ready to return to the Pellman's home. They were ready and she called the transportation office, spoke to Edward, and had the car brought around to take them back to the mansion. It had been a dreary day weather-wise and the forecast was for colder temperatures and more snow.

9

"Visiting the Past"

Newport, Rhode Island, Tuesday 23rd of December

This was the day for their Boston excursion. The three of them were up early, had breakfast with Ben and Lucy, and had Edward take them in the Pierce-Arrow Town Car to the train station. The Newport Line express departed at 8:15 am and arrived in Boston around 10:15 am. The guys were booked into the Parlor Car with lounge seating. The two-hour ride was easy and enjoyable. The Rhode Island and Massachusetts countryside was gorgeous with all features being covered with 3 inches of snow. The temperature was hovering right around 27°F and the wind was light and variable.

They arrived at the Back Bay station at 10:21 am and walked up the ramp and into the terminal. There was an information desk and they stopped to ask about transportation to the USS Constitution. The gentleman behind the desk was very helpful and told them that the Constitution was tied up right near the Navy Yard, which was across the Charles River and about a 30-minute bus ride from the Back Bay Station. He told them to look for a bus that displayed a Chelsea Street sign in its overhead panel and that would take them to their destination. They thanked him for the info and proceeded across the vast station and out the main door to the street. There were signs which indicated a bus stop so they hovered close to it and watched for the Chelsea Street bus. Sure, enough, within ten minutes a bus displaying the Chelsea Street line pulled up to the bus stop. They boarded, paid their twenty-five-cent fare, and took seats close to the front of the bus. The bus took them through downtown, past the Boston Common, past city hall then up into north

Station, a hub for busses. After a short wait for other passengers to board, the bus crossed the Charles River on Washington Street onto Chelsea Street. As they approached 5th street, the driver called to them that this was their stop. The driver stopped at the corner of Chelsea and 5th street, opened the front door and they stepped off once again into the cold. It was only a two-block walk south to the main building which housed the headquarters of the visitor's center for the USS Constitution.

As they entered the main door, they spied a first-class boatswain's mate sitting behind a desk. As they approached him, they each produced their military I.D. Paul first spoke to the boatswain's mate. Paul saw his nameplate on the desk.

"Petty Officer Battaglia," he said, "we are three active-duty naval officers just visiting Boston and would like a tour of the Constitution, if possible."

Showing him his I.D., he continued, "I'm Lieutenant (JG) Day, this is Lieutenant (JG) Pellman," and pointing to Bob, "that is Lieutenant (JG) Fitzwater."

Petty Officer Battaglia responded, "Well, Sir, our tours usually start at 1300, but since you're one of us I guess we can make an exception. Let me find Petty Officer Anson. He is one of our tour guides and he will be glad to take you through the ship. Why don't you take a little walk around the museum here while I go and find him?"

Soon Petty Officer Anson arrived and introduced himself.

"Gentlemen," he began. "The Constitution has just completed refurbishing and is set to begin a 40-city tour of the United States in a month or two. You are lucky to have chosen this time to see her. Let's walk down to the ship. I will guide you through and explain her place in naval history."

The tour was extremely fascinating. The most interesting to these naval officers was the length of overseas tours some of these crews had to endure. Petty Officer Anson described one tour as lasting four years while another lasted three. He described the battles and tactics used against the Barbary pirates. They observed first-hand how the officers and men lived aboard this ship during their tours of duty. It was interesting how the ship got her nickname "Old Ironsides". The extra thick oak planking on her sides prevented most cannonballs fired at her from penetrating the hull, thus the name "Old Ironsides." The tour lasted about two hours and time was approaching 1300.

On completion of the tour, they all thanked Petty Officer Anson then left the base and walked back up to Chelsea Street to catch a bus back into Boston.

"How did you guys enjoy the tour?" Walt said.

"Hey, Buddy, that was great. I really enjoyed it, but right now my stomach thinks my throats been cut. How's about we find someplace for lunch?" Bob interjected.

Paul chimed in, "I saw a possible good restaurant while the bus was waiting at north Station on the way out here. The sign said *Tavern in the Square.* Could be good or bad but we could give it a try."

"That's better than nothing,"Bob answered.

"Sounds good to me," Walt seconded. "Let's give it a try. Beats looking for something else."

The inbound bus arrived at the stop, and they boarded for the short trip into the center of the city. They soon arrived at the North Station, and when they got off the bus, there the restaurant was, right in front of them. They entered and were immediately seated. Wasn't much of a crowd as the main diners had already eaten and gone back to work. It was mainly a seafood menu, so they all ordered the Tempura Shrimp with a noodle bowl. They lingered over lunch and most discussion centered on the USS Constitution and the harsh conditions naval personnel had to endure during their tours. They finished lunch off with a caramel apple pie.

"The train back to Newport leaves the station at 3:15 so we have only 45 minutes to kill. What do you guys want to do until then?" Walt asked.

"I think we should just go back to the terminal," Paul said. "By the time we catch a bus and get to the station, we probably won't have more than 20 minutes to spare."

They caught the bus which displayed the "Back Bay" sign and within minutes were at the train terminal. Since they already had their tickets, they walked through the terminal and found track six which served the Newport Line.

The train from Newport pulled into the station right at 2:50 pm and within minutes the conductor called out "all aboard."

They boarded and found the parlor car. Exactly at 3:15 pm, the train began to move down the track and out of the station. Speed was limited within the city, so the train moved very slowly. As the conductor moved through the car collecting tickets, the snack bar opened for business.

Walt asked, "You guys want a drink of something. The snack bar is open, and I thought I would get a glass of "hot" apple cider."

Bob and Paul both opted to have a glass, so Walt got up and moved up to the snack bar.

When it was Walt's turn to order the server asked, "May I help you, Sir?"

"Yes please," he responded. "Three glasses of "hot" apple cider."

"Would you like large or small?" the server asked.

"Three large will be just fine," Walt said.

The server poured three large glasses of cider and placed them on a round metal tray.

"That'll be 30 cents please," he said.

Walt reached into his pants pocket and found a quarter and a nickel. He gave it to the server, and grabbed the tray and wandered back to the area where Bob and Paul were sitting.

"Here ya go," Walt said as he placed the tray on the table. "You guys owe me big time. This cost me all of 30 cents."

"You can put it on my tab," Bob offered.

"And we're even, old Buddy," Paul said. "I paid for the gum the other day, without reimbursement I might add."

It was just the Naval Aviator banter they were learning to hone, nothing serious, just something to keep egos in check. It continued as the train lumbered on headed for Newport.

The schedule called for their arrival in Newport at 5:15 pm. As the time approached, Walt wondered out loud, "I guess we'll have to catch a taxi back to the house. I didn't tell Edward what time we were arriving back in Newport."

After the train came to a stop in the Newport station, they disembarked, walked through the terminal and began looking for a taxi.

Paul thought he spied Edward standing beside the Pierce-Arrow Town Car. "Hey, guys, isn't that Edward over there?" he said.

"It sure as heck is," Walt said. "I never would have believed it but I'm glad he's here.

As they approached, Bob spoke first, "Boy, Edward, I'm sure glad to see you."

"Yes, Sir. It's nice to see you," he said. "I'm glad the train was on time. I've been here only about five minutes. So, get in and I'll get you back to the house in no time at all."

After they boarded and settled in, Walt asked, "How did you know what time we would arrive?"

"Miss Marilyn called me and gave me the time," Edward offered.

"I'll have to remember to thank her when I next see her," Walt said. "I would have hated to have had to stand around waiting for a taxi."

"Yes, Sir. It's mighty cold," Edward said. "The thermometer at the house said 10°F when I was leaving for the train station."

"Damn, that's almost Eskimo weather," Bob said. "I think I'm going to love the Pensacola weather when we get back."

"Come on, Bob, you being from Minnesota and all? 40°F is a summer heatwave," Paul said.

Bob couldn't let that stand, "And Paul, you being from Michigan makes 40°F cold, I expect, or is that your summer high temperature?"

"It's actually too hot for us in Michigan at that temperature," Paul said with a big smile.

"Okay, you guys, that's enough. You're beginning to sound like a couple of 16-year-olds, so stow it. We're almost home and we need to keep it civil or at least bring our banter up to an adult level," Walt interjected.

They all started to laugh when Bob added, "and the horse you rode in on, old Buddy."

They arrived at the house, and after Edward stopped the car at the front door, they jumped out, thanked him for the lift, and entered the house. Jason was there to greet them.

"Gentlemen, let me take your jackets," he said. "Mr. Pellman is back in the study waiting for you. Would you care for a hot buttered rum?"

They all agreed that would be nice. They proceeded back to the study where Ben was sitting and drinking what looked to be a hot buttered rum.

Welcome back, boys," Ben said. "Did you have a nice day in Boston?"

"Yeah Dad, we had a great day. The tour of the Constitution was unbelievable, and we had lunch at the Tavern in the Square. We didn't see much of the city though except the bus ride," Walt said. "The train ride was a nice diversion which I think the guys will agree was very comfortable."

"Yes, Sir," Bob said. "All in all, we had a great day, and please thank Marylin for making all the arrangements."

"Ditto to Bob's assessment of the day but I plan to come back one day and see some more of the historical sites." Paul added.

"Yes, Paul, you should make it back when the weather is warmer, and the historical sites are open. You should put Concord Bridge and Lexington on your to-do list."

Jasons entered the room with the hot buttered rum and the historical discussion continued. The conversation was hot and heavy, and they never noticed Lucy enter the room. She startled them when she spoke.

"I see you all are enjoying your time together," she said.

"Oh, hi Mom," Walt said, "We didn't hear you come in. Sorry, we missed you when we returned."

"You didn't miss me as I was downtown doing some late Christmas shopping. I just got back. Did you boys have a nice trip?" She asked.

"Yeah Mom, we were just telling Dad about our trip," Walt said. "We had a great day in Boston."

"That's very nice, Walt. You boys can tell me all about it over dinner."

She walked over and gave Ben a peck on the check. "Hi, darling. I hope you had a nice day."

Ben kissed her back and answered, "I had a great day, sweetheart. Did you have a nice day?" he asked.

"Yes, I enjoyed my trip downtown. Ran into Katherine Kelley. She and Bill are having a few guests tomorrow evening for drinks and Hors de oeuvres and she told us to stop by. I said I would let her know in the morning. I told her we had guests and she said to bring them along, so we are all invited."

"That sounds good, darling," Ben replied.

"I am going to check on dinner. Is there anything anyone needs?" she asked.

"I think we have everything we need, right now, Mom," Walt said

"Okay, I'm headed for the kitchen then," Lucy said

Shortly, they went into the dining room for dinner. It was salmon steak with all the trimmings and pumpkin pie for dessert. After dinner, they all adjourned to the study and settled in with a glass of Drambuie. It was well past ten when the discussion slowed, and everyone decided it was time for bed. They all said goodnight and retired to their beds for a good night's sleep.

Next Morning

Walt stirred about 7:30 am. He put on his robe and hit the bath- room first then checked on Paul and Bob. They were both still fast asleep, so he went downstairs and headed towards the kitchen. He passed the household staff, who were in the main living room putting the final touches on the Christmas tree. When they first noticed him, they all paused and almost in unison wished him a good morning, which he returned in kind.

The first person he ran into was Jason.

"Good morning, Mr. Pellman," he said. "Your mother is back in the study. May I get anything for you, Sir?"

"Yes, Jason, how about a cup of coffee," he said. "I'm joining my mother back in the study, so I'll have it there please."

"Yes, Sir. We just have a fresh pot," Jason answered.

Walt walked back to the study where he found his mom. She was reading a woman's magazine and sipping her tea.

"Good morning, Mom," Walt said, as he slipped in next to her and gave her a peck on the check. "You're up early."

"I couldn't sleep. Had some things to have the staff do before tonight, and had to make sure they got done. Did you sleep well?" she asked.

"Yeah, I slept like a log. My bed is a lot more comfortable than those Navy beds I've been sleeping on," Walt noted.

Jason entered the room and brought Walt's coffee. As he set it down next to him, he asked, "Ma'am, I can take your order for breakfast if you're ready?" he said.

"We'll wait for Walt's friends to come down before we're ready for breakfast, Jason." she said.

"Yes, thank you, ma'am. Is there anything else I can get for you at this time?" he asked.

"No, we're good for now," she answered.

Walt and Lucy continued their conversation while sipping their drinks. Shortly thereafter, Ben appeared, followed quickly by Paul and Bob.

After all had their morning coffee, they adjourned to the dining room and had breakfast. Ben indicated he needed to go into the office, but promised Lucy he would be home for lunch to spend the rest of this day with the family. The boys decided that was a great idea so they indicated they too would just lounge around the house.

Ben soon departed and Lucy and the boys sat in the dining room finishing breakfast and chatting about Christmas things.

Christmas Eve, Newport, Rhode Island

Ben had returned in time for lunch and spent the better part of the afternoon playing pool with the boys, smoking a good cigar, and just getting to know them better.

They were having an early, light dinner as they were having to dress up for Bill and Katherine Kelley's get-together that evening. Dinner consisted of a light salad plate with a side plate of baked ham and banana pudding for dessert. They finished dinner around 6:00 pm and all headed up to their bedrooms to get dressed for the shindig at the Kelley's. At 6:50 p.m. they met in the foyer near the front entrance ready to depart. Dress for the evening was a white shirt, navy tie, gray wool slacks with a navy blue blazer, and black shoes. The boys had also found in their closet a woolen navy-blue overcoat for the cold weather, a white silk scarf, as well as a black Stetson hat, and black leather/wool gloves. They looked like three brothers in their matching outfits. Ben was similarly dressed while Lucy was a knockout in her elegant white silk dress covered only by a full-length black woolen coat with a white silk scarf coiled around her neck.

They walked out the front entrance and boarded the Pierce-Arrow Town Car, Edward is driving with Walt in the jump seat, Ben and Lucy behind them, and Paul and Bob in the third seat. Edward had warmed up the car before bringing it around to the front entrance, so it was toasty-warm when they boarded. It was only a ten-minute drive to Kelley's mansion. The road was packed down and a little slippery. The temperature was still hovering around 10°F.

Within 10 minutes they arrived at this beautiful stone mansion, which was quite a bit larger than the Pellman's. As they pulled in under the porte cochere, two servants came to the car, opened the doors, and assisted Ben and Lucy out onto the driveway. It was only a few steps into the house, and they were followed by Walt, Paul, and Bob. Just inside the front doors, they were assisted with their coats, scarfs, hats, and gloves. They then took a couple of steps into the main foyer where they were greeted by Bill and Katherine Kelley.

Lucy introduced Bob and Paul as colleagues of Walt's. Greetings were exchanged and all were directed into a great room towards the back of the house. It was a huge room normally used for banquets or large dinners probably big enough to hold 75 to 80 people. Tonight, it was open with chairs along two walls, tables of food along a third wall, and a string quartet at the head of the room. There were at least 10 wait staff to serve drinks to people who were either standing on the floor talking or sitting in the chairs provided. Prohibition was not even a consideration.

Ben told the boys to mix with the crowd and enjoy themselves. He and Lucy would be joining Bill and Katherine once they had greeted all their guests. Bob, Paul, and Walt hailed one of the servers and ordered drinks. After the drinks were delivered, they wandered over to the food tables to see what hors de' oeuvres were available. They soon became aware of three beautiful women, about their age, standing at the end of the table so they eased their way in that direction to meet them. Bob was the first to reach the area. He leaned into their circle and asked, "Can anyone of you ladies recommend what food here is the best for my beautiful complextion?"

The three giggled. "Excuse me, for not introducing myself, I'm Bob Fitzwater. I'm here as a guest with the Ben Pellman party."

The first lady smiled and said, "Well, I'm Susan Kelley my parents are hosting this party. These are my friends Karen and Louise."

By this time, Paul and Walt had eased into the group and Bob introduced them to the ladies. The conversation was quite animated with the exchange of greetings, work, and hobbies. The ladies were impressed that the three guys were all in training to become Naval Aviators. Likewise, the guys were impressed that the ladies were all college graduates with Susan being an administrative assistant to a vice-president on the New York Stock Exchange while Karen and Louise were teaching school.

They all visited the buffet table then sat in a circle of chairs off in the corner and chatted while they finished their food.

The string quartet was still playing so the guys asked the ladies to dance. They danced most of the evening with each dance with a different lady. Around ten o'clock, the string quartet announced the last song, and the guys and ladies had their last dance.

A short time later Ben came over and announced they would be leaving in about thirty minutes. The guys and gals wandered out to the foyer and sat on the benches waiting for Ben and Lucy. The guys expressed to the gals what a great evening they had and hoped they might get together again before they went back to Pensacola.

Ben and Lucy finally appeared. The staff brought them their coats. They said their goodbyes, and walked out to the waiting Town Car to take them home.

Lucy inquired as to whether the guys had a good time. They all agreed that it was a pleasant evening. The gals were pleasant to be around and were smart and pretty sophisticated.

They arrived back home, said their goodnights, and headed for bed. Lucy had told them that breakfast would be at 9:00 am so they should plan on it, followed by church. The guys discussed gifts before they reached their rooms on the second floor. Paul and Bob had their gifts for the Pellmans. They all said goodnight and went to bed. The staff had warmed the rooms as well as the beds so it was pleasant to crawl into bed.

The rooms cooled off during the night, but the staff came in quietly around 6:00 a.m. and stoked the fire in the fireplace, so by the time the guys awakened, their rooms were a toasty 70°F. By 7:00 a.m. they were all up and around. After the normal bathroom routine, Walt got dressed and knocked on Paul's and Bob's room. They were both in the process of finishing dressing.

"Bout time you guys got your butts out of bed," Walt said as he entered the room.

"We've been up for hours." Bob chimed in. "We already played a round of golf, ran two miles, and swam the English Channel before you even thought about getting out of bed."

Walt could see this was going to be a Naval Aviator banter conversation.

"Hell, I flew two missions over Mobile during the night, played six games of pool and had a date with Susan Kelley, then went back to bed," Walt responded.

"And I rode with Santa Claus, delivering gifts for a couple of hours," Paul interjected as the three of them started to laugh.

"Okay, I surrender," Walt said. "Let's go down to breakfast."

The three of them went downstairs and were greeted by Jason.

"Merry Christmas," he said to all three. "Mrs. Pellman is back in the sunroom and I expect Mr. Pellman will be down shortly. May I bring you a cup of coffee while you wait for breakfast?"

"Well, a Merry Christmas to you, Jason, and yes I would like a cup of coffee," Paul said.

Bob and Walt did likewise and also asked for coffee. They proceeded to the sunroom where Lucy was sitting, drinking her tea.

"Good Morning, Mother. Merry Christmas," Walt said.

"Merry Christmas, boys. Come sit down. Ben will be down shortly."

Bob and Paul each in turn wished Lucy a Merry Christmas which she acknowledged.

"I hope you slept well?" she asked.

"Slept like a log, Ma'am," Paul said.

"Same here," Bob added. "The bed is quite comfortable and the room temperature was just right for sleeping. You sure are spoiling us. It's going to be tough getting back to Pensacola and sleeping in those Navy beds. Although anything beats sleeping in those shipboard bunks we used to have."

"I'm glad we can give you boys a break from the rugged routine you're in right now," Lucy said.

Jason entered the room carrying three cups of coffee. He set each on the available table nearest each of them. They thanked him for the coffee.

"Is there anything else I can get you?" he asked.

Lucy responded for the group, "Thank you, Jason. I think we have everything we need right now."

They chit-chatted for a short while and soon Ben entered the room.

"Good morning, everyone, and Merry Christmas," Ben said as he entered. "And how is everyone this morning?"

Lucy spoke up. "I believe we are all doing great, Ben. We were just finishing our morning beverages and I believe we might just be ready for breakfast."

Ben walked over, gave Lucy a peck on the cheek, took her hand, and said, "Well let's get to it then."

Ben escorted Lucy, followed by Walt, Paul, and Bob, into the dinning room. Jason took their orders, filled their drinks, and soon they were enjoying their Christmas breakfast. The conversation centered around the previous evening's festivities. As they were finishing breakfast, Lucy announced that Christmas services at St. Peter's Lutheran church started at eleven o'clock and anyone wishing to join her was welcome. Turns out Bob and Paul were both Lutheran so they all agreed to go with Lucy to the services. They met in the foyer at 10:40 a.m. all dressed for the cold. When they stepped out to get into the Town Car, the temperature was still hovering in the low twenties. It was only a 10-minute drive to the church. On arrival, they proceeded into the church where they found a pew to allow them all to sit together. Pastor Weideranders welcomed them all to the celebration of the birth of Christ. His sermon was inspiring and urged them all to help their fellow man during this holiday season and hard times because of the Depression.

When the service was over, they filed out and were greeted at the door by the pastor who wished them all a blessed Christmas. Because of the cold, few people stopped and talked outside so they all piled into the Town Car and drove back up the Main Street to the mansion. As they entered the foyer, Ben told everyone to go back to the study where they would have the gift-giving and a Christmas drink.

Bob and Paul made a quick trip up and back to their bedroom. They brought their gifts for the Pellmens to be given at the appropriate time.

Once settled in the study with their chairs surrounding the Christmas Tree, Jason served a fine-tasting Christmas drink, a brandy flavored eggnog. Ben stood and approached the tree where the gifts were sitting. He spoke of how he was enjoying having the boys there and how much he loved his family and especially his beautiful wife Lucy. He picked up a small beautifully wrapped package and handed it to Lucy, culminating with a peck on the cheek and telling her that he loved her very much. Lucy took the gift and unwrapped it. As she opened the box her face brightened with a huge smile followed by a few tears. She jumped up, and hugged Ben and planted a big kiss on his lips before he could even say a word. She expressed her love for him and they showed the boys the gift. It was a three-strand diamond bracelet with seven stones set in each row and mounted in an 18-carat gold setting. The boys commented on how beautiful it was.

Next Ben grabbed three small beautifully wrapped packages and gave one each to Walt, Bob, and Paul. All three opened their gift which turned out to be a Rolex self-winding watch called the Oyster. Turns out it was the first automatic self-winding watch and later became known as the Oyster Perpetual. They were overwhelmed and each stood and shook Ben's hand and thanked both Ben and Lucy for the beautiful gift. There was one more gift under the tree and Lucy picked it up and handed it to Ben. It was a long but narrow box. Ben smiled and thanked Lucy as he took it and began to unwrap it. When he opened the box there was a padded canvas sleeve which he unbuttoned and reached into and pulled out a Greener 12-gauge shotgun. He had a big smile on his face. He first opened the action, being sure it was unloaded, then closed it and placed it in his shoulder, looking down the barrel as if to shoot it. Turning to Lucy he said,

"It's a beauty darling, thank you." Grasped her around the waist and kissed her. His only disappointment was he would have to wait until spring to try it out.

Bob stood with his gift in his hand as did Paul. Paul began, "We have a gift for each of you to show you our appreciation for what you have done for us. Opening your home and allowing us to spend the holidays with you and your family means a great deal to us."

Paul gave his gift to Lucy and Bob his to Ben.

Lucy opened hers first. It was a large variety pack of tea from China.

"That was very thoughtful of you boys. It is a very practical gift for all of us. We will certainly enjoy our tea." Lucy said.

Ben opened his gift and smiled. "I have been wanting to try this particular cigar," he said. "I just haven't gotten around to getting these but now I have four boxes. I am sure we will enjoy them later. Thank you for thinking of me." Ben said.

The family sat around finishing their eggnog and chatting about their gifts. Lucy announced they would skip lunch. Snacks would be available, but dinner would be early, around 4:00 pm so the staff could be home with their families for dinner.

The men went into the game room for a game of pool while Lucy went into the kitchen to supervise the preparation of dinner.

10

"Winter Sports"

Newport, Rhode Island, Next Morning

The boys were up early as they wanted to depart around 7:00 a.m. It was a 10-hour drive to Lake Placid, and with stops along the way they figured to arrive before 7:00 p.m. They were already packed for the trip and the staff had brought the valises down to the foyer. After breakfast, they grabbed their winter jackets and proceeded to the foyer. Lucy came down the stairs and wished them a safe trip. Walt kissed his mom goodbye and the three of them walked out to the waiting car. Edward had picked up the Cadillac V-16 from the company garage before 6:00 a.m. and had it warmed up in the porte cochere. The staff had loaded the luggage so they climbed in with Walt in the front passenger seat and Paul and Bob in the back. Edward headed towards Providence then into Massachusetts and on up to the road which would take them to Albany and finally Lake Placid.

Edward told them he would probably stop for gas in Albany which should be around lunchtime. They started to discuss finding a restaurant, but Edward interrupted them and told them the staff had prepared lunch which he had stowed in the trunk. That would save them time on the road and they could get to Lake Placid a little sooner.

They passed through Providence and were shortly into Massachusetts. It was a little hillier and the roads were just a little bit icier. Edward had slowed down some just to be careful. Around noon they crossed the Hudson River bridge just east of Albany.

Edward was looking for a gas station. He spied a Socony station and pulled up to the pump. While the attendant pumped the gas, the guys got out of the car and went in to use the restroom. Edward retrieved the lunch from the trunk and put it on the front seat. He then went inside the station and gave the owner a company voucher to pay for gas.

They got back on the road, and after passing through Albany, Walt broke out the lunch and shared the sandwiches and coffee with Edward, Paul, and Bob. The road they were on took them into the Adirondack Mountains so there were more twists and turns to the road. It was approaching 5:30 p.m. and Edward told them they were about 15 miles out of Lake Placid. It was just starting to get dark and within 20 minutes they were entering the outskirts of the village. The population was reported to be 2930 people and the village was a quaint rural place. The center of the village had a few stores and two restaurants. There was also a village hall where the government offices were located. Just about 600 yards on the outskirts was the Lake Placid Club.

Edward pulled into the driveway of the club and stopped at the entrance. The three of them entered the club while Edward stayed with the car and talked to the club staff. When they stopped at the check-in desk, Walt did the talking.

He introduced himself, "I'm Walter Pellman. I have a reservation for three people for four days and will be checking out on the 30th." "Welcome to the Lake Placid Club, Mr. Pellman. Let me check your reservation," the clerk said.

He looked through his card file on his desk. "Yes, Sir here it is. We have you booked into Cottage #12. Your packages have arrived and we have already sent them over to Cottage #12. Your stay here has already been paid-in-full. Any charges made while you are here can be settled when you check out. Here is your key. The outside staff will direct you to Cottage #12. Our dining room will remain open until 8:30 if you wish to have supper. It is here in the main building. Are there any questions I can answer?"

Walt took the key to the cottage, "No questions at this time," he said.

"Have a nice stay," the clerk responded.

The three of them walked back out to the car. They told the staff where they would be staying and the staff, in turn, directed Edward how to get to Cottage #12. Turns out it was directly behind the club building set on the shore of Mirror Lake. Edward drove around the building and parked in front of the cottage. There was staff there to greet them and assist them in off-loading all their luggage.

When they entered the cottage, they came into a large room the width of the building. It appeared that this room served as a living room and dining area, with a kitchen, set directly behind the dining area. There was a central hallway that led back to two large bedrooms and a bathroom.

The staff set the luggage in the hallway outside the bedrooms leaving Walt, Paul, and Bob to sort through it and take their luggage to their room. One bedroom had a double bed while the other had two single beds. So, as usual, Bob and Paul would bunk together and Walt would have a bedroom all to himself.

Walt tipped the staff and then sent Edward off to his accommodations. Marilyn had found a boarding house for Edward with a room and bath with meals provided. It was in the village and was only a five-minute drive from the club. Edward took off and Walt went back into the cottage.

Bob and Paul were already unpacking and had discovered their ski clothes as well as more winter dress clothes for indoor occasions. Just inside the main entry door, they had seen six pairs of skis sitting against the wall, three pairs of cross-country and three pairs of downhill skis. Each package of clothes had been labeled on the outside with their names so each had the proper size clothes and shoes.

Walt went into his room and also found his packages with his clothes, shoes, and ski boots. He unpacked them and stowed them in the small closet available in his bedroom. He walked over to Bob and Paul's room.

"Hey, you guys, how about we get some dinner before we get all this stuff put away. I'm really hungry," he said.

"I thought you'd never ask," Paul said as he put away his ski jacket.

Bob acknowledged with a, "Yeah, let's eat. My body thinks it's been starved long enough."

They all put on their ski jackets and walked over to the main hotel. It was only about a hundred yards but man was it cold, -8°E.

As they entered the hotel, signs were directing them to the dining room. It was called *The Adirondack Room*. The maitre d' welcomed them and seated them at a window table. It was already dark outside so there wasn't much of a view of frozen Mirror lake. The menu was sparse so they all ordered the meatloaf dinner with mashed potatoes and canned corn. Eor dessert, there was apple pie. After they scarfed down their dinner, they discussed what they would do tomorrow while they sipped their hot tea.

Next Morning

After breakfast, the three young aviators put on their winter clothing. They had decided to try cross-country skiing this morning. After putting on their ski boots, they grabbed their skis and ski poles and walked over to where the trails started. There was a shack at the head of the trails and they needed to check in before they began their hike.

They were welcomed by the starter. "Good morning gentlemen. I see you would like to try our trails this morning. What's your choice?" he asked as he continued, "Trail A is 5 kilometers; Trail B is 10 Kilometers and Trail C is 20 kilometers. We have a special treat this morning, our Biathlon Team is practicing and we could fix you up to try it if you like." "What the hell is Biathlon?" Bob asked.

"Well Sir, it is 20 kilometers in length with two shooting stations. We can furnish you with a 22 caliber rifle which you will shoot standing at 10 targets and prone at ten targets. The course is 5 kilometers and you have to ski four laps shooting prone, standing, prone, and standing for the four laps. Would you like to try it?"

Paul thought they should stick together so they opted to give Biathlon a try. The starter issued them each a rifle and 20 rounds of ammunition. After strapping on the rifle, they started down the trail. After they had gone about two kilometers, Walt thought to himself *"Boy this was stupid. We should have skied a few other trails before trying this."* Anyway, at two and a half kilometers they came upon the shooting station. Targets 1 through 15 were prone and 16 through 30 were standing. Each took his place on a station, dropped down into a prone position, and fired five shots, one at each target. The targets were scored either hit or miss. If hit, a white paper dropped down in front of the target indicating a hit. Over the years Walt had developed a technique to control his heartbeat. He paused for about 20 seconds before he fired all five shots of hits on each. After completion, he jumped up, readjusted his rifle over his shoulders, and put on his ski poles. He got back on the trail and continued. He was beginning to enjoy this little exercise. He was followed quickly by Paul and Bob on the trail. The three of them were in great shape from their exercise regimen in flight training so they were having very little difficulty attacking this course of skiing. They went around the course the required four times with Walt missing the target 2 times, Paul 3 times, and Bob 4 times. They ended this course in about 50 minutes and finished at the starter's shack.

Once they caught their breath, they turned in their rifles and set their skis in the rack provided outside the shack.

The starter asked them to wait a minute. He introduced them to the captain of the biathlon team. After exchanging introductions, he asked them, "Would any of you like to join our team? You had some fantastic scores and times around the course this morning. Our team is in its infancy and we need members."

Bob responded. "I can speak for my fellow compatriots," he said. "The three of us are currently in flight training at Pensacola, Florida, to become Naval Aviators and we don't have the time to pursue this activity. We are only here on vacation over the Christmas holidays and will be returning to Pensacola at the end of the week. Thanks anyway for the invitation. It is a compliment that you would consider us for membership on your team, but we must decline."

"I understand your situation," the captain said. "Just thought I would give it a try. We are training for the Olympics which will be held here next year and we want to make a good showing."

"We appreciate your consideration of us and it is a great compliment that you would even consider us for your team. Thanks again," Paul said.

They all shook hands and the captain departed.

"How about a little lunch before we try this again this afternoon?" Walt offered.

"Sounds good to me," Bob said.

"Me too," Paul added.

Walt turned to the starter. "How about we leave our skis here while we get some lunch," he asked.

"That will be fine," he said. "Just put them over there in the ski rack." He pointed to a ski rack over in the corner of his shack.

"Thanks," Walt said.

The three of them stacked their skis in the rack and headed off to the dining room in the club.

After lunch, they relaxed in their cabin for about an hour then headed out for another round of cross-country skiing. This time they took the 20-kilometer trail and spent the afternoon just enjoying the outdoors on the trails. They returned to their cabin around 5:00 pm. It was just turning dark. They got cleaned up and dressed for dinner. After dinner in the club dining room, they decided to take a walk into the village. There were a few lights on and the two restaurants were doing a land-office business. On the way back to the club they decided to stop in at the club and sit around the fireplace for a couple of hours. They had a fireplace in their cabin but were a bit lazy to drag in some wood and light their fire.

The club was built with hewn timbers with large supports for the walls and roof. It was finished, but also had the feel of a large rustic wooden lodge. They found a place near the fireplace and settled in some big old stuffed chairs set on a rough wood frame which added to the rustic appearance of the lodge.

They spoke to some families with small children as well as a few unattached young ladies who were accompanied by their chaperone.

Next Morning (28th)

The boys awoke early and had breakfast. Today they had decided to give downhill skiing a try. Walt had alerted Edward to pick them up around 8:00 am. He would then take them to the downhill ski slopes, which were some 15 miles from the club. When they arrived at the slopes they were in awe of how big this area was. They had been told of the construction, which had been going on over the summer to make Lake Placid a world-class ski area for the upcoming winter Olympics. The upper reaches of the downhill skiing and slalom course had not been completed but would be done the next summer in time for the winter games. The bobsled run was finished and would be in use this winter.

They checked in at the ski lodge and then took to the slopes for some great downhill skiing. There was a tow lift as well and a double chair lift to get them to the top of the slope to make their downhill runs. The three of them were considered advanced skiers and they took advantage of all the difficult runs. By the end of the day, they were ready to give it a rest. Edward pulled into the parking lot around 4:30 pm and they made the short drive back to their cabin at the club.

Tonight, they decided to take advantage of a restaurant in town. They picked the Black Angus, which offered choice steak dinners. Edward dropped them off at 6:30 pm and was scheduled to pick them up around

9:30 pm. The restaurant was quaint and had a cozy family atmosphere. They were seated at a table in the rear, which was quiet with few people occupying the remainder of the seating.

Each had a steak dinner with a baked potato, green peas, and a side dish of canned tomatoes. Dessert was apple pie washed down with freshly roasted coffee. They finished their dinner around 8:30 pm and sat and discussed their day on the slopes and their upcoming training when they returned to Pensacola. They were looking forward to being finished by March the 1st, getting into a fleet fighter squadron and flying off one of the new carriers the Navy had purchased.

Edward picked them up at 9:30 pm and dropped them back at their cabin. They were beat from the day's skiing so they just went to bed once they got inside.

The next day was a repeat of the previous day on the downhill slopes and the weather was beautiful. They returned to the cabin dead tired as they had gone all-out for most of the day.

After dinner, they went back to the cabin and packed their skis and winter gear for shipping to Newport, then finished packing their everyday clothes to take back to Newport with them in the car.

Next Day(30th)

They had breakfast at 6:30 am and, while they ate, Edward had the staff pack the car, so by the time they were finished, he was already out-front waiting for them so they could depart immediately.

Walt checked out at the front desk, turned in the key to the cabin, then climbed into the front seat of the Cadillac V-16. Paul and Bob occupied the rear seat and they departed for Newport. Eleven hours later they arrived in Newport. Edward pulled up under the porte cochere where they were met by the staff. They walked into the house and were greeted by Lucy.

"Welcome back," she said, as she walked over to hug Walt. "Did you have a good time?"

Bob answered first. "We had a great time, Mrs. Pellman. It was a beautiful trip."

"The weather was absolutely gorgeous and the scenery was awesome," Paul chimed in.

"The accommodations and people were very gracious," Walt said.

"That's great. You'll have to tell us all about it, but meantime have you had any dinner?" she asked.

"No, Mom, we haven't eaten since lunch," Walt said

"Okay, go ahead and get washed up and I'll tell the staff to find you, boys, something," she said.

"Thanks, Mom," Walt responded.

The boys went upstairs, stowed their valises, washed their hands and face, and came back down very quickly. The staff directed them into the dining room where they sat down and were served a hot roast beef sandwich with some homemade fried potatoes and hot tea. While they were eating, Ben and Lucy entered the room and joined them at the table. They inquired about their trip and the discussion was all about what they had done on their journey to Lake Placid.

Sunday, January 3rd, 1931

The previous three days were all a blur. They all had celebrated New Year's Eve at the Kelley's residence. The boys had dressed in their Mess dress uniforms for the occasion and had a great time with the young ladies they had met previously at the Christmas party.

The next two days had been spent ice skating with the ladies, and having them over to the Pellman's for evening dinner, and then just sitting by the fire in the den and enjoying their company.

This morning they were off early, back to Pensacola. Ben was going along as he needed to look into some problems which had developed in the oil fields in Oklahoma. He would drop them off and then continue his journey.

After breakfast, they said their goodbyes to Lucy then thanked the staff for everything which made their visit remarkable.

They rode the Pierce-Arrow Town Car up to the airfield where the Ford Trimotor was loaded with their personal gear.

Once again, their pilot was Eric Olson and copilot Darius Young. Eric told them they were ready to depart, so they all boarded the aircraft, got strapped in, and readied themselves for departure. Eric started the engines, taxied out to the end of the runway, checked the mags and props, and taxied onto the runway. He added the power smoothly and rolled a couple of thousand feet before lifting off. He made a left turn out of the traffic pattern and headed south-southwest for Roanoke, Virginia. After some six hours in the air, he set the plane down at a somewhat countrylike airport to refuel. The airport was nestled amongst the small peaks of the Appalachian Mountains just south of the city of Roanoke. The temperature was in the 50s and they were all kind of glad to be heading south.

There were also a few low-hanging clouds on the mountains, but generally, the clouds were a broken layer and offered no obstruction to their flight.

With refueling complete, they all boarded the plane and were once again winging their way to Pensacola. This route of flight took them along the eastern side of the Blue Ridge Mountains. Soon they were passing Asheville, North Carolina, then down into Georgia. The scenery was beautiful. The mountains were topped with snow and the sky was now CAVU. That is ceiling and visibility unlimited. Walt was particularly enjoying the trip as it allowed him to visit with his dad. They broke out the lunch the staff had prepared for them and had a Coca Cola to wash it down.

Into Georgia, the mountains gave way to less hilly country and they passed 50 miles west of Atlanta. In the late afternoon familiar country began to appear, scrub pines and a few palmetto trees. Eric came back to the cabin from the cockpit and told Ben they would be in Pensacola about 5:15 pm. The boys tidied up the cabin and stowed the trash. Within 10 minutes they heard Eric reduce the power and begin his descent into Pensacola. Eric observed the wind out of the southwest so he set himself up for a landing on runway 25 at Pensacola. His touchdown was soft and smooth, and he taxied to the FBO Hangar to unload.

After shutdown of the engines, Darius came back and opened the rear door for deplaning. Walt was first off and he told Bob and Paul he would bring the car around so they could load their luggage. Meanwhile, Eric and Darius offloaded all the luggage.

When Walt drove up, Bob and Paul were having a conversation with Ben.

Bob was heard to say, "Thank you, Mr. Pellman, for everything. We can never repay you for all you have done for us to make this a beautiful Christmas leave."

"Glad to do it for you, boys," Ben responded. "It was great to have you for the holidays. I know Mrs. Pellman was extremely pleased you chose to spend them with us. I know you are ready to get back to flying, so be careful and let us know if you need anything."

Paul chimed in "Yes, Sir, we are ready to get back in the air. I echo what Bob has said. We enjoyed our time with you and Mrs. Pellman and hope one day we can treat you to a nice holiday."

"Why thank you, Paul. We were glad you chose to spend the holidays with us. I hope you are successful in your quest for your wings," Ben said.

Walt gave his dad a big hug. "Thanks for everything. Love ya Pop," he said. "I'll drop you a line pretty soon and let you know how we're doing. Be careful on your trip to Oklahoma."

The luggage had been loaded into the car and Walt, Bob, and Paul climbed into the car and drove off for Corry Station.

11

"A Taste of Gunnery"

The three young aviators got a good night's sleep. They had checked the flight schedule before they had retired for the night and were not on the schedule for Monday. After breakfast, they walked down to the Hangar.

They stopped in the training office to see what was in store for them. Training determined they would have about three or four flights just to get reacquainted with the airplane. They would also have two half-days of ground school for gunnery orientation. The training petty officer also had a note for Paul telling him to report to officer personnel as soon as possible.

Bob and Walt decided to accompany Paul to officer personnel. Each suspected it was Paul's promotion, but none of them verbally expressed it for fear it may not be true.

They arrived at officer personnel and Paul checked in with the Chief Yeoman. The Chief indicated that yes, they had received paperwork to promote Paul to Lieutenant Junior Grade effective November 1st, 1930. The Chief told Paul he would make an appointment for Tuesday at 1:00 pm with the Commanding Officer who would have a short ceremony marking the promotion followed by lemonade and a few snacks.

The three of them left the office and went back to the BOQ. There was not much to do so they just relaxed in Bob's room talking flying.

Next morning, they awakened, and after checking the weather, found out it was going to be crappy all day. They checked with training and the flight schedule was scrubbed for the day so it was another day for relaxation except for the 1:00 pm appointment Paul had with the Commanding Officer.

At 12:45 pm the trio showed up outside the Commanding Officer's office.

The Commanding Officer's petty officer told them to take a seat and as soon as the Commanding Officer was available. He would check to see if it was okay for them to witness the promotion.

They were cleared for the ceremony, and when invited, walked into the Commanding Officer's office. The Commanding Officer looked up from his desk and spoke, "Mr. Pellman, nice to see you again, and who are your two Friends?" he asked.

"Sir, this is Lieutenant Junior Grade Bob Fitzwater and Ensign Paul Day," Walt said.

"It's a pleasure to meet you, gentlemen. Ensign Day, I understand you are here to finalize your promotion to Lieutenant Junior Grade," the Commanding Officer responded.

"Yes, Sir. I have been looking forward to this day for a few months now," Paul said.

"Sounds good to me," he said, turning to Petty Officer Morrison. "Morrison, do we have the paperwork ready?"

"Yes, Sir, Skipper, you can swear him in first then we'll get both of you to sign the papers," Morrison said.

The Commanding Officer began, "Step forward Mr. Day. Raise your right hand and repeat after me. I, say your full name."

"I, Paul Fredrick Day."

The Commanding Officer continued, "Do solemnly swear that I will perform the duties of Lieutenant Junior Grade to the best of my ability. That I will obey the orders of all officers placed over me. That I will defend the Constitution of the United States against all enemies foreign and domestic, That I will bear true faith and allegiance to the same, so help me God."

Paul repeated the oath after which the Commanding Officer shook his hand, "Congratulations, Lieutenant Junior Grade Day."

"Thank you, Sir," Paul said.

Petty Officer Morrison gave Paul a pen and indicated where to sign the paperwork.

Paul dipped the pen in the ink well and signed his full name. Petty Officer Morrison indicated to the Skipper where to sign the paperwork, which he did.

The Commanding Officer wished Paul well and indicated to all present that the ceremony was over and they all had a drink and some snacks.

The three of them were ecstatic. All were now bonified, Lieutenant Junior Grade. Once again, they checked the flight schedule for Wednesday. They were all on the schedule for a morning and an afternoon flight and at the same time. Back at the BOQ, they sat around in Bob's room planning their flight for tomorrow.

Wednesday Morning

The day broke CAVU. It was going to be a great day for flying. The temperature was in the 50s and on its way up as they manned their aircraft. Bob taxied out first followed by Paul with Walt as tail-end Charlie. Engine checks were completed and Bob took the runway followed quickly by Paul and Walt. After take-off, Bob commenced a right turnout. Paul and Walt made a running rendezvous and were joined up in right echelon before Bob rolled wings level heading out to the training area north of Corry Station. They had decided to do a little formation flying before they broke up individually to practice some airwork and landings before returning to base.

They flew in parade right echelon for about fifteen minutes. Once they felt comfortable, Bob gave Paul and Walt a pre-agreed upon the signal of left echelon with a circular motion of the hand. They had dreamt up flying a parade V-formation stepped down 10 feet. Paul and Walt dropped down 10' and Paul slid over into left echelon while Walt assumed Paul's previous position in right echelon 10' off Bob's wing. They flew this V- formation making turns and climbing and descending. Bob headed for Silverhill outlying field so they could get some landing practice. As he descended to field landing pattern altitude, he signaled Paul to assume a right echelon position. Walt slid out to allow Paul to assume the number two position in the formation while he assumed the number three position. As they entered traffic, Bob kissed off and took interval on the downwind traffic. Paul kissed off and followed Bob leaving Walt to assume interval on Paul. Each of them made five touch-and-go landings then broke out of traffic and proceeded on their own to do some airwork. After completing some stalls, Walt decided to give his acrobatics a try. He started with a loop followed by an Immelmann turn then right into a barrel roll to the left. He was really having a great time and enjoying getting back in the air. After one final barrel roll, he completed an aileron roll and headed back to Corry Station.

Back in the Ready Room he met Bob and Paul, had a cup of coffee and they sat and rehashed the flight they had just completed.

They grabbed a sandwich at the Gedunk and took it back to the Ready Room where they fixed themselves a hot drink then settled down for lunch. Their next flight wasn't until 2:30 p.m. so they just relaxed in the Ready Room going through their emergency procedures. Walt walked down to the Training Office to check on when ground school was going to start. He reported back to Bob and Paul that they were scheduled for the following Monday for two half days of gunnery school.

The afternoon flight was a repeat of what they did in the morning. This time their formation was a lot crisper with fewer adjustments needed and landings a lot smoother.

The rest of the week was spent with each of them standing Squadron Duty Officer. It was much easier than standing watch aboard ship. All they had to do was react to situations as they developed and ensure that all planes returned safely from their scheduled flights.

The following Monday found them in ground school learning how to operate the 30 caliber gun mounted under the wing of their aircraft and how to fly the gunnery practice pattern. Preflight of the aircraft was a little more complicated, requiring checking the machine gun on the aircraft for proper installation and loading.

Tuesday was another half day of ground school. After lunch, they reported to the Hangar and prepared for their first gunnery flight. Lieutenant (JG) Tom Woolcock was their instructor. He briefed them on the flight procedures. He would take off first, dragging the gunnery sleeve. Jack Wilson was once again part of their flight. The four of them would follow him, and after takeoff, they would join up in right echelon and proceed to the rendezvous point on the coast. When Tom passed them, they would then proceed due south for ten minutes and then circle at 6000' waiting for him to arrive. Flying with the sleeve slowed the aircraft considerably so it took him some time to arrive on station.

Tom arrived at the circling aircraft. As he passed them heading south, Paul, who was leading the formation, paralleled his course, flew alongside the sleeve, and when he passed Tom's aircraft, he started a climbing slight left turn and leveled the formation when he was 1000' above and one-quarter of a mile left on a parallel course. Paul steadied the formation and matched Tom's speed. Paul signaled for a left echelon and as soon as they were steady, he made his machine gun unsafe, kissed off, and began his gunnery run on the sleeve. He banked right at 45°, let his nose drop, and as he came abeam of the sleeve, reversed his angle of bank and brought his gunsight into firing position. He had a good lead with the sight and let it drift back toward the sleeve as he pressed the trigger down and fired. As the firing position continued to drift back on the sleeve, he was now pulling 4Gs. As the nose passed the end of the sleeve, he ceased firing, eased pressure on the stick, and leveled his wings when parallel to the sleeve. He added power to the engine and once he passed Tom's aircraft, he headed over towards the formation. Once to their left, he climbed up and joined the formation in left echelon.

Each of the four pilots made eight runs at the sleeve. After the eighth run, Paul turned the flight north and headed back to Corry Station. Approach and landing were uneventful and they each, in turn, parked their aircraft and shut down. As they were gathering on the flight line, they observed their instructor approaching the field at about 30 feet and just right of the runway. After the first 100 feet past the approach to the runway, he released the sleeve, which floated to the ground and was picked up by the ground crew in a waiting pickup truck. The pilots walked into the Hangar where they awaited Tom.

The ground crew brought the sleeve into the Hangar and placed it on a long narrow table where they stretched it out flat. Tom arrived and told them to start counting their hits. Each student pilot had a different colored tip bullet. Bob had red, Paul green, Walt blue, and Jack purple. It took quite a while to do the counting. Each had fired 257 rounds at the sleeve. Bob had 86 hits, Paul 65, Walt 110, and Jack 77. Tom told them that was not bad for the first time. He cautioned them about pulling too many Gs and getting fixated on the sleeve. He indicated a mid-air collision with the sleeve was not good for either plane and he didn't like silk landings, especially in the Gulf of Mexico.

The rest of the week went very well. On flight G5 everyone in the flight had over 170 hits on the sleeve, a remarkable feat.

The last phase of Gunnery was bombing. There were only two flights in this phase. Bombing was done with 20-pound practice bombs which were lit up by a shotgun shell when they hit the ground. Spotters on the ground recorded the placement of the bomb visually using binoculars as they were positioned well off the target for observation.

Bombing runs started from 4000' with pullout at 2000'. Each pilot had eight practice bombs and made two practice runs before releasing a bomb. The final score was figured by averaging the distance for eight bombs. Bob had the lowest distance with a 23.5' average, Walt averaged 24.6', Paul finished at 27.8', and Jack was last with 30.4'. Not bad for the first time.

Day two was a repeat of day 1 with averages about the same.

With the Gunnery phase complete, the only thing left was carrier qualification. The Training Officer scheduled a briefing for the four airmen in the Ready Room at 10:00 on Thursday the 22nd.

The 22nd rolled around and all who were invited were present. The Training Officer, Lieutenant Bill Bounds, entered the room and all stood at attention. He told them to be seated. He began by telling them that the target date for carrier qualification was set for February 16th on the USS Langley out of Norfolk, Virginia. That gave them four weeks to qualify in a new plane, the VE-9. The training unit had acquired the last 15 of them remaining in the Navy. The plan was to have them qualify in this aircraft, practice carrier approaches and landing on the field, then fly to Norfolk and qualify on board USS Langley before flying back to Pensacola in time to graduate and get their wings on March 1st. Lieutenant Bounds admitted it was a tough schedule since it was still winter and weather would be a governing factor in the completion of this plan. The student aviators were instructed to familiarize themselves with the aircraft, which were parked on the west end of the ramp just past the last Hangar. Specifications on the aircraft were available at the training office. As he was finishing his briefing Lieutenant Bounds asked if there were any questions.

Paul raised his hand and was recognized. "Sir, Lieutenant (JG) Day. I was wondering if there was going to be any ground school?"

"Good question, Mr. Day. No there will not be a formal ground school but you will have a few classes here in the Ready Room to learn the signals from the Landing Signal Officer and a briefing on how to fly the carrier landing pattern," Lieutenant Bounds replied. "Any other questions?"

Walt raised his hand and was recognized. "How many flights will we have before we are field qualified in carrier approaches and landings?"

"We will try to fly as many sorties as our budget will allow right up to our departure date for Norfolk on the 14th of February. There will be two familiarization flights and then we will commence Field Carrier Landing Practice. Any more questions?"

"One more question, Sir," Walt said. "What kind of navigation charts do we have for flying to Norfolk?"

"That's a great question, Mr. Pellman. There are no navigation charts, only road maps, which are in short supply. Your flight leader will probably have the only set of charts."

There were no more questions and the group was dismissed.

As they were walking out, Walt piped up and said, "Let's go take a look at this bird we're going to be flying. It's almost on the way to BOQ." "Sounds like a good idea," Paul added.

Bob added his two cents into the conversation "Yeah, might as well look at this old piece of shit."

"What do you know about it, Bob?" Walt asked.

"There were a couple attached to the USS Chicago and Nevada when I was in the Atlantic Fleet. They were built back in 1921 and used as trainers before they converted them to fighters," he said.

"Hold the horses, Bob. Let's don't judge them before we see them," Paul said.

"Okay, okay, don't get your knickers in a twist guys. I just know they're older than Admiral Dewey," Bob said.

They arrived at the most western Hangar and viewed the VE-9s tied down on the ramp next to the Hangar. They approached the first one in line. "They look pretty good," Walt observed. "The paint job looks new and I suspect they just went through overhaul and got new cotton covering on the whole airplane. Walt hopped up into the cockpit. Bob got up on the wing on the starboard side and Paul was on the port wing.

Walt observed, "Not much difference in the cockpit instrumentation. Looks like overhaul did a nice job on refurbishing inside. I see there's a handle here to drop the tailhook, I guess. I wonder how you get the hook back up and locked?"

"There is probably a deckhand who has to do that manually," Paul said. "Yeah, Walt, go ahead and release it and I will see if I can lock it back up."

Paul jumped off the wing and went back to the tail of the aircraft. In the cockpit, Walt pulled the handle back and sure enough, the hook dropped down to the ground.

Paul called out for Walt to reset the handle to an up and locked position. He grabbed the arm near the hook and pushed it back up towards the locked position. Sure enough, the hook lock sprung back and grabbed the hook, and locked it in the up position.

"Well, that worked as advertised," Walt said. "I don't see much else different in the cockpit so it shouldn't be much different flying. I guess we'll just have to learn the power setting of this new engine and the flight speeds."

"Yeah, sounds good, Buddy. I've seen enough. Let's head back to the Q," Bob said.

Walt dismounted the aircraft and the three of them headed off to the BOQ. When they reached the BOQ, Walt had an idea.

"Hey, guys," he said. "My old man's company makes all kinds of road maps. Why don't I ask him for a set of maps for all of us to fly to Norfolk?"

"Hey, Buddy, that sounds like a life-saving idea," Paul said.

That evening Walt wrote his dad and asked him to send 5 sets of state road maps for Florida, Georgia, south Carolina, North Carolina, and Virginia.

12

"Carrier Landing Practice"

Corry Station, Pensacola, Florida

The plan presented to the student aviators now took on a sense of urgency. They had a deadline to meet because the only date to carrier qualify was the 16th of February. Walt, Paul, and Bob needed to get the factory specs on the VE-9. However, they weren't quite sure of where to find the performance characteristics. These would be needed to fly the aircraft properly. It was early morning, but they decided to visit the Training Office to see what information they had on the VE-9. Upon arrival, they met with the petty officer 1st class, who handled all the training material. After telling him what they needed, he went to his storage locker and pulled out some papers. When he returned, he handed each of them a copy of the VE-9 specifications and a three-page document which described *"How to fly the VE-9."*

They thanked the petty officer and proceeded to the Ready Room. After grabbing a cup of coffee, they began studying the specifications.

Paul broke the silence "Hey, guys, did you see this SOB has the Wright-Hisso E-4 engine and delivers 220 horsepower? She ought to have some speed to it."

Bob chimed in, "Yeah, and they say the max speed is 118 mph."

Walt added, "It cruises at 100 mph. That's a big change from the NS-1s we've been flying."

The three of them went on to study the pamphlet they had been given on the performance and *"How to Fly the VE-9."*

"Hey, guys," Walt said. "This aircraft stalls at 42 mph? That means takeoff speed should be about 45 to 50 mph. I don't see anywhere in these documents where it says what takeoff speed should be."

"I didn't see that anywhere either, but I have been reading about how to fly the landing pattern. It says pattern speed should be 60 mph and approach speed is 55 mph with final speed at 50 mph," Bob said.

"Yeah and after takeoff climb speed is 65 mph," Paul added. "Those speeds are all we need to worry about."

"I was also readingabout stalls. The pamphlet says level flight stalls are gentle, but steep turn stalls especially to the right can be violent and result in a spin. Caution should be used in that case," Walt observed. "It also says controls are sensitive to the touch. That sounds good."

"I guess we just need to go out and try this stuff for ourselves and see what this baby can do," Bob said while looking at his Rolex. "How about we do lunch. I'm starving."

They all agreed that lunch would be great so they hustled off to the BOQ.

Next Day

The Training Officer decided each student aviator would get two familiarization flights. Arrangements were made that if a third flight were necessary, the student needed only to ask. Training also assigned an open book test on the aircraft specifications as well as performance factors. Walt, Bob, and Paul stopped in the Training Office and were issued their test. They went down to the Ready Room to complete their assignment. It took them only about an hour and a half because of the research they had done the day before. They compared answers before turning them into the Training Office. It would take a day or so before the tests were graded, and with no duties assigned, the three of them sailed Paul's sailboat out on Pensacola Bay. It was still winter, but the daytime temperatures were usually in the 50's.

Finally, after a couple of days, their tests were graded and all achieved 100%. They were all scheduled for familiarization flights. The three of them were scheduled for the same time with the first flight at 8:00 a.m. and the second at 1:00 p.m.

An early breakfast and a brisk walk to the Hangar, were followed by a change into flight uniform and then a trip down to maintenance. Each, in turn, signed out their assigned aircraft and they proceeded to the flight line. This morning they had decided each of them would proceed on their own on this flight to get the feel for the aircraft before they tried any of their wild formation stuff. The preflight was pretty routine. All the aircraft they had flown were built the same making preflight requirements similar.

Bob was the first to taxi out to the duty runway followed closely by Paul and Walt. Each checked their magnetos and engine performance. Bob taxied out onto the duty runway and added takeoff power to the engine. As he rolled down the runway, the aircraft veered to the right, but he made a nice correction and got airborne at 55 mph. Paul was next and he made a beautiful takeoff. Walt had been taking note of the way each of them had handled the aircraft and had decided that slow addition of power after releasing the brakes was the way to go. He taxied onto the duty runway, lined up, and slowly added power as he released the brakes. He anticipated the right drift and applied left rudder as he gained speed. His was a straight smooth-rolling takeoff. He lifted off at 55 mph, accelerated to 65 mph, and set his climb attitude. He made a right turn out of traffic and headed northwest to the training area to practice his stalls and slow-flight.

Walt did the slow-flight first. He slowed to 50 mph and completed some 180° turns with reversals. He practiced descending and climbing turns and finally leveled at 5000'. He judged the aircraft to be very sensitive on the controls and very responsive to input.

Next came a series of stalls. His straight-on stall was quick to recover, which he credited to his big 200HP radial engine. Next was a steep turn stall to the right followed by a steep turn stall to the left. The one to the left pitched him back to level flight while the one to the right tended to almost pitch him inverted.

Walt decided to give a spin a try to see how the aircraft reacted. He reduced the power to flight idle, pitched up the nose until the aircraft stalled then kicked in full right rudder and full back stick. The nose fell through and turned to the right. He did a full turn and a half then applied full left rudder and full forward stick. As soon as rotation stopped, he centered the rudder and pulled back on the stick until the nose of the aircraft was level on the horizon with power coming back up as he accelerated to 115 mph.

He next moved into his acrobatics and performed two loops, each beginning with a 2G pullup with zero Gs on top. He finished each loop back at 5000'. Next, he performed two Immelmann turns followed by a barrel roll to the right and left. His final maneuver was an aileron roll to the left.

He had been tracking his position and was almost to Silverhill Field. He descended to 800' and joined the landing traffic pattern. Eight touch-and-go landings were performed after which he departed the pattern and headed back to Corry Station. Landing was a full stop and taxi to the ramp where he parked the aircraft and shut down.

The aircraft was signed-in to maintenance with no discrepancies. He proceeded to the Ready Room and grabbed a cup of coffee. He no sooner had sat down when Paul and Bob entered the room. All three were excited about the flight just completed. They compared notes of their flight profile and aircraft performance. Each agreed the aircraft was sensitive to control input and the power of the Wright-Hisson-E4 engine was a great improvement over the NS-1 aircraft.

They grabbed a bite to eat for lunch and discussed their upcoming 1:00 pm flight. At 12:30 pm they began their routine for the second flight of the day. Turns out it was a repeat of the first but generally with more confidence, safety, and pleasure. Upon returning to base, they debriefed each other, changed into the uniform of the day, and called it a day.

Next Morning

An early briefing was scheduled with Lieutenant Bounds. They were up early and in the Ready Room by 8:15 a.m., patiently waiting for the 8:30 a.m. briefing to begin. Lieutenant (JG) Jack Wilson joined them once again to make up the fourth member of their flight.

Walt welcomed him, "Hey, Jack, how did your fam flights go?" he asked.

"Kind of shaky," Jack replied. "Damn thing was heavy on the controls and landings were rough. Seems like the nose kept falling through at slow speeds on landing."

Bob joined the conversation, "Jack, use the trim wheel when you get to slow speeds on landing. That will help you keep the nose up for touchdown."

"Thanks, Bob. I'll try that," Jack replied.

Bill Bounds entered the room and the flight of four stood at attention as he approached them.

"Be seated, gentlemen. How are things going this morning?" Bill asked.

Paul answered for the group, "I believe we are all doing fine, Sir. Just awaiting your briefing."

"Okay, Mister Day, thank you. Let's get started," Bill said.

He went to the chalkboard and began, "The four of you are designated flight CF-14. Mr. Pellman, you are the temporary Flight Leader. Let's begin with the approach to the carrier. The ship will expect us to be at 1800'. Look for the Baker or Charlie flag to be flying from the yardarm. Baker means orbit the ship at 1800'. Charlie means cleared for approach and landing. Descend from 1800' down to 800'. We will be in lower right echelon flying at 800'. Fly up the starboard side of the ship parallel to the ship's course, which should be into the wind."

Bill had outlined the ship and the holding circle on the board with the altitude requirements. He continued showing descent and course to parallel the ship.

He continued to sketch on the chalkboard as he described the next progression of the landing pattern.

"If there are other aircraft in the pattern, don't break until you have proper interval for landing. When you do break, 45° angle of bank and reduce power to slow the aircraft from break speed to downwind speed of 55 mph, and descend to 300'. Complete your landing checklist and ensure that your hook is down. As you approach an abeam point midship on the carrier, reduce your speed to 50 mph and begin your 180° turn, descending so you roll out just before you cross the fantail of the ship. You should be about 10 to 15 feet above deck height. From the 90° position on your turn, you should be set on speed and rate of descent. That's when you will pick up the Landing Signal Officer (LSO), who will be standing on his platform located here." He drew a stick figure on the port side of the stern of the flight deck.

"He will have two paddles shaped like this." Again, he drew the shape of the paddles. "And will signal what you need to do to get aboard or that you are doing okay. Once you roll out on final approach, you will receive one of two signals from the LSO. He will signal either a cut or a wave off, which means add full power on your engine, begin a climb and make a slight "S" turn to clear the deck. Fly up the port side of the ship and take interval on the landing traffic before you join the downwind at 300' and 55mph. If you receive a cut from the LSO, reduce power to flight idle, hold your attitude on the nose, and let the plane settle and stall onto the deck where your hook can catch an arresting wire. There are seven wires and you are trying for number two which is an above-average satisfactory landing. The flight deck crew will unhook you from the arresting wire. The crewman forward and on the port side of your aircraft will give you the hook-up signal, which means placing the hook release handle in the up and locked position. The flight deck crew will then signal you to taxi forward and probably pass you on to the next Taxi Signalman. Once you are stopped forward of the wires, the Deck Launch Officer will give you a two- finger turn-up signal, which means hold your brakes and push your power up to just slightly below takeoff power," Bill demonstrated these signals.

"When the Deck Launch Officer hears your engine stabilize at power-up, he will give you the release brakes and launch signal. Squeeze your power up to takeoff power and fly the airplane off the deck. When airborne, climb to 300', taking interval on any traffic downwind for landing."

Having finished the brief, Bill asked, "Are there any questions?"

Paul raised his hand, "Sir, what if we don't catch a wire after we take the cut?"

"Great question, Mister Day. If there are aircraft parked forward on the deck, your only choice is to stand on the brakes and hope you can stop the aircraft. If you feel you can't, you will probably lock up the brakes and stand the aircraft on its prop. If the forward deck is clear, you can just take off and try again. There will probably be air group airplanes on the ship, so just follow the signals of the flight deck crewmen."

Bob raised his hand, "Sir, what about all the LSOs paddle signals. Do you have a handout?"

"Yes, Mister Fitzwater, we will have a sheet for all of you after the briefing is over. You will see them when you fly your field carrier landing practice flights."

Bill continued, "After you complete your seven arrested landings, normally your eighth will be your last where the deck crew will taxi you forward for refueling. After refueling, we will all return to the beach. However, if anyone takes a wave off, that will require another pass to get to seven so the rest of you can get an extra landing or two. You'll just have to follow the directions of the flight deck crew.

"Now let's talk about field carrier landing practice sorties. There are 11 planned flights. These are designed to duplicate carrier approaches and landings except for arrestment. The main difference is they will be touch and go landings on the field. We will use Perdido Field which is located off the west side of Perdido Bay, down towards the beach. It is a well- marked runway and will be easy to find. I will be your LSO on the field. My position will be at the end of the runway on your left side with a windscreen to simulate the shipboard LSO platform."

"Your flight will take off and join up in stepdown parade formation. You will climb to 1800', proceed to Perdido Field, Circle the field once, then descend to 800' and enter the break on the starboard side of the runway. Once you break, you will set up for a carrier pattern and execute a simulated carrier approach. As LSO I will pick you up at the 90 and wave you onto final and the cut position. After taking the cut, you will go around for another simulated landing. With the fuel onboard, you can make 12 FCLPs before you need to return to Corry Station. Are there any questions?"

There were no questions. "Gentlemen, that completes your briefing. Tomorrow we begin two flights a day until we get our 11 FCLP flights complete. We have three weeks to complete this schedule and if the weather holds, we will be on schedule for the 14th of February to qualify on the USS Langley."

13

"A Secret Exposed"

A Bright New Day

The group had picked up the sheet with the LSO paddles signals before they left the Hangar. The figures were all charcoal pencil sketches depicting each signal. They had studied all day until they retired for the night. Today was the day they would need to know them without fail and error. If they missed or misinterpreted a signal it could end up in a crash so they were all a little apprehensive.

They checked the flight schedule for today and Flight CF-14 was scheduled for FCLP 1 and 2. Lieutenant Bounds entered the Ready Room and sat down at the briefing table with the four of them.

He began his briefing, "Gentlemen, after takeoff you will join up and proceed to Perdido Field, circle and check the signal flag which will be flying on the LSO platform at the end of the duty runway. Does anyone remember what flag clears your flight to descend into the FCLP pattern and to commence your landings?"

Bill pointed at Jack. "What flag should you see?" he asked.

"Sir, Bravo flag continue to circle. Charlie cleared to descend and enter the landing pattern," Jack said.

"That's one above average for Mister Wilson. Okay, you see a Charlie flag and descend to 800' and enter the break parallel and to the starboard of the duty runway. Hard break and descend to what altitude?" Bill asked.

"Mr. Day, I'll bet you can give us that answer," Bill said.

"Sir, descend to 300' on the downwind and slow to 55kts," Paul replied.

"100 percent correct, Mr. Day," Bill responded. "Okay, from the 180 slow to 50kts and pick up the LSO at the 90. I will be your LSO and what we want is for you to roll out of your turn at about 20' over the threshold of the simulated deck of the carrier where I will give you either a cut signal or a wave-off. After you complete 12 landings, I will give you this signal with my paddles," Bill stood and demonstrated with both hands extended at waist level in front of him he moved his hands up and down.

"This means make this a full stop landing, taxi off onto the grass on the port side, and park next to the vehicles behind the LSO platform. We will debrief and refuel the aircraft there if necessary. Mister Pellman, I believe you are the Flight Leader for today. Are there any questions?"

"Seeing none." Bill said, "Okay, let's get this thing moving."

The students manned their aircraft. Walt was having trouble getting his engine started. The Plane Captain hand-propped the engine twice with no response. He gave Walt the signal to turn off the magnetos so he could prime the engine again. The Plane Captain pulled the prop through two more times and gave Walt the signal to turn on the magnetos and called out "contact." Walt responded with "contact" and turned on the mag switch.

The Plane Captain spun the prop once again and this time the engine roared to life. Walt gave the Plane Captain the signal to pull the chocks, saluted and taxied out to the duty runway. Bob, Paul, and Jack were sitting at the end of the duty runway waiting for Walt. He stopped, ran up the engine, checked the magnetos and RPMs, and all were normal. He turned and checked for any traffic then faced the tower where he received a green light, which cleared the flight for takeoff. Walt was off first, followed by Paul, Bob, and finally Jack. He leveled at 1800' and maintained 65kts until each plane had joined up in parade formation at right echelon. Walt gave the signal to accelerate to cruise speed and slowly added the power to reach 100kts. He headed directly towards Perdido Field and within five minutes was entering the holding circle at the field. He observed a bravo flag flying from the LSOs platform. He continued circling and observed Bill landing his plane and taxing back and parking behind the LSO platform. On his next circle, he observed a Charlie flag so he began his descent to 800'. As he was passing the LSO platform on the downwind leg, he turned left and entered the break for runway 25 just starboard and parallel to the runway. At the halfway point of the runway, he kissed off to Paul, who was number two in the formation and broke left at 45° angle of bank while descending to 300' and slowing to 55kts. As he approached the point abeam the LSO platform, he began a shallow banked descending left turn towards the runway. At the 90° position of his turn, he picked up the LSO. The signal from the LSO was arms extended straight out to the sides and level with his shoulders. This meant "Roger" everything looks good. As he continued, the signal changed to "Come on" which was signaled by bringing the paddles arms level to the front and then back to fully extended to "Roger." Walt squeezed on the power just slightly, and as he rolled out wings level at the threshold, he received a "cut" from the LSO. Walt reduced his power to flight idle and let the aircraft settle while it slowed towards the runway. It stalled at a foot above the runway. Right after touchdown, Walt added the power and took off. He accelerated to climb speed and looked for downwind traffic. Jack was just approaching the upwind end of the runway so Walt took interval on him and leveled at 300' downwind for another try.

As Walt was making his twelfth approach and just as he was rolling out over the threshold, Bill gave him the full-stop signal immediately followed by a "cut." Walt took the cut and landed, slowed the aircraft, and turned left off the runway onto the grass. He taxied back to the LSO platform and parked his plane next to Bill's airplane. Eventually, Bob made a full stop landing, Paul was next, and finally Jack. After all the planes were parked Bill met them behind the LSO Platform. They all took off their leather flight helmets and sat down on the grass in a semi-circle. The petty officer who had been assisting Bill handed him his notepad and went to help the ground crew with the aircraft. Bill flipped open the pad and began his debrief. The petty officer had documented each approach and landing as dictated by Bill for each student. Walt's passes were pretty much roger with a couple of slow speed approaching the groove. All in all, everybody got satisfactory to above average grades on their flying.

After a little relaxation, Bill once again had them airborne and practicing their FCLP skills. After the twelfth landing, Walt was given the signal to climb up into a circling position around the field at 1800'. He did so until the other three members of the flight joined up in formation and he then proceeded back to Corry Station. As he passed south of the Station he signaled a step-down right echelon. He brought the flight into the break over runway 27, made his break, and circled to land. After landing, he taxied back to the ramp and shut down. The flight members gathered on the ramp and walked back to the Hangar. In the Ready Room, they had a cup of coffee while they waited for Bill. They were very animated in their discussion of the two flights they just completed. Paul seemed to have trouble maintaining his proper speed while Jack was having difficulty getting his angle of bank set up to roll out in the proper position at the cut. Walt and Bob on the other hand were getting pretty much roger passes and were having a ball.

Shortly, Bill came into the room and sat down with them at the briefing table.

"Gentlemen, all in all, I would say those were two highly acceptable flights." He opened the notepad with the approach and landing documented.

"Mr. Day, you need to work on your speed control and use caution about diving for the deck when you get the cut. That can cause the aircraft to porpoise and on the carrier to miss the wire. Not really bad though. Mr. Wilson, you seem to be having difficulty getting the appropriate angle of bank for your approach. On the carrier, the wind will be straight down the deck so your angle of bank should not change all the way around the approach. Here on the field, a slight cross-wind may cause you to need to vary your angle of bank slightly in each 90°. Just remember your crosswind techniques from basic flights. Mr. Pellman and Mr. Fitzwater, just keep doing what you're doing with slight improvements each flight. Does anyone have any comments or questions?"

"No questions, I'll see you maybe tomorrow. Depends on the weather."

Next day

Sure enough, the weather was bad and the flight schedule was canceled for the day. With not much to do, the guys sat around the Ready Room most of the day drinking coffee and reviewing their flight procedures. Before they secured for the day, they checked the flight schedule. They were scheduled for FCLP flights 3 and 4 starting at 8:00 am.

They awoke the next day and it was raining cats and dogs. When they went to breakfast they saw the sign on the board outside the dining room. *"All flights canceled for today."* It would be another day of just sitting around.

Turns out this storm lasted three days, and finally on the fourth day, the weather broke and skies were broken clouds with visibility ten plus miles. However, the winds were slightly gusty, up to 18kts. This would make for an exciting couple of hours in the FCLP landing pattern. Flight CF-14 completed their two flights for the day, but all performance elements of their flights were rough and difficult to control. On debrief, Bill stated what everybody else had already deduced. They didn't get much out of these two flights and were somewhat a waste of time.

Flight CF-14 finished their twelfth FCLP flight by the 8th of February and Bill pronounced them all ready for their carrier qualification. Bill indicated they would have a briefing on their cross-country flight to Norfolk, Virginia, the next day at 10 o'clock in his office.

After breakfast, Walt went back to his room and retrieved the package his dad had sent him in the mail. Paul, Bob, Walt, and Jack arrived at Bill's office in the Hangar at 9:50 am. Just about 10 o'clock they were ushered into his office.

"Please, gentlemen, have a seat and make yourself comfortable. The reason for the meeting is to plan our trip to Norfolk, Virginia."

They all took out their note pads to record any pertinent facts they needed to remember.

Bill continued, "Planning is for us to leave here on the 13th of February. We will fly to the Naval Air Facility Norfolk, Virginia, with fuel stops in Macon, Georgia; Columbia, South Carolina and Fort Bragg, North Carolina."

Walt stopped Bill. "Sir, my father was gracious enough to supply each of us with road maps for this flight." He opened the package he had been carrying and sorted out a set of maps for each one present and handed them out.

"That was very nice of your dad to do that," Bill said. "You can lay out your course of flight later. Right now I want to finish out how our trip will proceed. Once we arrive at Norfolk, we will check into the BOQ. On the morning of the 14th, we will proceed down to the USS Langley and take a tour of the ship. I am sure we will meet the LSO and the Operations Officer, who will brief us on the schedule for the 16th. If weather delays us, the tour will shift to the 15th. Qualifying day will be the 16th. The ship is scheduled to depart on the morning of the 16th at 0700 hours. We will take off at 0900 and should be over the ship by 0930. After everyone has qualified, we will refuel and return to NAF Norfolk and remain overnight. Weather permitting, we will depart for Pensacola the morning of the 17th."

Pensacola, Florida February 13th

Bob was up about 5:00 a.m. He washed and shaved before he awakened Paul, then knocked on Walt's door and rousted him out of bed. The three of them had packed the night before so they had plenty of time for breakfast. By 6:00 a.m. they were out the door and walking to the Hangar where they received their assigned aircraft. They changed into their winter flight clothing, then proceeded to their aircraft and stowed their baggage in the plane. Next, they conducted a preflight of their aircraft and stood by awaiting Bill Bounds.

Bill arrived shortly and briefed them on the weather en-route to Macon, Georgia. It would be broken clouds with a base at 4000', visibility over 10 miles, and winds on the surface out of the northwest at 5 to 10mph. Sounded like a pleasant leg of the flight. Bill had filed a trip itinerary with the squadron and had alerted base operations of their planned flight.

They all manned their aircraft with Walt the designated leader. The formation for the day was four abreast at 200' interval, altitude 2000'. After takeoff, they joined up climbing to 2000' with Paul on the left-wing and Bob and Jack on the right. Bill took up a position 200' behind the formation between Walt and Bob. This way he figured he could keep an eye on all four of them fairly easily. Walt leveled the formation at 2000' and set power to maintain 100kts. He leaned his fuel mixture until he had a 10° rise in cylinder head temperature. That would give him the best cruise setting and best distance.

The flight to Macon, was uneventful and the flight landed for fuel. It took about 30 minutes and shortly after they were airborne again on their way to Columbia, South Carolina. The road maps Walt's dad had sent were very valuable and Walt was having little trouble determining his position. They soon crossed the Savannah River and were into South Carolina. After two and a half hours in the air, the flight sighted Columbia. The airport was located southeast of the city and they joined in parade formation, right echelon. They executed a left break on runway 32 and were soon on the ground being refueled. The five of them walked over to the airline terminal and found a vendor selling sandwiches and iced tea. After purchasing some lunch, they found a table and chairs and ate their lunch.

After lunch, they walked back to their planes. Bill settled up for the gas and they were on their way to their next stop, Fort Bragg, North Carolina. They arrived after a 2-hour flight, quickly refueled, and were back in the air headed for their final destination, Chambers Field, Norfolk, Virginia.

It was late in the afternoon as Flight CF-14 approached Norfolk, Virginia. Walt had been watching for smoke on the ground and had determined that the wind was out of the west-north-west. Chambers field was still under construction so he wasn't sure what runways were completed. He spotted the field off to the north so he set up his approach from the southeast. He signaled the flight to join up in right echelon. It appeared that runway 27 had been completed so he turned into the break, steadied on heading 270° and proceeded over the runway at 800'. The tower was alert and saw them approaching and signaled a green light. Walt kissed off and broke left establishing himself downwind at 600'. He completed his landing checklist, and as he approached the position abeam his point of intended landing, he commenced his 180° descending turn for landing. The tower signaled a green light and cleared him to land. He touched down smoothly and taxied over to the tower. His flight was right behind him and they parked in a row right next to the tower. Bill was the last to park and they quickly assembled near Bill's aircraft. As he climbed out of his aircraft, they were met by a Lieutenant (JG) who was the Air Operations Duty Officer. Bill took point on the situation and explained their purpose for being there. The duty officer acknowledged the situation and had his line personnel chock and tie down the aircraft. Since construction was not yet completed on the base BOQ, he told them they would have to stay at the Norfolk Naval Base BOQ. He arranged transportation to that facility. They all retrieved their travel kits and boarded the vehicle to take them to the naval base BOQ.

At the BOQ they settled into three rooms. Walt bunked with Paul, Bob with Jack, and Bill to himself. The group had decided they needed some supper and the Mess stayed open until seven o'clock. They all changed into their civilian dress and made it to the Mess before it closed.

After dinner, everyone agreed they were beat from the long day's flying and were just going to go to bed early. They would assemble the next morning after breakfast at 8:00 a.m. in the lobby. Everyone except Walt made it to breakfast. He was late getting up and by the time he got dressed the Mess was closed. He grabbed a cup of coffee in the lobby and was sitting waiting for them when they exited the Mess.

"Good morning," Bob said. "About time you got your butt out of bed. Missed ya at breakfast."

"Yeah, I know but the extra half-hour of sleep was worth it," Walt said. "I'm good for another sixteen hours now. Are we ready to go?" he asked.

"I'm going to check on transportation," Bill offered.

He went off to the lobby check-in desk to talk with the person manning the desk. Within a few minutes, he returned to the group and said, "It appears the Langley is tied up about three blocks from here so we can walk over there when we're ready. Our scheduled time is 9:00 a.m. for our tour and briefing so there's no rush to get there," Bill said.

The group decided to sit around for about thirty minutes in the lobby of the BOQ. The temperature for this February 14th was considered mild at 44°F but the VE-9 didn't have much room for their flight bag so they were without their trench coats, which were capable of staving off the cold temperatures. Their dress blues would be warm enough as long as the wind didn't blow very much.

At 8:35 a.m. they decided it was time to head down to the Langley. It was a brisk three-block walk and they arrived at the ship in about 10 minutes. They walked up the gangplank and saluted the flag flying from the yardarm. Then they saluted the Officer Of The Day (OOD) and requested permission to "come aboard." Bill Bounds told the OOD they were there to meet with Lieutenant Commander Coors. The Assistant OOD picked up the mic of the 1MC, "Lieutenant Commander Coors, lay up to the quarterdeck. You have visitors." Within a minute or two, Lieutenant Commander Coors arrived and introduced himself to Bill Bounds. Bill in turn introduced Walt, Paul, Bob, and Jack. Lieutenant Commander Coors invited them up to the officer's wardroom where they had a cup of coffee and were offered sweet rolls. The only one to partake of the sweet rolls was Walt as he was the only one to have missed breakfast.

Lieutenant Commander Coors began, "Before I take you on a tour of the ship, let's go over the op-plan for the 16th. First of all, we have a special guest scheduled. Rear Admiral McMillin will be here to observe flight operations."

Walt smiled to himself. He figured he would finally have to reveal his meeting with Admiral McMillin on the golf course in Pensacola.

Lieutenant Commander Coors continued, "The ship is scheduled to weigh anchor at 0900 but if the Admiral is late of course our departure will be delayed. You should plan your departure to rendezvous with the ship after we clear the mouth of the bay. That should take us about an hour. You can circle the ship until we proceed downwind and then commence landings when we turn into the wind. After every pilot has made seven landings, after the eighth landing planes will be taxied forward and parked for refueling then respotted aft in preparation for launch. If some of the pilots are waved-off during qualification and you have made your eight required landings you can make additional landings or you can circle the ship until we start parking aircraft, then make your final landing. Lieutenant Bounds, you can wave your pilots as LSO if you wish, but Lieutenant (JG) Orille will be the designated ship's LSO and will be supervising you back on the platform. That's about all I have for you at this time. Let's go back to my office. I'll get Chief Edwards to give you the tour of the ship."

They departed the wardroom and went down one level where by chance they ran into Chief Edwards.

"Chief, how about giving these gentlemen the nickel tour of the ship. They are going to qualify in carrier operations on the 16th." Turning to the group, "Gentlemen, please introduce yourselves. I will see you later. Have a good tour."

Bill extended his hand, "I'm Lieutenant Bounds, and these are my fledglings, Lieutenant (JG) Pellman, Lieutenant (JG) Day, Lieutenant (JG) Fitzwater, and Lieutenant (JG) Watson."

They all shook the Chief's hand and he started the tour. They looked in every nook and cranny of the ship it seemed. They started on the Hangar deck and ended on the flight deck. That is what most interested the student pilots.

"Damn, it sure looks short and narrow," Paul exclaimed.

"More like a parking lot than a runway," Bob added.

"Well, they do have seven arresting wires," Walt observed. "And since there won't be any parked aircraft forward, you can go around if you miss a wire, except on the last landing, maybe. I don't know about you but I intend to catch #2 or #3 on every approach."

"Yeah right, you'll probably have your eyes closed on every pass," Bob said.

Bill chimed in, "Just remember, guys, if you take a wave off, be sure to jog left and fly up the port side of the ship. The deck crew doesn't appreciate straight ahead wave-offs. Also, remember to move your hook handle to the up position as soon as you come to a stop on arrestment. The deck crew will unhook the wire and move your hook to the up position."

Paul asked, "Lieutenant Bounds, I noticed the ship has one catapult. Will we be launched by it on any of our takeoffs?"

"No, Mister Day, no catapult for you. There is plenty of deck for a deck launch. The ship will probably be steaming at 10 knots and if you add wind speed to it, that's plenty of headwind to shorten your takeoff distance," Bill remarked.

Chief Edwards indicated the tour was complete and he would answer any questions. The group had no questions so he led them down to Lieutenant Commander Coors office.

"Did you all have a good tour of the ship?" Lieutenant Commander Coors asked.

"Yes, Sir," Bill responded. "Thank you for arranging things and making this possible for my students to qualify," Bill shook his hand.

Lieutenant Commander Coors said, "You're welcome. Glad to have you aboard. If you'll check-in with me when you come aboard on the 16th I'll hook you up with Lieutenant (JG) Orille and you two guys can work out your plan for the day."

"That will be great, Sir. I guess we will be going ashore now. Thanks again," Bill responded.

With that, the group proceeded to the Hangar deck and over to the quarterdeck where they saluted the OOD and asked permission to leave the ship. Each officer in turn saluted and asked permission to go ashore. After "permission granted" they turned and saluted the flag flying on the yardarm then proceeded down the gangplank. Once ashore they decided to visit the Ship Stores which usually had a Gedunk where they could get some lunch. It was only a four-block walk and as they entered, they spotted the Gedunk. Most of them ordered a bowl of hot soup, a sandwich, and a drink. As they ate their lunch, the topic of the morning was discussed in great detail. The fledglings were all impressed with the ship and its crew. They were looking forward with great anticipation to their carrier qualification flight.

The remainder of the day and the next day were spent just relaxing around the BOQ. Late in the day of the 15th, the four student pilots sat around after dinner and discussed the plan for the next day. Bill was going to report to the Langley before 0800. They decided not to take off before 10 o'clock. The ship would leave port at 0900 and steam out of the bay at 3 to 5 knots. Once clear of the entrance, they would turn downwind and increase speed 10 knots, which would put them about 11 nautical miles from Chambers Field at takeoff time. What Walt said they would do is fly to the mouth of the bay and head downwind. That should put them overhead Langley about 20 minutes after takeoff. From then going forward, they would follow the ship's/LSO's signals.

Walt decided now was the time to tell his story he had kept from his friends for months.

"Guys," he said. "I want to come clean on something that happened a few months ago, which I didn't feel I needed to tell you but I do now because I don't want you to be surprised if it should happen."

Bob interrupted, "So, you finally proposed to Zimmy."

"No, that's not it," Walt answered. "I played golf with Admiral McMillin and a few other important Naval Aviators a few months ago. Then I was invited to the Commanding Officer of NAS Pensacola's quarters for dinner where Admiral McMillin was present. I want you to know just in case we meet the Admiral and he remembers me."

"Walt, you sneaky bastard, Here you have all these bigwigs as friends and you don't even tell us," Paul said.

"I didn't think of it as a big deal and I wanted to keep it low key so I didn't tell you guys. I'm sorry, maybe I should have told you," Walt said.

"Well, who else of importance did you meet?" Bob asked.

"Besides Admiral McMillin, there was Lieutenant Commander Charles E. Rosendahl, Senior Lighter-Than-Air expert, and Captain Frederick J. Horne, Commanding Officer, USS Saratoga," Walt said.

"And who won the golf game?" Paul asked.

"I was lucky enough to have scored best," Walt said.

"You can bet Admiral McMillin is going to remember you, a snotty-nosed Ensign beating all the high-priced help," Jack offered.

The banter continued for most of the evening. They all were not about to let Walt forget how he treated his buddies, even though it was great fun. In truth, they were proud of him but would never acknowledge that to him.

They all hit the hay by 9:30 p.m. with great anticipation of the next day's activities.

14

"Carrier Qualification"

Everyone was up very early and dressed ready for breakfast when the Mess opened at 6:00 a.m. The five of them sat together and Bill gave them some final words of wisdom and information.

"Before I forget, I have arranged transportation for you all out to Chambers Field departing here at 8:00 am. Now one final word on your flight today. I will be your LSO on the platform so just follow my signals. Remember what we drilled in your 12 FCLP flights and you will be just fine. The main thing which is added today is the hook. Drop it on the downwind and make sure the handle is in the up position right after arrestment on deck. Also, the launch officer will give you the flag turn up before he gives you the release brakes and launch signal. Nothing else should be any different than what you already have learned. Good Luck."

After breakfast, they all went back to their rooms and changed into their flight uniform. At 7:30 a.m. they rendezvoused in the BOQ lobby and sat and waited for their transportation to Chambers Field.

At exactly 8:00 a.m. their vehicle pulled up in front of the BOQ. The four of them piled in and the driver headed off to Chambers Field. It was only a twenty-minute drive when they arrived at base operations. They walked in and looked for the Aerology office. Since Walt was the designated flight leader, he spoke for the group. He asked the duty weatherman what the weather was going to be all day in and around the Chesapeake Bay area especially out in the Atlantic within 50 miles of the entrance to the bay. The weatherman scanned his latest chart and his teletype messages with the forecast from the U.S. Weather Bureau. He then briefed them on the current Chambers Field weather.

It was a 3500' ceiling of broken clouds with a higher overcast at 8000'. Visibility was 10+ miles, the temperature currently 45°F and winds out of the southwest at 5 to 8 mph. The forecast for the next 8 hours is expected to remain the same with the temperature reaching a high of 52°F and wind increasing to 8 to 10 mph out of the west. Winds up to 3500' where expected to be westerly at 10 mph.

Walt asked if he had a water temperature within 50 miles of shore. The weatherman checked his teletype and he had a ship report a surface water temperature of 50°F.

Walt thanked him for his briefing and walked over to the Air Operations Duty Officer. He briefed the duty officer on what his flight was scheduled to do when they would depart and approximately when they expected to return. He didn't know whether the Langley would pass any flight information back to him or not but he should expect none.

The flight gathered and began walking to their aircraft. Along the way, Walt stopped by the line shack and asked for four able-bodied Plane Captains to get their engines started. The line chief designated four Plane Captains who then walked out with Walt to their aircraft. While the pilots pre-flighted their aircraft, the Plane Captains untied the aircraft, removed the pitot tube cover, and removed the tarp covering the cockpit. The pilots checked the oil and double-checked the fuel tanks, taking a sample of each tank checking for water. Next, they donned their life preserver and strapped on their parachute before climbing into the cockpit. The Plane Captain assisted them in connecting their seat belt and shoulder harness then standing by in front and to the port of the wing awaiting the engine start signal. Walt checked his watch. It was approaching 10:00 a.m. so he gave the Plane Captain the signal to start the engine. The remainder of the flight was observing Walt's Plane Captain and when he moved to prime the engine, they in turn, gave their Plane Captain the start engine signal.

Walt's Plane Captain turned over the prop 2 complete revolutions. He then yelled "contact" and Walt responded "contact" and turned on the mag switch. The Plane Captain then pulled the prop through and Walt's engine sputtered to life, then roared and stabilized at 700rpm. He checked the engine oil pressure gauge which showed pressure rising. He checked his flight to see their status. All engines were up and running. Walt sat there until his cylinder head temperature reached operating range. Next, he gave the Plane Captain the signal to pull the chocks. The Plane Captain pulled the chocks and gave Walt the signal to taxi, saluted, and stepped out of the way. Walt taxied in front of his flight who all gave him a thumbs up so he headed out towards runway 25. His flight followed and they all stopped short and checked their engine and mags. Everything was normal. Walt turned directly facing the tower and received a green light, *"cleared for takeoff."* He taxied onto the duty runway followed by his flight, Paul was number 2, Bob number 3, and Jack tail-end Charlie. They all stopped, staggered out one behind the other. As soon as Walt added power and released his brakes, Paul counted to 10 then added power and released his brakes followed by Bob and Jack each at 10-second intervals. Walt climbed straight ahead to 800' before commencing a righthand turn. Before he reached 2000' and rolled out heading east, his flight had joined on his wing and slid over into left echelon. He gave Paul the signal to move to right echelon with Bob sliding into Paul's spot and Jack remaining on Bob's leftwing.

The flight proceeded on an easterly heading. They passed over Fort Story and finally Virginia Beach. Walt had climbed to 3000' hoping for greater visibility. Within a minute or two he spotted the USS Langley steaming east southeast. She was about 11 miles out of the mouth of Chesapeake Bay. He signaled the flight into right echelon and began a descent to 1800'. As he arrived on scene and started to enter a holding circle around the ship, he spotted the Bravo flag. After two complete circles, Langley made a 180° turn along with the plane guard destroyer following her. As she steadied out on heading 280°, the Bravo flag was lowered and Charlie flag raised. As soon as Walt spotted the Charlie flag, he began a descent to 800'. He approached heading 100° and commenced a tighter turn ending up parallel to the ship's course. He brought the flight up the starboard side of the ship, and after passing upwind, he counted to five, kissed off, broke port at 45° angle of bank descending to 300' while slowing the aircraft to 55 knots and completing the landing checklist including hook down. He could feel his heart start to race. This would be his first carrier landing. Passing midships on the Langley, he started a gentle descending left turn slowing to 50 knots. As he passed the 90° point in his turn, he picked up the LSO. His signal was Roger. He was extremely careful to maintain his speed and angle of bank. As he approached the groove, the LSO gave him a wings level signal followed by a cut. He reduced power to idle and stalled the aircraft just as it touched down on the deck. The aircraft caught number 3 wire and abruptly brought the aircraft to a stop. Walt placed the hook handle in the up position. The flight deck crew released him from the arresting wire and placed his hook in the retracted position. The Taxi Director signaled to taxi forward then passed him off to the next Taxi Director. He was directed into a parking position forward on the starboard side of the flight deck and given hold brakes signal. The flight deck crew chocked the aircraft then gave the cut engine signal. Walt wondered what the hell was going on. He released his shoulder harness and climbed out of the port side of his aircraft. He placed his parachute and life preserver on the wing of the aircraft just as Paul was parked behind him and likewise chocked and cut engine. Next came Bob followed by Jack. They in turn were parked next to Walt and Paul. After Jack parked his aircraft, it was a lot quieter on the deck and a crewman told Walt to report to the port side squadron Ready Room. Bill met them in the port catwalk and they followed him down into the Squadron Ready Room. Lieutenant (JG) Orille accompanied them and told them to be seated. Admiral McMillin had requested a meeting with them.

As Admiral McMillin entered the Ready Room accompanied by the Skipper, Lieutenant (JG) Orille called them to attention. The Admiral began to speak, "Gentlemen, be seated," he said, glancing around the Ready Room. "Mister Pellman, what a nice surprise. Nice to see you again."

Walt stood. "A pleasure to see you again, Sir," Walt answered.

"I'm told you were leading this flight. That was a very nice landing you made," the Admiral said.

"Thank you, Sir. I was doing my best just to get it smoothly on deck," Walt responded.

"Please introduce your fellow pilots. I have already met Lieutenant Bounds."

"Yes, Sir." Walt pointing to Paul, "This is Lieutenant (JG) Day." Paul stood and the Admiral extended his hand.

"Next to him is Lieutenant (JG) Bob Fitzwater," Walt said.

Again, the Admiral extended his hand, Bob reciprocated and said, "a pleasure to meet you, Sir."

"And finally, Sir, we have Lieutenant (JG) Jack Wilson," Walt said. The Admiral also shook Jack's hand.

The Admiral began, "Actually the reason I came down to Norfolk was to check on the operational status of the ship and to get a briefing on the upcoming Caribbean operation. Seeing you do your initial carrier quals is a real bonus. You are proving to me that our training syllabus is about right in training Naval Aviators. Has anyone any comments I can pass along?"

Walt raised his hand. "Yes, Mr. Pellman," the Admiral asked.

"Sir, two things are lacking. One, solid instrument flying, and two, plane to ground and plane to plane radio communications. We could operate a lot safer if we had those two things," Walt pointed out.

"Yes, Mr. Pellman, those are two priorities we are working on. Within six months I expect all control towers to be fitted with transceivers. Starting with advanced trainers and working backward, we will retrofit all aircraft with a VHF transceiver. We are also looking at a low-frequency radio range receiver along with placing an artificial horizon in all aircraft. It's going to take a while so you'll need to be patient. Takes time and money," the Admiral said. "I wish all of you success the rest of the day with your quals."

As the Admiral turned to leave, Lieutenant (JG) Orille called out, "Attention on deck."

They all stood at attention until the Admiral departed, then relaxed and once again sat down.

Lieutenant (JG) Orille spoke, "Your planes should be respotted by now and we should be ready to resume flight operations. The ship has been cruising east southeast this past hour so we should be at least 25 miles off the coast. When we commence flight operations, the ship will once again turn into the wind so that when you complete your eight landings, we should only be about a mile or two from the entrance to the harbor at Norfolk. This way you can depart overhead with plenty of gas to bingo to Chambers Field."

Lieutenant (JG) Orille called Pri-Fly on the 1MC, and shortly thereafter, the speaker in the Ready Room blared, "Pilots man your planes."

The flight moved up to the flight deck and spotted their planes parked aft on the deck. They once again donned their life preserver and parachute, climbed into the cockpit, and started their aircraft. The flight deck crew taxied Walt forward first where the Launch Officer gave him the hold brakes and waved a small flag in his hand indicating add power for takeoff. The Launch Officer faced forward, lowered his flag to shoulder level, and knelt on one knee while giving the release brake signal. Walt pushed the throttle all the way forward and lurched forward gaining speed. He was airborne well before he reached the end of the deck. Climbing to 300' he banked left for the downwind leg and another arrested landing. He turned for his approach to the ship, he spotted Jack's plane still parked aft on the fantail of the ship. As he passed the 90° position he picked up the LSO who was signaling a Roger with his paddles. Jack's plane was launched and Walt now had a clear deck for landing. The last of the arresting cables were rigged and, in the groove, he received a cut. He caught the number three wire and came to a stop. He moved his hook handle to the up position, the arresting cable was released and he was once again launched for another landing.

This procedure went on for another six landings. After his eighth landing and after launch, he climbed to 1800' and entered the holding pattern around the ship. After Paul's next landing he too joined Walt in the holding pattern. Bob and Jack both had two wave offs so they needed two more passes to record their eight landings. After completing those landings, they joined the formation at 1800'. Walt put the flight in parade right echelon and made one more circle and a pass straight down the flight deck as a salute to the ship for a job well done. He climbed to 3000' and headed west for the beach. As he reached 3000', he spied the shoreline and recognized Virginia Beach. He was about a mile south of the entrance to the bay so he headed directly for Chambers Field.

15

"Wings Of Gold"

Corry Station, Pensacola, Florida

Flight CF-14 had safely returned to Corry Station from Norfolk, Virginia, having successfully completed carrier qualification. Bill had given them permission to report to the Squadron Training Office after noon the next day so they all slept in late, had lunch and headed for the Hangar. They were ecstatic and excited to pin on their wings and get to a fleet fighter squadron. Their conversation was highly positive and happy that they had completed their flight training.

They arrived at the Training Office and were given their check-out sheet and flight log book. They were invited into the training officer's office for a short congratulatory speech and a date for their winging, which would be Wednesday the 25th of February in the Commanding Officer's office. They left the Training Officer's office and were still very animated in their discussions. Check-out was almost enjoyable and nothing seemed to bother them. All offices they needed to visit were done on the 19th, which would give them six more days to enjoy their accomplishment.

Prohibition was still in effect so they put a stealth plan into operation. Since Jack had become an integral part of their recent success, Walt, Paul and Bob invited him to join the alliance, kind of like D'Artagnan joining the three Musketeers. They traveled to mainside Pensacola and went to the base exchange. Each ordered an aviation green uniform with a set of embroidered wings sewn over the left jacket pocket. The tailor fitted them and measured them for alterations. The uniform consisted of green cover for their cap with the gold braid, a khaki shirt with black tie, a green button-down jacket with black braid for rank on the sleeve, jodhpurs, and knee length leather brown boots. While they were at it, they all ordered a pair of metallic 18k gold wings and two sets of embroidered wings for their dress blues and khakis. Having completed that chore, Walt drove over to the BOQ. He caught Moses, the grounds keeper, just as he was finishing his work for the afternoon.

Walt hailed him, "Hey Moses, Lieutenant (JG) Pellmen. How are you doing?

"I'z doin' just fine, suh," he said.

"Do you remember me?" Walt asked.

"Yassa, I remembers yo," Moses answered. "We done some exchangeun a while back."

"Well Moses, I need a favor. Can you get me a couple of pints of White Lightnin'. Walt asked.

"Yessa, I can do that. When might you be needin' that?" Moses said.

"I'd like to pick it up tomorrow, if possible," Walt said

"That's fine suh, I'll have it fo you tomorrow, anytime," Moses responded.

Walt gave Moses a couple of dollars and then went on his way. He met the guys in front of the BOQ and they drove off to Corry Station. Their plans were to have a party on Paul's sailboat over the weekend so they needed to get some supplies.

Walt had taken care of the booze, so now they needed something to mix it with. After thoroughly discussing the subject, they decided orange juice would be the easiest to handle. They still had an ice chest so Friday afternoon they would get some ice, buy a couple of quarts of orange juice and place them in the ice chest. For snacks they settled for potato chips and popcorn. For lunch they decided they could pull up on the beach and cook hot dogs and hamburgers.

Friday turned out to be a busy day. Walt and Paul first drove to the Mainside BOQ, found Moses and picked up the White Lightnin'. After lunch they took off and in town bought some ice, orange juice, hot dogs, hamburger meat, rolls and all the condiments necessary. At th hardware store, they found a suitable pan for cooking and some cheap tableware in case they needed it. On the way back to the base, Walt came upon a farmer's food stand alongside the highway so he stopped and bought a couple dozen eggs for breakfast. Arriving back at Corry Station, Walt parked in the shade and they left all their supplies in the car so the next morning they wouldn't have to pack again.

Saturday morning arrived and they piled into the car with their bathing suits and a few blankets. When they arrived at the Marina, Paul went aboard and readied the sailboat while Walt, Bob and Jack stowed everything they brought neatly in compartments in the boat, except for the ice chest. In short order they were off on their weekend adventure. It was a pleasant February morning with sky partly cloudy and temperature in the mid 50s. Wind was out of the southwest at 5 to 8 mph which made sailing pleasant and easy.

By noon they were hungry so they beached the sailboat on a deserted strand of beach and cooked hamburgers. None of them was used to drinking so they rationed the White Lightnin' to a pint each day for the four of them. Just enough to give one a buzz but not enough to consider being drunk. After lunch they headed back on the water for an afternoon of sailing. Towards evening they once again beached the sailboat, gathered some firewood and started a fire. Using their survival skills, they built a windbreak with driftwood logs and placed them upwind from their fire. This made for a warm place out of the wind. They all curled up in their blankets and talked well into the night. Sleep finally overcame them and all dozed off into a deep sleep.

Bob was the first to awaken. He gathered some firewood and rebuilt the fire. By then the others were awake. Walt broke out the pan and cooked some eggs for breakfast. After breakfast, they packed the boat and headed out into the Gulf for another day of sailing. By late afternoon, Paul had the sailboat headed into Pensacola Bay and back to the Marina. Once tied up, Paul secured the sailboat while the others cleaned up the boat and disposed of the trash. Once the tarp was in place on the sailboat, they piled into Walt's car and headed back to Corry Station. They all agreed the weekend had been fun and pleasant and the memories would last a lifetime. They would be friends forever.

On Tuesday they picked up their uniforms at the Base Exchange. Their green uniforms were all tailored and fitted, and after trying them on, the tailor shop packed them in a soft bag for them to carry. There was the usual banter among them on how ugly each looked with the breeches and jodhpurs. In fact, they were four handsome young guys who were about to go out into the aviation world as fighter pilots.

Wednesday rolled around and by noon they were anxious to get on with the winging ceremony. They were all dressed in their dress blue winter uniforms and had given an extra shine to their black shoes. Each had their wings in their pocket as they headed off to the base admin building. They checked in with the personnel office and the Chief Yeoman escorted them to the Commanding Officer's Office. It was not quite 1:00pm yet so they all took seats in his outer office. While they were waiting, Lieutenant Commander Osborn, Commanding Officer of Training Squadron 2, entered the room.

"Good afternoon, gentleman," he said as he took a seat.

"Good afternoon, Sir," they all responded.

"I'm pleased to see you all here this afternoon. I guess you thought this day would never arrive," Lieutenant Commander Osborn said.

Bob answered for the group, "Yes, Sir, it's been a long 15 months."

"And how did you enjoy your flight to Norfolk and the Langley episode?" Lieutenant Commander Osborn asked.

Walt spoke up. "Sir we had a blast. The ship's crew really treated us great, and we got to meet Admiral McMillin. As for the carrier landings, it was a great experience and I am sure all of us are looking forward to making many more."

"Well, I'm sure your next squadron will be glad to have you aboard," Lieutenant Commander Osborn said.

The Commanding Officers door opened and all were invited in. Commander Claude Nordhill greeted them as they fell in line. Each in turn introduced himself and exchanged greetings with the Commanding Officer. Commander Nordhill and Lieutenant Commander Osborn exchanged a few words while the young officers to be winged formed a line abreast facing the Commanding Officers desk.

The Chief Yeoman called out, "Attention to orders."

He then read the citation ending with "takes great pleasure in designating Lieutenant (JG) Walter Pellman, United States Navy; Lieutenant (JG) Paul Day, United States Navy; Lieutenant(JG) Robert Fitzwater, United States Navy; and Lieutenant (JG) John Wilson, United States Navy, from this day forward Naval Aviators in the United States Navy."

Lieutenant Commander Osborn preceded Commander Nordhill down the line. As he did, each passed his wings to him, then he in turn gave them to Commander Nordhill who pinned them on the left breast of each officer's uniform, followed by a handshake. The Chief Yeoman followed with a certificate, with a cover letter signed by Admiral McMillin and a wallet sized leather holder with a Naval Aviator's certificate in it.

After the ceremony was complete, Commander Nordhill said a few words commending them for their fine work in completing this rugged course and their outstanding performance. Turns out they were the highest graded aviators to complete Navy flight training to date with Walt scoring the highest Naval Aviator ever at 3.99.

The Commanding Officer wished them good luck in their next assignment and with that they departed and followed the Chief Yeoman back to the personnel office. Bob was handed his orders first which read "Proceed and report to Commanding Officer Fighter Squadron Two Bravo currently deployed aboard USS Saratoga. Authorized ten (10) days leave enroute.

Bob turns to the others with a big smile. "How about them apples?" he said.

"Hey, Buddy, that's great," Walt replied.

"Good for you," Paul said. "Just what you wanted, right?"

"Yeah, great stuff," Bob answered.

Next up was Paul. His orders read, "Proceed and report to Commanding Officer Fighter Squadron One Bravo, currently deployed aboard USS Saratoga. Authorized ten (10) days leave enroute."

"Holy shit, Bob, we're going to be in the same air group on Saratoga," he shouted.

"Hey, Paul, that's great," Bob said.

Now it was Walt's turn. The Chief Yeoman handed him his orders which read, "Proceed and report to Chief, Bureau of Aeronautics, Washington, D.C. for duty involving flying. Authorized ten (10) day leave enroute. Walt had a big frown, "I wonder what the hell that's all about," he said.

"Well, that sure as hell sounds disappointing," Paul said.

"Bummer, Walt. You never know how these things work out though," Bob noted.

"Hey, it is what it is. At least I'll be where they issue the orders. Maybe I'll have some influence where I go next so I can get assigned to a real squadron," Walt observed.

The three of them were advised that checkout day was Sunday, March 1st. Paul and Bob were advised to check back the next day to find out where they would meet the ship. After leaving the personnel office, they decided to wander back to BOQ and just chill out for a while. Paul believed that he would be flying the F8C-4 Helldiver, a 450 horse Power biplane capable of 119 kts, while Bob would be assigned to fly the F3B-1 capable of 135 kts max speed. They knew the Saratoga was assigned to the West Coast and was based in San Pedro, but didn't know the deployment schedule and area of deployment. They had heard Fleet Exercise XI was going on currently, but it could be either the Caribbean or Hawaii. Either way they would probably need to go to San Pedro to await its arrival.

Walt was pretty sure the Bureau was located at the Washington Navy Yard whose physical location was in southwest Washington, D.C. Also, the flight test center for all Navy aircraft was located at the Naval Air Facility Anacostia, Maryland, right across the river from the Navy Yard so he might have a chance to fly a few aircraft from there. He would wait and see what was in store for him.

The next day Bob and Paul found out the Saratoga was scheduled to be in Norfolk, Virginia, in May for the Presidential Review and they were designated to meet her there. In the meantime, they would be assigned to the air wing at Chambers Field and could check out in their respective airplanes while waiting for Saratoga to arrive. They had scheduled the train to Norfolk and decided not to travel home during the winter in Minnesota and Upper Michigan.

Walt was going to pack his car and drive to D.C. and look for a place to live. Maybe the BOQ at the Navy Yard would be available.

On Sunday morning the three of them checked out of the BOQ and Walt drove Bob and Paul to the train station at NAS Pensacola. At 9:45 a.m. Paul and Bob said their goodbyes to Walt and boarded the train. They all had kind of a lost feeling. They had been close buddies for 16 months and had grown to be almost like brothers. The train pulled out at 10:00 a.m. and they waved goodbye. It was a sad time in breaking up the close knit family, but a happy time looking forward to flying fighters.

16

"Admiral's Aide"

Washington, D.C.

It took Walt four days to drive to Washington. On his road map, there was an inset expanded view of Washington so it turned out to be easy to locate the Navy Yard. He checked through the main gate and was given directions to the BOQ. He checked in and was assigned a large room with an attached bath. There was a Closed Mess so he joined and paid for a month. He unpacked his car and settled in.

He took the first couple of days to tour the city, enjoying many of the national monuments. He was interested in his new assignment and wondered what he was doing here.

The next morning, he walked over to the Bureau of Aeronautics and checked in. He went through the usual check-in procedures with his last stop the Chief of the Bureau's office. After he received his orders, he realized Rear Admiral McMillin was head of the Bureau and would be his boss. He wasn't sure if he would be working directly for the Admiral, but surely the Admiral was the ultimate decision-maker at the Bureau. He entered the Admiral's outer office and was greeted by a beautiful young woman.

"Yes, Sir, may I help you?" she asked.

"Yes, I'm Lieutenant (JG) Pellman and I am checking in. I guess I need to see the Admiral before I am completely done with my check-in?"

"Yes, Mr. Pellman, we've been expecting you. My name is Gloria Bestwick. Please have a seat and I will tell the Admiral you are here."

"Thanks, Gloria. They call me Walt."

Gloria went into the inner office and returned shortly. "The Admiral is busy and will be with you shortly."

"Thanks, Gloria. I'm not going anywhere."

He sat back and tried to take in all the trappings. The building was fairly new and had solid oak panels, doors, and molding. The chandeliers in this office were of the finest quality and the furnishings were all first class.

After waiting some 30 minutes he was ushered into the Admiral's office by Gloria. Walt spoke first. "Good morning, Admiral. It's nice to see you again, Sir."

"Mr. Pellman, it's great to see you again and so soon after our meeting on the Langley. Did you enjoy your carrier quals?" he asked.

"Yes, Sir, I enjoyed it immensely. Turned out to be a great day," Walt said.

"I was standing just behind the LSO most of the day and it looked like you were enjoying yourself. Seemed like that was some great flying, Mr. Pellman."

"A lot of practice before we got there, Sir, and a great instructor, Lieutenant Bounds was the best," Walt observed.

"Speaking of Lieutenants, excuse me for a moment," the Admiral said.

On his intercom he said, "Gloria, would you bring in Mr. Pell- man's paperwork?"

Gloria answered., "Yes, Sir, right away."

Walt was at a loss as to what was happening.

"Mr. Pellman, I have conferred with the Chief of Naval Personnel and the Secretary of the Navy. I need a new aide which requires the rank of Lieutenant, so you have been selected for the job. So, raise your right hand and repeat after me," the Admiral said.

The Admiral administered the oath and when he finished shook Walt's hand.

"Congratulations, Lieutenant, and when you get your uniforms updated, don't forget to get your aiguillettes. That will get you into a lot of places you might otherwise not be allowed. Now sit down and let's talk about things. The reason I brought you on board, besides your keen mind and expertise in engineering, is I need a personal representative I can depend on to report back to me on some of the projects I want you to monitor. We have activities right here at Anacostia. We will be testing the N2Y and the XF9C-1. I want you to help with the tests and get a thorough check out in those two aircraft. Of course, they are both related to the

ZRS4 and ZRS5 projects. And by the way, Mr. Pellman, ZRS4 is now known as the USS Akron. Parts for both dirigibles are being fabricated at the Naval Aircraft Factory in Philadelphia and being assembled in Akron at the Goodyear-Zeppelin factory. I want you to familiarize yourself with all aspects of the construction of the dirigibles. We eventually plan to homeport them in Lakehurst, New Jersey. We will need input from there on the ground handling capabilities and what is needed for safety. I expect you will need to travel to all those locations, meet the people and make recommendations. This is a big job and it is important to me to be kept up to speed on how things are progressing."

The Admiral paused, "Have I overwhelmed you yet Lieutenant?" he asked.

"Yes, Sir, you have certainly laid out some lofty goals for me. However, I believe I can accomplish what you desire. I believe the easiest place for me to start is at Anacostia. Why were the N2Y and XF9C-1 chosen as aircraft for the ZRS4 and 5?" Walt asked.

"Well, the opening for the Hangar on those airships is T-shaped and is only 30-foot wingspan, 10-foot tailplane, and 34-foot overall length. We didn't have sufficient funds to develop a new aircraft so the two that fit the bill were the N2Y and the XF9C-1," the Admiral explained.

"Thank you, Sir, for clearing that up for me. That gives me some basis to start from in my file folder on that aspect of the operation," Walt said.

"I think you now have enough background information to get started. When you have something to report or need more guidance, come back and knock on my door. Check with Gloria before you leave, she will have more information for you," the Admiral said.

As Walt got up to leave he spoke, "Thank you Sir for your trust and confidence in me. I will not let you down."

The Admiral shook his hand. "Trust me, it won't be an easy job." Walt left the office and stopped at Gloria's desk.

"He really surprised you didn't he, Lieutenant," Gloria said. "He expects a lot from you and I know he trusts you. He talked about you a lot in the past two weeks. I also believe he respects your accomplishments and needs your expertise around here."

"You are absolutely correct on the surprise part," Walt said.

"Before you leave, we have a few papers to sign and then I will show you your office," Gloria said.

She picked up a file from her desk and placed a paper in front of him.

"You need to sign your promotion papers first," Gloria reiterated.

After he completed that task, she led him into an adjoining office. It was half the size of hers and was furnished with a large oak business desk accompanied by a huge leather-covered matching oak chair and a large leather couch. The desk had a dual stand desk lamp with green shades and a large green blotter encased in a leather holder. Also on the desk was a dual ink holder with two pens. The last item he noticed was an intercom box on a small table behind his desk. Walt was impressed with how neat the office was kept. Gloria pointed to another door in the office.

"That door is the closet and this door is a direct entry into the Admiral's office. That way you don't have to go through me when you need to talk to the Admiral. That completes the tour," Gloria said.

"Gloria, you have been extremely helpful and I appreciate that. Now all I need is the office telephone number and I'll get out of your hair."

They went back into her reception room and she wrote a couple of numbers on a piece of paper.

"We have only two numbers here in the office," as she handed him the paper.

"Thanks, Gloria, I will be on my way. When I am out of the office I will try to keep you advised where I will be and what my schedule will be. Right now, I am going to change into my aviation green uniform then go to the Base Exchange and have my uniforms altered. I should be back in the office this afternoon."

Walt went to the BOQ, changed into his aviation greens, and headed off to the Base Exchange. He stopped in the tailor shop to have his blues restriped and fitted for aiguillettes. The tailor inquired who he was the aide for. After determining it was for Admiral McMillin, the tailor told him they would be fitted for the left shoulder and two gold loops would be required for a Rear Admiral. On his khakis, all he needed was a snap fastener so he could attach the aiguillettes, that way they would be interchangeable between his blues and khakis. While he was there, he also purchased another set of dress blues, had the tailor mark them up for alteration, striping, and fitted with a snap on the left shoulder for the aiguillettes. Walt purchased a pair of embroidered gold wings and brought them back to the tailor to be sewed onto his new set of dress blues.

Walt's next stop was the stationary desk. He asked whether they handled business cards. They said they could order them and that it would take a week to get them. Walt gave the clerk the information for the cards and told her to call him when they were ready and he would pick them up.

His next stop was the Gedunk where he had a baloney and cheese sandwich with a pot of tea. About one o'clock he returned to his office and began to get organized. He found the BuAer phone directory and he highlighted those offices he thought to be important. It also listed those people associated with that function so he was able to learn a lot about the organization. He decided his first task would be finding out about "Flight Test" at Anacostia.

He walked out to Gloria's desk.

"Gloria, I plan on going to Anacostia tomorrow morning and it may turn into an all-day affair, so I may not see you until Thursday."

"That will be fine, Lieutenant."

Wednesday Morning

About 8:30 a.m. Walt hopped in his automobile and headed across the Anacostia River for the Naval Air Station. It was only a 15-minute drive when he arrived at the main gate. He asked directions to Flight Test and within five minutes was parking in front of the Hangar housing the Flight Test Division. Offices were located on the second deck on the west side of the Hangar. Walt found the office marked Director and he walked in. He asked to see the Director who he found out was Lieutenant Commander John Becker.

He was invited into John Becker's office and introduced himself. He explained who he was and what his interest was in Flight Test. They talked about what kind of testing was necessary for XF9C-1. Landing and takeoff speeds needed to be determined for airship work along with spin test certification. John indicated he was short of test pilots and he would be glad to work Walt into their testing program. John detailed the flights necessary for certification. Flight Test had an N2Y assigned for familiarization. It would later need to be fitted with a skyhook, but for now, it was a transitional aircraft for pilot training. It had been determined that the N2Ys, which had been in NAS Pensacola, were being sent to the Naval Aircraft Factory to be fitted with a skyhook then tested for adaptability. Flight Test had determined that one flight was all that would be necessary and could probably be accomplished at NAF in Philadelphia.

As for the XF9C-1, the plane had not yet been turned over from the factory, but this plane would need certification from the bottom up. A complete acceptance program needed to be conducted by Flight Test. Walt volunteered for this program. John detailed the flights necessary for certification. John said he could schedule Walt for a familiarization flight on Wednesday the next week and that he should draw a new flight helmet with headphones installed. This was caused by the installation of the new ten-channel VHF transceiver now being used for tower/plane communications and cross-country for CAA stations communications. Walt thanked John for everything and said he would see him next week.

He drove back across the Anacostia River to the Navy Yard. When he entered the building, he headed for the office of Commander Charles J. Fuller, head of the Lighter-Than-Air Design section of BuAer. He planned to learn as much as possible about the history and development of Lighter-Than-Air in the United States Navy. He learned that Charlie Fuller was "Mr. Lighter-than-air" in the Navy and had been at it for over ten years. He was not an aviator but an engineer and he held the key of knowledge for all this Lighter-Than-Air stuff. After meeting him and explaining his position, Charlie opened up all his files to Walt so he could learn the history and progress of the dirigible in the Navy. During the next two months Walt would read every file, report, and seminar he could get his hands on.

On Monday he picked up all his uniforms from the base exchange tailor shop and left his green uniform jacket for restriping. The tailor told him he could pick it up on Tuesday.

Tuesday rolled around and he was decked out in his new dress blue uniform. As he walked into the outer office, Gloria looked up from her desk.

"Now don't you look sharp in the proper uniform. About time I'd n say.

"You can't say I haven't been trying to get it together. The base exchange tailor shop was just a little slow."

About that time Admiral McMillin entered. Both Walt and Gloria welcomed him with a "Good morning, Sir."

He replied with, "Good morning, Lieutenant Pellman. Come in my office for a few minutes and update me."

Walt followed the Admiral into his office.

"Have a seat young man and tell me what you have been up to," he said.

Walt told him about being integrated into the Flight Test program for the N2Y and XF9C, that he had also been in touch with Commander Fuller on all matters Lighter-than-air.

The Admiral asked him to find out about what the USS Los Angeles was up to. He had heard they were participating in the Fleet Exercise XII down in Panama since February and were due back at NAF Lakehurst in March.

Having finished their short discussion, Walt went to his office to try to figure out the best way to find out about the Los Angeles.

He finally figured the best way was sending a message to the Commander overseeing the Fleet Exercise. He drafted the message and walked it down to the Communication Center. It was a priority message so he didn't expect an answer for at least 24 hours.

He had received many files from Commander Fuller so he sat down on his couch and began reading from the beginning, the policy and thinking behind the direction the development of Lighter-Than-Air was going in the U.S. Navy.

17

" Spins "

Tuesday Morning

When he arrived at the office, the first thing Walt checked was the communications traffic. Sure, enough, there was a message from Commander Task Force 2.2, which read in part "USS Los Angeles proving her worth in our scouting role. Summary of her value to the fleet outlined in my final report should be available next week."

Since the Admiral was away at an aircraft procurement conference, Walt attached a note and had it placed in the Admiral's in-basket.

He filled the remainder of his day doing more research on Commander Fuller's files. On his way back to the BOQ, he picked up his Aviation Green uniform.

Wednesday

Walt was up early, dressed, and was on his way to NAS Anacostia. He arrived about 8 o'clock and made his way up to Lieutenant Commander Becker's office.

John greeted him, "Are you ready to fly, Mr. Pellman?"

"Yes, Sir, I am. I brought my flight helmet to exchange for a new one," Walt responded.

"That's great. Let's go down to the equipment shop and I'll let them take it from there. Just a quick brief, however. Our operating area is east and south of the field. Just stay clear of Dalghren Ordnance Depot as they are usually testing some big guns down there. Also, stay clear of Washington. The pols get excited if we fly over the city. Other than that, have a ball. The N2Y you will be flying today has had the hook mechanism attached for hookup on the dirigibles. That's the main reason it's here for testing. I suggest you stay away from any spins as that will be the subject of our tests and for that, you will need a chase plane," John said.

They arrived at the equipment shop. "Petty Officer Alexis, this is Lieutenant Pellman. Fix him up with a new helmet and check him out on the new VHF transceiver gear in the N2Y."

Answering Lieutenant Commander Becker, "Will do, Sir." Then turning to Walt, "Mr. Pellman, let me have your old helmet."

Walt handed him the helmet and he threw it in the discard bin. He went over to his storage cabinet, opened it, and retrieved a new helmet with headphones installed in it.

"See if this one fits, Sir?" the petty officer asked.

Walt tried it on and it fit perfectly. He took off his green jacket, placed it in his flight bag and donned his white scarf and winter flight jacket. The two of them walked over to maintenance control and Walt signed out the N2Y on the yellow sheet. They found the N2Y parked on the back of the flight line where a Plane Captain was already removing the tie-downs and pitot tube cover. Walt climbed into the front cockpit and the equipment petty officer showed him how to plug in his headset and change channels. There was a placard mounted on the instrument panel listing the 10 channels and what station was on each channel. He also showed Walt how to select guard channel which was the emergency channel. Walt thanked him for the checkout and climbed from the cockpit. He took the parachute from the airplane and placed it on the wing and did a preflight. This plane was not much different from the NYs he had flown in the training command. After the walk-around, he checked the fuel for water and engine oil for amount. Everything looked good so he donned his parachute and climbed into the front cockpit once again. He held the brakes, turned on the fuel, and signaled to the Plane Captain for engine start. The Plane Captain pulled the prop through three complete revolutions then yelled "contact." Walt responded, "contact", and placed the mag switch to both. The Plane Captain once again spun the prop and the engine roared to life on the first pull. The engine settled at ground idle rpm and Walt signaled for the chocks to be pulled. Walt found the mic switch and called

Anacostia tower for taxi instructions. He thought to himself, *"these radios are going to take something to get used to."*

The tower gave him instructions to runway 34. After reaching the south end of the field, Walt did his engine runup and everything checked out. He called the tower for takeoff and was cleared for takeoff with a right turn out of the traffic pattern.

After takeoff, Walt turned out of the pattern and headed to the east. The weather was scattered clouds at 8000' so he leveled his plane at 5000'. He slowed to 50kts and practiced his slow flight. The plane handled beautifully. Next he did some steep turns and finally a few stalls. He had gained enough confidence so he put it through a series of acrobatic maneuvers ending with an aileron roll. He had been in the air about 50 minutes so he decided to practice a few landings. He headed for Anacostia and called Anacostia tower. They cleared him for the break on runway 34, which he executed at 800' entered downwind and made 5 touch-and-go landings and a final full stop landing. He taxied back to the parking ramp where a Plane Captain assisted him with parking, then chocked the plane and reinstalled the pitot tube cover. With the plane secured, Walt checked back in with maintenance, signed the yellow sheet, and went up to John Becker's office. John invited him into his office and offered him a cup of coffee.

"Well, how did the flight go, Walt?" he said.

"It was a very nice flight. Comfortable plane to fly, but a little short on the horsepower end," Walt reported.

"Yeah, I think that Kinner engine puts out only about 115 hp," John said.

"It is what it is," Walt said. "Anyway, I feel fairly comfortable flying it so I think we could go forward on the certification testing."

"That's great, Walt. We can schedule the spin test for next Monday, if that fits your schedule," John said.

"That'll work for me. Let's make it late morning. That way I can discuss the flight test procedures with you beforehand. How about we plan to meet at 9 o'clock?" Walt asked.

"That sounds like a good plan, Walt. I'll put you on the schedule for Monday."

"John, are there any other items we need to do for certification?" Walt asked.

"Yeah, Walt, we need to record stall speeds and safe approach and landing speeds."

"I already recorded those on my flight today. I have them in my flight notebook if you would like them," Walt said.

"That's great. Let me get you a test flight form to fill out and we can certify that portion of the flight," John said.

Walt completed the paperwork, and handed it to the petty officer working in the director's office and headed back to the Bureau.

He figured it was about time to meet the Admiral's, Chief of Staff, Captain Martin. His office was directly across the hall from the Admiral's so he popped in there and asked the Captain's administrative assistant if the captain was in. Seems like everyone forgot to tell him that Captain Martin was on a trip until Tuesday morning.

Walt went over to his office and checked the communication clipboard. Commander Task Force 2.2 had ordered USS Los Angeles detached from the exercise and to proceed back to NAF Lakehurst. He studied more of Charlie Fuller's files on the Navy's Lighter-Than-Air program, who got into the testing of the practicality of an airplane hooking up to a trapeze on a dirigible. Flight testing was being done with the Los Angeles and had been successful with a Vought UO-1. Lieutenant Commander Fred Nichols was the current officer at the Bureau in charge of the development of the trapeze and hook-up aircraft. He had already made a couple of successful hookups to the Los Angeles, but right now the trapeze was at the Naval Aircraft Factory for modifications and the Los Angeles was in Panama.

Lieutenant Duane Harrison, a Naval Aviator, had been ordered to report to NAF Lakehurst as one of the first pilots assigned to fly off the USS Akron when she was commissioned and launched. That would be a little while yet in coming. Lieutenant Harrison, Naval Academy class of 1922, became a Naval Aviator in 1927 and had been assigned to a group whose pilots were to make up the squadrons flying off the yet-to-be-completed aircraft carriers Lexington and Saratoga. He helped develop the techniques for landing on these carriers and made the first arrested landing on the Lexington. He then served two years with the "Red Rippers" of

Fighter Squadron Five aboard the Lexington, becoming a flight instructor at Hampton Roads for a year before moving to Lakehurst. When Harrison arrived at Lakehurst, there were no N2Ys or XF9C-1s so he settled for checking out in the UO-1.

Monday rolled around and Walt headed off to Anacostia. At midmorning he met with John Becker in his office and was introduced to Lieutenant Ed "Butch" Harmon. Butch would fly the F4C-2 chase plane for the spin test.

John briefed them both of the parameters of the flight and test procedures. The flight would proceed to the east after takeoff, climb to 10,000', and perform six spin maneuvers, three to the left and three to the right. If a flat spin developed and recovery was not completed by 5000', bailout was the emergency procedure recommended. Those spins were all that would be required to certify the aircraft for hook-up duty.

Both pilots manned their aircraft and were soon airborne, headed east and climbing. Upon reaching 10,000', Walt radioed he was ready to commence the test. Butch took a position ^ of a mile starboard and 500' lower than Walt.

Walt reduced power to flight idle on the engine and retrimmed the aircraft as he slowed the aircraft. He maintained his altitude, and when the airspeed reached 39 kts, it stalled. He kicked in full left rudder and held the control stick all the way back. The nose fell through and he entered a left spin. After 1-1/2 turns Walt applied full right rudder and full forward stick. As the spin stopped, he neutralized the rudder, and as the plane accelerated, he began easing back on the stick. Engine power was applied and level flight was regained. He made some notes on his notepad and then began a climb back to 10,000'. After two more left spins were complete he performed three spins to the right. At the completion of all maneuvers, Butch joined up on his wing in right echelon and they returned to Anacostia.

As they were walking back into the Hangar, they were discussing how well the aircraft performed, no glitches or extreme aircraft reactions. They settled down in Flight Test debriefing room and wrote up their reports. With the reports, complete, Butch went back to his office and Walt stopped by John Becker's office. Upon meeting in John's office, Walt explained that he would be available to deliver the N2Y to Lakehurst as he had business there in the next week. John told Walt he would advise him when the aircraft was released for transfer and he would be grateful for him helping with delivery.

Walt returned to his office at BuAer. He wrote a short note to Admiral McMillin outlining the progress on the N2Y and approximate delivery timetable. The next day he stopped in Captain Martin's office. He was ushered in by the administrative assistant and he introduced himself.

"Good morning, Sir," Walt said. "I'm Lieutenant Pellman. Sorry, we haven't made contact before this but I guess our schedules just didn't mesh."

"It's nice to meet you, Lieutenant. So you're the hotshot Naval Aviator the Admiral has been bragging about," the Captain said.

"Well, Sir, I don't know about the hotshot part but I always try to perform at my best when I'm flying," Walt responded.

"Don't be modest, son, I read your training jacket. Top scoring aviator ever to graduate from Pensacola. That record has to be worth something," Captain Martin said.

"Yes, Sir, I'm very proud of that. I did work hard to accomplish it, but I guess your reputation is only as good as your last flight," Walt said. "The main reason I stopped by this morning was to let you know I am here to help in any way I can."

"I appreciate that, Lieutenant. I will tell you now I am not a big fan of Lighter-Than-Air but always support what Admiral McMillin wants us to accomplish, so feel free to knock on my door at any time. I will help you in any way possible. Now that we got through all the bullshit, glad to have you aboard. I know the Admiral has given you a tough assignment and we can get it done by working together," Captain Martin said.

"Thank you, Sir. I appreciate your candor. I will keep your comments in mind," Walt said as he excused himself and departed the Captain's office.

Walt was almost finished reading Charlie Fuller's papers so he turned to study the progress on the construction of USS Akron at the Goodyear Zeppelin factory in Akron, Ohio. The reports were few and sometimes confusing so he decided a trip to Akron was in the making to give Admiral McMillin a clear picture of Akron's construction progress.

A few days passed and he received a phone call from John Becker at Flight Test over at Anacostia. John told Walt the N2Y-1 was cleared for delivery to Lakehurst. Walt's local schedule was clear for a couple of days so he told John he could take the plane on March 26th.

On the night of the 25th, he packed his flight bag including his dress blue uniform, and headed for Anacostia. Upon arrival, he parked in the back lot and headed for John Becker's office. John had completed all the necessary paperwork and handed Walt a packet with the aircraft logbooks along with the airworthy certification. Walt walked over to base operations and received a weather briefing. The weather to Lakehurst was broken clouds at 3500', visibility 10 plus miles and surface wind northwest at 4 to 6 mph. He filed a visual flight rules flight plan for a 2 hour and 36-minute flight.

Walt manned his aircraft and was airborne for Lakehurst. He climbed to 2000' and headed northeast. His flight took him over Annapolis where he spotted the U.S. Naval Academy. He flew across the Chesapeake Bay into Delaware where he passed just south of Dover, then across Delaware Bay and into New Jersey. He flew over Vineland then across the low country of New Jersey. After some 2.3 hours of flight, he spotted Hangar #1 at Lakehurst off to the north and headed for it. When he was within 10 miles of Lakehurst, he called the tower for landing instructions. He was cleared for the break on runway 34 so he descended to 800' and came up the slot over the runway, broke left, and completed his checklist. His landing was normal and he taxied over to Hangar #1. There was a UO-1 parked outside on the flight line so he taxied up and parked next to it. The tower had alerted the ground crew and they arrived quickly and chocked the aircraft. After shutdown, he asked for directions to maintenance. He gathered his flight bag and uniform and headed for the maintenance office. As he entered, he was greeted by one of the pilots assigned to the flight unit.

"Hi, I'm Lieutenant Harrison," he said. "You can call me Duane." "Hi, I'm Walt Pellman. I brought you an N2Y for your unit."

"I appreciate that. That's Dick Koenig over there. He's our Maintenance Officer. I'm sure he can assist you in transferring the aircraft," Duane said.

Walt presented the aircraft logs and flight certification to Dick.

Turning to Duane, "And what's your job around here?" Walt asked.

"I'm supposed to be O-in-C of the flight unit for ZRS4, but currently I'm the only one assigned. We are developing flight procedures for hookup to ZRS4 whenever she is commissioned but right now we're doing that with USS Los Angeles since they reinstalled the trapeze. Are you with Flight Test at Anacostia?" he asked

"Actually, I am assigned as Aide to Admiral McMillin, but he has me flying with Flight Test, among other things. Most of my duties are monitoring developments associated with the dirigibles and associated aircraft. I expect they will have me involved with the certification and acceptance of the XF9C-1 Sparrowhawk," Walt said.

"Do you know anything about the trapeze we are currently using on the Los Angeles?" Duane asked.

Yeah, I read all about it in Lieutenant Commander Fuller's papers. For the Akron's trapeze, I have been in that discussion for about a year. I suggested stabilizing the aircraft after hookup on the trapeze, but I think it needs further improvement," Walt offered.

"Well then maybe you'd like to witness a hookup first hand," Duane said. "We are going to run some on the Los Angeles tomorrow. You could fly the N2Y-1. I am going to fly the UO-1. How about it? You game for some excitement?"

"That sounds like something I'd like to add to my resume," Walt added.

"Great, where are you staying tonight?" Duane asked.

"I was hoping to get a room at the 'Q'," Walt said.

"That's good. I have a room there so why don't we meet for dinner, say six o'clock, and afterward we can discuss the flight for tomorrow," Duane said.

18

"The Sparrowhawk"

Next Morning

Walt met Duane for breakfast and afterward headed off to Hangar #1. When they arrived, the ground crew was just moving Los Angeles from the Hangar. The crew was using an experimental procedure that could later be used on ZRS4 for ground handling. There was a tractor pushing out a portable mooring mast with the bow of the Los Angeles attached. The stern was coming out first with a set of wheels attached to the lower fin and guided by the ground crew. Once well out of the Hangar, the crew detached the wheels and allowed the airship to swing into the wind. There was only a 2 to 3 mph wind, so it swung very slowly.

The flight crew was already on board, and once the Commanding Officer had the airship at neutral balance he called for "Up ship." The bow was released from the mast and the engines came to life. The Los Angeles moved slowly away from the mast and began to gain altitude. It was a beautiful sight to behold, and Walt was impressed.

Duane and Walt had planned and discussed the flight and procedures for hookup to the Los Angeles, so they manned their aircraft and taxied for takeoff. Duane took the lead with Walt on his right-wing. The Los Angeles had headed east and they would intercept her just off the coast. Rendezvous was at 5000'. After takeoff, Duane and Walt had switched their VHF transceiver to channel 4, which was air to air frequency. Duane called Los Angeles and gave them his position. When Duane and Walt passed the coastline, they spotted the Los Angeles headed south. Duane called Los Angeles and gave them an estimated time of intercept. As they approached, Los Angeles accelerated to fast cruise speed so the plane could hook up at about 50 kts. Walt dropped down a couple hundred feet to observe Duane's techniques on the hook. The plan was for Duane to make five hookups followed by five hookups for Walt. After that, they might try a few more depending on their fuel state.

The air was smooth and Duane had little trouble on his hookups. Now it was Walt's turn. He approached the trapeze from below and matched the speed of the Los Angeles. Approaching from below kept the plane out of the turbulence created by the Los Angeles engines except for the last five feet. Then it required adding slight power on the engine to break through and make the hookup. Walt was a smooth pilot and had no trouble hooking up five straight times without a wave-off. Because of that, Duane ascertained that they had enough fuel to make a couple of more hookups, so each took turns and made three more each. After that Walt joined on Duane's right-wing and Duane signed out with the Los Angeles and headed for Lakehurst. Los Angeles' Navigator had given them their current position and provided a heading back to Lakehurst. Duane settled on 330° to get him back to base.

The duo switched to Channel 2, which was the frequency for Lakehurst tower. At 20 miles from base, they both spotted Hangar #1. At 10 miles Duane, contacted Lakehurst tower and he was cleared for the break runway 34. They descended to 800' and proceeded straight into the break. Approach and landing were normal as were taxi and shutdown. The pilots met in front of their aircraft and headed for the maintenance office.

"Well, Walt, what did you think about the hookups?" Duane said.

"Hey, Buddy, that was one hell of an experience. Easier than carrier landings. Hooking up at zero differential airspeed makes it a piece of cake," Walt said. "That prop turbulence from the engines is a little hairy the first time, but after that, I knew what to expect so I was able to anticipate it," Walt added.

"I liked the way you handled things today, Walt. Why don't you think about joining the team?" Duane asked.

"I'd like that, Duane, but I don't know how Admiral McMillin would take it. I'll have to ease him into it. Maybe after the ZRS4 is launched he might turn me loose," Walt answered.

"Well, you won't miss much. They are going to take the trapeze off the Los Angeles, adapt it and use some parts for the ZRS4, which probably won't be ready until August, so we won't have much to do around here until then," Duane said.

"Let me see what I can do. Meanwhile, I need to go to the Communications office," Walt said.

"Why don't I take you and afterward we can go to lunch," Duane offered.

"Sounds good, Duane. Let's change back into our uniforms, and then we can be on our way," Walt said.

When they arrived at Communications, Walt sent a message to the Senior Resident Naval Officer at the Goodyear-Zeppelin plant in Akron saying he would arrive in two days for an update conference on the progress of the USS Akron.

Walt and Duane went to lunch and had a great discussion on what they envisioned for the aviation unit assigned to fly off the Akron and yet unnamed ZRS5. Duane dropped Walt at the BOQ, said his goodbyes, then went back to the Hangar. Walt settled in and called the Central Railroad of New Jersey to check on train connections to Akron. He found he could take either the Delaware, Lackawanna, and Western to Buffalo, New York, then transfer to the New York Central, or take the New York Central from New York City to Buffalo then on to Cleveland, Ohio. He decided to take the DL&W to Buffalo and stop there for a day to visit the Curtis Aircraft Factory. That evening he had dinner with Duane and advised him of his plan to visit Curtis-Wright Corporation in Buffalo and check on the progress of the XF9C-1 Sparrowhawk.

The next morning, Duane drove Walt to the Central Railroad of New Jersey terminal where he caught the local at 10:35 a.m. which would take him to Hoboken. There he would transfer to the Delaware Lackawanna and Western Railroad, which would deliver him to Buffalo, New York, the next day about 2:16 p.m.

When he arrived in Buffalo, he took a taxi to the Statler Hotel, which was located on McKinley Circle and Delaware Avenue in the heart of downtown Buffalo. Upon checking in, the desk clerk asked if he was with the Admiral McMillin party. He said he was attached to the group, so the clerk put him on the same floor as the Admiral. He knew the Admiral would be coming back to the hotel for dinner, so he waited until 5:50 p.m. then called the Admiral's room. Of course, the Admiral was surprised to hear from him. Walt explained to the Admiral what his plan was and where he was headed. The Admiral invited him to attend dinner with him since the Curtis-Wright executives were wining and dining him that evening. They met in the lobby at 6:30 p.m. where they were met by Glen Curtis and three of his executives. Two cars were waiting outside to take them to the Park Lane restaurant. Upon entering, the party was ushered into the dining room which featured a black onyx fireplace and walls hung with rose damask. The manager had selected real Irish linen, silver engraved with the name of the restaurant, and china in a Chinese design of black and white. The waiters wore black pea coats and long white aprons. Walt was really impressed. Glen Curtis ordered dinner for everyone. It was as delicious as the decor of the restaurant. The Admiral had introduced Walt to everyone, and by the end of the evening, he was almost a close friend with everyone present. Walt and the Chief Engineer, Rex West, were seated next to each other and they exchanged ideas all night on Curtis's aircraft. Walt was smart enough that he mostly listened, and in the process, learned a lot about aircraft development and testing. Rex told him to stop by his office tomorrow and he would brief him on the Sparrowhawk and get him a tour of the factory.

Next Morning

Walt met up with the Admiral and they boarded the car the Curtis Wright Company had sent to take them out to the factory. The ride allowed Walt to brief the Admiral on the progress with the N2Y and brag about his 8 hookups on the USS Los Angeles. He also gave the Admiral a copy of the report on the Los Angeles performance with Task Force 2.2 in Panama. He told the Admiral he was going to Akron to get a face-to-face progress report on the ZRS4. The ride was a straight shot out Genesee Street to the commercial airport where the plant was located.

Upon arrival, the Admiral was met and escorted to his conference by the Curtis Wright executives. Walt slipped away quietly and headed for the Chief Engineer's office. Upon arriving there, Rex greeted him and they dug into the XF9C-1's performance and specifications data.

Rex discussed the Wright engine installed. It was designated an R-975-E3 single row radial developing 415 horsepower and driving a 2-bladed prop. The aircraft's maximum speed was 153 knots and maximum range was 295 miles. Curtis Wright Aircraft corporation had completed the company certification and the Navy had signed off on its acceptance for delivery. They were only waiting for the Navy to notify Anacostia Flight Test to transfer it to Anacostia. Rex suggested Walt fly it while he was here since he could be considered one of Flight Tests' pilots. Walt beamed at that suggestion,so Rex made the arrangements for an afternoon flight. Rex also arranged for Walt to take the plant tour. He directed his assistant to conduct the tour. Matt Sobieski introduced himself and the two of them left Rex's office to began the tour.

After lunch, Walt donned his flying gear and one of Curtis' test pilots walked him out to the aircraft to conduct a quick interior and exterior checkout. He also had previously given Walt a card with the aircraft and engine limitations on it. When they finished the briefing, he asked Walt if he was ready to fly. Walt indicated in the affirmative, and donned his parachute and mounted the aircraft. Once in the cockpit, he completed the prestart items and gave the lineman the engine start signal. Chocks were pulled and taxi instructions received by the tower. Walt added power to leave the line. That's when he realized how much power this aircraft had. He hadn't flown an aircraft with such a powerful engine. It was difficult to see the centerline of the taxiway and he utilized the s-turn procedure to clear the area ahead of him. He reached the end of the runway, and holding short of the duty runway, he turned into the wind and ran the engine up to check the prop and magnetos. A variable pitch prop was new to him. He hadread about them but had never experienced one. Full low pitch was for takeoff and a higher pitch could be used at cruise altitude to reduce fuel consumption. Walt exercised the prop through its full range then reset it to full low pitch for takeoff. He set power for 1500rpms and checked both mags. The drop-in rpm was within limits, so he reduced power to ground idle, switched his radio to tower frequency, and asked for takeoff clearance. The tower cleared him, and he took a position on the duty, held the brakes momentarily then added power. As he passed 2000 rpm, he released the brakes and began his takeoff roll. He anticipated engine torque and added left rudder. As he gained speed, he eased the rudder, raised the tailwheel off the ground, and put back pressure on the stick as he passed takeoff speed. The aircraft leaped into the air. He reached climb speed and raised the nose further. The weather was scattered clouds, so he climbed to 5000' and headed in a northerly direction. Upon reaching 5000', he leveled the aircraft and accelerated to 135kts cruising speed. He spied Niagara Falls to the northwest and headed for them. He had never seen them before, and it was an impressive sight to behold. The American and Canadian Falls were glistening in the afternoon sun and the rush of water was hard to comprehend. He circled the Falls a couple of times, soaking in all its beauty. Finally, he turned north and followed the river where the white water in the rapids was incomprehensible. The white water ended at the whirlpool which again was beautiful. He followed the river once more until he passed the edge of the escarpment where the gorge of the river ended, flowing onto the Ontario plains.

Having done his sightseeing, Walt turned his attention to the intricacies of the airplane. He did his usual routine, a few stalls followed by slow flight. He determined this aircraft was extremely sensitive in the pitch axis. The fulcrum between the center of the pitch axis over the wing, coupled with the extremely short distance to the elevator, made the aircraft hard to hold altitude. Since this was an X-model, he decided not to spin it but instead completed a few acrobatics. Turns out they were a lot more fun at the higher speeds required of the aircraft with also a little more altitude required on the vertical maneuvers. After his last Immelmann turn, he headed back to the Buffalo airport. Landing was routine although this aircraft stalled at 48 kts and used a little more runway for landing. He returned to the flight line, shut down, and walked back to the locker room where he changed into his uniform and proceeded to Rex's office.

Rex greeted him, "Well, Walt, what did you think of our Sparrowhawk?" he asked.

"That's one fine airplane you have there," Walt said.

"Do you have any comments or suggestions?" Rex asked.

"I think the only shortcoming was the short coupling distance between the pitch axis and the elevator. It made for very sensitive altitude control. Have you spun it yet?" Walt asked.

"I appreciate what you are saying on the pitch control. Yes, we have spun the aircraft. It tends to spin a little flatter than most aircraft, but we didn't get any flat spins out of it," Rex commented.

"Well anyway, that's a good thing. Flat spins don't seem like they're much fun," Walt said. "Another thing I thought about but didn't try, what will she do when the power is jammed on from flight idle? Is there any kind of torque action in the airplane?"

"When you jam on full power, you can always expect some roll to the right. How much usually depends on horsepower and prop pitch. At full low pitch on the prop, expect quite a bit. I think that is something the Navy will have to determine," Rex reiterated.

"Anyway, I had a great flight, and thanks for setting me up with it," Walt said.

"Well, I have a surprise for you. While you were flying, I talked with John Becker on the phone, and he approved for you to ferry the plane to Anacostia," Rex said

Walt broke into a huge smile. "That was one hell of a nice thing for you to do. I sincerely appreciate that."

"Lieutenant, your reputation precedes you. Glad to do it and besides it saves the Navy having to send another pilot up here to fly it back. So, when might you be leaving?" he asked.

"I should get going tomorrow as I have another stop on my way back to Washington," Walt said.

"Good, we'll get all the paperwork done today so you can take it all with you. Flight Test will need it," Rex said.

"Okay, I'll check back with you early in the morning. I want to get an early start," Walt said. He shook Rex's hand and departed. Curtis Wright's transport took him back to the Statler Hilton.

19

"Meet The USS Akron"

Walt was up and dressed by 6:30 am., packed his bag, ate breakfast, then checked out and was ready for pickup by 7:30 a.m. Upon arrival at the plant, he checked in one more time with Rex, who provided him with the proper paperwork to transfer the plane to Flight Test at Anacostia. Rex provided him transportation over to the civilian air terminal where the U.S. Weather Office was located. He received a briefing on the weather between Buffalo and Akron. The meteorologist indicated low ceilings with light rain between Erie, Pennsylvania, and Ashtabula, Ohio, and the ceiling lifting enroute to Akron. Akron weather was forecast to be 2500' broken clouds with visibility 7 miles. Surface winds would be light and variable. Walt departed the Weather Office, walked over to the CAA office and filed a visual flight rules flight plan.

At the curb, the Curtis driver was still waiting to take him back to the plant. He hopped in the car, and they drove back to the flight line at Curtis-Wright. Upon arriving, Walt stepped into the line shack where some of the line crew were more than eager to take his luggage and valise out to the plane and stow it for him. Others removed the tie-downs and prepped the plane for flight. They even checked the fuel and oil levels and tested for water in the gas tanks.

With all the preflight completed, there was nothing more for Walt to do than man the aircraft and be on his way. Within minutes, Walt was airborne and winging his way to Akron. It would be a short flight as it was only a 200-mile flight from Buffalo to Akron. He estimated his arrival time at approximately 10:30 a'm. His cruising altitude was 1500'.

He quickly reached it and leveled off at a cruise speed of 135 kts. He reduced rpm to cruise and leaned the fuel mixture until he had a 10° rise in cylinder head temperature, which would put him at best cruise fuel consumption. His route of flight put him just south of Buffalo's city center. Lake Erie was just ahead, and he turned and followed the shoreline. Within a short time, he approached the city of Erie, Pennsylvania, where the cloud ceiling became solid and forced him to descend to 800'. He was just over the edge of the water and followed the shoreline very closely. He crossed over a spit of land at the entrance to Presque Isle Bay and was just over the water passing downtown Erie. He observed the Erie Airport just off his left-wing and within minutes was passing the city of Conneaut, Ohio. His next checkpoint would be Ashtabula, Ohio. As he approached the city, he was still over the water when the ceiling of clouds began to rise, and he made a gentle climb to 1500'. Soon the clouds were broken above him and patches of blue began to appear in the sky. *"The weather definitely is improving,"* he thought. Ashtabula was just a few minutes southwest from Conneaut, and on passing Ashtabula, he took up a heading of 200° and headed straight for Akron airport. Along the way, he passed the towns of Middlefield and Kent. He next spied Tallmadge and headed almost due south. The large hanger the Goodyear-Zeppelin company had built was located on the southside of the airport and was clearly visible at 20 miles. Here was where they were putting together the USS Akron. Walt called Akron tower and received permission to land runway 19. He came into the break for runway 19 at 1800' since field elevation at Akron was 1,067'. After landing, he rolled to the end of the runway, taxied off onto the grass and over to the Dirigible Hangar at Goodyear Zeppelin. This Hangar was a sight to behold. The building was a unique shape that looked like "half a silkworm's cocoon, cut in half the long way." Walt had been told it was 1,175 feet long, 325 feet wide, and 211 feet high, supported by 13 steel arches. He could see a control tower and radio aerial at the northeast end. At each end of the building were two huge semi-spherical doors that each weighed 600 tons. The doors rolled on 40 wheels along specially designed curved railroad tracks, each powered by an individual power plant that could open the doors in about 5 minutes. His plane was soon met by a line crew, and they parked him on the southeast side of this Hangar. He shut down his engine and climbed out to be greeted by Lieutenant Bruce Gordon, Senior Naval Representative at the site.

"I'm Bruce Gordon," he said.

"Walt Pellman. Pleased to meet you." As they shook hands.

"I've been expecting you for a couple of days," Bruce offered.

"Sorry I didn't get here sooner, Bruce. I was delayed in Buffalo at Curtis-Wright and met Admiral McMillin there. He needed me to consult with the Curtis-Wright people. One nice thing though, I brought the Sparrowhawk down here so everyone could have a look at what we are dealing with on our interface with the Akron."

"Yeah, the Goodyear guys will be glad to take a look at it," Bruce said. "Let's go into my office and discuss your visit."

Walt grabbed his travel kit and valise and followed Bruce into the Hangar and his office. He was impressed. Bruce's office had a couple of large windows, which looked into the Hangar where the partially finished Akron was under construction. It was a sight to behold. Construction on the Akron seemed to be progressing. The workmen was about half finished with putting the skin on the airship. The airship didn't appear as big as it was because of the size of the Hangar. The Akron was only 785' in length and in the 1175' Hangar, there was still plenty of extra space. Also, the height of the airship was 155' but the hanger stretched to a height of 211'.

"Bruce, the Admiral wanted me to get a first-hand report from you on the construction progress and any problems you have had and might have in the future that he could help with, keeping them in the family, so to speak, and not have the press or Congress on his back for answers. You know we already took a beating on the airship being overweight with conjecture by the press that it would never fly because of it. One-hundred percent bullshit, but you are aware that is what the Admiral is talking about."

"Well, let's get our latest fiasco out on the table then, Walt," Bruce said. "We just discovered this yesterday. One of our workmen, Paul Kassay, has been under investigation by the FBI. He is a Hungarian by birth and an admitted communist. It seems he likes to hear himself talk and has told his co-workers many tall tales. Two undercover FBI agents, while interacting with him asked him, why he spits on each rivet before he puts it into the dirigible. His answer was the spit freezes and then when it melts in the spring, it makes the rivet loose and weakens the structure of the ship. He is currently under arrest and we are starting an inspection of all his work. It will probably take a week to do but will not slow construction."

"Wow, Bruce, that is some tall tale. Do you want to fill in Admiral McMillin or do you want me to do that? Walt asked.

"Why don't you let me do that, Walt. That way it will come from official channels and the Admiral will know the Navy is officially involved in the inspection of Massey's work," Bruce replied.

"That sounds great. Now, how about a brief on your construction timeline, and then I would like a tour of the airship," Walt said.

"The Goodyear-Zeppelin company has determined that construction of the Akron should be complete during the middle of August. We have determined that the airship could be christened on August 8th and the first flight sometime around mid-September. That will give us a good month to complete the Navy's inspection and still make the first flight timeline. As you can see out in the Hangar, the outer skin is almost complete and the company has started to furnish the interior of the ship. Have you got any questions?" Bruce asked.

"Yes, Bruce, I have. Could I see the drawings for the trapeze, Hangar bay, and monorail system?" Walt asked.

They walked over to the large drafting table in the corner of Bruce's office where he had a pile of drawings for the Akron. He flipped through about 8 sheets and came to the Hangar bay drawing which depicted the bay, monorail, and opening for the planes to be lifted through. Walt studied them for a few minutes and then Bruce turned to the next sheet which showed the trapeze. He studied that drawing intently then said, "I see they have proposed to use the stabilizing bars to steady the aircraft after slowing the speed of the airship and bringing the aircraft aboard after engine shutdown."

Walt pointed out the bars to Bruce.

"Oh yeah, I see what you are talking about, Walt," Bruce answered.

"I had discussed this feature with Admiral McMillin and Lieutenant Commander Rosendahl about a year ago. I'm not sure that is the best design we can come up with. Maybe I'll talk with the Goodyear engineers before I leave about a new idea," Walt mused. "Let's go look at the airship."

Bruce gave Walt a safety brief before they left the office and then proceeded down on the Hangar deck and began a walkthrough of the airship. They first climbed into the control car, which was the center of control and operation of the airship. Besides the actual flight instruments, there were the engine and associated propeller controls. The Akron had four engines mounted on each side of the airship. The propellers were over 16' in diameter, were reversible as well as being able to swivel 90° to produce up and down thrust. Then there were the airship's control surfaces, huge control wheels for elevator and rudder, a control panel for monitoring and venting helium, and ballast, usually water. There was also a provision for a navigator's station in the control car.

Walt and Bruce spent an hour going over all the functions and systems monitored in the control car. They next went through the galley and wardroom. After inspecting these sections, they took a break for lunch. Walt's biggest comment during his tour was the strong smell of the dope which was being applied to the outer skin of the airship. Bruce told him they needed to apply four coats of dope, the last two with aluminum pigment mixed into it. The skin was made of standard aircraft cotton fabric, the same as used to cover current Navy aircraft.

After lunch, they continued the tour, inspecting the officers, enlisted, and pilots' quarters. They finished the tour looking at the Hangar deck and aviation workshops. The workmen had finished the opening in the bottom of the airship for retrieving the airplanes off the trapeze, but the trapeze itself had not been installed. The two of them went back to Bruce's office, sat down, and had a cup of coffee, and discussed what they had just observed and what was in store for Akron. Bruce asked Walt if he had made any sleeping arrangements. He indicated he had not so Bruce suggested they get a room at the boarding house where some of the Navy officers on the project were staying. It was known as "Mazie's Boarding House" and was located halfway to town. Breakfast and dinner were included in the price of six dollars a night. Bruce offered to call to see if he could arrange Walt's stay. Walt estimated he would be there four nights, so Bruce dialed the phone and arranged with Mazie for Walt's stay.

They spent the remainder of the afternoon drafting messages each for Admiral McMillin and the Navy Inspector General advising them of the Massey situation. They finished their work for the day. Bruce got his car, after Walt loaded his luggage, they headed off to Mazie's.

On arriving at Mazie's, they met her, and Walt was assigned one of the bedrooms on the 1st floor level. It was small, had a single-size bed with a closet, an armoire, and a dressing table with a washbasin. The bathroom was down the hall with a toilet and bathtub. Dinner was at 6:00 p.m. and served family-style. After dinner, the group went into the parlor and sat around discussing things that happened that day at work. Walt had met a couple of other Naval officers who were assigned to the plant and were working in the inspection section.

Walt got a good night's sleep, was up early, had breakfast, and he and Bruce were off once again to the Goodyear plant. They arrived at Bruce's office, had a cup of coffee, and sat down to decide what the plan was for the day. Walt decided he would visit with the engineers assigned on the trapeze portion of the project. Bruce provided him with directions on how to get to the engineering offices. It was about a half-mile walk from the Hangar.

When he entered the engineering space, he was greeted by a young lady who was manning the information desk. Since he was new to the property, he was issued an identification pass and given directions to the engineering section with whom he wished to talk. When he reached his destination, he was greeted by a secretary who directed him to a Mr. Charles Rowe. Upon entering his office, he was welcomed by a gentleman estimated to be in his fifties, sitting behind his desk smoking a Meerschaum pipe. He rose as Walt entered and introduced himself.

"Good morning. I'm Lieutenant Walt Pellman," he said.

Charles extended his hand. "I'm Chuck Rowe," he replied. "And what can I do for you this morning, Mr. Pellman?"

"Sir, I wanted to get your feelings on the trapeze for the Akron and possibly an engineering brief on its status," Walt said.

"Well, Lieutenant, have a seat, and let's see where we're at," Charles stated.

Charles broke out the studies which had been made on the trapeze including the installation on the USS Los Angeles and then invited Walt to come over to his drafting table. He unrolled a set of blueprints and placed them on the table so they could both see them and discuss them. Walt told him how he had discussed the trapeze with Admiral McMillin and Lieutenant Commander Rosenthal the previous year and how the discussion centered on the stabilizing bars to the aircraft. There was a pause in the conversation and that's when he sprung his surprise.

"Sir, after studying the stabilizer bar fix on the trapeze, I have come up with a new method for stabilizing the aircraft on the trapeze which I think will prove successful and easier to operate. Let me draw out a rough idea and I will let your team run with it from there," Walt proffered.

"Well by all means. Here's some paper and pencil. Give us an idea of your new development," Charles replied.

Walt took a pencil and paper and sketched out his new idea.

"Here it is. It is just an inverted saddle, padded on the inside so it won't damage the aircraft's skin. It is attached to the trapeze with the cross tube on the structure and extends out, so it comes down on the aircraft between the cockpit and the tail's vertical stabilizer. It probably can be designed to operate by electric winch or hand-cranked down by the Hangar deck crew. Once down on the aircraft, it will stabilize the aircraft in its longitudinal axis and make the aircraft safer to handle when bringing it up into the belly of the airship," Walt offered.

"Damn, that's so simple. I wish I had thought of it myself," Charles said.

"Sir, I know it is a design change that will take some months to integrate into the system, but I believe it will make everything safer and easier for the Hangar crew to handle. I'm aware of the bureaucracy this needs to go through, but it should solve the problem big time," Walt said.

"Let me work on the drawings and put the change into the system. We should be able to make the change early next year. Meantime we are stuck with the old system," Charles said.

"I understand it will take some time. Meanwhile, I have flown an XF9C-1 here from Curtis Wright in Buffalo. So, if your technicians wish to take some measurements and get a feel for what you are dealing with, it's parked outside the new Zeppelin Hangar over on the airport," Walt said.

"Wow, you brought us a lot of good stuff, Lieutenant. Thanks," Charles replied.

The two of them sat and chatted extensively on the progress of the trapeze for Akron. Two hours later, Charles indicated he had a meeting, so Walt excused himself and walked back to Bruce's office.

When Walt entered Bruce's office, Bruce was reading the morning *Beacon-Journal* newspaper.

"Well, Walt, the proverbial shit has hit the fan. The *Journal* picked up on the FBI arrest of Paul Massey and have a story in this morning's edition. I'm afraid by tonight it will be a national story. If you can reach Admiral

McMillin, I suggest you phone him and update him on the situation," Bruce suggested.

"You're absolutely correct, Bruce," Walt said. "Let me use your phone and I will try to contact the Admiral."

Walt dug Rex West's business card out of his wallet and picked up the phone. He got the operator and told her he wished to make a longdistance call to Buffalo, New York, and gave her Rex's number. In short order Rex picked up his phone and Walt told him he needed to speak to Admiral McMillin as soon as possible. Rex said he would transfer his call, but gave Walt the number where Admiral McMillin could be reached. It took about 15 minutes to switch the call. Finally, someone at Curtis Wright answered and Walt asked for Admiral McMillin.

Walt briefed the Admiral on the situation and told him that the Goodyear-Zeppelin people were all over it and were going to inspect all Massey's work to ensure everything on the Akron was satisfactory and safe and that any discrepancies if found would be corrected. He also told the Admiral he would be leaving tomorrow for Washington and would be in the office to brief him on Friday. Admiral McMillin told Walt he planned to leave Buffalo tomorrow, and would be in the office on Friday, and looked forward to receiving his briefing. Walt hung up the phone and turned to Bruce.

"Bruce, the Admiral suggested that you and Dr. Arnstein issue a joint statement explaining to the public that, with the overlapping inspection system in place between the company and the Navy, it would be impossible to sabotage the Akron. Also indicate the reinspection measures being taken on Massey's work ensure that no sabotage occurred."

"I'll get together right away with Arnstein and draft a press release. It may take us a couple of hours, but I think we can get it done today," Bruce said.

"That sounds like a plan. I guess you heard me tell the Admiral I plan on leaving tomorrow. I think I will spend the rest of the day writing my report for Admiral McMillin. I would ask that you coordinate with the appropriate personnel and get my plane ready for departure tomorrow. I think a 9:00 a.m. departure would be good," Walt said.

20

"Back To Washington"

Akron, Ohio

Walt and Bruce arrived at the Hangar about 7:30 a.m. After changing into his flying uniform and stowing his gear in the aircraft, Walt went over to the CAA Flight Following Office in the air terminal and filed a flight plan. He also stopped at the Weather Office and received a briefing of enroute weather as well as arrival at Anacostia. His flight time was estimated at 2 hours 25 minutes. He would have tailwinds most of the way with winds out of the northwest at 15-20 mph at cruise altitude of 2500'.

He checked out with Bruce when he arrived back at the Hangar. Bruce briefed him on the latest story coming out of the press coverage of the Massey story. The Akron *Beacon-Journal* had run a front-page story of the joint press release and things looked good from that point of view.

Walt said his goodbyes, manned his aircraft and departed Akron bound for Anacostia. He was cruising at 2500' and it was a gorgeous day for flying. He soon passed just north of Pittsburgh, Pennsylvania. Within a short time, he spotted Hancock, West Virginia, about 29 miles off to his north. His next checkpoint was the city of Martinsburg, West Virginia, just 5 miles south of his track. He crossed the Blue Ridge mountains and finally his last checkpoint in West Virginia was Harper's Ferry. His course of flight took him directly over the city and into Virginia. Next, he crossed the Potomac River, which meandered along left of his track then passed under his track and right of his route of flight. He once again crossed over the river and into Virginia then into the suburbs of the Washington DC area. He called Washington National Airport for permission to fly through their airspace then asked permission to switch over to Anacostia

Tower. Permission was granted and he entered the break for runway 01. Approach and landing were normal. He taxied over to the flight line, and parked and shutdown his aircraft at Flight Test. It was exactly 2 hours and 31 minutes of flight time. He had now logged almost five and a half hours in this experimental fighter and it felt good.

John Becker was in the maintenance office when Walt entered.

"I see you brought us a new bird to check out," he said to Walt. "How was your trip?"

"It was great, John. I had a nice flight to Lakehurst. I even got to make 8 hookups to the USS Los Angeles while I was there. Then took the train to Buffalo, New York. Just happened Admiral McMillin was visiting Curtis Wright so I got to fly the Sparrowhawk while I was there. They asked me to bring it here for acceptance. I did take a side trip to Akron as I needed to check on the construction of the USS Akron. I guess I logged a total of 5-1/2 hours in that aircraft."

"Hey, that's great, Walt. How about writing up a short report on your general observations and opinions on the aircraft when you have time," John asked.

"I can do that, John," Walt said. "I'll see you later."

Walt changed into his dress blues and headed for the Washington Navy Yard. He stopped by his BOQ suite, dropped off his travel bag, stopped to have lunch in the Mess, then headed over to the office. Upon arrival, Gloria was at her desk and greeted him.

"Well, Mr. Pellman it's nice to see you once again. I hope you had a nice trip," she said.

"Hi, Gloria," he said. "Yes, I had a great trip. I will tell you about it when I get some time. Right now, I have about three reports to finish before the Admiral gets back."

"Do you know when that will be? He has been out of touch for a day or two and I don't know his exact schedule. SecNav called this morning, to have him call," Gloria said.

"First of all, the Admiral said he would be in the office tomorrow. Second, be prepared for a hectic time for a few days. I believe we will have our hands full dealing with this situation," Walt said. "By the way, would you get me a copy of today's *Washington Post*?"

"I'll see what I can do, Sir," she said.

He went into his office, and broke out his yellow legal pad and started to write. He had been writing for about an hour when Gloria came into his office.

"Here's a copy of today's *Post*." She said as she placed it on his desk.

"Thanks, Gloria. I'll read it in a few minutes. I just remembered, how about you call SecNavs office and tell them Admiral McMillin will be in tomorrow and will call as soon as he arrives in the office," Walt said.

"Yes, Sir, I'll take care of that," she said

Walt set his pencil down, grabbed the *Washington Post,* and started searching. He was looking to see what they were reporting on the Massey situation. Sure, enough the joint statement by Goodyear-Zeppelin and the Navy had not made it beyond Akron but sabotage of the USS Akron made it to page two. Walt finished his Akron/ Massey report then worked on his complete trip report for the Admiral. When he finished, he asked Gloria to type them both up. Within an hour she had them ready. Walt reviewed them, signed both, and placed them on the Admiral's desk. He was really beat as it had been a long day so he retired to the BOQ and got settled down for a good night's sleep.

Morning broke early and Walt was in the office by 7:30 a.m. He wanted to be there when Admiral McMillin arrived. He was sipping a cup of coffee when the Admiral came through the outer doorway.

"Good morning, Admiral," Walt said. "I hope you had a productive trip?"

"Good morning, Lieutenant. Good Morning, Gloria, and yes, I had a productive trip. I expect the newspapers went crazy over the Paul Massey story?" he asked.

"Yes, Sir, they certainly did. I included most of the update in my report on your desk, but I haven't researched it this morning, Sir, I will while you are getting up to date on things," Walt said.

"Good, Lieutenant. You can brief me later this morning," the Admiral responded.

He went into his office and Gloria followed with his usual cup of coffee. Walt went into his office and found the morning's *Washington Post* which Gloria had conveniently put on his desk as she knew he would be looking for it first thing this morning.

Walt didn't need to look past page one. It was on the bottom half of it and furthered the sabotage story. The journalist quoted a few congressmen and senators who suggested it was some kind of foreign conspiracy, which they failed to identify who it could be. It was a typical snow job used to inflame the public.

Walt had a call from John Becker at Flight Test. He wanted Walt to be the main pilot involved in acceptance testing of the XF9C-1. They worked out a schedule and John indicated they would draft all the paperwork for the tests while Walt would do all the flying. He was keen on that. It would give him more flight time. They set a date for the following Monday for the beginning of testing. It would require most of the day so he wrote it into his calendar.

Mid-morning Gloria delivered the mail. In it was a letter from Paul Day. He and Bob were still at Norfolk flying with Fighter Squadron 5, flying the F8C Curtis Helldiver. The Saratoga was due in port in a week so they would soon be reporting to their respective squadrons. Paul said they would like to get together before they leave for the West Coast and was asking Walt when might be a good time and place. He decided he would need to figure that one out. His intercom came on and Gloria told him the Admiral was ready to meet with him so he should go right in. Walt knocked on the door to the Admiral's office and opened the door. The Admiral directed him to come in and sit down, which he did.

"Well, Lieutenant, give me an update on the Massey situation."

"Sir, the Navy Inspector's office in Akron is conducting a further investigation and the Goodyear people along with the Navy are inspecting all of Massey's work. The national newspapers are calling it sabotage and the joint statement by Goodyear and the Navy still hasn't made its way to the national news. The *Washington Post* has a story on the bottom half of its front page this morning quoting congressmen and senators that this is a conspiracy of foreign origin to destroy the U.S. Navy's Lighter-Than-Air program," Walt reported.

"I just talked with SecNav and he is getting the same reports as are reported in the *post*. He wants us to put out the fire so how about calling the *post* and having one of their reporters working this story come over and I'll do an interview. Maybe that will put some sense to this narrative.

Also, tell me about the change you proposed to the trapeze for the Akron and about your 8 hookups on the Los Angeles," the Admiral said.

Walt first described his proposed change of the trapeze and then, with obvious pride and excitement, told the Admiral how exhilarating the hookups on the Los Angeles were.

The Admiral responded, "It sounds like you were having too much fun, Lieutenant."

"Sir, I have to admit I was certainly enjoying the experience. There is nothing to match attaching your airplane to a moving dirigible at 3000' in the air."

"I like your idea on the change to the trapeze. It sounds like it will not only be safer but easier for everyone all the way around. The downside will be the bureaucracy it needs to go through to get accomplished. We'll be lucky to have it incorporated into the system by next May," the Admiral said.

"Yes, Sir, I understand that process. If you have nothing further for me I will get busy on setting up an interview for you with the *Washington Post* reporter," Walt said.

"Get to it, Lieutenant," the Admiral responded.

Walt went back to his office and made a few phone calls before he reached the reporter who was handling the Akron story. He set up an interview with the Admiral for 10 a.m. Friday. He also did some more research on how other newspaper outlets were handling the story. Seems like they were all carrying the same line, a foreign conspiracy trying to shutdown America's Lighter-Than-Air program.

Walt drafted a note to the Admiral updating him on all he had discovered in his research and advising him of the time of the proposed interview.

Friday, Washington, D.C.

Friday was upon them and at 9:45 a.m. Edward R. Anderson of the Washington Post entered the Admiral's outer office. He was greeted by Gloria where he introduced himself and told her he was there to interview the Admiral. She asked him to be seated while she entered the Admiral's office and briefed the Admiral on the situation. Within minutes, Mr. Anderson was admitted into his office where he conducted his interview.

After some 45 minutes, he exited the Admiral's office, and excused himself, and departed the building.

In discussion with the Admiral, he expressed his view that the interview went okay. They would just have to wait and see what the *Post* reported.

Walt was still in a quandary about visiting Paul and Bob in Norfolk. Finally, he came up with a plan. He would fly the first acceptance test of the XF9C-1 on Monday and ask John Becker if he could take it on a cross-country flight on Wednesday to Norfolk. He could stay and visit Thursday and return to Anacostia on Friday, then catch up on the office work before the weekend.

He went into the office on Saturday morning. When he arrived, Gloria was already there making coffee.

"Good morning, Gloria," he said. "What are you doing here on a Saturday?"

"The Admiral had a lot of typing for me and wanted it done before Monday morning so he asked me to work today," she responded.

"Was there a *Washington Post* delivered this morning?" Walt asked.

"Yes, here it is." As she handed it to him, "You better be sitting down when you read the story I think you're interested in reading."

"It's that bad?" Walt said.

"I wouldn't paint it as good, even fair," she said.

"Well, I better get on and read it before the Admiral gets here so I can brief him," Walt said.

He went into his office, sat at his desk, and opened the paper to page 1. There it was on the lower half. He read the story, which ran over onto page 3. It was quite a long article. When finished reading, he wrote a few notes. He concluded that Mr. Anderson had reported exactly what Admiral McMillin had told him. It was a good article and would go a long way to tell the Massey story the way it was.

Walt next turned to the editorial page. He quickly scanned the content, and sure enough, another journalist had written a column about the front-page article alluding to the fact that Admiral McMillin had requested the interview, which could be judged as the Navy trying to cover up the truth. His conclusion was the Navy was trying to cover up the fact that a foreign country was trying to destroy the U.S. Navy's Lighter-than-air program. Conclusion, the Admiral would not be happy.

Gloria broke the mood. She entered his office with a cup of coffee.

"Lieutenant, the Admiral just arrived," she said as she set his coffee on his desk.

"Thanks, Gloria, I'm almost finished with my report. I'll brief the Admiral in a couple of minutes," Walt answered.

He finished his report then knocked on the Admiral's door and entered. He briefed the Admiral then left the morning *Washington Post* for the Admiral to read. He could tell the Admiral was pissed. He had expressed his displeasure at learning of the editorial written on the opinion page which went back to spewing that same old stuff about the Massey story being a foreign plot against the U.S. Navy.

Walt went back to his office and wrote the Admiral a note telling him of his first acceptance flight in the XF9C-1, then asking permission to fly to Norfolk on Wednesday, returning on Friday morning, and planning on being in the office on Friday afternoon. He gave the note to Gloria to send to the Admiral. Later in the day, it was returned to him with a hand-written note directing him to plan a trip to the Naval Aircraft Factory in Philadelphia to check on the progress of the trapeze for the Akron.

Sunday, Washington, D.C.

This morning, after breakfast, Walt decided to explore the base. He had been there over a month and hadn't even driven around all of the waterfront. He put on casual clothes to be comfortable but warm. It was late April but there was a bit of a chill still in the air. He wore sporty khaki long pants with a short-sleeved black cotton shirt and a long-sleeved light brown V-neck wool sweater. As he toured the waterfront, he came across the base marina. Here is where military personnel could keep their boats in a safe dockage for a small fee for recreational activities. He parked his Alfa Romeo RM Sports car and stepped out to have a closer look at the boats tied up. As he was strolling down one of the docks, a couple of young ladies were having difficulty with the lines mooring their sailboat. He stopped to chat and asked if they needed help. Of course, they readily accepted and he helped them untie and launch their sailboat. It was a beautiful 19' Lighting built for racing. As the sailboat left the pier, the ladies waved a thank you to him for the help. He waved back and continued his stroll.

Walt had a relaxing day just sightseeing and sitting around. He decided to have dinner at the Officer's Club. Dress was blue blazer and gray trousers with shirt and tie. As he entered the club, he was accosted by the same two young ladies he had helped with their sailboat earlier in the day.

"Hi, again, sailor. My sister and I didn't have a chance to thank you personally for the help this morning. My name is Candice and this is my sister Lydia."

"Hi, ladies. I'm Walt Pellman. Pleased to meet you. It was my pleasure helping you this morning."

"Are you meeting someone?" Candice asked.

"No, I'm here by myself," Walt responded.

"Why don't you join us for dinner. My mom's over there and my dad is parking the car. He'll be right in and we will be ready to sit down for dinner," Candice said.

"Thanks anyway, but I wouldn't want to impose," Walt said.

"You wouldn't be imposing and I'm sure my family will be glad to meet a considerate young man of your stature," Lydia interjected.

"Well, if you insist," Walt answered.

"Come over and meet our mom," Lydia said.

The three of them walked over to where the girl's mother was sitting just as their father arrived.

"Mom and Dad, this is the young man we told you about who helped us with the boat this morning. I'd like you to meet Walt Pellman," Candice said.

Candice's father extended his hand, "I'm Admiral Willis Lee and this is my wife, Enid."

"I'm Lieutenant Walter Pellman, Sir. It's a pleasure to meet you. I hope I'm not imposing on your family dinner, Sir."

"If the ladies invited you that's just fine, so let's move into the dining room," The Admiral said.

They were greeted by the maitre d', "Good evening, Sir. We have your table ready."

"That's fine. We have a fifth for dinner," the Admiral said.

"We can set another place, Sir. Please follow me," The maitre d' said.

They followed him to the table where the staff was already moving another chair into place and putting another table setting on the table.

The wait staff took their order for dinner. Walt ordered the shrimp cocktail and crab cakes for an entree. When all orders had been taken, the Admiral turned to Walt, "Mr. Pellman, and what is your present assignment?"

"Well Sir, I'm a Naval Aviator and I am Admiral McMillin's aide," Walt said.

"Oh yes, now I remember. I've heard of you. You're that hotshot aviator, graduated 1st in your class, highest scoring pilot we ever trained," the Admiral said.

"Guilty on all counts, Sir. Not sure about the hotshot part though," Walt responded. "I just go out prepared for every flight."

"Nothing to be ashamed of, son. Reputation will go a long way in this man's Navy," the Admiral said.

"Yes, Sir, your shooting resume has certainly made you a national figure. I remember learning about your accomplishments when I was at the Naval Academy," Walt said.

About that time the appetizers were served and they all began eating. Walt was seated between the two ladies and the conversation settled between the three of them. The entrees were brought out and dinner was now well underway.

~ 21 ~

"Reunion"

Monday, Washington, D.C..

Walt arrived at Anacostia before 8:30 a.m. His flight was not scheduled until 10:30 a.m., but he wanted to get a head start on the procedures required for the flight as well as review the paperwork. He discovered it consisted of performing the routine maneuvers and recording the data. He wrote some of the parameters in his flight notebook in preparation for the flight.

He checked in with John Becker where John gave him the paperwork to review. This would be a simple flight except for the service ceiling test. He would need an oxygen mask and bottle to take the plane up to an altitude as high as possible at maximum power of the engine.

With all the information needed for the flight, Walt manned the aircraft and was airborne by 10:35 a.m. He climbed out to 5000' where he put the aircraft through a series of stalls and he recorded stall speed and fuel remaining. He next put the aircraft through slow flight and recorded the results. His next item was to check service ceiling. He donned his oxygen mask and added climb power. As he was approaching stall speed, he began recording fuel remaining, outside air temperature, and barometric pressure. As the plane stalled, he recovered from the stall and recorded the altitude.

"Wow, 19,286'," he thought. That's the highest he'd ever flown and first time he'd used oxygen. Just another event to chalk up to experience.

He brought the plane down below 10,000', and stowed his oxygen mask then proceeded back to Anacostia to make five precision landings while recording speeds and fuel remaining. After his fifth landing, he taxied back to the flight line and shut down his aircraft. He checked through maintenance and went to the pilot's Ready Room. Drawing a cup of coffee, he sat down to fill out all the paperwork. After recording his statistics from the flight, he answered the opinion questions. When finished he turned in the paperwork to Flight Test and stopped by John Becker's office.

"Good morning, John," he said.

"Good morning, Walt. How did your flight go?" he asked.

"It was smooth as a baby's bottom," Walt responded. "I have a favor to ask. I need to go to Norfolk on Wednesday and was wondering if I could fly the Sparrowhawk down there. I would be back on Friday early if that's okay?"

"I don't have a problem with that," John responded. "She's your project so nobody else is going to fly her. Let's plan another test flight next week, however. We need to spin test her next. So, when are you available?"

"My schedule should be open on Thursday next week. I need to get some things done for the Admiral since I'm neglecting them this week," Walt said.

"Okay, I'll put you on the schedule for next Thursday and you have a good trip to Norfolk," John said.

After changing back into his uniform of the day, he proceeded back to headquarters. It was way past lunch and he was hungry, so he stopped at the Gedunk and purchased a sandwich. He then headed back to the office. Gloria was there but the Admiral was over on Capitol Hill lobbying for more money for the department.

Walt had a document in his in-basket, which Gloria had put there this morning, so he grabbed it and began to read. It was from Bruce Gordon, that the result of the inspection of Paul Massay's work had yielded nothing. His work was flawless, and as a result, the judge in the case threw out the charges as Massay was only guilty of a big mouth but had not committed a crime. Nevertheless, Massay was let go for the good of the project. *"The Admiral will be glad to hear this story,"* Walt thought.

Walt next pulled out his file folder on the christening of the USS Akron. It was now scheduled for August 1st and he had been assigned various tasks as they related to the Admiral's personal schedule that week which he would need to schedule and confirm. In the meantime, the Admiral wanted to travel to Akron and check on the construction of the air ship personally. Walt coordinated with the Goodyear-Zeppelin people on dates, times, and accommodations. He would accompany the Admiral on this trip as well as a few other bureau people. The Navy had acquired a brand-new Ford Trimotor, also known as a JR-3, so Walt contacted the Commanding Officer at Chambers Field, in Norfolk, to schedule the dates of the Admiral's trip when the JR-3 would be needed. Turned out it would be a late May trip.

The Admiral arrived at the office and Walt briefed him on the Massay affair. They both hoped this would put an end to the press coverage that Akron had been sabotaged.

Walt advised the Admiral of his intended trip to Norfolk commencing on Wednesday and indicated he would doublecheck on the availability and schedule of the JR-3 for the upcoming trip to Akron.

The Admiral also inquired how the Flight Test was proceeding on the XF9C-1. Walt gave him a rundown on his morning flight and what was in store the next couple of weeks. He estimated completion and certification by the end of the month. When their conversation was finished, Walt went back to his office and buried himself in his paperwork.

The next morning, he was in his office when Gloria brought in the day's mail. In it was a report from Akron from Bruce Gordon. Walt opened it and began to read. It was another bombshell. Two civilian workers had contacted the Navy Department and were now claiming the Akron was the victim of inferior materials and shoddy workmanship. He indicated that two Navy Construction Corps Officers had been assigned to do an investigation and that he would keep the Admiral advised of the progress of the investigation. Walt knocked on the Admiral's door, entered and briefed the Admiral on the new issue which had developed in Akron. The Admiral's only comment was, "when is this bullshit ever going to stop." Walt agreed and excused himself. He spent the rest of the day coordinating their plans for the trip to Akron at the end of the month.

Wednesday Morning

It was a bright, sunny spring day and the sun was well up over the Eastern Shore as Walt manned the Sparrowhawk and taxied for takeoff. Once airborne, he headed down the Potomac River towards Chesapeake Bay. He would follow the Bay to Norfolk. The 431hp Wright engine was purring along just like a kitten and his speed was about 170 knots. "*What a great machine,*" Walt thought. Within a short time, he had the city of Norfolk in sight. He flew directly over it and headed southeast to Chambers field. As he did, he switched channels on his radio and keyed his mic.

"Chambers Field, this is Navy 731. Two miles for landing, over."

"Roger, 731, you are cleared for the break, runway 14, wind south 6 miles per hour, altimeter 29.96."

"Roger, Chambers Tower, altimeter two niner niner six."

He hit the break on speed, broke sharply to port, and entered downwind at 800'. His landing was smooth as the plane stalled just as the wheels touched down. He requested taxi instructions to Fighter Squadron Five's flight line where the line crew parked his aircraft. He told the line crew he would be here a couple of days and would appreciate it if they could refuel the plane before Friday. His next stop would be the pilots' locker room where he could change into his dress uniform.

After getting squared away in his dress khaki uniform, he scouted out the Commanding Officer's office. He knocked on the door frame as the door was already open. Lieutenant Commander Armstrong looked up from his desk and instructed Walt to enter.

"Good morning, Sir. I'm Lieutenant Pellman."

Lieutenant Commander Armstrong extended his hand, "Duke Armstrong, pleased to meet you, Lieutenant," he said. "And what may I do for you?"

"Sir, I am Admiral McMillin's aide and I wanted to touch base with you just in case you were wondering who was occupying space on your flight line with that funny-looking airplane. I flew the Sparrowhawk from Anacostia this morning to do some business with the base Operations Officer and thought that while I was here, I would visit with my two good friends Lieutenant (JG) Day and Lieutenant (JG) Fitzwater. I hope you don't mind, Sir."

"Not at all Lieutenant, although I haven't seen your funny airplane yet," Duke said.

"Well, Sir, it's funny in that it has this crazy hook on top vs on the lower tail. It is designed to hook up to the trapeze on the airship USS Akron when it's finally commissioned. We are in the process of certifying it at Flight Test right now," Walt said.

"That'll be something different, I guess. Is it going to be a difficult maneuver compared to an arrested carrier landing?" Duke asked.

"No, Sir, I don't believe so. I have eight traps aboard USS Los Angeles and it was a lot easier than my arrested landings aboard USS Langley," Walt said.

"Sounds good, Lieutenant. I think Lieutenant (JG) Day and Lieutenant (JG) Fitzwater are out flying right now but should return shortly. Why don't you go down to the Ready Room, and have a cup of coffee and wait for them there? Just turn right out of my office and it's at the end of the balcony."

Walt stood, extended his hand, "Thank you, Sir. It's been a pleasure meeting you." And with that Walt left Duke's office headed for the Ready Room.

He had barely settled down with his coffee when Paul and Bob burst into the room. They spotted Walt immediately and rushed over with hugs all around.

Paul spoke first. He was almost tongue-tied as he was more surprised than shocked.

"What the hell is this posing as a Lieutenant. Are you some kind of spook?" he said.

"Yeah, great to see you too, Paul," Walt said.

Bob chimed in next, "We need to sit down so you can tell us all about this, Buddy. Are you really a Lieutenant?" he asked. "And what about all this gold braid shit on your shoulder?"

"Okay, okay. Here's the deal. When I reported to Washington, the Admiral needed an aide. To fill the slot required a Lieutenant so he promoted me to Lieutenant. The aiguillettes denote an aide for a Rear Admiral," Walt said.

"So, you were a Lieutenant (JG) for three months," Paul exclaimed.

"Yeah, I guess so," Walt replied

"How'd you get here and how long are you here for?" Bob asked.

"I flew down in an XF9-C Sparrowhawk and I'm going to be here until Friday morning," Walt answered.

"How the hell are you flying an experimental plane?" Bob asked.

"I'm coordinating all Lighter-Than-Air activity for Admiral McMillin. This is the plane that's going to be flown aboard USS Akron as soon as it's commissioned. I am also assigned to Flight Test at Anacostia and doing all the acceptance tests on the Sparrowhawk for the Navy," Walt said.

"What else are you doing for the Navy?" Paul asked facetiously.

"I'm working on a plan for ladies on every ship, you ninny," Walt replied.

They all had a good laugh.

"Why don't you guys get changed into your uniform of the day so we can go to lunch, and while you are doing that, I need to run over to base operations and talk with the Ops Officer for a few minutes. I'll meet you back here and we can make plans for today and tomorrow. I need to get back to Washington Friday morning," Walt said.

"Okay, Buddy. We'll see you in a few," Paul said.

Walt walked over to base operations while Paul and Bob headed for the locker room to change into their uniforms.

Walt located the Operations Officer's office and knocked on his door. He was welcomed in and introduced himself to Lieutenant Commander Jerry Elliott.

"Sir, Admiral McMillin is planning a trip to Akron, Ohio, to inspect the progress on construction of the new dirigible and will need transportation for six people. The Admiral would like to depart Washington on the 24th of this month and return on the 29th. He sent me to check on the availability of the JR-3 to make the trip."

Jerry pulled out his planning calendar and scanned the dates. "Lieutenant, I am certain we can accommodate the Admiral on those dates."

He wrote that onto the calendar. "We will pre-position the JR-3 at Anacostia on the 23rd and be ready for departure on the morning of the 24th."

"That sounds great, Sir," Walt said. "I will have the Navy office in Akron make reservations for accommodations for five nights for your crew. I presume that will be for 4 people?"

"Yeah, we'll have a pilot, co-pilot, Plane Captain, and an orderly," Jerry replied.

"I'll take care of the snacks and you can handle the coffee and water," Walt said. "I will send you a message confirming all the details once I have coordinated with Akron."

"I appreciate that, Lieutenant," Jerry said.

"Yes Sir, thank you for the help. I will be in touch," Walt said as he rose, shook Jerry's hand, and departed his office.

He headed back to Fighter Squadron Five's Ready Room. When he arrived, Paul and Bob were already waiting. They headed out to the parking lot. Paul and Bob had jointly purchased a used car. It was a 1931 Model A Ford Sports Roadster. When they got to the car, Walt was puzzled and asked Paul, "Where am I going to sit?"

"Where do you think, you dummy. In the rumble seat," Paul said

Before Walt could ask any more questions. Paul grabbed the handle on the panel behind the front seat, turned it, and pulled back until it rotated down and exposed the rumble seat.

"To get in, just step up on that pad on the rear bumper and climb into the seat," Paul directed.

The three of them got settled with Paul driving, Bob in the passenger seat, and Walt in the rumble seat. They headed to the Officer's Club for lunch. They were seated at a table and ordered the daily special, tomato soup and a grilled cheese sandwich with a glass of sweet, iced tea.

Over lunch, they caught up on what they had been doing. Paul and Bob had mainly been learning to fly fighter tactics, shooting their 30 caliber machine guns, and dropping a few bombs. They had also flown a few Field Carrier Landing Practice sorties, but had made no carrier landings since there was no carrier available.

Walt brought them up to speed on what he had been doing. They were particularly interested in his hookups to the USS Los Angeles. He told them about the construction of USS Akron and invited them to be his guests at the christening. Paul and Bob were all excited about possibly attending.

For the next day and a half, the three of them were inseparable. They spent most of Thursday at the officer's swimming pool just relaxing and enjoying each other's company. On Wednesday and Thursday nights, they sampled the local cuisine in Norfolk.

Friday rolled around and Walt donned his flying uniform. Paul and Bob accompanied Walt to his plane. They said their goodbyes and Walt took off for Anacostia.

22

"Spinning The Sparrowhawk"

Washington, D.C.

Walt spent the weekend working at the office trying to catch up on his paperwork. He wrote a memo to the Admiral giving him the details of the trip to Akron at the end of the month and reminding him they were scheduled to depart on the 24th and return on the 29th. In another memo, he summarized the progress of acceptance of the Sparrowhawk and included his spin test next Thursday. He estimated he would be ready to deliver the Sparrowhawk to Lakehurst the first week of June.

Monday rolled around quickly and he was early to the office. The Admiral arrived around 8:30 a.m. and Walt knocked on the Admiral's door about 9:00 a.m.

"Good morning, Sir," he said.

"Good morning, Lieutenant. I see you have been busy. How was your trip to Norfolk?"

"I had a great trip, Sir," Walt replied. "I completed all the arrangements for our upcoming trip to Akron and visited with my two friends in Fighter Squadron 5. Is there anything you need, Admiral?"

"No, Lieutenant, I read both your memos so I am up to speed on those items. However, you might check to see when Flight Test is going to receive an N2Y for recertification after they attach the trapeze hook. That will probably be your next project at Flight Test."

"Yes, Sir, I'll do some checking around and see the status of that project. By the way, Sir, they already have an N2Y at Flight Test and I have already flown it."

Walt stood and departed the Admiral's office. He went into the outer office and chatted with Gloria for a few minutes before he returned to his own office.

He began checking on the location and status of the N2Ys. They were scheduled to be delivered to the Naval Aircraft Factory (NAF) in Philadelphia from Pensacola, late in the summer, probably August, to be retrofitted with skyhooks, after which they would be delivered to Lakehurst. It was determined they would not need to be recertified before delivery. He also discovered that a team from the NAF would be coming to Ana- costia and retrofitting the N2Y with a skyhook. That would save Flight Test some time in not having to fly the plane to Philadelphia and return.

Walt determined that the XF9C-1 would also need to be refitted with a modified skyhook before delivery to Lakehurst. This would delay delivery until late June. He was a little relieved as that would be more of a leisurely certification schedule at Anacostia.

The week had gone by quickly. It was a never-ending battle just to keep up with all that was happening in and around Washington and Akron. Walt had caught up on his office work, and when Thursday rolled around, he was ready for his next flight in the XF9C-1. He arrived early at flight Test, changed into his flight uniform, and proceeded to John Becker's office for a briefing. John was already there, and soon thereafter, Lieutenant Chad Edwards arrived.

John greeted everyone and began his briefing.

"Gentlemen, today we will conduct the spin capabilities of the XF9C-1. Curtis-Wright has done a spin test and reported favorable results. However, you know that the factory wouldn't report anything else. In this aircraft, it could be a very dangerous maneuver. The short coupling between the longitudinal and lateral axis could result in a flat spin making recovery difficult. You will begin your test at 10,000'. If recovery is not complete by 5000', Walt, you are directed to bail out. No ifs ands or buts about it. Don't second guess yourself and say you can do it. These are your instructions. If your first spin recovery is successful you will conduct a second and third spin to confirm the spin characteristics. Chad you are the controlling factor of these tests. If you observe anything unsafe, you will direct the cessation of the test, understood?"

"Yes, Sir, understood," Chad replied.

"Walt, do you have any questions on what your responsibilities are?" John asked.

"No, Sir, no questions, and I understand the parameters of the test and my responsibilities," Walt replied.

"Okay, go do it and try to bring it back in one piece," John said.

"Will do, John. Don't worry, we got this," Walt reiterated. "Okay. Good luck," John said.

Chad and Walt grabbed their gear and proceeded down to maintenance where they drew their parachutes and signed out for their aircraft. Walt for the XF9C-1 and Chad for the F3C-3.

Taxi and takeoff were normal with Walt leading the formation. He climbed to 10,000' while proceeding east from Anacostia. Upon reaching 10,000', he directed Chad to assume the safety plane's position, which was 500' abeam and 1000' below Walt's altitude. Walt's first spin attempt would be to the left. He reduced the power to flight idle, turned on carburetor heat, and retrimmed the aircraft as he slowed the aircraft while maintaining altitude. Chad matched Walt's procedures. When Walt slowed below 90 knots, he ceased trimming the aircraft and held back pressure on the stick while maintaining altitude. The aircraft finally stalled at 53 knots. He kicked in full left rudder and pulled back on the stick. The aircraft began a spin to the left. Chad pushed his nose over into a dive and began to circle the spinning aircraft. After completing 1-1/2 turns and a loss of 1200', Walt applied full right rudder and forward stick. After another ¾ turn, the aircraft stopped spinning and recovered where Walt neutralized the rudder pulled back on the stick, and added full power on the engine. The aircraft momentarily leveled at 8000', then began a climb as Walt retrimmed the aircraft. Chad rejoined Walt's right-wing and commented, "Nice recovery, Walt. That spin didn't seem too bad."

"Yeah, Chad, pretty standard reaction in the aircraft. How about you slip over on my left-wing. This one will be a spin to the right," Walt said.

Passing 9000', Chad peeled off and stabilized 500' abeam Walt's position. Walt leveled the aircraft at 10,000'. Once again, he reduced power to flight idle, carburetor heat on, and retrimmed as he slowed the aircraft. The aircraft stalled at 52 knots as he applied full right rudder and full aft stick. The aircraft began to spin and immediately the tail went down into a flat spin. The wings rolled over about 30° from level. Walt recognized the situation and immediately applied full left rudder and full forward stick. The flat spin continued. Walt applied full power to the engine. Still no change in the aircraft. Walt reduced power and applied full left-down aileron. The aircraft was now shuddering and shaking. Chad shouted in his microphone, "Walt, you're passing 6000'."

Suddenly the nose of the aircraft fell through. Walt neutralized the aileron and rudder. The aircraft stopped spinning and Walt recovered by pulling back on the stick while adding full power to the engine. His recovery altitude was 5080'.

"That was a close one," Chad said.

"Yeah, Chad, but I learned a lot from it. Let's go back up to 10,000' and try it again."

"You sure are a glutton for punishment," Chad replied.

"Yeah, but we have to make these things known to pilots of lesser ability so they are aware of what the airplane can do," Walt said.

Walt arrived at 10,000' and once again entered a right spin. Just as quickly as the flat spin developed he applied left aileron and the nose pitched down and he recovered at 7,800'.

"I told you I learned a lot on the first one, Chad. Not bad for a second attempt."

"Yeah, looks like you nailed that one," Chad replied.

"Let's take 'er home, Chad. You take the lead."

Chad brought them into the break at 800'. He kissed off and broke left. Walt counted to five and broke left. As he passed abeam the end of the runway, he turned and began his descent for landing. His touchdown was smooth and right on speed. He and Chad taxied back to the flight line, parked, and shut down. As they walked back to the Hangar, Chad broke the silence.

"That was some fine flying, Walt. How the hell did you know what to do in that flat spin?" he asked.

"Trial and error, Chad. I tried everything. All that was left was applying aileron. On the first one, it worked, but I also found out adding power only aggravated the spin. On the second try, I applied what I learned on the first and it worked just fine," Walt said.

"Man, if it were me, I would have bailed out on the first one. You were so damn close to 5,000' I was just about to tell you to bail out," Chad replied.

"Well, everything worked out and we learned a lot. That's all that counts.

They both settled into the Flight Test Office and wrote up their reports. For Walt, it was a long report what with all the data he needed to include. The majority of this information would later be incorporated into a flight handbook for the pilots who would fly the aircraft. Walt finished his report, changed into his dress uniform, and headed for the bureau.

During the next couple of days, he transcribed notes from Bruce Gordon's report into a usable document for the Admiral to rebut some of the stories now circulating in the national news. The press releases that the Admiral made helped to cool the rhetoric and the news media supported the Navy's position on the truth.

Walt completed the final flight on the Sparrowhawk, and as soon as a skyhook was reinstalled, he could make one final flight and complete the certification. After that, and with approval by the Bureau of Aeronautics, it would be ready for delivery to Lakehurst.

The 23rd rolled around, and later in the day, Walt had snacks delivered to Anacostia to be loaded on the JR-3 when it arrived. The next morning, he was up early and stopped by the Gedunk where he had breakfast and picked up sandwiches and fruit cups for lunch on the plane going to Akron. He then proceeded to Anacostia, and after parking his car, he met with the flight crew of the JR-3 and had the orderly stow the lunch he had brought for all hands. The pilot, Lieutenant Jack Fisher, briefed him on the weather forecast enroute to Akron and a flight time of 2 hours 59 minutes. By 8:30 a.m. the pilots manned their assigned positions in the aircraft while the flight engineer and orderly waited outside the aircraft with Walt for the arrival of the Admiral's party. Just before the Admiral arrived, Captain Charlie Fuller walked up with two officers from the Bureau's certification office. Walt saluted, and greeted them and told them the Admiral would be arriving within five minutes and they were free to board the aircraft. They climbed aboard just as the Admiral's car pulled up. Walt greeted the Admiral while the orderly gathered up the Admiral's travel bag. He stowed it on board, and they all boarded the aircraft, except for the flight engineer. He pulled the landing gear locking pins, chocks and stowed the boarding ladder. Just as he closed the rear door, the number three engine roared to life. Walt took a seat near the Admiral and handed him the morning edition of the *Washington Post*.

Soon they were winging their way to Akron. The pilot leveled the aircraft at 3500' and the orderly supplied the Admiral with a cup of coffee. There were some sweet rolls and the other passengers partook of them.

Walt and Admiral McMillin discussed the accusations of shoddy workmanship and inferior materials which had been leveled against the Navy in the construction of the Akron. It had been debunked and the story was now 26th-page news in the *Washington Post*.

The Admiral settled in, sipping his coffee and reading the *post*. As the time passed 11:00 a.m., the orderly began soliciting the passengers concerning lunch. Everyone opted for a sandwich and a fruit cup as there would be no time for lunch as they would "hit the ground running."

The orderly cleaned up the remnants of lunch, told Walt the pilots had opted to have their lunch after arrival at Akron. Soon power was reduced on the engines and the pilots began their approach to the Akron airport. They landed on runway 26 then taxied on the grass over to the Goodyear Dirigible Hangar. They were met by the flight line crew, who parked the aircraft then helped with the luggage after shutdown.

There was a gaggle of VIPs, naval officers, and civilians all waiting to greet the Admiral and his entourage. Adolph Schmidt, CEO of the Goodyear-Zeppelin Company, and his staff greeted the Admiral first, followed by the naval detachment who were lined up in formation. The Admiral shook each man's hand after honors were rendered in the form of a hand salute.

Walt and the Admiral had some final words before the Admiral boarded the CEO's car and departed. The Admiral would be staying with Adolph Schmidt at his residence while Walt and the crew would hunker down at Mazie's Boarding House. The Admiral's entourage chose to stay at the Portage Hotel in downtown Akron, but were going to conduct some routine business with the Goodyear-Zeppelin people before they traveled downtown. With everyone taken care of, Walt joined Bruce Gordon and walked over to his office. They sat down over a cup of coffee and discussed the operation's plan for the christening of the USS Akron on the 8th of

August. It was very detailed, and Bruce took copious notes as it was his responsibility to coordinate the Navy's participation in the festivities. There was a committee forming to handle the christening activities. The executive director under Adolph Schmidt was the chairman with other members from the various departments of the company, along with the mayor of Akron and a representative from the Ohio Governor's office. Lieutenant Commander Rosendahl, Commanding Officer, of the Akron, would be arriving shortly from Washington, D.C., to assist Bruce in scheduling the Navy activities.

It was getting late and Walt needed to get over to Mazie's before 6 o'clock to make it to supper. Bruce had a Navy vehicle come around to the Hangar to drive him to Mazie's.

Walt arrived at Mazie's at 5:45 p.m., just in time to sign up for his room and get into the dining room in time for supper. The JR-3 flight crew was already seated and Walt joined them at their table. During their discussion over dinner, the crew asked Walt if they could get a tour of the factory and the USS Akron. Walt said he could arrange that for the next day and they should plan on riding together over to the plant in the morning.

After dinner, Walt changed into some sports clothes and went back downstairs. He joined the crew out on the porch where they all sat in rocking chairs and just relaxed. As usual, there was a lot of hand flying and sea stories as the evening progressed. It got dark around 9:00 p.m. and Walt was beat. He would have a busy day tomorrow so he told the crew he would hit the sack.

Walt met the JR-3 flight crew in the dining room about 7:30 a.m., had breakfast, then they all piled in a Navy staff car and headed for the Hangar. When they arrived, they walked into Bruce Gordon's outer office. Walt talked with Bruce's administrative assistant who nodded and indicated to Walt that she would get the crew a tour of the plant and dirigible. Walt passed that info to the flight crew and then walked into Bruce's office. He remained there only long enough to tell Bruce he was headed to Chuck Rowe's office and he would see him later in the morning.

With that, Walt began the half-mile walk through the factory to Chuck's office. When he arrived, he checked in with Chuck's assistant who then ushered him onto Chuck's office.

"Good morning, Lieutenant. It's nice to see you again. How's everything going on your end?" he asked. "may I get you a cup of coffee?"

"Yes, coffee would be great. Things are proceeding smoothly, although you know changes are inevitable in our situation. I just wanted to stop by and see how things were going on the change to the trapeze we discussed the last time we talked," Walt said.

Chuck asked his assistant to bring them each a cup of coffee.

"Well, we got the drawings completed and sent in to the Bureau. It's going to take a few months before it comes back approved and then we'll have to get NAF into the picture as they will need to make the change to the trapeze. I'm sure the Akron will be at Lakehurst by then so it will be an easy fix to make. Let me pull out the drawings for you to look at," Chuck said.

Chuck's assistant brought them each a cup of coffee. Walt took his black while Chuck added a little cream and sugar.

Chuck broke out the blueprints and found the correct page, which he rolled out on his drafting table.

"It sure made it easy for us to draw this with you having flown the XFC9 here and our draftsmen being able to get some measurements from it. I think you'll like the final product," Chuck said.

The two of them poured over the drawing.

"This really looks great, Chuck. I can't wait to see it in action. I'm sure it is a great improvement over the stabilizing struts we originally had," Walt noted.

"Yeah, of course, we haven't had any reports yet since we haven't even launched the Akron, but I'm sure the pilots will give us feedback when they test it," Chuck observed.

"I'm hoping to be one of those pilots, Chuck. I haven't told the Admiral yet, but I'm bucking for a transfer to the Aviation Unit at Lakehurst, may be late in the year," Walt said.

"That may be good timing, Lieutenant. I hear the trapeze won't be installed until later this year," Chuck said.

"Great. Thanks for the info, Chuck."

"Is there anything else you would like to look at?" Chuck asked.

"No, Chuck, I guess we've covered everything I wanted to see. I guess I'll go back over to the Hangar. Thanks for everything. It's been a pleasure seeing you again," Walt said as he shook Chuck's hand and departed his office.

It took Walt about 15 minutes to walk back to Bruce's office.

"Bruce, I am going to go aboard the Akron and study some of the systems. If you need me, that's where I'll be," Walt said as he left the office for the Akron.

23

"Carrier Quals"

Akron, Ohio

Walt spent the next couple of days with Bruce helping develop the operations plan for the christening of the Akron. Both Naval Officers could see this was going to be a mass undertaking. They agonized over some of the details, but they needed to get it right so everything went off without a hitch.

Walt didn't have much contact with the Admiral, but they were scheduled to leave Akron at 9 o'clock on Friday. The Goodyear-Zeppelin company would provide the food, coffee, and water for the trip back to Washington, D.C. All details were finalized, and Walt was ready for the flight home. He and the JR-3 crew were up early on Friday, and after an early breakfast, headed for the airport. They arrived by 7 o'clock and started their preflight preparations. At 7:20 a small truck pulled up and delivered lunch along with coffee and water. Once the food was stowed, Walt just needed to await the Admiral's arrival. To bide away his time, he accompanied the flight engineer on his pre-flight preparations to learn more about the JR-3. It was natural for him as he was interested in any type and model of airplane in the Navy.

At 8:45 a.m. Admiral McMillin and his entourage drove up in a fleet of company cars. The Admiral was accompanied by Adolph Schmidt. Walt greeted the Admiral while the crew took all luggage aboard the aircraft.

"Good morning, Sir," Walt said as he saluted the Admiral. "I hope you had a fruitful visit."

The Admiral returned Walt's, salute, "Yes, Lieutenant, it was a successful visit, and how was your visit?"

"Sir, I discussed the trapeze with the Goodyear engineers and reviewed the drawings. It looks good for the changes we suggested," Walt said.

"Sounds like a great improvement. I can't wait to see it," the Admiral said.

While they were talking, Commander Fuller and his assistants climbed aboard the JR-3 and settled into their seats. The Admiral was the last to board except for Walt and the flight engineer. Walt followed the Admiral aboard and found his seat. Meanwhile, the flight engineer pulled the landing gear locking pins, chocks, climbed aboard, and secured the rear cabin door. At that point, the starboard engine roared to life, followed by the number one and number two engines.

The pilot taxied out to the duty runway, performed his engine check, and was soon airborne for Anacostia. He leveled off at 3500' where the air was smooth and cool.

Walt provided the Admiral with the morning paper from the Akron *Free Beacon*. The orderly furnished the Admiral and Walt with a cup of coffee. Most of the passengers dug into the sweet rolls except for Walt. ETA Anacostia was 12:35 p.m. so everyone settled down for a couple of hours. Walt joined the Admiral at his table where they discussed the preparations for the christening of the Akron. The Admiral made a couple of decisions concerning the proceedings. He would escort the President of the United States while Walt would escort Amelia Earhart. He also wanted the banquet scheduled the night before the christening.

Time was approaching 11:30 a.m. and the orderly was asking people about lunch, which consisted of a ham and cheese sandwich and a fruit cup. By the time everyone finished their lunch, the pilot began his descent into Anacostia.

On arrival and after shutdown, Walt made a quick trip to the cockpit and thanked the crew for the great flight. He escorted the Admiral to his waiting car, then gathered his own gear, walked over to his car, loaded it and headed for BuAer headquarters. It was a Friday, so he didn't stay long, then was off to his quarters. For the upcoming weekend, he planned to just relax and get his mind cleared of all the hectic stuff he had endured during the last few days. He was determined he was not going to think about anything which transpired the past week. Monday would be soon enough to dig into all he needed to do between now and the 8th of August, the christening date now set for Akron.

Monday Morning

Walt was into the office early. No one had arrived yet, so he settled in his office and began reviewing his messages. Gloria had taken a call from Flight Test. They needed Walt to call John Berger at his earliest convenience. He decided to call John after 8:30. There was a final report of the possible sabotage from Bruce Gordon. Walt had already discussed this in person with Bruce and this was just a formal report to put it to bed. He attached a note to Gloria to route it to the Admiral then to the appropriate people within the bureau. Hopefully, they were past all the negative stuff concerning Akron and could now concentrate on positive things.

Walt came across a report that the Saratoga had been sent out from Guantanamo Bay, Cuba, to the eastern Caribbean to search for a missing luxury yacht, which had been caught in a storm and hadn't been heard from for some four days. The yacht belonged to the Astor family who were on a trip to Jamacia. They had visited the Leeward Islands and had departed Barbados four days earlier. The Saratoga was searching the Caribbean from Jamacia out to Barbados. The Saratoga's arrival at Norfolk was now to be determined. It would once again delay Paul and Bob from joining their fighter squadrons aboard Saratoga.

At 8:30 Walt called John Berger at Flight Test. John picked up on the third ring.

"Lieutenant Commander Berger," he said.

"John, Walt Pellman here returning your call."

"Hey, Walt, great to hear from you. Heard you were in Akron for a few days. How was your trip?" John asked.

"It was pretty good. Got a lot accomplished but a lot to do yet for the christening of the Akron," Walt responded.

"Anyway, the reason I called is that we need to run carrier suitability tests on the XF9C-1. We can get an hour allotted to us on the Langley on the 3rd of June. Do you think you could make that time slot?" John said.

Walt checked his calendar, "Yeah, John, it looks like I'm free for a couple of days. I believe I can make that time slot."

"Okay, Walt. I'll contact Langley and lock us in on that schedule.

While I got you on the phone, let me run down what we need to do next. After we certify carrier suitability, we need to get the plane up to the Naval Aircraft Factory for reinstallation of the skyhook then deliver it to Lakehurst. They took the hook off for upgrade and reconfiguration. Right now, it looks like the 2nd week in June for delivery to NAF, then a week for reinstallation of the skyhook, and the 3rd week for delivery to Lakehurst. How does that schedule sound?"

"John, I will lock it into my schedule so we can plan on it happening," Walt responded.

"Okay then, I'll call you later today with the schedule for the Langley," John reported.

"Roger that," Walt said. "Talk to you later."

Walt hung up and scribbled some notes on his calendar.

The Admiral arrived at 9:30 and Walt knocked on his door and entered.

"Good morning, Sir. I just wanted to bring you up to speed on the Sparrowhawk. I talked with flight test earlier and we need to certify it for carrier suitability. Wednesday, Flight Test will have one hour allotted on the Langley for us to conduct the suitability testing. Next week I will need to deliver it to NAF for reinstallation of the skyhook and the following week to Lakehurst. After that, my Flight Test schedule will be clear so I can concentrate on the christening of the Akron," Walt said as he continued, "Sir I also wanted to update you on the Saratoga. She has been dispatched to search for the Astor's yacht which has been out of communication for about four days. They are searching starting at Jamacia and running a course out to Barbados. They Astors departed Barbados four days ago headed for Jamacia. I will keep you up to date as the situation unfolds."

"Oh crap, is that the only thing we have to do with our limited budget is search for some rich bastard's yacht." the Admiral retorted. "I guess he's a friend of the President, so we're bound to do it. Thanks, Lieutenant, for the update. By the way, we may have to visit the White House later this week and I want you to attend with me so keep Thursday and Friday open."

"Yes, Sir, I'll block them out right now," Walt said as he departed the Admiral's office.

He went back to his own office and took out his calendar. His phone rang. It was John Berger.

"Walt, John here. I got our time slot confirmed. It is for 1400 hours on the third. I will leave it to you to figure out where you will rendezvous with the Langley."

"Thanks, John, I'll plan my trip to Norfolk. Looks like I can depart in the morning, refuel at Chambers Field, then fly out to the ship and come back directly to Anacostia from Langley. I have to be in the office on Thursday and Friday for a possible meeting in Washington so that'll work for me."

John hung up and Walt went back to work.

Wednesday Morning

Walt was on his way to Anacostia by 8:30 a.m. finding very little traffic on the streets of Washington. The depression was building and taking its toll on all aspects of normal life. He was not affected very much by it, and he was thankful for being able to fly and continue in his career in the Navy.

He arrived at Anacostia, parked his car, and proceeded to his locker in the Hangar. He changed into his flight uniform then checked in with John Berger at Flight Test.

He greeted John as he entered his office. "Good morning, John. How are things going this morning?" Walt asked.

"Hey, Walt, great to see you this morning. Yeah, we're going to be busy with this new Curtis fighter we just took delivery of. Are you all set for your carrier suitability test this afternoon?"

"I should be in Norfolk by 11:30, get a little lunch and be over the Langley by 1400. If things go right, I'll be back tonight before supper," Walt offered.

"Maybe you should plan on being back a little later. Your Bureau has put out a new requirement of 20 hours night flying each fiscal year. How are you doing on that?" John asked.

"I don't have any night flying yet this year. I guess I should plan some night flying. After the christening of Akron, I should have a little more time in my schedule. Anyway, I'm off to Norfolk. I'll leave my report on your desk tonight when I get back. Let me know the plans for delivery of the Sparrowhawk to NAF," Walt offered.

He left John's office, and went out on the flight line and manned his aircraft. The line crew got him started and sent him off for his flight to Norfolk. He took the usual route to Chambers Field, down the Potomac and then just follow the Chesapeake Bay south to Norfolk. It was only an hour and a half, and he switched to the Chambers Field tower frequency.

He keyed the mic, "Chambers Field, Navy 8731 five miles north for landing, over."

"Roger 8731, you're cleared to enter the break runway 28, winds 300° at 7 mph. Altimeter 29.97," Chambers tower reported.

"Roger altimeter 29.97," Walt answered.

He entered the break and completed his landing. The tower switched him to ground control and cleared him to taxi to the flight line alongside the tower. The line crew parked him where he shut down the engine and the line crew chocked the plane. After he exited the airplane, he directed the line crew to refuel the aircraft.

Walt walked into the Operations building and stopped to talk with the Operations Duty Officer.

"Good morning," Walt said. "I'm Walt Pellman." As he extended his hand.

"Good morning, Lieutenant. Is there anything I can do for you?" he asked.

"You sure can," Walt answered. "I am going out to the Langley this afternoon and need to know her steaming course from Norfolk, so if I may use your phone, I will call 2nd Fleet operations."

"Sure, come around here and use the phone in my office," the Duty Officer said.

Walt proceeded around the counter and entered the office behind the Duty Officer. On the desk next to the phone was a hand-printed list of phone numbers, one of which was 2nd Fleet Operations.

Walt picked up the phone and dialed the number. The 2nd Fleet Duty Petty Officer answered. Walt identified himself and told the petty officer his mission and his 1400 time slot to fly aboard Langley. The petty officer then put the Duty Officer on the phone and Walt repeated his request. The Duty Officer checked Langley's planned operation schedule for today.

"Lieutenant, she's operating south and East of the mouth of the Bay. She was scheduled to depart Norfolk at ten hundred hours. Her proposed DOT should be heading 135° true, which will put her approximately 45 miles off the coast," the duty officer reported.

"Thank you, Sir, I got it. I should have no trouble finding her this afternoon." And with that Walt hung up the phone.

He turned to the Operations Duty Officer. "Thanks for the help," Walt said. "I think I'll get some lunch."

"The Gedunk is just a couple of blocks up the main street from here. If you just walk straight out our street-side door, that will take you to it," The Duty Officer reiterated.

"Roger that, Sir. I'll see you after lunch."

Walt walked back out to his plane and retrieved his dress blouse for his green aviation uniform. Flying uniforms were not allowed on base except for the Hangars and flight line. He also retrieved his hard hat which was part of his dress greens. He thought since he had some time, he would walk over to Hangar Thirty-One and check on Bob and Paul. They would be pissed if he didn't check in with them at least since he was this close.

He checked in with the Fighter Squadron Five Duty Officer who determined that by chance Bob and Paul were both out on carrier quals to Langley. What a coincidence he thought. *"I'll probably see them on the ship."*

The Gedunk was hardly occupied as it wasn't quite lunchtime yet. He ordered the soup and sandwich, and after he received his order, sat down to eat his lunch.

Back at base operations, he filed a flight plan out to USS Langley. It would be only a half-hour flight to the ship, so he decided to depart Chambers Field about 1315 hours. As his departure time approached, he put on his life jacket and parachute and manned his aircraft. The line crew got him started and pulled the chocks. He contacted ground control and followed their instructions out to the approach end of runway 28. After engine run-up to check the magnetos, he called the tower and received permission for take-off. The plane seemed to leap into the air and accelerate quickly. He reached climb speed and headed out of the pattern climbing to 2500' while enroute to Langley. His compass heading was due East until he reached the mouth of Chesapeake Bay, then he turned to 135°. At cruise speed, Walt figured it should only take him about twenty minutes to reach Langley. Sure enough, fifteen minutes out he spotted Langley, at ten miles, off to his port.

He was already on Langley's operating frequency, so he called.

"Langley this is Navy 8731 entering your 'Charlie' pattern at 2500'. Over."

"Roger 8731, deck is fouled continue Dog. Will advise," Langley answered.

It looked to Walt like they were recovering aircraft and parking them forward on the deck, which meant they were probably going to refuel the aircraft before commencing flight operations. Within minutes Walt observed the Charlie flag and Langley called on the radio.

"Navy 8731, you're cleared to enter the landing pattern. Your signal is Charlie."

Walt answered, "Roger, Langley. Signal Charlie. Will call the break."

Walt circled until he was abeam, downwind of the ship. He descended to 600' and turned in to approach the ship on the starboard side. She was headed into the wind, which was blowing about 7-8 miles per hour. The ship was now making 18 knots so landing deck speed would be about 35 mph.

"Langley, 8731 at the break," Walt broadcast.

No answer was required since Langley was flying the Charlie flag. There were two aircraft in the pattern on the downwind leg for recovery. Walt took interval on the 2nd plane. As he passed abeam the plane's position, he counted to five then broke smartly at 45° angle of bank while descending to 300' and slowing his aircraft to 55 knots. Passing abeam the ship, he began his left descending turn. He double-checked his hook down then visually picked up the LSO. He was passing the 90° of his 180° turn into the ship. Since this LSO had never waved a Sparrowhawk before he would have to carefully maintain his speed. He slowed to 52 knots and maintained it throughout the remainder of his turn. The LSO gave him a roger throughout his approach. Once he rolled out in the groove, the LSO gave him the cut signal. He reduced power to flight idle and the aircraft stalled just as it touched down on the deck catching the number two-wire. Walt held the brakes as the flight deck crew released the wire and raised his hook. As he looked up to his right, a yellow shirt was signaling him to taxi forward. He picked up the second yellow shirt who brought him to a position near the edge of the starboard side of the flight deck, where his plane was chocked and he shut down his engine. Walt unstrapped, left his parachute in the plane, and climbed out. The flight deck crew were already pulling out the hoses for refueling the aircraft, so Walt made his way over to the port side of the ship, jumped down into the catwalk, and entered the squadron Ready Room. As he entered, the first one to spot him was Paul.

Paul called out, "Gentlemen, let me have your attention." Everyone quieted down. "We have a Washington desk jockey with us this afternoon. Let me introduce Lieutenant Walt Pellman, a well-known Naval Aviator, mingler with the high muckety, mucks, and aide to Admiral McMillin. He usually travels only with the higher ranks, but he's stuck with us low-class guys today. How the hell are you old Buddy? All kidding aside, this is my friend Walt so be nice to him while he's aboard," Paul said.

"How about my autograph, Paul?" Walt joked.

All the pilots got up and shook his hand, except Bob. When he reached Walt, he gave him a big bear hug and said, "We miss you old friend. What are you doing here today?"

"I needed to bring the Curtis Sparrowhawk aboard for certification in carrier adaptability. We can't accept it into Navy inventory until we certify it completely and this is the last step in certification. How long have you guys been aboard?" Walt asked.

"We just flew out this morning. We have twelve traps to make and then we're off to Chambers Field this afternoon," Bob answered. We just finished eight traps and have another four to go then we're off to the beach. How many traps do you have to make?"

"We have no set number, but a minimum of five is all we need for certification." Walt said.

About that time, Lieutenant (JG) Jim Orille entered the Ready Room. As ships' LSO, Jim had waved all the earlier traps.

"Hey, you guys settle down," he said. "Let me debrief each of you individually on each of your passes so we can see what you need to work on for the last four landings."

He called each pilot by name who then went to where Jim was sitting, and from his notebook, he went over each approach and landing, advising them what needed work.

Bob and Paul came back to sit with Walt when Jim shouted out, "Who was flying that last bird in the pattern to land?"

Walt raised his hand. When Jim saw who it was, he smiled.

"Nice to see you again, Lieutenant Pellman. That was a nice approach and landing you made. What was your speed past the ninety?" he asked.

"I was set at 52 knots. She stalls at 48," Walt said.

"What the hell is it you're flying anyway?" Jim inquired.

"It's a Curtis XF9C-1 Sparrowhawk," Walt responded.

That caught everyone's attention. Now everyone was listening as they were interested in what this new plane was destined for in the Navy.

"Well, tell us all about it, old Buddy," Paul said.

"Okay, guys, we're in the process of certifying the plane at Flight Test at Anacostia. After we're complete, the Naval Aircraft Factory is going to put a skyhook on it and we're going to fly it on and off the new Navy's dirigible the USS Akron. There will be a flying trapeze attached to the underside of the Akron which we will use for hookup. The Akron has a Hangar deck for three aircraft with one on the trapeze so we can operate with three aircraft at any one time," Walt said as he was interrupted by one of the pilots.

"What will be your mission?" he asked.

"Primary mission will be scouting. Secondary mission, defensive protection of the dirigible," Walt said

"What's your top speed?" someone asked.

"We haven't determined that as yet, but I have flown it as fast as 191 knots," Walt interjected.

"Damn that's pretty fast," Bob said.

"Yeah, the reason it was selected for dirigible work is the wingspan and overall length. We were limited by the size of the opening in the diri-gible to bring it into the Hangar deck. As you can imagine it is a little squirrely in pitch in the longitudinal axis. The short coupling of the elevators with the lateral axis makes it difficult to control," Walt said.

Over the 1MC circuit, the following message blared, "All pilots man your planes."

As they all filed out of the Ready Room, they wished Walt good luck in his test program.

Up on deck all planes had been respotted aft. The Sparrowhawk was at the back of the pack so Walt knew he would be last to launch.

He climbed into his plane, and after attaching himself to his parachute, he strapped into the plane and waited for the flight deck crew to assist him in starting his aircraft. In short order, a crewman approached and yelled switch off. Walt checked the mag switch in the off position and gave the crewman a thumbs up. The crewman pulled the prop through three times then shouted "contact." Walt replied "contact" and the crewman pulled the prop through once again. This time the engine roared to life and stabilized at ground idle. After a short interval, Walt ran the engine up to 1500rpm and checked the magnetos and all other related engine gauges. He once again reduced power to ground idle and sat waiting his turn for launch.

The last plane ahead of him was launched and he taxied forward a short distance. The launch officer gave him the hold brakes and two-fingered turnup. Once engine power stabilized at take-off power, the launch officer signaled release brakes and proceed to launch. The plane lurched down the deck, grasping for lift, then suddenly becoming airborne well before reaching the end of the deck.

Walt climbed straight ahead until reaching 300'. He spied the last plane on the downwind in the landing pattern and took interval on him, turning downwind and paralleling the reverse direction the ship was steaming. He dropped his hook and checked his shoulder harness locked and carburetor mixture full rich. He reached the 180° position and began his descending turn at 55 knots, slowing to 52 knots by the 90° position. He made a roger pass, took the cut, and after the flight deck crew released the wire and raised his hook, he taxied forward to repeat another trip around the ship. After the other planes made their fourth landing, they climbed to 2500' in the Charlie pattern until they all were joined up, then departed to the west and Chambers Field. Walt made one more arrested landing, and after takeoff departed the ship, climbed to 3500' and proceeded on a 315° heading for Anacostia. It was just about 6:15 p.m. and the sun would set in 8 minutes. He was only about 20 miles from the beach. He soon passed over the beach and could see the lights of Newport News to the south. He reached the Chesapeake Bay in a couple of minutes, then turned north until he reached the mouth of the Potomac River. He turned northwest and followed the river until he passed Dahlgren then called Anacostia for landing. At five miles, Anacostia turned on their runway lights and the tower gave him permission to enter the break for runway 34. He broke over the numbers and made a sweet as you please approach and landing. After parking and shutdown, he proceeded to John Berger's office. His report was short and to the point. His conclusions were the same as had previously been suggested, that the XF9C-1 was unsuitable for carrier landings due to its high wing and power loadings. In other words, it was a hot plane. He also included in his report that the wing was set too low. It interfered with forward vision during all landings, including carrier landings. Having completed his paperwork, he went home for a good night's sleep.

24

"Presidential Visit"

Washington, D.C., Thursday Morning

Walt put on his dress Khaki uniform and attached all his accouterments. He wasn't sure if he needed to accompany the Admiral to the White House today, so he wanted to be ready just in case.

After breakfast, he made his way over to the office. As he entered, he was greeted by Gloria.

"Good morning, Lieutenant. How was your flight yesterday?" she asked.

"Good morning, Gloria. My flight was great, but don't let the Admiral know that. He thinks I'm having too much fun, which I am," Walt responded. "Anything hot on the docket this morning?"

"Yes," she said. "You and the Admiral are scheduled to be at the White House at 10 o'clock this morning to meet with the President. Also, there is a message from 2nd Fleet concerning the USS Saratoga."

"Okay, I guess I need to check the message board before the Admiral gets here," Walt mused. He got a cup of fresh coffee and walked into his office, hung up his hard hat, and sat down at his desk. The message board was on his desk, so he began to peruse the new messages. The top message concerned the status of the USS Saratoga and the Astor's yacht. The Saratoga had reached the Leeward Islands and had sent a two-plane sortie to Piarco, Trinidad, for mail and some supplies. Lo and behold, there tied up at one of the docks was the Astor's yacht. They had decided to take a side trip without checking in with anybody, so the search was called off and Saratoga was returning to Guantanamo Bay.

A second message was an update from the Naval Aircraft Factory. They were beginning to work on the trapeze for Akron, but were having difficulty getting some of the required parts to complete the work. They were projecting completion work on the trapeze in late October.

Walt knew the Admiral would not be happy with that news. Next message really intrigued Walt in that it concerned research and development work of retractable landing gear for some of the fighters now on the drawing board. This would be a great step forward, he thought, giving planes more speed when not in the landing configuration. The remainder of the messages were routine communications, which Walt read very quickly.

As soon as the Admiral arrived and got settled in his office, Walt knocked and entered his office to brief him on current events within Naval Aviation. The Admiral was still upset about the Astor's yacht wasting the Saratoga's time and assets because of some stupid yacht master not following the rules. He was more interested in Walt's assessment of the Sparrowhawk for carrier aviation.

"Lieutenant, give me your assessment of the Sparrowhawk's performance on and around the ship?" the Admiral asked.

"Sir, it's a squirrelly plane to fly. With all the power, it has it tends to want to run off the runway to the right on takeoff due to the torque produced. Then on wave offs at slow speeds, it tends to want to roll inverted, which in my opinion is highly dangerous, especially around the carrier. Then the coupling between the elevator and the lateral axis is too short. It makes the plane difficult to control even in just level flight. That makes it seems like it just wants to porpoise. As far as a fleet airplane, I don't think we should buy anymore. On all my carrier approaches yesterday, I was constantly moving the controls trying to fly a steady pattern."

"I appreciate your passion on the issue, Lieutenant, but we are stuck with it for the dirigible flying so I guess we will order six more just for that purpose," the Admiral said.

"Yes Sir, I understand. One good thing is we won't have brand new Naval Aviators flying them. I am sure all the pilots in the Aviation Units for Akron and RS5C will all be seasoned pilots." Walt said.

"You are absolutely correct, Lieutenant. I am putting you in charge of all pilot selection, along with Lieutenant Harrison for our manning of our dirigible aviation units. You and he can set up any selection process you wish so work it out with him," the Admiral said.

"Yes Sir. I will take care of that," Walt said. "Your car will be out front for us before 9:30 to go to the White House."

At exactly 9:25, Walt and the Admiral exited the front door of the building and entered the waiting car to take them to the White House. The ride took them up Virginia Street to Independence then over 17th street and around the corner to the South Gate of the White House. Once there, they were checked through security and escorted by a Marine Guard to the waiting area of the Oval Office. Exactly at 10:00, the door to the Oval Office opened and they were invited in.

The Admiral spoke first, "Good morning, Mr. President."

"Good morning, Bill. A pleasure to see you again," the President responded. "And who is this young man with you this morning?"

"Sir, this is my aide Lieutenant Walter Pellman," Admiral McMillin replied.

"It's a pleasure to meet you, young man," President Hoover said.

"Thank you, Sir. It's a pleasure to meet you," Walt replied.

Turning to the other person in the room the President spoke, "This is my Chief of Staff, Hal Holbrook."

Hal approached and shook hands with Admiral McMillin and Walt.

The President directed everyone to take a seat in the lounge area.

"Would you all like a cup of coffee?" he asked.

They all answered in the affirmative, so Hal stepped out to have the steward bring the coffee.

"Bill, I wanted to talk to you face to face. I need to have the straight word on the dirigible program. You know some in Congress are uneasy about the Navy spending so much money on the Lighter-Than-Air program. They feel the money would be better spent on building another carrier. I am quite interested in the program as I think it has more of a future than just in the Navy. I believe it can be adapted to civilian airline use, especially for overseas travel and the movement of goods. What's your assessment of the Navy's current progress on your dirigible program?" the President queried.

"Mr. President, we are making great strides in getting the first dirigible into the fleet. Once we launch the USS Akron, we have set up a development program to make the best use of the capability of the dirigible and her airplanes. We have worked out most of the construction problems and the appearance before the media should be a positive thing from here on out."

"That sounds positive, Bill. Some of the press reports have been negative for the past year giving the dirigible program kind of a bad name," The President observed.

"Yes, Sir. We have had a few incidents which detracted from the reputation of the Akron, but all reports on them proved to be false and we have rebutted them fairly well in our responses," Admiral McMillin replied.

"So, tell me about the planes you're going to fly from the dirigibles? How will they add to the mission?" the President asked.

"Sir, let me throw this one at my Aide as he is my expert on that particular section of the puzzle."

Walt took a deep breath, exhaled, and began. "Mr. President, the plane we intend to fly off the Akron is built by the Curtis-Wright Corporation. It is called the Sparrowhawk. Its formal designation is currently an experimental fighter, the XF9C-1. Its scouting capability will extend the area covered by the Akron to millions of square miles not now in the Navy's realm of capability. We have tested the skyhook feasibility on the USS Los Angeles and that is a proven maneuver that is within our scope of operations. I personally have made 10 hookups to the Los Angeles, and they were straight-forward and a fairly simple maneuver."

The Admiral spoke up, "Mr. President, it's easy for the Lieutenant to say it's easy. He is one of our best Naval Aviators in the fleet today. I would say it is a maneuver our pilots can be trained to safely accomplish. Are there any questions I can answer at his time, Sir?"

"No, Bill. I think we have enough information so Hal here can write up a briefing paper for me just in case the journalists ask me about the program," the President said.

The Admiral interjected, "Sir, we have one other item to discuss with you this morning. We are planning on christening the Akron on the 8th of August. I know we had previously said the 1st, but we have had a few setbacks in our schedule and that is the earliest date we can be sure to meet."

The President turned to Hal. "Hal, what is our schedule for the 8th of August?"

"Hal responded, "Mr. President, looking at our calendar, we will be on our western trip touring some of the National Parks and a stop at Stanford University."

"Damn, I hate to miss the christening, Bill, but that trip is very important to me. I have an idea. How about having Mrs. Hoover christen the Akron?" the President offered.

The Admiral answered, "Sir, that would be awesome. We can coordinate with Hal and Mrs. Hoover's Chief-of-Staff and work out the details."

"Excellent plan, gentlemen. Make it happen. Thanks, Bill, for coming over this morning. I appreciate the briefing. Always good to see you," the President offered.

Admiral McMillin and Walt shook the President's hand and said goodbye to Hal then departed the Oval Office.

The Admiral's car was waiting for them when they reached the exit to the White House. They entered the car and headed back to the Navy Yard.

On the ride back Walt observed, "Well, Admiral, that seemed to go fairly well."

"Yes, it did, Liieutenant. I'm glad we had a chance to pitch our program to the President. Nice job on your presentation. That was pretty good for an off-the-cuff offering," Admiral McMillin said as he smiled.

"Thank you, Sir. I didn't expect to have to do that," Walt said.

"I knew you could handle it. No one else knows more of the nuts and bolts of the Sparrowhawk program than you so I was sure you could handle a short briefing of the President," the Admiral responded.

"I will coordinate with Mr. Holbrook and the First Ladys' Chief- of-Staff on the details of her plans for the christening and give you a report when I have that, Admiral," Walt added.

Washington, D.C.

A week had passed since the Admiral and Walt had visited the White House. Walt had already been in touch with Hal Holbrook and Mrs. Hoover's Chief-of-Staff. Hal had pretty much stepped out of the picture and let Walt and the Chief of Staff handle everything, thereby having less confusion in the planning and details of Mrs. Hoover's trip.

The Saratoga had suffered an engine room fire at Guantanamo Bay and was now on indefinite hold until her boilers and steam plant could be checked out and repaired. Walt briefed the Admiral on the situation, which made him quite unhappy. He always wanted the best for Naval aviation and a positive face to the higher-ups and Congress. A preliminary report had been sent on the damage, but everyone was waiting for the final report so the damage could be repaired.

Walt received a message from John Berger at Flight Test that the Sparrowhawk would be ready for delivery to the Naval Aircraft Factory in Philadelphia by the 6th of June. That was just a couple of days away so Walt contacted John by phone and determined he would fly the plane up there on Friday. John would send Chad Edwards up in the N2Y to pick him up. Their difference in cruising speed made it almost impossible for them to go together. So, they would meet at NAF and fly back to Anacostia.

Walt called Bruce Gordon in Akron and gave him the latest news on Mrs. Hoover now being the guest of honor to do the christening of the USS Akron on the 8th of August. Bruce inquired about required lodging for the Hoover entourage. Walt advised him that was yet undetermined. He further advised Walt that the crew of the Akron was already reporting in and being housed at the Portage Hotel in downtown Akron. Lieutenant Commander Charles E. Rosendahl would be the Skipper of the Akron but was not scheduled to arrive in Akron until July 1st. The Executive Officer, Lieutenant Commander Frank Johnson, was due to report next week. Some of the division officers had already reported in and were handling the enlisted crew. They further discussed more of the planning for the week of the christening. Walt guaranteed Bruce he would pin down Mrs. Hoover's schedule as soon as possible so they could move forward on the details.

Friday arrived and Walt traveled over to Anacostia. He met John Berger and received all the logbooks and paperwork for the transfer of the Sparrowhawk to the NAF. He was soon off in the Sparrowhawk winging his way to Philadelphia.

Weather enroute was beautiful and Walt just cruised along and enjoyed the scenery. As he approached Philadelphia, he called the tower at the

Naval Aircraft Factory and was cleared for approach and landing as there was no traffic in the pattern.

After landing, Walt was directed to the end Hangar on the field which served as one of the final assembly areas for NAF. He parked as directed by the line crew and proceeded into the maintenance office. There he turned over the logbooks and NAF accepted the aircraft for modification. Walt decided since he was there, he would check on the progress of the construction of the trapeze for the USS Akron. The maintenance chief directed him to another building where he met Henry Jones, a supervisor for all things Akron.

After introducing each other, they discussed the construction and delays in completing the work on the trapeze. Henry told Walt not to expect completion of the trapeze before December 1st as the acquisition of parts would take until October 1st. Walt also asked if NAF had received the modification of the trapeze yet from the Bureau of Aeronautics. Henry indicated they had not yet received that and would go ahead with the original design until the modification was received. Walt was truly disappointed that it would take that long for the mod to arrive, but the recession was slowing everything down, almost to a standstill.

Walt had a little time before Chad would arrive in the N2Y, so Henry gave him an abbreviated tour of the fabrication area where the fuselage rings for the new dirigible, ZRS5 were being manufactured. He was impressed at the size of the rings being made from aluminum.

After finishing the tour of the plant, Walt wandered back over to the Hangar and talked with the supervisor whose crew would put the skyhook on the Sparrowhawk. He asked for an estimate of the finishing date so they could alert Lieutenant Duane Harrison in Lakehurst when it was ready for pickup.

Chad Edwards arrived in the N2Y and Walt hopped into the rear cockpit. Chad didn't even need to shut down the engine, so after Walt gave him a thumbs up, he taxied out to the duty runway and took off for Anacostia. The flight took twice as long over the same route Walt had just flown in the Sparrowhawk. The flight was without incident as Chad handled it in his usual professional manner. After 2-1/2 hours of flight, they arrived back at Anacostia. Walt changed into his dress khaki uniform and proceed back to the Naval Station and his quarters in the BOQ.

Washington Navy Yard, Monday Morning

After breakfast in the officer's Mess, Walt walked over to his office at headquarters. Gloria was already in the office and he stopped to chat with her for a few minutes before pouring himself a large cup of coffee. Gloria pointed him to a message in the communications traffic giving an update of the Saratoga.

Walt settled into his office and first drafted a message to the attention of Lieutenant Duane Harrison at Lakehurst. He infoed NAF indicating Duane would be picking up the Sparrowhawk when it was ready for delivery.

Next, he checked his messages and the communications board for any action items for him. Mrs. Hoover's Chief-of-Staff had sent him a memo with her itinerary. She would arrive in Akron on the morning of the sixth. Her mode of travel would be by rail, and she would be traveling in the Presidential railroad car. It was a plush car with all the amenities needed during her stay. The Chief-of-Staff indicated there would be two cars dedicated to the First Lady and her staff. If possible, she wished to stay in the President's railcar during her stay at Akron. Walt would need to work out the details to make that happen.

He perused the communications clipboard and briefed himself on the status of the Saratoga.

Finally, he took some time to finish his report on the delivery of the XF9-C to NAF. He took it to Gloria and asked her to type it up for him so he could sign it and she could then mail it to Flight Test. While Gloria and Walt were discussing his report, Admiral McMillin walked through the door.

"Good morning, Admiral," Walt said.

"Good morning, Lieutenant," the Admiral responded. "Come in my office and fill me in on the latest happenings in Naval Aviation."

"Yes, Sir. Let me grab my notes off my desk," Walt said.

Walt grabbed his notes and entered the Admirals office. He gave him the rundown on the Saratoga, XF9-C, and the status of Mrs. Hoover's itinerary for the christening of the USS Akron. He also covered the construction of the trapeze at the Naval Aircraft Factory. The Admiral was disappointed that the projected delivery date for the trapeze was late

November, early December. He also asked Walt to check on the parts required for the Saratoga. Two months of downtime seemed excessive and Naval Aviation really needed the Saratoga for qualifications and training.

Back in his office, Walt placed a call to Bruce Gordon in Akron. Bruce's secretary answered and put Bruce on the phone.

"Good morning, Walt. How are things in Washington?" he asked.

"Good morning, Bruce. Seems like things here are snowballing to a crescendo with the christening front and center. Listen, I need to update you on Mrs. Hoover's itinerary."

"Okay, Walt, give me what you have," Bruce said.

"Mrs. Hoover will arrive by train on the 6th of August. There will be two railcars dedicated to her entourage. She wishes to stay in the railcar as they have all the amenities she needs. What think you?" Walt asked.

"Walt, we have a couple of rail sidings over near the factory. I'm sure we can accommodate her there. We will need to have a platform built as the company does not have that structure as part of the rail system at the factory. We will also need to ensure we have electricity to plug into the rail cars. I can take care of that, no problem," Bruce said.

"We will also need a few more staff cars during her stay. I know the Admiral will probably be in Akron earlier that week, just don't have a firm date right now, but he will need a staff car and Mrs. Hoover and staff will need a couple. I will leave the details up to you," Walt said. "Is there anything else I can help you with right now?"

"Yeah, get me a list of those personnel from Washington who will be attending the dinner on the 7th. We are limiting the guest list to 1000 people. Right now, we are planning on having it on the Hangar deck away from the Akron as that is the only place we have enough room to host it. The christening ceremony will be on the other end of the Hangar. We will open the Hangar doors and have chairs all the way out on the grass if necessary. The mayor's task force will be handling most of the details for all this so the sooner we get them stuff the better chance we have of them getting it right," Bruce said.

"I understand the urgency, Bruce, and I will compile a list as soon as I can and send it to you. I'll be in touch," Walt said and hung up the phone. He went back to his notebook and updated it with the current information.

Walt wrote the Admiral a note and asked him for guidance on compiling a list of Washington attendees for the christening. He also called Mrs. Hoover's Chief-of-Staff and filled him in on the plans for Mrs. Hoover's stay in Akron.

The following weeks were filled with the christening planning front and center. During this time, Duane Harrison had picked up the Sparrowhawk from NAF and had delivered it safely to Lakehurst. Walt advised Duane he should fly the Sparrowhawk to Akron and arrive at least by the 6th. He would not be required to fly it while he was there but only put it on display. He could then schedule his return to Lakehurst after the 8th.

The Saratoga was estimated to be back in service on September 1st, but was now scheduled to remain at Guantanamo Bay, until October 1st.

Walt had a short note from Paul in Norfolk that said he and Bob were now permanently assigned to Fighter Squadron Five. He wrote a note to Paul indicating he and Bob should try to be part of the Navy contingent flying the air show at Akron on the 8th for the christening of the USS Akron. It would be part of the Langley Air Group. Their air show would be over before the actual ceremony so he told Paul to make their way to the VIP seating and he would have seats for him and Bob.

One new development occurred. Six N2Ys had been transferred to NAF for fitting of a skyhook and would soon be ready for pickup and transfer to Lakehurst. He would have to get busy and screen more pilots to fly with the Heavier-Than-Air unit for Akron.

~ *25* ~

"Akron Once Again"

Washington, D.C.

The months of June and July seemed to all be a blur looking back at how fast they had passed. Almost all Walt's concentration was on the activities surrounding the christening of the USS Akron on the 8th of August. He had been so busy he had flown only three times during this period and that was a few simple acceptance tests on the new F8C-6 Curtis fighter.

As the end of July approached, he firmed up the Admiral's Akron schedule. The Admiral would arrive on the 3rd of August and be staying at the Portage Hotel in downtown Akron. He had a full schedule every day with the main event before the christening being the banquet on Friday the 7th to be held on the floor of the airship Hangar at the airport.

His schedule called for him to meet Amelia Earhart Friday afternoon and then spend the rest of the day escorting her wherever she wished to go. She would be flying in to Akron in her Kinner Sportster and arrangements had been made to park her airplane on the south side of the airship Hangar.

On a personal note, Walt's father had given him a new 1931 Alfa-Romeo Sport car, which was delivered on the 27th of July. It was a beauty. 17/95hp engine but only a two-seater, which was a change from his four- seat Alfa-Romeo. He decided this would be his mode of travel to Akron.

Walt informed the Admiral he would be leaving for Akron on Sunday and would meet his aircraft on arrival Monday afternoon.

Washington, D.C. August 2nd

Walt checked out with the duty officer on his Temporary Additional Duty orders, jumped into his shiny new car, and headed to Akron.

He traveled out across Fredrick, Maryland, then headed up to Pittsburgh and off to Akron. He stopped for lunch and bought some fuel at Socony, on a voucher, and arrived after dinner at Mazie's Boarding House. As he checked in, Mazie was standing there to greet him.

"Have you had any dinner?" she asked.

"No Mazie, I just didn't stop along the way," Walt answered.

"Well, come into the kitchen. I have some leftovers from dinner," she said.

"That'll be great," Walt said.

He finished checking in, dropped his luggage and travel bag in his room, and went back down to the kitchen. Mazie had heated some leftovers from dinner he really enjoyed them. He was famished and it sure hit the spot. There was one piece of rhubarb pie left and he finished that too.

"Mazie, that was absolutely delicious. I enjoyed that more than you will ever know," Walt said.

"You're welcome, young man. Always glad to give you Navy boys our best," Mazie answered.

Walt stepped over and gave her a big hug. She grinned from ear to ear. There was truly a bond between them, and both appreciated the situation.

Walt went up to his room, and stripped down to his underwear and stretched out on the bed. He was beat from the long trip and quickly dozed off into a deep sleep. He awoke early, about 4:30 a.m., and decided he needed a quick bath. He went into the bathroom and drew the bathwater. He jumped in the tub and had a rapid wash down. Then he was out, dried himself, cleaned the tub, went back to his room, and got dressed. It was almost 6:00 a.m and breakfast would start soon.

At 6:00 a.m. he went down to the dining room and took a seat in the corner at one of the tables. Many of the workers from the plant were there as they had to be at work by 7:30 a.m. Breakfast was family-style, so Walt had scrambled eggs, bacon, and a piece of toast. This was washed down with a large cup of coffee. He was soon joined by Bruce Gordon.

"Hey, Walt, great to see you once again. When did you get in?" he asked.

"I arrived just after supper. Missed you guys but had some leftovers in the kitchen with Mazie. I was really beat and just went back to my room afterward and crashed," Walt said.

"Well, what's on the schedule for today?" Bruce asked.

"The Admiral is coming in at 2 o'clock this afternoon and then he has a speech to a civic group with dinner tonight. I don't have to accompany him today except meet the plane when he lands, so I am here to help you as much as possible during my free time," Walt said.

"Great, let me finish my breakfast, and then we can go over to the Hangar. You can ride over with me if you like," Bruce offered.

"Yeah, that'll be great. Let me cover my car with the tarp before we go," Walt said.

Bruce and Walt arrived at the Hangar.

"Did you hear from Frank Hawks yet?" Walt asked.

"Yeah, he sent me his regrets. Jimmie Doolittle also sends his regrets as he is prepping for the National Air Races up in Cleveland," Bruce said.

"What's the order of arrival for the airshow?" Walt inquired.

"What I have so far is Lieutenant Colonel "Hap" Arnold is bringing 12 fighters up from Wright Field and Major George Brett has some 36 fighters coming down from Selfridge Air Base. The Navy is sending some fighters and scout planes in from the Langley Air Group. Not sure how many. They will all make flyovers, and all will return to base, except the Navy guys. The Navy guys will land and remain overnight and return to Norfolk on Sunday. They all know that flyovers will be completed by 2 o'clock as that's when the Hangar ceremony will begin," Bruce said. "We expect about a quarter of a million people for the ceremony. We have 50 rail cars of ashes to spread on the grassy areas of the airport to keep the mud to a minimum for parking cars.

"We have 48 homing pigeons to put in the nose compartment of the Akron which will be released by Mrs. Hoover when she officially christens the Akron. They were flight tested last week and everything was good."

"Where are we going to park all the airplanes?" Walt asked.

"We have over 50-line crew to park airplanes, and we are going to park them on the off-duty runway. Goodyear-Zeppelin has provided a blimp and the Akron chief-of-police is going to direct parking from the blimp," Bruce added. "In the Hangar, Goodyear is providing all the tables and chairs for the Friday night banquet and they will break down after the banquet and reset chairs for the ceremony. The city of Akron is providing all the decorations in and around the Hangar. The main committee is working on all the minor stuff and I'm sure the chairman has a handle on all that. As far as the Navy's responsibilities, I am certain we have everything covered," Bruce concluded.

Glancing out into the Hangar, Walt saw the crew of the Akron mustering on the Hangar deck. "I think I will go visit with the officers and crew of the Akron for a while. I'll be back here in time for lunch. See you then," Walt said.

Walt wandered out to greet some of the crew of the Akron. He met the navigator, Lieutenant Bill Grammer, and the communications officer Lieutenant Junior Grade Will Johnson. Both were Naval Aviators and qualified Lighter-Than-Air.

Walt inquired, "Has the Executive Officer reported aboard yet?"

"Yes, Sir, he checked in last Thursday. He's up in his cabin on the Akron," Will Johnson responded.

"And has Lieutenant Commander Rosendahl reported aboard?" Walt asked.

"Yes, Sir, he came in yesterday and I saw him at breakfast at the hotel, but I don't know his present location," Bill Grammer responded.

"Who is your Hangar deck officer?" Walt asked.

"That would be Lieutenant Junior Grade Torri Hudson, our ship's maintenance officer," Bill Grammer said.

"Do you know where I can find him? I would like to be briefed on the rail system along with the Hangar deck capabilities and aircraft handling procedures. If that's possible," Walt said.

"Let me get someone to find him for you, Sir," Will Johnson said.

He went off, and found a seaman and sent him to find Lieutenant (JG) Hudson. Within a few minutes, Lieutenant (JG) Hudson climbed down from the airship and came over to where Bill and Walt were standing.

As he approached, he saluted and introduced himself to Walt, "Sir, I'm Lieutenant (JG) Hudson."

"At ease, Mr. Hudson. I'm Lieutenant Walt Pellman, aide to Admiral McMillin. I would like a briefing on the rail system as well as the Hangar facilities."

"Yes, Sir. Let's go aboard and I can show you what we have." Torri Hudson said.

Walt turned to Bill Grammer and Will Johnson. "Hey, great seeing you guys, will talk to you later." He shook their hands, and he and Lieutenant (JG) Hudson climbed aboard Akron.

The two of them proceeded a short distance behind the gondola and reached the opening for retrieving the aircraft. Walt played dumb as if he didn't know anything about the trapeze, rail system, and Hangar deck to give Lieutenant (JG) Hudson free reign to explain in detail the three areas involved with aircraft recovery and storage. He wanted to be sure the airship crew knew what they were doing with aircraft recovery and storage. Lieutenant (JG) Hudson professionally covered the subject, was well versed on all aspects of the operation involved, and assured Walt they would be ready to recover and handle aircraft when the time came to do so.

Walt commended him for his professional handling and explanation of the system and told him he was confident that the airship crew would do a great job in handling aircraft.

Lieutenant (JG) Hudson went back to his duties. Walt stopped at Lieutenant Commander Frank Johnson's cabin and introduced himself. He indicated to him where he could be reached and where Bruce's office was located should he need any help. They had a short discussion about the ceremony on Saturday and Walt told him they would probably have a briefing later in the week on the overall situation.

Walt went back to Bruce's office where Bruce was ready to go to lunch.

"Bruce, I forgot to tell you earlier that I have Lieutenant Duane Harrison slated to bring the Sparrowhawk out from Lakehurst for the christening. He should be here early Thursday. I'll leave his parking to you where people can see but not touch his machine. He'll be one of my guests at the ceremony.

They traveled about a mile past Mazie's boarding house and Bruce stopped at a country-style restaurant that specialized in BBQ. They had great pork BBQ on homemade bread with a side order of cole slaw.

After lunch, they went back to the Hangar and firmed up more of the Navy's responsibilities for the christening. Time was approaching 1:30 p.m and Walt started to check up on the Admiral's transportation and accommodations. He had specified two sedans for the Admiral's party. Walt went down on the Hangar deck, and walked over to the south side and out the door, stopping in the line shack. The line crew were all ready for the arrival of the Ford Trimotor carrying the Admiral's party. At 1:25 p.m. the phone rang. It was the control tower letting them know the Trimotor was on short final and would be on deck at 1:28 p.m. The parking on the south side of the Hangar was being reserved for VIP aircraft and visitors who would be staying over for the christening.

As the trimotor taxied off the runway onto the grass and around the end of the Hangar, the line crew picked them up and taxied them to a parking spot close to the tower. As they did, the two sedans pulled up and stopped.

After shutdown, the Admiral deplaned first. He was greeted by Walt.

"Did you have a nice trip, Admiral?" Walt said as he saluted the Admiral.

"Yes, we had a fairly smooth ride, Lieutenant. How long have you been here?" he asked.

"I arrived on Sunday, Sir. The CEO sends his regrets that he could not meet you here. He said he has a meeting with the Zeppelin people which he could not postpone," Walt said.

He escorted the Admiral over to his sedan and ensured that the Admiral's luggage was taken care of. Lieutenant Commander Charlie Fuller was part of the Admiral's party and Walt directed him to the second sedan.

Walt climbed into the sedan with the Admiral, and they departed for town. It would be only about a twenty-minute ride as it was about 7 miles to town.

"Admiral, Bruce Gordon and I have been confirming the Navy's responsibilities for the christening and it looks like we have everything covered at this time. Frank Hawks declined with regrets our invitation as well as Jimmie Doolittle. Major Doolittle is tied up prepping his plane for the Cleveland Air Races. Mrs. Hoover's facilities are complete. The company had to build a platform where her railcar will be parked as they previously had none. We have four limos reserved for her and will be available for her use. It looks like we are in good shape for Saturday," Walt said.

"That is great to hear, Lieutenant. There is good news from Washington. The pending cancellation order for ZRS5 has been rescinded and we are a go for construction of ZRS5. That was just decided as I was leaving Washington, so no one here is aware of that news. You may tell others as you see fit."

"Yes, Sir, that's great news. I will tell the Navy detachment they will be here a lot longer," Walt noted.

They arrived at the Portage Hotel. The driver took care of the Admiral's luggage while Walt asked the driver of the other sedan to wait for him.

Walt accompanied the Admiral into the hotel, and once he was off to his room, Walt left the hotel, and climbed into the waiting sedan and returned to the airship Hangar. He burst into Bruce's office with a big smile on his face.

Bruce saw him and said, "Why the big grin, Walt?" "You better sit down for this one," Walt directed.

"What the hell is so important that I need to sit down?" Bruce asked.

"I just heard from the Admiral that the cancellation order for ZRS5 has been rescinded, which means you guys will be here for a lot longer than you thought," Walt said.

"That's great news, Walt. My guys like it here. Beats a destroyer at sea anytime," Bruce replied.

"I've got to tell the rest of the crew about this. I'll be back in a few minutes Walt."

Bruce took off to spread the word. Walt went back to working on arrangements for Saturday.

Thursday, Akron, Ohio

Walt and Bruce arrived early at the Hangar. They had planned a meeting of all major players in Saturday's christening. It was scheduled for ten o'clock. At 9:45 a.m. they both walked over to the attached classroom where Bruce set up the lectern with all his notes ready to brief the attendees. People were already streaming into the classroom. Lieutenant Commander Rosendahl was one of the last to arrive. He spotted Walt and walked upfront.

"Lieutenant Pellman, it's great to see you once again," he said.

"Great to see you, Sir. I guess it's been quite a while since we last met. Pensacola, over dinner at Captain McDonald's quarters, I believe," Walt said.

"Admiral McMillin's aide is a real change of pace," Rosendahl said.

"Thank you, Sir. Yes, it is quite a change from just flying airplanes. Congratulation on your new command Sir. I know you are excited about getting it underway," Walt noted. "Why don't you take a seat up front, Sir."

Lieutenant Commander Rosendahl took a seat and Bruce Gordon began his presentation. He went through the planned day on Saturday, step by step, ending with the slacking of the lines holding down the Akron just enough to raise it off the deck and signify the ceremony was finished and the Akron had been launched. The presentation was quite detailed and thorough. Bruce asked if there were any questions. One Akron officer asked if any tours of the airship would be allowed. Bruce indicated that only Mrs. Hoover would be allowed and presently she had not asked for a tour. Bruce adjourned the meeting and Walt walked out with Lieutenant Commander Rosendahl. They were having an animated discussion which continued out onto the Hangar deck.

Walt talked with the flight line crew and told them to expect the Sparrowhawk after lunch and to send Lieutenant Harrison into Lieutenant Gordon's office when he was all finished getting his plane settled.

Bruce and Walt had BBQ again for lunch and were now back in the office. Bruce had booked a room at Mazie's for Lieutenant Harrison for three nights, so everything was all set for his arrival.

At about 1:30p.m. Duane walked into Bruce's office. Walt espied him first and walked out to the outer office.

"Hey Duane, 'bout time you got here," Walt said. He shook Duane's hand, "Great to see you again."

"Yeah, Walt, great to be here," Duane said.

"How was the flight?" Walt asked.

"It was good. The weather was beautiful. I got delayed a little. I had to stop for gas in Altoona and their fuel system was intermittent so it took a little longer to pump gas into the airplane," Duane said. "I walked around the Akron getting to Bruce's office. That is one big mother."

"We'll take a tour in it tomorrow morning. Right now, we are securing for the day and getting you settled down at Mazie's," Walt said

The three of them walked out to Bruce's car and piled in.

"The Christening"

26

Akron, Ohio-Friday

Today was going to be a busy day for all hands. Bruce Gordon was completing some details and checking that minor glitches were fixed. He was coordinating the seating of Akron's crew as they would be the guests of honor. Walt was checking with the Baltimore and Ohio Railroad trying to determine the arrival time of Mrs. Hoover. He would have to meet with her staff and fill them in on some minor details of Friday's and Saturday's festivities. When he felt he had everything under control, he and Duane walked onto the Hangar deck and over to the Akron. He wanted Duane to get a feel for the airship they would soon be hooking up to.

As they boarded Akron, they ran into Lieutenant (JG) Torri Hudson.

"Good morning, Mr. Hudson. We were looking for someone who could give Lieutenant Harrison a tour of the airship," Walt asked.

"Sir, I have some time right now and I can do that," Torri said.

"Great, I'll leave him in your hands. Thank you," Walt said. "Duane, I need to go back to the office and check on a few things. I'll meet you there when you're finished."

"Okay, Walt. See you in a little bit," Duane answered.

Walt stepped down from the airship onto the Hangar deck. He looked around at the activity going on and was in awe at what he saw. It was like a bunch of ants searching for food. Banners were being raised all over the Hangar. Tables were being set up in the southwest end of the Hangar, while up near the Hangar doors of the northwest end, bleachers were being erected for the five high school bands who would play the next day. A VIP dais was being built for the speakers who would conduct the ceremony.

The airship workers were finishing the final touches needed to float the airship. Helium was being topped off for that purpose.

After arriving back at Bruce's office, Walt needed to check on the Admiral's schedule for today and the status of Amelia Earhart's arrival in Akron. He decided to call the airport tower, in West Lafayette. In discussion with the personnel manning the tower, he determined that Amelia had filed a flight plan for Akron and was about to depart. Her estimated time enroute was 3 hours 12 minutes. It was now 10:25 a.m which should put her in Akron at about 1:40 p.m.

The Admiral would be having a luncheon with the American Legion, then an afternoon meeting with the CEO of Goodyear-Zeppelin Corporation. They were scheduled to arrive together at the Hangar for the banquet at 5:45 p.m. with dinner to start at 6:00 p.m. sharp.

Walt then received a call from the Baltimore and Ohio Railroad dispatcher who estimated Mrs. Hoover's arrival at the company siding around 1:30 p.m. This development called for a quick change as to who would meet Amelia Earhart when she arrived as he had to meet the Hoover train. About that time Duane walked into the office and a light went on in Walt's brain.

"Hey, Duane. How was the tour of the Akron?" he asked.

"It was great. What a beautiful ship she is. I can hardly wait to make some hookups and take a cruise on her," Duane said.

"I felt the same way when I first toured her, but right now I have a task for you to perform. It's a tough job, but I am sure you will be able to handle it," Walt said with a slight smile.

"You know me, I can handle tough jobs. What is it?" Duane asked. "Here it is. Are you sure you will be able to handle it?" Walt teased. "Yeah, yeah, what is this tough job?" Duane asked once again.

"Okay, here it is. Amelia Earhart will be arriving at around 1:40 p.m. and you need to meet and escort her while she is here," Walt said.

Duane broke out into a huge smile. "That's going to be the toughest job I've had in the Navy, Walt, but I think I can handle it." Inside he was thinking *"I'm going to meet and escort the greatest lady flyer of our decade. Holy shit!"*

"Great Buddy. They will be parking her over on the southeast corner of the Hangar right near where the Sparrowhawk is parked. I was supposed to escort her, but Mrs. Hoover's train will be arriving around the same time so now it is up to you to maintain the reputation of all Naval Aviators," Walt said "I promise I will uphold that reputation," Duane responded.

"She may want to get some lunch. You can take her either to the BBQ joint out past Mazie's or the dining room at the Portage Hotel where she will be staying. Just play it by ear. Also, ask her about pickup time for the banquet which starts serving at 6:00 p.m. here in the Hangar. Just keep the staff car so it's available to you, but make sure the driver gets lunch and dinner if needed," Walt said. "Anything else you can think of?"

"No, I think you covered everything," Duane said.

The three of them decided they would go to lunch early to be back in time to get to their various activities and responsibilities. Bruce had a meeting in town at 1:30 p.m. while Walt and Duane were engaged with their tasks about the same time.

A couple of staff cars pulled up to the southeast door of the Hangar. Walt left in one at about 1:00 p.m. Duane stood by in the Line shack awaiting the arrival of Amelia Earhart in her Kinner Sportster.

Walt reached the railroad siding at 1:25 p.m. There were already several Baltimore & Ohio Railroad employees on scene. They had doublechecked the track, platform, switches, and reported to Walt that everything was in order. At 1:35p.m. Admiral McMillin and Adolph Schmidt arrived unexpectedly.

Walt saluted. "Good afternoon, Admiral."

The Admiral returned the salute. "Good afternoon, Lieutenant. How is your day going?"

"Everything is progressing fine, Sir. Mrs. Hoover's train is scheduled to arrive around 1:42p.m." Turning to Mr. Schmidt, "Good afternoon, Sir. Great to see you again," Walt said.

"Great to see you again, Lieutenant," Adolph Schmidt responded. "We've been looking forward to this day for a few months. Hope all goes well."

"I believe everything is under control and will come off just fine," Walt answered.

About that time the train was in sight and would be on the siding momentarily. The Railroad crew switched the train onto the siding. The large steam engine backed the cars onto the siding and stopped in the exact spot it needed to be. The engine decoupled from the cars and moved down the track. Meanwhile, the railroad crew attached electricity to the rail cars.

Everyone in the greeting party moved up on the platform. Mrs. Hoover's Chief-of-Staff stepped out and greeted everyone and invited them into the parlor car to meet with Mrs. Hoover.

Walt passed on the details of activities for Friday and Saturday to the Chief of Staff. He indicated to the Admiral he was going to depart. The Admiral nodded his approval and Walt left for the Hangar. As he approached the Hangar, he spotted the Kinner Sportster parked next to the Sparrowhawk, so he knew Amelia Earhart had arrived. He also noted that the workers had finished spreading the ashes on the grass to help keep the mud down.

When Bruce returned, Walt told him he was going back to Mazie's and take a bath and change into his fresh uniform. He was all hot and sweaty and his shirt was such it did not meet his standard of a neat dress uniform. He needed to look his best at the banquet.

Walt took a staff car to Mazie's. He undressed in his room, threw on his bathrobe, and headed for the bathroom. He drew his bathwater but didn't make it too warm. He wanted to cool off some from the hot humid weather. Temperature at the time was 87°F and humidity at 90%. He just soaked in the bath for a while, and after he had cooled down some, he soaped and rinsed. He finished drying himself and walked back to his room. He stretched out in his underwear on his bed. It was really relaxing, and he could have taken a nap, but he knew that was not an option, so he just relaxed for about an hour. He knew it was time to get dressed so he put on his fresh dress khaki uniform but carried his blouse which he would put on when he arrived at the Hangar.

After arriving at the Hangar, he walked over to Bruce's office. Everyone had secured for the day, so he went in, turned on the fans, and sat down for a few minutes. At 5:15 p.m. he put on his blouse and walked out on the Hangar deck. People had started to arrive and were taking their seats for the banquet. Some seats were reserved while others were open seating. The largest group to arrive was the crew of the Akron. The enlisted crew looked really sharp in their dress whites while their officers were adorned in the dress khakis. They were all seated at the tables in front of the dais. The hanger was soon swarming with guests. Walt took a position on the end of the dais where he could greet people as they arrived. There were 40 VIP seats on the dais. He had added a seat for Duane Harrison so he could sit next to Amelia Earhart. Walt would sit on the other side so they could both talk with her during dinner. At 5:50 p.m. the Admiral arrived. He made his way to the dais where Walt took up a position next to him. They stood and chatted awaiting other VIPs. Adolph Schmidt was next to arrive with his wife followed shortly by the Mayor of Akron and his wife. Lieutenant Commander Rosendahl had arrived with his crew, and he made his way to the dais. John Glenn, the local Congressman, arrived just before the guest of honor Mrs. Hoover. Everyone made their way to their seats and the Admiral took to the microphone. He welcomed everyone and called on the preacher from the local Methodist church to give the blessing for the food. Everyone stood silently and bowed their head while the preacher gave the blessing. The Admiral told everyone to take their seats. This was followed by the food being served.

During dinner, Walt and Duane were kept busy answering and asking questions of Amelia. They were all enjoying themselves. When dinner was over, the festivities began. The Admiral, acting as master of ceremonies, started by welcoming everyone to this extraordinary celebration, and he introduced the guest of honor, the First Lady, Mrs Hoover. She gave a stirring speech, telling the Akron's crew of their place in the history of the U.S. Navy. She acknowledged the Goodyear-Zeppelin Corporation for its ability to design and build such a beautiful airship. Finally, she thanked the City of Akron for hosting this event and that she was pleased to have been invited to attend. The Admiral then introduced each VIP who stood and gave a short speech. Speeches were mostly directed at the historic importance of the day and the place in history the USS Akron would take when launched.

Saturday, Akron, Ohio

Walt was awake by 7:00 a.m. He along with Bruce and Duane, had decided they didn't have much to do before 11 o'clock so they slept late and would get to the Hangar about 9:00 a.m. Walt changed his hard hat cover from Khaki to white in anticipation of wearing his choker-neck white uniform for the ceremony. He put his metallic gold wings on his blouse along with his shoulder boards, attached his gold buttons and placed his aiguillettes on his left shoulder. The uniform was already on a hanger, so he covered it with a cloth travel bag. He went down for breakfast where he met Duane and Bruce. After breakfast, he went back to his room, grabbed the travel bag, hard hat, and shoes, and headed back downstairs. He had decided to wear civilian clothes this morning and change into his uniform after lunch. Bruce and Duane had elected to do the same.

Duane drove his staff car to the Hangar, and Bruce and Walt went in Bruce's staff car. When they arrived, the workmen were putting the finishing touches on the area for the ceremony. There were chairs and benches in the Hangar as well as out on the grass. They discovered that people had been arriving since early morning and the parking area was already filling up. The roads were clogged bumper to bumper with people coming from Akron, Toledo, Cleveland, Erie, Columbus, as well as Pittsburgh. A quarter of a million people were expected to witness the ceremony. The Hangar doors had been opened, which allowed the sun to shine into the Hangar.

A company blimp was already circling the airport with Sam Williams, the chief of police on board, directing traffic. Mayor Wiel had declared the day a holiday and there had been dances as well as movies honoring the upcoming christening. The National Guard, American Legion, and Boy Scouts were recruited to assist the police in the parking.

Duane was concerned about getting Amelia Earhart to the ceremony because of the traffic blocking the roads. Walt called the sheriff's office and explained the situation. It was decided to send Duane in a sheriff's car to pick up Amelia. Duane changed into his uniform and was off to the Portage Hotel. It took about 40 minutes to make the round trip. Amelia and Duane arrived, and they were directed into Bruce's office where it wasn't so hectic.

Someone had thoughtfully brought them some baloney and cheese sandwiches for lunch, and they had placed an icebox in the outer office filled with Nehi soda, so everyone at least had a little bit to eat and drink.

Outside the airshow had begun. Lieutenant Colonel Hap Arnold and his fighters from Wright Field had made a couple of low passes, in formation, over the field followed by Major Brett and his 36 fighters from Selfridge Field who did the same. Right now, the Navy fighters and scout planes from the Langley contingency were doing acrobatics. Walt would have liked to see them, but he knew Bob and Paul were doing them in formation since they had done them with Walt during flight training. The final act was a couple of air racers from Cleveland making a few high-speed, low pass over the runway.

After their show, the Navy fighters and Scout planes landed and were parked on the off-duty runway. Bob and Paul secured their planes and then walked over to the Hangar. It took them a little while until they finally found someone who knew where Lieutenant Pellman could be found. They made their way through the ever-increasing crowd to Bruce's office, walked in and there was Walt.

"Hey, Buddy, we made it," Paul said.

"Hey, you guys. So glad to see you. Come on over and meet the people," Walt said. "Hey everyone, these are my two best friends. I want you to meet Bob Fitzwater and Paul Day. Please introduce yourselves."

Bruce, Duane, and Amelia came over and introduced themselves. Bob and Paul were blown away meeting America's greatest woman aviator. Of course, they ignored Walt and hovered around Amelia asking her questions as well as answering her questions about their careers and what squadron they were flying with.

It was approaching the two o'clock hour when the ceremony would start so they moved out onto the Hangar deck once more to find their seats.

There were five high school bands from Akron high schools taking turns entertaining the crowd while challenging the bad acoustics of the large Hangar. As Mrs. Hoover and the official party took the podium under the bow of the dirigible, Rosendahl and his crew fell into formation in front of the control car. At 2 o'clock the bands joined together and played "Anchors Aweigh." Paul Litchfield took to the podium. As the first speaker, he paid tribute to the pioneers of Lighter-Than-Air as Lansdowne, Scott, and Maxfield. When he finished his remarks, he introduced Admiral McMillin.

The Admiral thanked Mrs. Hoover and the crowd for attending, providing evidence the Lighter-Than-Air had now become part of the aviation community. He hoped this airship would provide incentives for the development of a commercial fleet of dirigibles carrying freight and passengers around the world. As his words faded, Mrs. Hoover picked up the microphone and said, "I christen thee Akron!" She reached above her and pulled the red, white, and blue cord, which opened the nose compartment of the Akron and released the 48 racing pigeons. Simultaneously the combined bands struck up the Star-Spangled Banner as workmen slacked off the airship's tethering cables and floated the Akron, completing her "launching."

There were cheers and applause from everyone present. The crowd was both pleased and proud of their new airship.

Within a short period of time, people walked through the Hangar just trying to see or take a photo of the new dirigible, after which the crowd began to disperse.

As soon as things quieted down and the area between the Hangar and the runway was clear, Amelia Earhart, in her flying gear, climbed into her Kinner Sportster and departed for West Lafayette, Indiana. Duane, Bob, Paul, and Walt were there to see her off and thanked her for coming. She was pleased to meet all of them, and she told them she had a great time just hanging out with a bunch of Naval Aviators like them.

Bruce, Walt and Duane were not responsible for the cleanup and rearranging of things. They were joined by Bob and Paul and went back to Mazie's and changed clothes. They decided to have dinner at Mazie's, and after dinner, Walt, Bob, Paul, and Duane went out on the porch to relax after a busy day.

Bruce was already there so they continued their relaxing conversation. They all felt the ceremony went very well and pretty much without a glitch.

"How did your part of the air show go, Bob?" Walt asked.

"I thought it went pretty well," Bob said. "Paul and I joined up in formation and gave the crowd a couple of loops, Immelmann turns, and a minimum radius turn inside the airport boundaries. Then we made a low pass, pulled straight up, and Paul broke east and I pulled over west. We made opposing low passes a couple of times then did opposing barrel rolls finishing with opposing aileron rolls. Then we joined up in formation with two other fighters and made a low pass in parade formation with our hooks down, then broke over the duty runway for landing. I thought it was a good show."

"Sounds like you guys did great," Duane said. "What kind of training have you guys been doing back in Norfolk?"

"We've been out to Langley for carrier quals a couple of times," Paul said. "Got our traps to over twenty now. We have done some gunnery and bombing. We also did some strafing of trucks and things over on Wallops Island. Our next cycle is going to include fighter tactics."

"Wow, sounds like you guys are learning everything," Duane noted.

"Yeah, we should be well-rounded fighter pilots except for a little combat," Bob answered. "What are you into Duane?"

"I'm O-in-C of the Heavier-Than-Air unit flying off the dirigibles. We are just starting to build up the unit. Walt and I are choosing the pilots in the next few months," Duane said.

"That sounds like it is going to be interesting and delicate work," Paul observed.

"Yeah, it is, Paul, and a lot easier than carrier landings. Walt and I made some hookups to the Los Angeles earlier in the spring and we had a ball," Duane said.

"Yeah, Duane and I made 12 hookups in about an hour and a half. We had a great time," Walt chimed in.

Bob stood up, "I'm really beat, and we have to muster a 7:30 a.m. tomorrow morning then fly back to Norfolk. I'm going to bed." Paul joined Bob.

"We'll see you guys about 6:30 a.m. for breakfast. Somebody will give you a ride to the airport," Walt said. "Goodnight, guys."

Walt and Duane remained on the porch for a little bit. Walt indicated they needed to discuss some business before they parted ways. He presented his plan for them to fill the pilot positions in the Heavier-Than- Air Unit. Walt would have an ALLNAV sent out to all aviation commands within the Navy and invite qualified Naval Aviators to volunteer. Both Duane and Walt would be on the contact list and would receive applications of volunteers. They both would review the applications, and each make recommendations to the other, with Duane having the final say in who was selected as he was the Officer-in-Charge of the unit. They set the final figure at 6 including Duane. As for enlisted manning, they came up with 18 enlisted billets. All this was based on a 10-plane inventory, five F9C-2s, and five N2Y-1s. The Vought UO-1 was excess and would probably be transferred to another command. As soon as the trapeze was delivered to Lakehurst, Walt would begin to have the pilots transferred to Lakehurst. With all that settled, Walt and Duane said goodnight and went to bed.

27

"Time For a Breather"

Sunday, Akron, Ohio

The guys all met for breakfast and afterward, Bruce said he would take Bob and Paul to the airport since he needed to go to the office for a little bit. Bob and Paul donned their flying gear, piled into Bruce's car and headed to the airport.

It was a quiet Sunday morning and Duane was not scheduled to return to Lakehurst until Monday, so he and Walt and he decided to take a trip up to Cleveland for the day to see the airfield and the preparations going on for the National Air Races. Walt wanted to drive his new sports car since it had been sitting covered up for over a week.

After breakfast, they pulled off the tarp, folded it, and placed it behind the front seat, and climbed in.

"Where did you get this baby, Walt?" Duane asked.

"My old man decided I needed a new car, so he had this one delivered to me two weeks ago," Walt answered.

"Damn, I really like it. It is beautiful," Duane said.

"Yeah, I really like the white paint job," Walt said. "Reach in the glove box, Duane. There is a road map of Ohio, and you can do the navigating".

"You gonna' need gas for this thing?" Duane asked.

"No, I tanked up when I got here so we have enough for the trip," Walt said.

Duane got out the map and they drove through Akron and joined Federal Highway 21 which took them into Cleveland. The trip took about an hour and fifty minutes. They proceeded to the waterfront to find the waterfront airport. The wasn't much flying going on, but a couple of

Hangars had their doors open so Walt parked the car and the two of them walked into the Hangar. There were a couple of civilians working on an aircraft that appeared to be an unknown airplane to Walt and Duane.

Walt asked one of the people working on the aircraft.

"What is the designation of this airplane? "This airplane is known as a Laird Super Solution," the man said as he stepped down from the work stand. "I'm Jimmie Doolittle."

"I'm Lieutenant Walt Pellman, Major. Sorry I didn't recognize you. This is Lieutenant Duane Harrison," Walt said as they both shook Jimmie's hand.

"Glad to meet you," Jimmie said. "I recognize your names. You're the two hotshot Navy pilots working on the USS Akron project."

"Yes, Sir, and we missed you on the christening yesterday in Akron," Walt said.

"Yeah, I hated to miss that, but I need to get this plane ready to go. I'm leaving tomorrow for the West Coast. The Bendix race starts in a week, so I have to be ready," Jimmie said.

"Sir, we understand completely, and I know the Admiral did also, although he was disappointed you couldn't make it," Walt said.

"If you are looking to see some of the other racers, I think there is only one Lockheed Orion left here that hasn't yet gone to the West Coast." Jimmie offered.

"Thanks for stopping to talk with us, Sir," Walt said as he and Duane shook hands with Jimmie then left the Hangar.

They drove off and headed downtown. They figured they might as well see the city if they were there. Their route took them along the waterfront. Lake Erie was loaded with ships plying their trade on the Great Lakes. There were many iron ore ships headed for Ashtabula and the steel plant while the grain ships were docking in Cleveland and off-loading into the grain elevators to be transferred to General Mills and made into flour.

They came into the Italian neighborhood of Cleveland and saw a delicatessen open. They stopped, hoping they might be able to get lunch. They checked the menu board as they entered and sure enough the special for the day was a Rueben Sandwich. They each ordered one and a soft drink. There were tables outside for eating. They occupied one and had their lunch.

After lunch, they drove through the city center and admired the beautiful buildings under construction. It was great the city was putting people back to work during this terrible depression.

They headed back down Route 31 to Akron. Back at Mazie's, they relaxed on the porch and discussed all facets of what was planned for their future in Naval Aviation. It lasted several hours and soon it was time for supper. Mazie had a great supper. Of fresh caught Walleye with mashed potatoes and fresh-picked corn on the cob. Dessert was some plain chocolate pudding. The dinner was great.

Once again Duane and Walt sat out on the porch until the mosquitos drove them inside. On the radio in the sitting room, they listened to Lowell Thomas followed by J.V. Kaltenborn. After that, Amos and Andy came on followed by Eddie Cantor, then Guy Lombardo did his thing coming in on CBS from the Roosevelt Hotel in New York City.

It was almost 11 o'clock when they decided to call it a night. Duane was departing about mid-morning, so they didn't have to rise very early.

Monday, Akron, Ohio

Walt got Duane off in good time. He would be in Lakehurst by 2 o'clock. He then went into the Hangar to talk with Bruce. He was busy in the plant, so Walt called the Airport Tower to see if they had a flight plan on the Trimotor coming in to pick up the Admiral and his party. Their estimated time of arrival was 1 o'clock. Walt then called the Portage Hotel where the Admiral and his party were staying. The Admiral answered the phone and Walt advised him of the ETA of the Trimotor and asked him what time he would like to depart the hotel. The Admiral said 1:30 p.m. was early enough. A 2 o'clock departure would put them at Anacostia by 5:30 p.m. He hung up the phone, dialed the motor pool and checked on the two staff cars which would transport the Admiral's party to the Hangar.

Having finished all his required work, Walt waited for Bruce to show up and they could go to lunch. As they drove back to Mazie's for lunch, Walt said, "Bruce, now that we have Akron christened, I guess the next step will be the first flight. I will need you to send me a daily status report with past 24-hour activity and when the first flight is imminent. I know the Admiral will be on my case to give him a daily briefing on the Akron."

"I can do that," Bruce replied.

"Also, the Admiral is scheduled to depart at 2 o'clock. I need to go down to the Portage Hotel to pick him up at 1:30 p.m. and escort him to the airport. Why don't you plan on meeting us at the plane and be there for his departure?" Walt said. "You might check to see if Lieutenant Commander Rosendahl is available as he should probably be there too to see the Admiral off."

After lunch, Walt took a staff car and headed for the Portage Hotel. On arrival, he went up to the Admiral's room, accompanied by two bellhops. He knocked on the Admiral's door and was invited in. He greeted the Admiral and asked if his luggage was ready for transport. It was and the bellhops gathered the luggage and carried it down to the lobby via the elevator. The front desk called the room and advised Walt that the staff cars had arrived. He returned and advised the Admiral they were ready to depart for the airport, whenever he was ready.

Walt and the Admiral went down to the lobby and the others in the Admiral's party were there waiting. Walt approached Lieutenant Commander Charlie Fuller and asked him if he would mind driving his staff car to the airport. That way he could ride with the Admiral. Charlie was amenable to that arrangement.

All-hands boarded the staff cars with the Admiral boarding last. During the drive to the airport, Walt and the Admiral discussed each of their schedules for the next two days. The Admiral indicated he was taking Tuesday and Wednesday off while Walt said he was driving back to Washington, D.C. on Tuesday and would also take Wednesday off. They agreed they would meet once again in the office on Thursday.

As they arrived at the airport, Walt could see that the Trimotor had arrived and now appeared to be ready for departure. There was a welcoming party consisting of Lieutenant Commander Rosendahl, Lieutenant Bruce Gordon, and the Trimotor Pilot in command. The enlisted flight crew was standing by to handle the luggage.

On arrival, the Admiral talked with Rosendahl for a couple of minutes while the luggage was being loaded and other passengers were boarding the aircraft. As soon as those tasks were complete, the Admiral boarded the aircraft. Engines started, and the Trimotor was off for Washington.

Walt thanked Lieutenant Commander Rosendahl for coming and told Bruce Gordon he would meet him in his office. He returned his staff car to the motor pool and was then driven back to the Hangar. He and Bruce spent some time discussing the post-ceremony details of the christening. They decided which letters the Admiral needed to sign thanking certain participants and which letters Bruce could handle. Bruce gave Walt the list for the Admiral and a rough letter. It approached time to secure for the day. Walt and Bruce climbed into Bruce's staff car and headed back to Mazie's for dinner.

Tuesday Morning

Walt uncovered his car, loaded his luggage, and headed for Washington, D.C. After passing Pittsburg, rain was in the forecast so he pulled over onto a driveway to a farm and put up the top on his convertible. Sure enough it started to rain once he was backon the rode. It was a warm gentle summer shower which was scattered to isolated. As he approached Hagerstown, Maryland, the showers stopped, and the weather was scattered clouds. He entered Gaithersburg just as the sun passed down behind the Blue Ridge Mountains. He turned on his headlights and continued into Washington. The roads were almost deserted and he made good time.

He arrived at his quarters at the Washington Navy Yard and settled in for the night. In the morning he went down to the dining room for breakfast. After breakfast, he went back to his suite and wrote some letters. His letter to Zimmy was mostly apologetic since he had neglected her for some time because of his busy schedule. He promised her they would get together in person soon. He also told her how much he missed her. His next letter was to his Mom and Dad, mostly telling them about the christening of the Akron and how much he enjoyed driving his new car there and back. Thanks, Dad he wrote.

Having finished his letter writing, he headed off to the Smithsonian Castle to look at the exhibits. Afterward, he walked over to the Washington Monument and climbed the stairway to the top. The view was spectacular of the city where many new buildings were going up. Time was approaching dinner time, so he went back to the Navy Yard and had dinner in the Mess. Afterward he went back to his quarters and just relaxed. He had all his windows open and a floor fan going to try to move the air around and maybe cool off a bit. August in Washington was hot and humid. Today's temperature had been a high of 95°F and it was still 90°F going on 10:00

p.m. He stripped down to his underwear and stretched out on top of the sheets and turned the fan in his direction to try to cool off. He was beat and now that the stress of the Akron christening was over and done, he slipped into a deep sleep.

He was awakened by the sound of rain beating down on the side of the building and some thunder in the distance. He arose and glanced out of his window towards the southwest. Sure, enough he could see some thunderstorms moving in his direction with lightning hitting the ground. He put on his dress khakis and went down for breakfast. After breakfast, he went back and picked up his raincoat as it was still thundering and lightning with medium to heavy rain. In the lobby, he picked up the phone and dialed the office. Gloria picked up.

"Good morning," she said. "Admiral McMillin's office. Gloria speaking. May I help you?"

"Gloria, this is Walt, I'm over here at my quarters and I think I may wait until this storm blows over before I try to walk over to the office. Is the Admiral in yet?" he asked.

"Oh, Walt, good morning. No, the Admiral is not in yet. Why don't I send the staff car over to the BOQ to pick you up?" Gloria said.

"If that's not too much trouble, that would be great. Thanks, Gloria. I'll be out front out of the rain waiting for the staff car," Walt said.

"It's on its way. See you in a few minutes," Gloria responded.

Walt hung up his phone and headed down to the lobby to await his transportation.

The staff car arrived and drove under the canopy in front of the BOQ so he didn't get wet. They drove over to headquarters and Walt entered and went to the office.

"Thanks, Gloria, for helping me keep dry," Walt said.

"Glad to help. I left the message board on your desk along with a couple of telephone calls," Gloria said.

Walt started reading the messages. The first one of any importance was from Bruce Gordon. In it, Bruce laid out the series of tests the Akron needed to be put through before she would be certified to fly. These tests included general and overloading's, hogging and sagging, a strength test of the bridge across the airplane compartment, and ground testing of the elevator and rudder. It also included testing many of the internal systems and controls.

Bruce, along with his assistant and a Goodyear-Zeppelin engineer, took on the task of training 250 civilians to act as a ground crew for the Akron.

The second message concerned the status of the USS Saratoga. She was estimated to be back in service about September 10th. The Chief of Naval Operations directed that she proceed directly back to her home port on the West Coast via the Panama Canal.

Walt thought, *"The Admiral will be pleased to hear that."*

The remaining message traffic was of little importance since it didn't require his attention.

Walt then checked his phone messages. There were a couple from John Becker, so he picked up the phone and dialed John's number.

"Flight Test, Lieutenant Commander Becker."

"John, Walt Pellman here returning your call."

"Hey Walt, just wondering when you might be available to give us a hand here. We have a couple of certification tests on our new fighter which needs to be done and we're receiving a new prototype from Vought which we are going to put through the paces," John said.

"I should be available next week, John. I just need to clean up a few items from the christening of the USS Akron and I'll be ready to lend you a hand," Walt said.

"That will be great, Walt. You know me, I just like to try to keep ahead of these acceptance tests we are charged with doing. By the way, how was the christening?" John asked.

"The christening went off without a hitch, but we're still a way off before the first flight. Had a great time, however. Met Amelia Earhart and Jimmie Doolittle," Walt said.

"Sounds like pretty good duty for a Lieutenant," John noted.

"Yeah, it was a great week. Anyway, I'll let you know my availability for next week by Friday so you can adjust your schedule. I'll give you a call Friday," Walt said as he hung up the phone.

Walt turned to write his reports and briefing notes for the Admiral when he returned to the office.

28

"First Flight"

Washington D.C.

The next three weeks were filled with all kinds of exciting situations. Some good and some bad. In Akron, the testing was going smoothly. The nation was excited by the christening to have the Akron fly. They could hardly wait for the first flight and could not understand the testing requirements holding this action up. As the days became weeks and now extended for three weeks, the media began to grumble. Goodyear- Zeppelin Corporation only added to the media's frustration by announcing a delay in the first flight because of strains caused by the testing required building more localized strength into the Akron.

Media and public impatience only added to the old rumor that Akron was flawed and in trouble of never flying. More frustration was exhibited on August 26th, Winds were favorable, and Bruce Gordon put the ground crew through a dress rehearsal by opening the large Hangar doors and moving Akron in and out of the Hangar. The nation was wondering why didn't the Akron fly.

Labor Day provided a macabre illustration of this strange attitude of the public toward Akron. Lieutenant Commander Rosendahl and his crew were guests of the Air races in Cleveland. During the races, he was called over the public address system that he had a phone call. He was notified that Lieutenant Feldman, the designated ground handling officer of the Akron, was injured in a crash of his glider. The media received word of his phone call and the crash, and of course, it came out in the papers and radio that the Akron had crashed.

Walt was having a hard time keeping up with all the various happenings concerning the Akron, but somehow, he managed to keep the Admiral briefed, and fortunately, the Admiral took all these things in stride and didn't let them put this off track to get the Akron flying and operational.

Lieutenant Scotty Peck was recruited from Lakehurst to replace Lieutenant Feldman as ground handling officer for Akron. He had been one of the early qualified as a Lighter-Than-Air pilot. Lieutenant Commander Marc Miller had strong-armed him into Heavier-Than-Air training, so he was one of the few airship pilots who was dual qualified. During this evolution of Akron, he was the designated navigator.

It was now well into September and Bruce Gordon advised Walt that the inaugural flight of the Akron was at hand. He promised he would keep him advised of the exact date, as far in advance as was humanly possible. Walt had advised Bruce that SECNAV, his assistant, Admiral McMillin, and the Board of Inspection and Survey would be present as passengers on the first flight and probably others as determined to be necessary. This would be a logistical nightmare for Walt as transportation would need to be on standby for all these dignitaries to travel to Akron at a moment's notice. He coordinated with SECNAV's office. They agreed Admiral McMillin would travel with SECNAV's party and the Board of Inspection would handle their transportation.

On September 16th the call from Bruce Gordon finally came. Akron was scheduled to make her first flight on the 21st. SECNAV's office scheduled transportation departing from Anacostia at 9 o'clock on the morning of September 20th. Walt advised Admiral McMillin of the travel plans and planned for ground travel for them to arrive at Anacostia at 8:45 a.m. The flight to Akron was uneventful and Walt got the Admiral settled into his suite at the Portage Hotel. Walt wanted to stay at Mazie's, but it turned out to be more convenient for him to stay at the Portage.

Early on the 21st, the decision was made to reschedule the flight for the 22nd because of low clouds, rain, and high winds. Walt spent his time with Bruce Gordon while the Admiral was preoccupied with SEC-NAV. They spent most of their time with Adolph Schmidt, CEO of the Goodyear-Zeppelin Corporation.

The 23rd dawned and Lieutenant Commander Rosendahl and his meteorologist checked the weather. Winds were down and the rain was predicted to end sometime around noon. Sure enough, around noon conditions for launch were within limits. Lieutenant Commander Rosendahl ordered the Executive Officer to man the ship and prepare for flight.

The large Hangar doors were rolled back and Lieutenant Scotty Peck ordered his ground handling crew into position. The airship was pushed out on her tailwheel and portable nose mast. The ground crew manned their lines to restrain and steady the airship and helped guide it out onto the launch circle. The picture appeared that the Lilliputians had captured this big airship. Scotty Peck gave the command to slack the lines and the Akron was allowed to swing around into the 4-knot wind. The guests for the flight boarded, and after checking the balance of the ship, Lieutenant Commander Rosendahl gave the command, "Up ship". The Akron was released from her mast and tail wheel and was airborne. Her engines roared to life and she was on her way for her first flight. Cheers echoed from the 200,000 people who had gathered to witness the first flight. A 21-gun salute was fired by the Ohio National Guard. Rosendahl circled the field and headed for downtown Akron. He passed over the hospital whose roof was crowded with many staff people wanting to see the Akron flying. Rosendahl dropped a note for Lieutenant Feldman who unfortunately was bedridden in 20 pounds of plaster of Paris. He next headed toward Cleveland while checking out the systems of the huge airship. On the ground there was chaos. Cars were stopping right where they were and drivers getting out just to see the Akron as she flew by. Traffic jams were the norm. Passing Cleveland, Rosendahl headed for Pittsburgh then back to Akron. Docking was normal and the airship was rolled back into her Hangar.

Walt and Bruce Gordon greeted the VIPs as they debarked from Akron. The comments from SECNAV and Admiral McMillin were nothing but high praise for the performance of the Airship and crew.

Washington, D.C.

The next month was hectic for Walt. Bruce was great in keeping him up to date on Akron's activities. Akron made a series of local flights, checking out systems and training the crew. On the 18th of October, she took a long cross-country flight down the Ohio River to St. Louis then up to Chicago/Milwaukie area, and back to Akron a distance of 2000 nautical miles. It involved flying at night, which in and of itself could sometimes be a hairy experience. It was a great success when compared to the performance of the Ford Trimotor which could do 500 miles at best.

On October 21st, Akron launched from the airship Hangar for the last time and headed for Pittsburgh, then on to her permanent home, Lakehurst, New Jersey. When she arrived, she experienced the new ground handling system, which was mechanical versus human. There was a huge tractor for the forward mast and a two-wheeled trailer for the tail. The airship approached the landing circle, headed into the wind. Its nose cable was attached to the mast and reeled in, making the nose tight to the mast. The trailer was attached to the tail fin of the airship. The trailer was then rolled along the rails of the landing circle until the airship was aligned with the axis of the Hangar, then rolled into the Hangar alongside the USS Los Angeles. The doors were closed, and Akron was home.

Washington D.C.

Walt turned his attention to the trapeze. It was under construction in the bowels of the Naval Aircraft Factory in Philadelphia. During his last conversation with NAF, it was determined that planning was for the installation of the trapeze on Akron in early December. Walt passed that word to Duane Harrison and they decided they needed to man the Unit with a few more aviators. The names of Lieutenant JG Paul Day and Lieutenant JG Bob Fitzwater were floated into the discussion of possible candidates. Walt discussed this situation with Admiral McMillin. The Admiral shocked Walt by telling him he thought a good move would be for him to transfer to the Unit in Lakehurst. The Admiral assured Walt he would still be his aide when he visited Lakehurst and flew on the Akron. The Admiral thought Walt should transfer to Lakehurst before December 1st, which should be in time to be there for the first hook-ups to Akron.

Walt was elated and smiling inside while expressing his sorrow for not being able to serve the Admiral in Washington. However, the Admiral assured him his job would be even harder as he would be expected to keep him updated on all happenings regarding Akron.

Lakehurst, New Jersey 27 October 1931

The 27th was Navy Day and was the designated day for commissioning the USS Akron. The civilian radio networks had been experimenting with remote broadcasting. CBS and NBC took on the task of setting up a network so every one of importance could participate in the commissioning remotely. At 8:00p.m. announcer Phil Graham interviewed Lieutenant Commander Rosendahl, followed by, Paul Litchfield from New York City. Navy Secretary Adams delivered a short speech from the deck of the newly renovated USS Constitution in Baltimore Harbor. He was followed by Admiral McMillin from Washington D.C. Assistant Secretary Ingalls offered his remarks at the site in Lakehurst, New Jersey. When he finished, he turned the dais over to Commanding Officer Captain Wes Shoemaker of Lakehurst. He was responsible for turning over the airship to Lieutenant Commander Rosendahl. Captain Shoemaker read his orders and asked Rosendahl if he was ready to accept the command. Rosendahl replied, "I accept the ship, Sir," and directed the Executive Officer to set the watch. A bosun's pipe shrilled throughout the Hangar and the crew marched aboard while a band played the Star-Spangled Banner. All external lights on the ship came on, signaling the new status for the Akron.

Washington, D.C.

With the commissioning of the Akron now out of the way Walt settled down to the more mundane problems of Naval Aviation and keeping the Admiral up to date. One of the responsibilities handed to him by the Admiral was the selection of Naval Aviators for the Heavier-Than-Air unit for the Akron. The All-NAV had attracted 33 names of volunteers. Walt added Paul and Bob to the list. He had advised them earlier that he would put them on the volunteer list. He communicated with Duane and advised him of Admiral McMillin's decision that he be attached to the Unit and report to him right after Thanksgiving. He also recommended Paul and Bob as the first Aviators who should be added to the unit. Duane concurred and Walt set out to have orders issued to Paul and Bob to report to Lakehurst no later than June 1st, 1932.

Duane recommended two other Naval Aviators whom he knew to be part of the unit. He sent their experience and other info to Walt. He reviewed them and concurred with Duane that they too join the unit. Walt took care of the orders for these two Naval Aviators to report to Lakehurst no later than June 15th, 1932.

As November rolled around, Walt began to clear items from his schedule. He talked with John Becker at Flight Test. John said he would be sorry to see him leave, but asked if he would do one more test before he left Washington. It was related to the new Curtis fighter, the F8C-6. It required a check of the bombing capability of the aircraft. He would need to go to Norfolk and load a couple of bombs then fly to Wallops Island bombing range and check out the aircraft's capability in its bombing mission. Walt completed this test during the first week of November, dropping six bombs on Wallops Island target. Three runs were glide bombing and three runs were dive-bombing from high altitude. He returned to Anacostia and completed his report, then checked out with John Becker.

On the 20th of November, he said his farewell to Admiral McMillin and Gloria. It was a sad day as he had really enjoyed his time there even though sometimes it was hectic. He planned to visit his family in Newport for Thanksgiving then report to Lakehurst by the 30th. The Navy shipped his belongings to Lakehurst, and he took his travel bag and uniform in his car to Newport. On the 21st he drove up through Maryland, New Jersey, New York, and Connecticut. He arrived in Newport, Rhode Island, late in the afternoon. He pulled up into the porte cochere about 5:30 p.m. Jason stepped out of the front door.

"Welcome home, Master Pellman," he said. "I hope you had a good trip. Mrs. Pellman is in the drawing-room, but your Dad is not home from the office yet. I'll have someone take your belongings up to your room so don't worry about it."

"Thanks, Jason. Yes, I had a nice trip from Washington," Walt said.

"That's fine Sir. I will have Edward take your car to the garage," Jason said.

Walt entered the mansion and went directly to the drawing-room where his mother was relaxing. As he entered, he approached her, giving her a big hug.

"Hi, Mom. How are you doing?" he asked.

"Oh, Son, it's wonderful to have you home." She returned his hug.

"Are you hungry?" she asked. "If you are, we can get you a snack. We were planning to eat dinner around 7 o'clock. Your Dad should be home soon. He just went to the office for an hour or two to catch up on a few things."

"I'm okay, Mom. I think I may just have a cup of tea for now. I can wait for dinner," Walt said.

Jason was handy and Lucy told him to bring a pot of tea for the both of them.

"Did you have a nice trip?" she asked.

"Yeah Mom. I left Washington about 7:00 a.m. I stopped for gas and some lunch in Newark, so the trip went smoothly. The countryside was bleak however since all the leaves have fallen from the trees," Walt said.

Jason brought the tea. Lucy and Walt sat and drank their tea and continued their conversation. About 6:30 Ben arrived home and stuck his head into the drawing-room. He spied Walt and came over and shook his hand.

"Welcome home, Son. Great to see you again," Ben said.

"Thanks, Dad. It's great to be home if just for a couple of days," Walt said.

Ben walked over and kissed Lucy on the cheek.

"Hi, sweetheart," Ben said.

"Would you like some tea?" Lucy asked.

"Yes, that would be very nice," Ben responded.

The three of them continued their conversation until Jason entered and announced that dinner was ready to be served. They walked into the dining room and were seated. The kitchen staff served dinner, after which the family moved back into the drawing-room for dessert and an afterdinner drink. Around 10 o'clock Walt arose and said he was going to bed as it had been a long drive and he was beat.

Walt had a great night's sleep. He awoke around 8:00 a.m., showered, and dressed casually. When he arrived downstairs, his Mom was already having a second cup of coffee and Pop was reading the *New York Times.*

After breakfast, he and his dad decided they would go hunting for a few hours. They put on their hunting clothes and Edward brought around their Model A Ford Pickup. After loading their shotguns into the truck, Ben climbed into the driver's seat and Walt took the passenger seat.

They drove out north of town to some land Ben owned. It was leased to a farmer who usually planted corn and soybeans on 20 acres. The remainder was forested. Ben and Walt decided they would hunt for ruffed grouse. The grouse usually hung out along the hedgerows so, after loading their shotguns, they started to walk the hedgerows with Walt on one side and Ben on the other. On the first hedgerow they didn't flush any birds, but as they started down the second, Ben flushed two grouse. He raised the gun and fired. His first shot took down a grouse. He fired again but this time the grouse was out of range and he missed. He walked over, picked up the bird, and stuck it in the back pouch of his hunting coat.

"Nice shot Pop," Walt said. "What happened on the second?"

"I got greedy, and the bird was out of range by the time I fired," Ben said.

They continued down the row. Walt flushed a male pheasant. He fired one shot and took down the bird. The next hedgerow was very productive with Ben bagging two more grouse and Walt one. They decided five birds were enough for a couple of meals, so they walked back to the truck and returned to the mansion. When they arrived, they turned over the birds to Jason who passed them on to the kitchen staff. Walt took the guns into the gun room and cleaned and oiled them before he returned them to the gun cabinet.

It was mid-afternoon, so after changing into some casual clothes, he went down to the drawing-room where his mom and dad were sitting. Mom was knitting and Dad was reading the Sunday edition of the *New York Times*. He joined them.

"Walt, your Dad says you were very successful in your hunt today and that we're having grouse for dinner," Lucy said. "I'm looking forward to it."

"Yeah, Mom. The old man got lucky today and shot three grouse," Walt said.

"And I missed only one shot, so I would say more skill than luck," Ben replied.

"Yeah, you're still pretty good with that gun," Walt answered.

"Not to change the subject, however. You might want to look at these articles in the *Times*. They are about your new airship," Ben said.

"Are they good or bad, Pop?" Walt asked.

"Read them and make up your own mind," Ben replied.

Walt sat down and took that section of the paper to read. The gist of one story recapped most of the flights the Akron had made and concluded that the airship was so far successful. The other story was somewhat critical of the Navy and how it had not been determined what her overall mission would be. It asked the question of whether this was a ship of the navy with planes or whether it was a flying aircraft carrier. Walt concluded that the question would certainly rile up many of the Lighter-Than-Air officers since he already knew many of them and they wouldn't cotton to being there only to serve as an aircraft carrier. He knew right then and there it would be like a running gun battle and not one he wanted to get into.

The dinner hour approached, and Jason announced that dinner was ready to be served. The three of them walked into the dining room and took their seats. The first course was a lentil soup followed by the grouse. It was baked then served on rice with mushrooms and hazelnuts. The green vegetable was Del Monte green peas. All agreed that it was tasteful, and they thoroughly enjoyed it. Dessert was apple pie with a scoop of vanilla ice cream.

After dinner, they adjourned to the drawing-room and had a libation of Tia Maria. Ben turned on the radio and they listened to Amos and Andy and H. V. Kaltenborn followed by Lowell Thomas. These were followed by the Jack Benny Show.

The next day Ben asked Walt if he could get their sailboat out of the water and put it into storage for the winter. He said he would, After breakfast, he recruited Edward to drive him to the marina and go sailing for a couple of hours before they had the sailboat hauled out for winter storage. The temperature was mid 50° F at mid-day and the water on Narragansett Bay was only a little choppy in the 5-mph wind. By 1 o'clock they had the boat in storage inside the large barn at the marina and Walt took Edward to lunch before they returned to the mansion.

The remaining days Walt spent just relaxing and clearing his mind from the past busy summer and fall he had just gone through with the Akron happenings. Thanksgiving dawned as a typical fall day in New England. The family had invited the Kelleys to dinner, so the staff was busy prepping everything for their arrival. Walt stayed out of the way in the drawing-room, reading the *New York Times* and listening to the radio.

Dinner was scheduled around 4:00 p.m., so at 3 o'clock he went up to his room and dressed for dinner.

Bill and Katherine Kelley arrived along with daughter Susan. The Pellmans met and welcomed them in the foyer, and all walked back into the drawing-room.

Walt homed in on Susan. "Hi, Susan. It's been a while since last we met," Walt said. "What's been happening in your life?"

"I've been busy with work," Susan answered. "And what is happening in your life.?"

"It's been a busy year for me. I have been Admiral McMillin's aide and we have been mostly dealing with the Navy's new dirigible. Washington is a zoo and administrative work is not my thing, although I have been able to fly a lot testing new aircraft for the Navy."

"That sounds like interesting work, Walt. Are you headed back to Washington after Thanksgiving?" Susan asked.

"No, I'm headed to Lakehurst, New Jersey, to do some flying and working with the dirigible USS Akron," Walt replied.

"I guess we'll be seeing you in the news then," Susan mused.

"Gosh, Susan, I hope not. I want to stay away from publicity as much as possible."

Jason interrupted the conversation, announcing that dinner was served. Everyone moved into the dining room and took seats. Walt and Susan found seats together so that could continue their conversation. Ben said the blessing and the staff began serving the dinner. The first course was soup followed by a shrimp cocktail. The turkey had already been carved by the chef and was served by the staff. Each person was asked what they would like on their plate and the staff served it from carts set behind the seated family and guests. There was more food than was humanly possible to eat. After the main course, dessert of pumpkin pie or New York cheesecake was available. Coffee or tea was also available with dessert. Dinner lasted about an hour and a half. After everyone was finished with dessert and drink the group adjourned to the drawing-room. Ben offered Bill and Walt a cigar. Walt declined but Bill and Ben decided to smoke so they moved to the solarium accompanied by Walt. It was cozy and warm as the staff had lit fires in all the fireplaces to take the chill off the mansion. Bill queried

Walt on his new assignment and the discussion centered around the Navy's dirigible program.

After a short time, Walt excused himself, walked back to the drawing-room, and found Susan. They moved off into a corner closer to the fireplace. Their interaction was animated, and Walt found a liking to Susan. She was quite interesting along with being a great-looking woman. He and Susan had an enjoyable time and hated to end the evening. Around 10 o'clock Bill told Ben and Lucy it had been a great dinner and evening, but it was time for them to get back home as everyone was tired. Everyone walked toward the foyer. They were met by the staff and Jason supervised assisting the Kelley family in putting on their coats in anticipation of moving out into the cold while boarding their vehicle for the ride home. Goodbyes were exchanged and the Kelleys departed.

"Well, that was a pleasant evening. The Kelleys are always fun to be around," Lucy observed. "Did you and Susan enjoy yourselves?" She asked.

"Yeah Mom, we hit it off pretty good. It's too bad I'm leaving tomorrow. It would have been enjoyable to see her again," Walt said.

"Oh, I had forgotten you were leaving tomorrow Son. What time will you be departing?" Ben asked.

"I'll probably leave after breakfast. It's only about four hours to Lakehurst," Walt answered. "I guess I'll hit the hay now. Goodnight," he said as he kissed his Mom on the cheek and then turned and went up the stairs to his room.

29

"First Hookups"

On the Road to Lakehurst

Walt left Newport at about 9:30 a.m., driving through Connecticut, New York City, into New Jersey, and was now heading down U.S. 1 to Lakehurst. He arrived at the gate to the base around 1:30 p.m. He received a temporary base permit for his automobile then proceeded on base to the BOQ. He checked in and was assigned a room on the first floor. He unloaded his car and settled in. There was a closed Mess, but he could not join it being a weekend. He would have to wait until Monday to join so he purchased a dinner ticket as a guest. After dinner, he wandered back to his room and stretched out on the bed. After relaxing for an hour, he turned on the light at his desk and sat in his chair to jot down a few things he and Duane needed to decide.

Monday, November 30th Lakehurst, New Jersey

Walt set out in his dress blue uniform to find Akron's administrative offices so he could report in for duty. Even though he was in a separate aviation unit, Akron was responsible for all administrative duties for the unit. The Akron had established offices in the large Hangar housing the airship. Walt found himself a parking spot and proceeded into the Hangar. He located the personnel office in the southeast corner of the Hangar and entered. He presented his orders to the first-class Yeoman who endorsed his orders and checked him on board. Walt was given a check-in sheet of the places he needed to visit.

He departed the Hangar and drove up to the base security office, the first place on his check-in sheet. At security, they registered his automobile and issued him a registration number. This was to be displayed when entering and leaving the facility. His next stop was the post office. Here he filled out a card with his assigned duty station and forwarding address at the BOQ. That was where he would receive his mail. His next stop was the BOQ office where he joined the closed Mess. There were a few other routine stops which he completed, then returned to Akron's admin office and turned in his check-in sheet. Now he could find Lieutenant Harrison's office and get to work.

Duane was in the same place he had been when Walt first visited and had flown with Duane on hookups to the USS Los Angeles. As Walt entered the office, Duane looked up from his desk and espied Walt.

"Hey, Buddy. Great to see you," Duane said. "Are you here permanently?" he quired.

Walt shook Duane's hand. "Great to see you, Duane. Yes, I am at your service, Boss," He jested.

"Well, that's great. It's nice to have some company and someone to work with and of course, serve me coffee," Duane smirked. Walt smiled, "Yeah, I'm good at the coffee stuff," he said. "Speaking of which, where are you hiding the coffee urn?"

"It's down the passageway. The Akron officers have a coffee mess in their Ready Room. You can pay by the mug or join each month for three dollars," Duane said.

"Okay, I'll get some after lunch. Right now, where will my desk be located?" Walt asked.

"I see you're still wearing your aiguillettes. Are you still Admiral McMillin's aide?

"Yeah, Duane, the Admiral felt I should be his aide when he is here in Lakehurst or flying in the Akron."

"I procured a desk for you. It's over there in the corner. Let's grab it and put it right here facing each other. That will make it easier for us to yell at each other in softer tones," Duane answered. They both laughed.

They got the desk settled and found Walt a chair. He and Duane began to discuss the Unit and manning level of enlisted personnel. Duane told him they already had 13 of the 20 men assigned to the unit. ACMM

Schoonderwoerd was the senior enlisted man who would be the only Chief Petty Officer assigned to them. He was already on board and was organizing the maintenance department. Duane told Walt they had 8 planes already assigned. There were six N2Ys, the Vought UO-1, and the XF9C-1. The UO-1 was soon to be turned over to the Naval Aircraft Factory. All the N2Ys had been retrofitted with the skyhook and were ready to fly.

Duane lamented that the planes needed to be flown, and up until now, he was the only pilot available to do so. Walt chimed in, "Well, there's two of us now so I guess we can do a lot more flying. Speaking of which, have you had a chance to take a flight on the Akron yet?"

"No, Buddy, I haven't. There have been so many VIPs around here taking flights there is never enough room to get aboard," Duane noted.

"Yeah, I know what you mean. Admiral McMillin has been here quite a few times already and I'm sure he will be here a lot more," Walt observed.

"As far as pilots for the unit, Bob Fitzwater and Paul Day are scheduled to report by June 1st. Our two other guys aren't due to report until June 15th. I guess it's you and me, Duane, for quite some time. By the way, have you heard anything about when the trapeze might be installed on the Akron?" Walt asked.

"We were promised to have it delivered here by December 1st, but I heard last week the date has been delayed until January 1st. The maintenance crew off the Akron have been directed to uninstall the trapeze from Los Angeles and ship it to NAF for use as parts for Akron's trapeze. We'll be lucky to see it by February, if you ask me," Duane noted.

"Let me put that on my to-do list, Duane. I will call the team leader on the construction of the trapeze at NAF and see if I can get us a firm date for delivery," Walt said.

"Sounds like a plan to me, Walt."

The Akron had flown its inaugural flight as a commissioned airship on November 2nd. Admiral McMillin had arranged for a few aviation writers to fly on this flight along with four NBC radio technicians who had made remote broadcasts during the flight. The Admiral hoped to get a better reputation for the Akron from it, but it never came to fruition.

During December Akron logged many hours. Duane managed to get onto a local test flight with the Akron checking her water recovery system.

Walt on the other hand flew on the Akron for an extended cross country flight. It took the Akron south across the southern states then up the Mississippi and Ohio rivers and finally back to Lakehurst. The flight lasted for 48 hours, and Walt was able to develop a rapport with the officers and men of Akron. During meals aboard the Akron, the conversation centered around the question, *"Does the Akron exist as an airborne aircraft carrier or does the Akron just carry planes to complement the scouting mission?"* The conversations were hot and heavy, but Walt being the diplomat, listened a great deal so as not to cause positions to harden. All in all, he enjoyed the flight, especially night flying.

In addition to these flights, Duane and Walt flew almost every other day when the weather was good. The planes developed maintenance problems when they weren't flown enough so they made it a point to vary flying the aircraft.

Christmas was soon upon them, and since they had no primary mission to perform, Duane shut down the Unit and allowed anyone who wanted leave to take it. Walt did spend a couple of days with the folks in Newport while Duane traveled to his home in Buffalo. They were both back at Lakehurst by the 2nd of January. Walt called his contact at NAF and was advised that the trapeze for Akron would be delivered by February 15th along with a crew to install it. He also found that the design change he had recommended would be implemented in the installation.

Lakehurst, New Jersey, February 22nd

During January and February, Duane and Walt cycled through flying all the unit's aircraft. The two of them were generally invited to Akron's department heads' meeting when she wasn't scheduled to fly. At one of these meetings, they learned that delivery and installation of the trapeze was delayed until the end of February. They were surely disappointed but settled down to the fact that it would be late. They spent many days working on the development of a Standard Operating Procedures manual for the unit, on airship protocols especially hookups and releases along with safety procedures. It was determined that they would keep the engine running after hookup if the plane was to be brought aboard the airship and stowed in the Hangar bay. This was in case the plane released from the hook accidentally it would have immediate power to keep flying. This was important in case the airship slowed after hookup below stall speed of the airplane. If a release of the hook happened, the plane would be stalled, and precious altitude could be lost trying to recover from the stall and restart the engine.

Then on February 22nd, disaster struck Akron. A brisk northwest wind of from six to fourteen knots was blowing. As the Akron was being pulled from the Hangar there was a strain on the cables which held the tail to the rear railroad car. The situation as viewed by the diesel engine driver pulling the mast decided to rush the procedure. As the mast cleared the Hangar door the tail broke loose from the rail car and danced upward. As it started down, water ballast was released but too late. The tail slammed down on the ground, damaging the tail fin. It bounced up and slammed down again as the airship swung around into the wind with the tail absorbing strong blows. To make matters worse, a congressional delegation was standing by to board her for the flight and were witness to the accident and subsequent damage. She was pulled back into the Hangar and her damage assessed. Serious fin damage and mainframe damage were logged. As a result of the damage, the airship's participation in the latest fleet exercise was canceled. The good news was that, during the downtime of March and April, the trapeze was finally installed. Duane and Walt were ecstatic. They would finally be able to complete some hookups to the Akron and compliment it in its scouting mission.

Finally, on May 2nd, all the repairs were completed and today was the day for the Unit to make history. The Akron took off just at sunup and headed out to sea to complete some minor tests of equipment and training of personnel.

At 7 o'clock, Walt and Duane manned their aircraft. They decided they both would fly N2Ys for their first hookups. Akron's point of intended movement was to fly east to the coastline then parallel it to the south. After takeoff, the two aviators joined up in parade formation and headed due south towards Atlantic City. Twenty-five minutes later, they passed over the city and headed south down the coast. The Akron would be cruising at slow speed at an altitude determined by the cloud base. Walt was the first to spot the Akron, and Duane and Walt switched to air-to-air frequency.

Duane called Akron, "Akron this is Navy 601 and 604, over."

Akron replied, "Navy 601 you are loud and clear. Go ahead "Akron, Navy 601 and 604 at 20 miles for hookup, over," Duane transmitted

"Navy 601 and 604, proceed inbound we are accelerating to hookup speed. Circle port side until cleared for hookup, over."

"Roger, Akron, Navy 601 proceeding as instructed," Duane responded.

As the two planes proceeded to catch up to Akron, Duane, who was leading, passed the lead to Walt. The two of them had agreed, since the trapeze was Walt's baby, he would have the pleasure of making history, the first hookup to Akron. Akron was accelerating to 50 knots, but hadn't quite reached it yet. Walt passed abeam Akron about 20' below on the port side. As he reached the bow, he began a shallow banked turn to the port. As he passed the tail abeam, he resumed his port turn and rolled out parallel to Akron's course sightly astern. Akron had reached 50 knots and Walt had matched her speed maintaining his position sightly port and astern.

Akron came up once again on frequency, "Navy 601 and 604 cleared to commence hookups."

Walt answered, "Roger, Akron, commencing hookup."

He maneuvered his section gently to the starboard of Akron, then kissed off from Duane and slid his plane directly under Akron, about 20 feet below. He accelerated a couple of knots until he was directly below the trapeze, then matched the speed of the Akron. He eased back on the stick slightly and began a slow ascent towards the trapeze. As he reached the prop wash from Akron, he jammed on a little power and continued his ascent. The hook snapped onto the trapeze and locked. Yea, his first successful hookup to Akron.

He reached up and pulled the hook release handle and the plane fell away. Walt stabilized his power and his position 20' low and slightly port and aft of Akron. He looked for Duane. He was just beginning his approach to the trapeze. Walt then shifted his position to the starboard side of Akron just aft of the trapeze. He watched as Duane skillfully maneuvered his plane for hookup. Duane mimicked Walt's approach to the trapeze and within seconds was on the hook.

Walt couldn't help himself, He broke radio silence, "Nice job, Duane."

Duane pulled his hook release, and it was Walt's turn again.

"That was a great hookup you made on your first try, Buddy," Duane said.

"Thanks, Duane. Here we go again," Walt said.

After each pilot had completed seven hookups, Duane transmitted to Akron, "Akron, 601 and 604 are at bingo fuel, Request recommended heading to base, over."

"Roger, 601, standby for heading to Lakehurst."

It took the Akron's navigator about a minute to calculate the heading.

"Navy 601, Akron. Recommended heading to Atlantic City 355° then 360° to Lakehurst."

"Akron, 601 roger copied. 601 and 604 departing," Duane reported.

After an hour and forty minutes, Duane and Walt arrived back at Lakehurst, and headed for the office. After changing uniforms, they sat down at their desks.

"I don't know about you, Duane, but that was an exhilarating few hours," Walt said

"You know it. I didn't have time to think about it while we were hooking up, but man that was some experience," Duane answered.

Jokingly Walt said, "Yeah we need to do that again sometime soon. How about tomorrow?"

"Why not, how about we do it again tomorrow?" Duane quipped.

"If I didn't know better, I'd think we're addicted already," Walt answered. "It sure was a hell-of-a-lot of fun."

"Okay, let's get serious, Walt. We need to plan our next steps in this development."

"I already thought of how we should proceed. We need to discuss our plan with the Akron Ops Officer. I guess that would be Lieutenant Commander Bill Stoddard. What we need to do is for both of us to qualify the Sparrowhawk on the hook first and qualify the aircraft handling crew of the Akron. I figure one of us can fly six hookups in the Sparrowhawk, then have the trapeze crew bring us both aboard where we can switch planes then launch for six more hookups. We can have the trapeze crew bring us abord as many times as they would like to get them comfortable handling aircraft," Walt said.

"Okay, Buddy, that's our plan now let's go to lunch," Duane noted.

30

"Spring Trouble"

Lakehurst, New Jersey

The Akron was due to arrive just before sunset. Walt had to meet the Admiral, so he donned his dress khakis and drove down to the Hangar. It was only 7:15 p.m. He had plenty of time before Akron arrived. Sunset was 7:53 p.m. so he went to the office and worked a little on the op-plan he and Duane had developed earlier in the day.

It was approaching sunset and he walked out into the Hangar as the huge hanger doors rolled open. The docking mast was already in place in the outer hauling circle and the machines to haul the airship into the Hangar were in place. This is where the passengers would disembark as soon as the airship was locked on the mast.

The humming of her engines was heard before the Akron was in sight. Walt spotted her at about 25 miles from base. She was cruising at about 1500' at 25 knots. Wind at the mast was northwest at 3 knots. One of the ground crew lit a smoke bomb and dropped it on the ground. It would give the Akron pilots a good idea of what the wind was doing. Walt figured Lieutenant Commander Rosendahl was probably commanding the bridge and issuing commands as necessary to tie up to the mast. As she approached the mast, her engines reversed the propellors and brought her to a stop within 16" of the mast where the Akron was attached and pulled up tight to the locking mechanism. The tail trolly was swung on the railroad tracks until it was under the tail fin of Akron. The ground crew secured the tail fin to the trolly and was now ready to be pulled into the Hangar.

Before that would happen, the stairway to the control car lowered and the VIP passengers disembarked. Admiral McMillin was first down the stairs. He was greeted by Walt.

"Good evening, Sir," Walt said as he saluted. "Did you have a nice flight?"

The Admiral returned his salute, "Good evening, Lieutenant. Yes, we had a great flight. Did you have a great flight?" he asked. The Admiral already knew the answer to that question, but he just wanted to hear what his favorite Lieutenant had to say.

"Sir we had a great flight. Lieutenant Harrison and I made seven beautiful hookups to Akron without a hitch. I think things are working out just right. Next flight we are going to test the trapeze handling crew," Walt said.

"I watched the two of you make your hookups and they were beautiful examples of smooth flying by great Naval Aviators. By the way, who made the first hookup you or Lieutenant Harrison?" the Admiral asked.

"I made the first one, Sir. Lieutenant Harrison let me do it because he felt I earned it," Walt answered.

"Looks like you will now go down in the history of Naval Aviation as making that first hookup to the Akron," the Admiral said.

They continued to talk as they walked over to the Admiral's waiting Trimotor. He was returning to Washington tonight.

As they parted, Walt saluted and said, "Thank you Sir for putting your trust in my ability. I could not have made my hookups without your support and direction."

The Admiral returned his salute. "You earned every part of this yourself Lieutenant. Just be prepared for more tough assignments."

He turned and boarded his flight. Walt stood on the tarmac until the Trimotor roared off the runway. With his responsibilities to the Admiral, complete, Walt went back to the BOQ for some well-deserved rest.

The next day he and Duane walked down to the Akron operations office. They found Lieutenant Commander Stoddard to discuss further aircraft trapeze operations. They all agreed that exercising the trapeze crew should be done on a local training or maintenance check flight and not on an operational mission.

The next day for the Akron crew would be a day of rest or maintenance, but the following day was scheduled for a six-hour flight to test the water recovery system once again. The three of them decided that would be a good time to train the aircraft handling crew, along with exercising the trapeze and rail system onboard the Akron.

Following day

All hands were up early and ready to fly. Today Duane and Walt needed to hook up with the XF9C-1. They flipped a coin and Walt won the toss. He elected to fly it first, then switch with Duane after they were both on board the Akron so Duane could bring the Sparrowhawk home.

Walt manned the Sparrowhawk and Duane selected one of the N2Ys to fly.

Akron was pulled out of the Hangar and took off right about sunup. Walt and Duane departed about 15 minutes after Akron. They caught up to her as she passed over the coast. After radio contact, they were directed into a holding pattern, like the previous flight, awaiting the Akron to accelerate to landing speed. Once up to speed, the flight was cleared to land. The first two hookups were scheduled to be full stop landings with transfer aboard on the rail system. The plan was to capture the Sparrowhawk, followed by the N2Y, then launch both aircraft. After the second evolution, Walt and Duane would switch aircraft and repeat the cycle twice more, then depart for Lakehurst.

The Akron reached aircraft recovery speed and Walt broke off and made his first hookup. He reached up and pulled the hook release lever. The hook failed to release. He pulled it another six or seven times but each time the hook failed to release. Lieutenant Ellis, the trapeze officer, after a conference with the bridge, decided someone needed to crawl down to the Sparrowhawk and try to release the hook. Lieutenant Ellis volunteered to do that, and after attaching a safety line to his body, he began crawling down the trapeze mechanism toward the Sparrowhawk. One thing the bridge had decided was they could not land with the Sparrowhawk on the trapeze, so Lieutenant Ellis needed to be successful. After 20 minutes he reached the aircraft and began prying the locking mechanism on the hook release. After 10 minutes of work, he finally broke the Sparrowhawk loose. The Sparrowhawk was stalled, and Walt pushed the nose down while adding power. He lost about 800' of altitude but was never in danger of crashing. Akron advised the aircraft section to return to base as both aircraft were just about down to bingo fuel.

Walt and Duane landed at Lakehurst and parked their aircraft.

Chief Schoonderwoerd was called to the flight line to inspect the possible problem with the hook mechanism. Walt and Duane changed uniforms and waited in their office to receive a briefing of what the Chief had found. In a short time, Chief Schoonderwoerd entered their office.

"Well, Chief, what did you find?" Duane asked.

"Sir, the mechanism works just fine right now. Of course, we didn't have a load on the release latch, but I believe this is what happened. The Sparrowhawk weighs a lot more than the N2Y and because of the extra weight, the design on the hook release mechanism would not allow it to release. A possible fix could be a stronger spring on the side of the release latch, which will solve the problem. I think we should run it by Engineering Departments at Goodyear/ Zeppelin, Curtis Wright, and Naval Aircraft Factory to get the opinion and possible fix."

"Okay, Chief, that's a great analysis. I'll draft a message to all concerned and ask them for their opinions and possible fix," Duane said.

"If we have any more hookup flights, I guess we'll use our N2Ys only, for a while," Walt said.

They decided to have another conference with Lieutenant Commander Stoddard concerning any more hookup flights. The Akron was going out the next day. Duane proposed he and Walt would make four hookups a piece and the aircraft handling crew would take the planes aboard and test out the rail handling system. Lieutenant Commander Stoddard agreed that would test the handling crew and give them the appropriate training they needed.

Wednesday, May 4th

The Akron was off exactly at sunrise followed shortly thereafter by Walt and Duane in their N2Ys. Duane was leading the flight, and after the Akron reached aircraft recovery speed, he kissed off and proceeded to make his first hookup. He kept the engine running while the crew lowered the inverted saddle to stabilize the aircraft on the trapeze. The handling crew cranked up the trapeze and Duane was slowly brought up into the Hangar deck opening. As he cleared the outer hull, he shut down the engine. The crew then brought him aboard Akron and pushed him onto the rail system. As soon as he cleared the trapeze, the crew brought it down into recovery position. The whole evolution took about 15 minutes. Lieutenant Ellis was keeping time and indicated to the crew they were striving for 10 minutes by the end of the day. Walt made his approach and a beautiful hookup. He too kept the engine running until the plane cleared the outer hull. Once the engine was secured, the aircraft handling crew cranked him aboard and transferred him to the rail system.

Now it was time for the crew to undo what they had just done. They reversed the procedure and pushed Walt onto the trapeze. Once there, Walt gave the crewman the signal to start his engine. He turned on the fuel and signaled to prime the engine. The crewman hand-cranked the prop three complete revolutions. Next, he called "Contact." Walt switched on the mag switch and the crewman pulled the prop through once again. The engine roared to life and the handling crew continued to crank the trapeze down into the slipstream. The crew retracted the saddle. Walt waited until he was above stall speed then released the hook from the Akron. All-in-all it took 13 minutes to bring him aboard and 12 minutes to launch him. It looked like the crew was learning as they went along and just might reach the 10-minute threshold before the day was out.

Walt took up position starboard and slightly aft of Akron. He observed as Duane was brought down and engine started. Within minutes he was in position and released his hook. He dropped in altitude then began a climb to a wing position on Walt who was now leading. He kissed off and began his hookup. The whole aircraft handling procedure was complete when he was safely aboard and on the rail system. Total time 12 minutes. Duane and the handling crew repeated the procedure. Eleven minutes from start to finish. The crew was ecstatic. Walt and Duane made two more hookups and recovery. On the last one, the crew achieved a time of ten minutes and were commended by Lieutenant Ellis.

After the last launch, Duane and Walt joined in parade formation. Akron's navigator came up on the aircraft frequency and gave them a heading to take them back to Lakehurst.

It took them approximately one hour to make it back. Duane called the break to the tower, and both made a safe landing. They taxied to the ramp and parked their aircraft. It was just about noon, and they decided to have lunch before tackling all the problems waiting for them back at the office.

Returning from lunch they read the message board. The Navy Department had dropped the perimeter flight around the United States, but still insisted on the Akron going to the West Coast. The planned date for departure was the 8th of May. Walt's comment was, "How in the hell do they expect us to get the Sparrowhawk ready by then."

The message stated the Unit would provide two aircraft for the West Coast deployment.

Further down the stack of messages, Curtis Wright had figured out a possible solution to the Sparrowhawk's hook release problem from the trapeze. They had shipped a stronger spring for the hook latch via special courier flying into Teterboro, New Jersey, tomorrow, arriving at 4:30 p.m. Someone from the unit would need to meet them and pick up the spring. Walt volunteered to drive to Teterboro, but Duane had a better idea. Take an N2Y and fly to Teterboro. That sounded like a great idea. Walt put it on the schedule for a 3:30 p.m. departure. He also contacted Chief Schoonderwoerd to accompany him. The Chief needed some flight time to qualify for his monthly aircrewman's flight pay.

Thursday, May 5th

The project's planning and execution never ended. Walt and Duane were on the phone or sending a message. Tomorrow Admiral McMillin was scheduled to arrive early and board Akron for her eight-hour flight, which meant Walt would need to be up early to meet the Admiral. Duane would need to fly the Sparrowhawk out to Akron and test the hook release. Unit maintenance would need to get the spring installed before going out in the morning to test it. They also worked on their Unit Standard Operating Procedures Manual for flying the hook.

The weather over New York and New Jersey had been lousy all day. Light rain and low clouds were covering the area. Departure time rolled around with no clearing or improvement insight. Walt and Chief Schoonderwoerd climbed into the N2Y and cranked the engine. The tower cleared them for departure to the southeast. Walt climbed straight ahead to 300' and headed to the coast. Upon reaching it, he turned north and began following the coastline. He was in and out of the clouds, but managed to maintain contact with the ground and determine his position. He entered the mouth of the Hudson River and flew up the river until he espied Central Park in New York. He called Teterboro Tower.

"Teterboro Tower, this is Navy 6244 four miles southeast for landing, over."

"Roger, Navy 6244. Are you VFR, over?" Tower replied.

"Teterboro Tower, Navy 6355 is VFR. Turning northwest at this time, over," Walt responded.

"Navy 6244, you're cleared for a straight-in approach and landing to runway 03. Report passing % mile. Weather Teterboro is 400' overcast, visibility 1 mile, winds northeast at 4 knots and altimeter 29.86", over."

"Tower, Navy 6244 copied altimeter 29.86," Walt said.

Walt spotted the road which ran to the airport. He turned northeast and slowed to approach speed. At % of a mile he spotted the runway slightly to his port, so he made a slight turn and lined up with the runway, and began a gentle descent. At % mile, he called the tower.

"Teterboro Tower, Navy 6244 at % mile for landing," Walt transmitted.

"Navy 6244 is cleared to land runway 03," Tower said

Walt touched down in the first 100 feet of the runway, and as he rolled out, he was cleared to switch to ground control. Ground control directed him to the General Operations area where he shut down.

He and Chief Schoonderwoerd climbed out of their airplane, and after checking-in, with operations, they walked over to the airline terminal.

The special courier was due in on American Airlines flight 828, ETA 4:45 p.m. They sat down in the terminal to relax for a few minutes until the flight arrived.

At 4:45 p.m. the flight arrived at gate 3. Walt and the Chief walked out and stood where deplaning passengers could readily see them. The courier could easily identify them as Navy fliers, and they could receive the package he was carrying. Within minutes, one passenger walked up to them and identified himself as the Curtis-Wright courier. They all shook hands and exchanged the package.

Walt and Chief Schoonderwoerd said their goodbyes and walked back to the base operations. Walt climbed into the cockpit while Chief Schoonderwoerd stood by to pull the prop through and get the engine started. Walt indicated he was ready to start.

The chief shouted, "Brakes on, mags off."

Walt responded, "Brakes on, mags off."

The Chief pulled the prop through twice and yelled "Contact."

Walt responded "Contact."

As the Chief pulled the prop through one more time, the engine roared to life. He then pulled the chocks and climbed aboard the N2Y.

Ground control cleared them to taxi to runway 03. After engine runup was complete, Walt switched to tower frequency and they were cleared for takeoff. As he climbed out, he turned southeast and headed for the Hudson River. He could see the weather was improving with the ceiling now 600'. He leveled off at 500' and headed down the river. He retraced his position down the Jersey coast until he could see a familiar place near the beach, then headed directly towards Lakehurst. At 20 miles he spotted the Hangar and called the tower for landing instructions. The tower cleared him for landing.

When Walt shut down the N2Y on the ramp, they discovered that the Sparrowhawk had already been pulled into the Hangar. Walt and Chief Schoonderwoerd walked into the Hangar with their precious package in hand. Two Aviation Machinist Mates (AMM) came out of the maintenance shop. The four of them met at the Sparrowhawk. The Chief had instructed them to remove the cover over the spring housing, which the AMMs had already accomplished. It now appeared to be a simple spring replacement job.

Walt went into the locker room to change into his uniform. He was aware the men worked better without a crowd standing by, and watching their every move. Walt had told the Chief he would be in his office, when the job was done to notify him there.

Within 15 minutes the Chief entered.

"Mister Pellman." he said. "The spring has been replaced and we cycled the release handle five times. Everything appears to be working properly. I guess our come-to Jesus moment will be when you hook up to the trapeze on the Akron."

"Thanks, Chief. I know you have done your best and I am sure everything will be okay when we operate the hook release. Go get yourself some chow and tell the men well done. It's been a long day and I'm ready for some rest."

Walt jumped into his car and headed for the BOQ. Tomorrow would be a long day as he needed to meet the Admiral upon his arrival. That would be around 7:00 a.m. as the scheduled departure time for the Akron was sunup, 7:35 a.m. to be exact. He wouldn't need to accompany him on board since he and Duane would be flying hookups in both the N2Y and XF9C-1.

Friday, May 6th

Walt had been up since 5:00 a.m. He had showered, eaten breakfast, driven to the Hangar, and changed into his flight uniform. By 6:45 a.m. he was ready for the Admiral's arrival. Duane had arrived and he too was ready for flying. The two of them walked out onto the Hangar deck where they were met by Lieutenant Commander Bill Stoddard.

"Good morning, gentlemen," he said. "Bad news for you. The Admiral has been delayed until 10 o'clock and he expects to be flown out to Akron. You will need to find us out at sea and rendezvous for your hookup. Let's go aboard Akron and look at the navigator's chart. He has laid out our proposed route to be flown and should give you a good starting point to find us.

Lieutenant George Masterson entered the navigator's space. He was the Assistant Navigator who would be doing the navigation today.

"Good morning, gentlemen. What may I do for you this morning?" he asked.

"Give us your estimated position for 10:20 a.m and your point of intended movement from there for the next two hours," Walt said.

"Our estimated position will be 39°16'18.0"N 73°58'12.3"W. Lakehurst Airship Hangar will bear 348° true. Course 018° and speed 35 knots." George said.

"Okay, George I copied all the information. Just make sure the old man does what you tell him to do," Walt said as everyone chuckled. They all knew that the Skipper of the Akron will generally fly the course the navigator recommends but nobody dictates to him.

Duane and Walt stepped off the Akron just as the Hangar doors rolled open. Akron was moved out to the outer handling circle and launched at 7:35 a.m. Duane and Walt went back to their office, When they arrived,

Walt stretched out on the couch to get some zzzs. Duane put his chair back and feet on the coffee table to relax. It was going to be a long day for them.

At 9:45a.m. Duane and Walt walked down to the flight line awaiting the Ford Trimotor carrying the Admiral. Right on schedule, the Trimotor was on short final. He landed and taxied over to the flight line alongside the Hangar. The Admiral was alone and he disembarked as soon as the door to the cabin was opened.

Walt and Duane saluted, "Good morning, Sir." Walt said. "Hope your flight was comfortable?"

The Admiral returned the salute "Good morning, gentlemen," he said. "What's the plan?"

Walt spoke up. "Sir, I am going to take you out to Akron. Lieutenant Harrison is going to fly the Sparrowhawk and we are going as a section in case either one of us has a problem. You and I will recover first, and Akron will bring us aboard and put us on the rail system. Lieutenant Harrison will then hook up on the trapeze and remain there until I am ready to commence practice hookups. Each hookup will be completed with a recovery onboard Akron by the aircraft handling crew. After three evolutions are complete, pilots will switch aircraft and make two more hookups, then remain on board until you are ready to depart for Lakehurst, at which time we will depart together for safety reasons."

"That appears to be a sound plan. I'm impressed. So, let's get on with it," the Admiral said.

"Sir, you can change into your flying uniform in the Akron's officer locker room. I have already procured two life preservers, which are already in the airplane. We're ready when you are," Walt said.

The Admiral went into the locker room and donned his flying uniform. Meanwhile, Walt and Duane pre-flighted their respective aircraft. The Admiral exited the Hangar and proceeded to the N2Y. Walt assisted him in donning his life preserver and told the Admiral to take the front seat. Walt climbed into the rear seat. The line crew quickly had the engines of the N2Y and Sparrowhawk started. Walt was the leader for this portion of the flight, so he taxied first followed by Duane.

Walt asked the Admiral if he would like to fly this leg since Walt had to do some maneuvering board navigation to reach the Akron. The Admiral was pleased and took control of the aircraft. Takeoff was normal and while making a right turn out of the traffic pattern, Duane had already made a running rendezvous and was in parade position on Walt's starboard wing. As they were climbing Walt pulled out his maneuvering board and was plotting his intercept of Akron. He had the Admiral take up a heading of 095° with an intercept time of 11:06 a.m.

The Admiral leveled off a 3500' and set cruise for 100 knots. While they were cruising along, Walt briefed the Admiral on how to fly the hookup pattern. As time was approaching 10:50 a.m., the pilots began visually searching for Akron. At 10:54a.m. Duane came up on frequency and announced he had Akron visually at bearing 110° at 3500'. Walt and the Admiral scanned that area of the sky and soon Walt told Duane he had the Akron insight.

Walt called Akron, "Akron, this is Acrobat 2 at 20 miles westnorthwest with two for hookup. I have Fangtooth aboard," Walt transmitted.

"Acrobat 2, you are cleared for hookup. Akron is now accelerating to hookup speed," Akron reported.

The Admiral oriented the flight to approach the Akron toward the stern. As he neared midship, he commenced a shallow port turn placing him ^ mile astern and slightly offset to the starboard side of the Akron. Akron was stable and cruising at 50knots. The Admiral kissed off and commenced a shallow port turn. When he was directly astern, he matched the Akron's heading and accelerated to a speed slightly above 50 knots. He then raised the nose of the N2Y slightly and began approaching the trapeze from below. Walt began talking the Admiral closer, and just as he entered the prop wash from the Akron, Walt told him to add power then reduce power as the bar from the hook slid up and the hook snapped locked. The Admiral reduced power. The trapeze crew lowered the inverted saddle which stabilized the aircraft on the hook. The aircraft handling crew then began to retrieve the aircraft into Aaron's Hangar bay. As soon as the aircraft passed the outer hull, Walt reminded the Admiral to cut the engine. He pulled the mixture to ground cutoff. The crew then continued to retrieve the N2Y and finally shifted it to Akron's rail system. Duane in the Sparrowhawk made his hookup and was also retrieved into Akron. The crew left the Sparrowhawk hooked up to the trapeze. The three pilots climbed from their aircraft and were met by Lieutenant Commander Rosendahl.

"Welcome aboard, Admiral," Rosendahl said. "That was a nice hookup you made. I guess you are now one of the *"men on the flying trapeze."*

"Yes, Skipper, I really enjoyed doing that. Thanks to my aide in the back seat, I didn't damage anything," the Admiral said.

"I'll take your life preserver, Admiral," Walt said.

He then assisted the Admiral in removing the life preserver and placed it on the rear seat of the N2Y.

The Admiral and Lieutenant Commander Rosendahl proceeded forward to the control car while Walt and Duane manned their aircraft. The crew helped Duane start his engine, and now was the moment of truth. Would the Sparrowhawk release from the trapeze? The crew cranked Duane back down into the launch position and he pulled the release handle. The aircraft dropped off the trapeze bar and maneuvered into the standard holding position aft and starboard of the airship. There were smiles all around with the hook release. Walt was shifted from the rail system to the trapeze bar, then after engine start, was lowered into the flight position. He released from the trapeze then maneuvered into a parade position on Duane's wing.

Duane and Walt each made another two evolutions then remained aboard after they were complete. Walt then climbed into the Sparrowhawk and made one hookup and release then made a hookup followed by recovery onto Akron. The Sparrowhawk remained on the trapeze. The aircraft were refueled and made ready for departure while Duane and Walt had some lunch in the officer's wardroom.

At five o'clock, word was passed down to Walt and Duane to be ready to launch. Walt would need to take Admiral McMillin back to Lakehurst because Akron still had three hours of test and certification of equipment before she would head into Lakehurst.

Five twenty arrived and Admiral McMillin stepped onto the Hangar deck. Walt retrieved the Admiral's life vest and assisted the Admiral in donning it. He went to climb into the rear cockpit, but the Admiral insisted he take the front cockpit and fly the flight. The Admiral said he just wanted to sightsee.

The two aircraft were lowered on the trapeze and unhooked. Walt followed Duane and they joined in formation and proceeded on heading

246°. ETA Lakehurst was 6:33. p.m. They maintained 3500' and the weather was beautiful.

The flight was recovered at Lakehurst, and once on the flight line, the Admiral boarded his Trimotor and was soon winging his way to Washington.

31

"Westward Ho"

Lakehurst, New Jersey

Walt had spent the evening packing his clothes and generally preparing for his deployment with Akron to the West Coast. He then packed his car and hit the hay. Morning broke early for him, and after breakfast, he drove to the Hangar where he unpacked his clothes and travel kit. He parked his car under the USS Los Angeles which was still stored in the Hangar. He then went aboard Akron and stored his clothes in his assigned stateroom. Next, he took his travel bag and carried it out to the N2Y he intended to fly that day.

Duane arrived and followed Walt's procedures. He stowed his travel bag in the Sparrowhawk. The Hangar doors rolled open and Akron was soon on her way down the coast. She would fly to Georgia then across Alabama, Mississippi, Louisiana, and into Texas.

Duane and Walt manned their aircraft, started the engine and headed out to the end of the runway. Engine runup was normal for Walt, but Duanes left mag turned out to be inoperable. There was a lot of silent cursing as they taxied back to the Hangar. They shut down and were met by Petty Officer First Class Galetta.

"What's the problem, Sir?" he asked

"Damn left mag appears to be inoperable, Galetta," Duane said.

"Why don't you relax in the Ready Room and have a cup of coffee, Sir. We'll check it out and keep you advised," Galetta said.

"Sounds like a plan," Walt interjected. "Let's go to the Ready Room Duane, I'll take my maneuvering board with me and do some calculating on intercepting the Akron."

The two of them sat down with their coffee and Walt pulled up his maneuvering board. He plotted the point of intended movement and estimated the Sparrowhawk would be flyable within two hours. He then calculated the flight section's speed and plotted on his board.

"If we get off here within two hours, we can joint up with Akron right near Richmond, Virginia," Walt mused.

"Sounds like a plan, Walt," Duane said.

Within thirty minutes Petty Officer Galetta appeared at the Ready Room door.

"Sir, your plane is fixed and ready for you," Galetta said.

"What was the problem?" Duane asked.

"The left mag switch was shorted out, Sir. We had a spare in the power plants shop so we just switched it with the plane, and it checked out okay," Galetta answered.

Turning to Walt, Duane said, "Well, let's get this show on the road, old Buddy."

"Okay, I'm ready to go," Walt said.

The two pilots manned their planes and were soon winging their way south. The weather was beautiful with scattered clouds. They passed east of Philadelphia then Washington, D.C., and into Virginia. They were looking for Akron as they passed Richmond. As they passed over Petersburg, Duane spotted Akron some 40 miles southeast of their present position. He turned slightly port and headed towards Akron. Walt had seen Akron also and Duane climbed to match her altitude. At 20 miles he called Akron on his VHF radio.

"Akron, this is Acrobat 1 and 2, 20 miles northwest your position for hookup, over," Duane transmitted.

"Roger, Acrobat 1. You are cleared for hook up. We are currently cruising at 50 knots, over," Akron said.

Duane approached Akron slightly below her altitude. He stabilized momentarily then kissed off and broke left. He matched Akron's speed and when he was directly behind and below the trapeze, he increased power slightly and approached the trapeze. When directly underneath, he eased up and his hook caught the trapeze. The aircraft handling crew brought him aboard, and as soon as he cleared the trapeze, the crew cranked it back down and Walt commenced his approach. He made his usual smooth approach and caught the hook on the trapeze. The aircraft handling crew brought him aboard and slid him down the rail system into the Hangar bay. He secured his aircraft and grabbed his travel bag. He and Duane made their way into the officer's berthing and entered their stateroom. After stowing their gear, they proceeded to the control car where Lieutenant Commander Rosendahl was in the Commanding Officer's chair. They reported to him and exchanged a few words.

Duane and Walt then proceeded to the officer's wardroom to have some lunch. Duane and Walt had nothing assigned to them to do while onboard. Duane decided to go back to his stateroom and work on the Standard Operating Procedures manual he and Walt had been writing. This manual would set the standard for making hookups to dirigibles in the future.

Walt made his way to the control car and received permission to observe the flying of the Akron. Lieutenant Commander Rosendahl had increased the speed of the ship to 65 knots, and they were soon approaching Georgia. Late in the afternoon, they passed Savannah and Rosendahl gave the order to change course to 270°. He was now headed directly for El Paso, Texas.

Walt talked with Lieutenant Commander Rosendahl for a short time. He told him that a friend of his at Paramount News had informed him that he had alerted his cameramen along the route of flight through Texas, New Mexico, and Arizona, that the Akron would crash, a story that they didn't want to miss as it would be a national disaster.

Rosendahl scoffed at the report, but told Walt the transit to the West Coast would not be easy. After spending some time with everyone in the control car, Walt's head was spinning with information and procedures on Akron's systems and flight characteristics. He wanted to learn all he could about the Akron so he could logically discuss operations between the dirigible and the aircraft tucked safely in her Hangar bay. He left the control car and headed to his stateroom. As he stepped onto the catwalk, there was a soft explosion on the port side of the ship. People started running towards the site, many with fire extinguishers and wearing protective clothing. Walt could smell the presence of gasoline, so he stood where he was and let the experts in the crew deal with the emergency. After some 30 minutes, people started moving back to their normal stations. As they passed Walt, he inquired as to the problem. One petty officer said that a fuel tank had burst but most of the fuel drained over the side, however, some fumes remained in the port keel area, but hopefully would dissipate in a short time. Walt figured the emergency was over, so he continued to his stateroom.

He and Duane had a lively discussion about the emergency then settled down and dressed for dinner.

Monday, May 9th

Walt and Duane had spent most of the day flying scouting missions for Akron. The Weather Service put out a report only twice a day so Walt and Duane would fly out the intended track of the Akron, gather the weather they observed and report back to Akron's weather officer.

Late in the day, they were crossing mid-Texas and approaching San Angelo. The mountain passes were clogged up with fog and Rosendahl spent about six hours maneuvering around lightning and thunderstorms waiting for the fog to clear. Around sunup, on the tenth, he decided to head towards Langtry on the Mexican frontier to see if the weather was any better, in hopes the Rio Grande Valley would be clear. However, a few miles west of town, the fog was still covering the mountains and valleys. Rosendahl retreated to Langtry. Here he picked up the Pecos River and was able to grope his way over the obscured ground - and equally obscured mountain peaks on both sides of the airship - to a better sky over the town of Pecos. The weather remained poor over Texas and into New Mexico. From here and into Arizona the airship was tested to the edge of her design. The air was turbulent due to the heating and vertical currents. This made for a rough ride. The Akron also had a tough time with the altitude as, in some places, the ground elevation was 5000' above sea level. The Akron was designed to fly over the water at lower elevations, so she struggled with some of the mountain passes.

The airship finally passed over the last mountain pass just west of Mexicali, California, and began its descent into San Diego. Its destination was Camp Kearney which had been set up with a temporary mooring mast. Here the Akron was due to refuel, and take on water and supplies, then participate in Scouting Pacific Fleet exercises.

Word was passed for Duane and Walt to launch their planes and land at Camp Kearney. Walt would be flying the Sparrowhawk while Duane, with Scotty Peck in the front seat, would fly the N2Y. Scotty Peck was the navigator for the Akron, but here he would be acting as mooring officer.

No airship had docked in San Diego since the USS Shenandoah last landed in 1924 so there were no experienced ground handling personnel and no mechanical equipment to handle the Akron. Because of this situation, the ground handling crew had been drawn from recruits at the San Diego Training Center.

The docking turned into a disaster. The Akron descended until she broke out of the fog at 1200' and headed for the mooring mast. She dropped her aft ropes which were attached to a spider. The spider provided two dozen ropes used to steady the airship and guide it to the mast. When the aft ropes were dropped nothing happened. Despite Scotty Peck yelling at the recruits to grab the ropes, they just stood there in awe looking at the giant airship hovering above them.

Akron made a second approach and this time the ground crew reacted to the situation and grabbed the ropes then guided the airship to the mast. At this time, the airship had only 5 tons of fuel remaining from the 50 tons she started with on her journey across the country. Then with the launching of the aircraft, she lost even more weight, so she was even lighter. As the nose of the airship was secured to the mast the tail began to rise. Rosendahl ordered the airship to be released. It rose to 1000' after he vented helium and reversed the propellors to try to get the tail of the airship down. The unfortunate part of the whole episode was the death of two of the ground crew who had failed to let go of the ropes and were carried aloft, then lost their grip and fell to their deaths. A third crewman had managed to wrap the rope around his feet and was saved when the Akron finally docked and was secured by its tail.

Camp Kearney had no helium, and since Akron was so low on helium, it was decided that joining the fleet was impossible. She would have to fly to Sunnyvale, where helium was readily available and any necessary repairs could be completed. Since they needed to lighten the airship further, Duane and Walt were ordered to fly to Sunnyvale on their own. Also, two officers and ten crewmen were flown to Sunnyvale in two Sikorsky amphibians.

Duane and Walt didn't mind proceeding on their own. It would give them a chance to see the countryside up close and personal. So, without an aeronautical chart, they flew along the shoreline up to Los Angeles then picked up the southern Pacific Railroad headed to Bakersfield, Fresno, then a trunk line that took them to San Francisco Bay, and finally to the base just northwest of San Jose. Airbase Sunnyvale, California, had just one runway. They set up and made the break, and after landing, taxied over to the parking ramp alongside the dirigible Hangar. It was an exact duplicate of the Hangar at Lakehurst designed to hold USS Akron. Construction of the base had begun in 1931 and was almost complete at this time.

Walt and Duane secured their aircraft and were transported to the BOQ. They got adjoining rooms with a shared bathroom. After settling in, they searched for and found the Officers Mess. They had changed into their dress khakis and were allowed to enter the Mess for dinner. After dinner, they checked with base operations to see if there was an ETA for the Akron. They were informed that the Akron was due in tomorrow after 2 o'clock.

Sure enough, about 2 o'clock Akron appeared over the mountains just east of San Jose. The ground handling crew had their heavy machinery in place and were ready to receive the giant airship. Winds were almost calm which should make for an easy landing. The road around the airbase began to fill with gawkers wanting to see this beautiful airship. Traffic was becoming congested and the crowd was growing.

Duane and Walt were standing near the open Hangar doors watching this evolution. Things went very smoothly, and Akron was soon being pushed into the Hangar. Duane and Walt went aboard and checked in with Lieutenant Commander Rosendahl. He inquired about their flight to which they responded, "It would sure be nice to have a navigational chart once in a while, but we flew IFR (I Follow Railroads) all the way up here and didn't have a problem."

The Navigator overheard the conversation and made a note to order additional navigation charts for the Akron's Heavier-Than-Air unit.

Duane and Walt went up to their staterooms and gathered some of their civilian clothes and extra uniforms. At this point, they weren't sure how long they would be in Sunnyvale, but would need a change of uniforms and clothes anyway.

Airbase Sunnyvale, California

The next couple of days, the airship crew and base maintenance crew went about trying to correct the discrepancies on the Akron. Walt and Duane found an empty office in the Hangar to do some work, but reported in every day to Akron's Operations Officer. The workload was light, and they had plenty of time to explore the San Francisco Bay Area.

One of the first things they did was schedule an early morning flight. They had decided that a flight around the perimeter of the bay would familiarize them with landmarks should the weather be marginal, and they would need to find the base. They manned their planes and were off about 8:30 a.m. Their flight took them over the city of San Jose after which they turned to a northerly heading reaching Oakland and Alameda, which were due east of San Francisco. They observed the beginnings of construction of the new bay bridge which would eventually connect Oakland with San Francisco via Yerba Buena Island, a small piece of land located in the middle of the bay. They next reached the city of Berkley where the University of California was located. Here the shoreline turned west so they followed it passing Napa and Sanoma and finally crossing Tiberon and the Golden Gate Bridge. They noted Alcatraz which housed the federal prison which was located just east of the bridge in the ship channel. Passing San Francisco, they noted the location of the airport as a possible alternate landing site. After passing the airport, they observed a salt reclamation project with dikes spanning a small area of the south Bay.

They were once again approaching the base and Duane called for a break and landing. After parking on the ramp next to the Hangar, they walked back to their office.

"Well Walt, what did you think of the Bay Area?" Duane asked.

"That is one hell of a complex, Duane. I saw some places we need to explore," Walt responded.

"We need to develop a priority list of things to do. No telling how long we're going to be here," Walt said.

They settled down in their office and shuffled a few papers but then decided to leave work and return to the BOQ. It was late in the day and they were bored to death. After dinner, they sat in the lounge and started to make plans.

"Duane, have you ever ridden a motorcycle?" Walt asked.

"No, but I think I could handle one if needed. Why do you ask? Have you got one of your sinister plots working in that weird mind of yours?" Duane responded.

"Yeah, how did you know?" Walt said

"Unfortunately, I'm beginning to understand what goes on in that mind of yours? Duane noted.

"Here's my plan. I'll get my old man to buy us a couple of motorcycles we can ride while we're here and then sell them when we leave and pay my Dad back. That way we will have transportation to get around and see things," Walt said. "I heard one of the servers in the Mess talking about this great state park of redwoods which is close by that we need to put first on our places to visit. It's called *Big Basin State Park*."

"Hey, that sounds like a plan. The second place we need to visit is the wineries up in Napa Valley. From what I saw during our flight the other day, it looks like a great place to visit and get a little grape juice," Duane said.

"Okay, tomorrow I'll call the old man and see what he can do for us," Walt said.

"Sounds great," Duane responded.

The two of them continued their discussion for a couple of hours. It was late and they were both tired, so they retired for the night.

Next Morning

After mustering in with the Akron Ops Officer, they went into their office in the Hangar. Walt picked up the phone and made a collect call to his dad in Newport, Rhode Island. Marilyn, dad's office manager, answered. She told the operator she would accept the phone call.

"Well, good morning, Mister Pellman. How are you doing this morning?" she asked.

"Good morning, Marilyn. I'm doing just fine out here in California. Listen I need to speak to my Dad. Is he in the office?" Walt asked.

"Yes, your Dad is here. Let me get him on the phone," Marilyn said.

Ben Pellman picked up the phone on his desk, "How are you Son, Great to hear from you."

"Hey, Dad, I'm doing great. How are you and Mom doing?" he asked.

"Your mother is doing just fine and I'm doing great except for getting more gray hair fighting this recession the economy is in right now,"
Ben said.

"Yeah, Dad. The rescession is hurting us now too. I'm glad you two are doing well," Walt said. "Listen, I have a proposition for you. My friend Duane Harrison and I are out here with the USS Akron. Not sure how long we'll be here, but we need transportation to get around and I was wondering if you could back us with the cash to buy a couple of motorcycles. When we leave, we could sell them then reimburse you for the fullamount you gave us in the beginning.How does that sound?"

"I think I could handle that. About how much wouldyou need?" Ben asked.

"I would estimate about$800 for two goodbikes," Walt said.

"Okay, Son, you got a deal. Let me put Marilyn back on the phone and she'll handle things from here. You take care of yourself," Ben said.

"Thanks, Dad, Hope to see you when we get back East. Love ya," Walt said.

Marilyn came back on the line. "Your Dad briefed me on what you need Mr. Pellman. Give me your phone number, and when I get things worked out, I will call you back," she said.

"Thanks, Marilyn. My phone number is Chestnut 56651. The best time to call would be before noon, your time," Walt said.

"How about later today?" she asked.

"I should be here until 7 o'clock your time," Walt answered.

"Okay, I got it. I will call you later," Marilyn said.

"Thanks, Marilyn. Goodbye for now," Walt said as he hung up the phone.

32
"Time for Relaxation"

Airbase Sunnyvale, California

It was close to 1:30 p.m. when the phone rang. Walt picked up, "Lieutenant Pellman speaking."

"Mr. Pellman, this is Marilyn."

"Oh, hi, Marilyn. Great to hear back from you so quickly," Walt said.

"I found a great BSA Motorcycle dealership in San Francisco and here is the setup. I purchased two BSA Blue Star bikes for you for $800. They will deliver them to you at the Hangar by 11:00 a.m. tomorrow. I wired them the $800 about a half-hour ago so they should give you a sales receipt when they deliver the bikes. Make sure you keep the receipt since they have also agreed to buy them back when you are ready. They have assured me they will give you a fair market price when you are ready to return them. They are also furnishing, with the bikes, a leather helmet, and goggles, so I believe you are all set. Do you have any questions?" Marilyn said.

"No questions here, Marilyn. You are a jewel for doing this for us. Thank you," Walt said

"Just doing my job, Sir. Enjoy your bikes. Goodbye for now," Marilyn said.

"Goodbye, Marilyn and thanks again," Walt said and hung up the phone.

Walt turned to Duane, "All set Buddy. We have two BSA Blue Star Bikes coming tomorrow. They will be delivered to the Hangar."

"Yer old man is a saint, Walt," Duane said.

"Yeah, he's always been good to me," Walt said. "Let's go check with Bob Stoddard and see what our commitment will be to Akron."

They walked out into the Hangar and boarded Akron. They found Bob Stoddard in his cabin. He was working on the flight schedule.

As they entered his cabin he looked up from his work:

"Good afternoon, gentlemen," he said. "What can I do for you?"

Duane asked, "We were wondering what flight commitments we are going to have for the next couple of weeks?"

"I'm working on the schedule right now. We are estimating Akron to be completely repaired and in an up status in about a week. After that, we have public relations stuff. There will be a flight to Redlands and another down the San Joaquin Valley flying over Sacramento. Later, we'll be making a flight up the coast to Seattle to introduce the people to Akron. We plan on you guys to be making hookups over the highly populated areas so people can see what our planes can do. Maybe you guys can make a couple of low passes over the towns to give the population a look at Naval Aviation at its finest," Bob said.

"I am sure we can handle that, Bob. Here's what we would like to do. Since we have no commitments for the next week, Walt and I would like to tour a few of the sights which are part of the beauty of California. We have a couple of motorcycles to do this, so I think we're all set except for getting your clearance to take the time off," Duane offered.

"I think we can handle that, Duane. Just make sure your planes are in an up status before you head out on your explorations," Bob said.

"We'll take care of that, Bob, and thanks for making this possible," Duane replied.

Walt and Duane took leave of their meeting with Bob and went back to their office. Chief Schoonderwoerd was waiting for them.

"Good afternoon, Chief," Duane said.

"Good afternoon, Sir." The Chief replied. "I was wondering what our schedule was for the next week?"

"Funny you should ask. We just got briefed ourselves. So here is the plan. We won't be flying for the next week. Plan on giving the men some time off during the week, but ensure that both planes are in an up status just in case we are needed. If you take some days off, ensure Petty Officer Galetta is briefed on the situation and leave him in charge if we're not available," Duane said.

The Chief acknowledged and went off to brief the men.

Duane and Walt decided what they would do for the next couple of days. They decided to make a day trip to Big Basin State Park and then planned an overnight, possibly two nights, to Yosemite National Park.

They walked out to the aircraft maintenance shop to check on activities there. The Chief had the men double-checking the aircraft. They were up and running an engine check. When that was finished, they shut down and inspected the engines for any leakage. Galetta had the men wiping down the engine while others were wiping down the wings and fuselage. The planes shone brightly in the intense sunlight and when finished, the engine looked like new as it was clean and dry.

Galetta reported back to the Chief that both engines checked out perfectly and the planes were in tip-top shape. He reported they had also checked the wing cable tensions and they were all within tolerance.

The Chief, Walt, and Duane were pleased with the report. They felt that the men had earned some time off.

Next day

Walt and Duane were excited in anticipation of the arrival of their bikes. At 11 o'clock, right on schedule, "BSA Specialties Dealer" arrived at the Hangar with their bikes. They met them at the door, and after a briefing on operating procedures and refueling, Walt signed for the bikes and accepted a Bill-of-Sale.

The agent from the dealership hung around until they started the bikes and took a little trip around the parking lot to become familiar with the riding techniques. Walt and Duane came back to the Hangar door and told the agent the bikes rode beautifully and would be just fine. After the agent took off, and they parked their bikes next to the Hangar.

After checking out with Bob Stoddard, the two of them proceeded to the BOQ to don their riding clothes. After that, they rode out to security at the main gate and registered the bikes to be able to get on and off the base.

Having completed registering the bikes, they then set off to find a Socony gas station. Walt had looked in the Bay Area phonebook and found the closest station to be in Redwood City. They left the base and entered onto Federal Highway 101 and proceeded to Redwood City. As they entered, they found a Socony Gas Station at the corner of Highway 101 and Maple Street. They pulled in and stopped by the pumps. An attendant came out and asked them what they needed. Walt told him to fill up both bikes. He entered the station and was met by the owner. He asked the owner if he could get a road map of California. The owner dug one out of the map case and placed it on the counter. The cost was 16 cents. Walt told him to add it to the cost of gas and that he would pay for it all with a company voucher. The owner was in somewhat of a shock. He asked Walt how come he had company vouchers. Walt was coy and finally told him that his father owned the company and supplied him with the vouchers.

The attendant came in and gave the owner the cost of the gasoline. He added the cost of the map and rang it up on his register. Walt filled out the voucher, signed it, and gave the top copy to the owner. The owner thanked him, and Duane and Walt looked at their route to Big Basin. They decided to take the scenic route across the mountains.

They took California Highway 84W through Woodside then up the mountain onto California highway 85. It was a beautiful, wooded highway with many oaks, birch, and conifers. Next, they turned onto Highway 9 into Big Basin. This highway was lined with Redwoods which seemed to get bigger and bigger the closer they got to Big Basin. Soon they were in the center of the park and arrived at the Ranger Station and Welcome Center. It was a weekday and had very few visitors.

They parked their bikes and checked in with the Ranger. He pointed out a nice easy hiking trail which he said should take them about two hours. That seemed like a reasonable exercise, so they set out on the trail.

They completed the trek in about 2 hours. The trees were gorgeous and the wildlife they saw was outstanding. Mule deer were all over the park. A few black bears had been seen wandering and even a cougar stalking the bears. It was an exciting time for these two Naval Aviators.

It was getting late, so Walt and Duane checked out with the Ranger, hopped on their bikes and headed back to Sunnyvale. This time they went down the mountain through Cupertino and into Sunnyvale then onto the base. They didn't feel like changing into their dress uniforms for dinner, so they stopped at the Base Exchange snack bar and had a sandwich and a cool drink.

The two of them settled down in Walt's room and discussed the events of the day. They agreed the bike ride to and from Big Basin was the most exciting because of the twisty windy mountain roads. The scenic beauty of the ride and the park were the highlight of the day.

The next morning, they put on their dress khakis, and after breakfast, headed to the Hangar. They met Petty Office Galetta who indicated Chief Schoonderwoerd had gone sightseeing for the day and had left him in charge. He reported that both planes had a thorough check and were in an up status. He in effect was just minding the store and answering the phone.

Walt and Duane walked over to Akron and climbed aboard. They found Lieutenant Commander Bob Stoddard and reported that they were there for the day. They still had four days until Akron's flight up the valley to Redwood City. They told Bob they would be going to Yosemite National Park and would be back in four days in time to make the Akron's flight schedule.

It took them about an hour to get packed and ready to depart the base headed for Yosemite. Their saddlebags on the bike were packed full and each had a sleeping bag they checked out from Recreation Services.

They headed East from the base, and when they got to Milpitas, they stopped for gas at a Socony station. Heading north, they passed Free- mont then Livermore and finally dropped down into the San Joaquin Valley through the towns of Tracey, Modesto, and Turlock. Highway 99 took them into Merced. It would be a good place to stock up on some food, so they stopped at a mom and pop store and grabbed a few items. Somehow, they found some space to store the food on their bikes and were off to Yosemite. They traveled up Highway 140. Once they passed Planada, the road started to climb, and after ¾ hour, descended into a foothill's valley. The land was plush and green with lots of trees. After crossing the valley, the road once again started to climb and became windier. Soon they were in a steep canyon that came down right against the road. After two hours on 140, they finally arrived at the entrance to the park. Signs directed them to the Ranger Station where they checked in and obtained a map of the park. The rangers directed them to the camping area next to the Merced River. They were told the water was clear and okay to drink. They picked a spot where previously someone had set three logs on top of one another and staked them with small logs to act as a windbreak. If they built a fire near it, the heat would remain between the logs and the fire and keep them warm during the night.

For the next two days, they enjoyed the scenic beauty of the park. They had found a dirt road that led up to Half Dome and gave them a panoramic view of the park and surrounding mountains. The falls within the park were running at full capacity and were gorgeous. Sadly, the two days went quickly, and they were now headed back to Sunnyvale and the business of flying the trapeze.

33

"Official Business"

Sunnyvale, California

Akron was preparing for liftoff, so Duane and Walt manned their aircraft in anticipation of a few hookups for the crowds in the cities they were to fly over. Akron was on her way about 8:20 a.m. followed shortly thereafter by her airplanes. She was headed east and over Milpitas and would turn north towards Freemont. With Duane in the lead, flying the Sparrowhawk they headed for Freemont. When they arrived over Freemont, Akron was still quite a way south. Duane began a gentle turn to the port to circle waiting for Akron to arrive. She soon appeared and Duane planned his intercept, so he and Walt rolled out just under Akron heading parallel to her route of flight. They took a final position abeam the control car with one on each side of the airship at eye level. Akron was cruising at 60 knots and ordered the airplanes to make hookups over Livermore. Walt slid his position slightly aft and changed his altitude just 20' below the trapeze. Duane then changed his position, and with Walt in sight, joined him in the parade position in right echelon. As the airship approached Livermore, the planes were signaled to commence hookup operations.

Walt looked over at Duane and kissed off. He stabilized his position under the trapeze, matched the speed of the airship then eased forward until he was directly under the trapeze. He added a burst of power when he entered the prop turbulence and made an "as beautiful as you, please" hook up. He remained on the trapeze for about 30 seconds then pulled the release lever and disengaged the hook. Duane observed the operation, and as soon as Walt cleared the trapeze, began his approach and hook up to the trapeze. He mimicked Walt's movements and again made a smooth hookup. When he released, he once again joined up with Walt in the parade position ready for another hookup.

As they approached Sacramento, Akron signaled for more hookups. Walt and Duane obliged once again and after two hookups each, Akron headed for Redwood, California. After passing over the city, Akron reversed course and flew back over Redwood. The planes did their thing on the trapeze.

When passing Sacramento headed south, Akron released her planes to make a couple of low passes over the city. The people were out in droves and cheered as the planes passed over them, followed by Akron. The same scenario was presented to the people of Stockton and Fresno. On the way back north, the pilots did a few hookups.

With all the hand waving completed, Akron headed back to Sunnyvale. She released her planes who flew directly to base and completed their flight. Akron arrived about thirty minutes later, and she too completed her flight with attachment to the mooring mast. Akron was then rolled in and secured in the Hangar.

The next hand-waving flight was scheduled in two days. It would be over San Francisco and a few of the Bay Cities. This gave Duane and Walt a day off and a chance to visit San Francisco.

They awoke early and were off on their bikes by mid-morning. They departed the base and hopped onto U.S. highway 101. This route took them into Mountain Home, Palo Alto, Redwood City, and San Mateo before bringing them into San Francisco. They visited Telegraph Hill, Golden Gate Park, and the Presidio. The views of the Pacific Ocean and the Golden Gate was spectacular. Since they were so close, they decided to ride across the Golden Gate Bridge into the village of Tiburon. It was a quaint little place with artsy shops and tea gardens. They stopped for a late lunch and had a small sandwich and some hot tea. It was a delightful change of pace from the Navy food they had been eating. During lunch, they decided to continue around the Bay to the eastern side and go back to Sunnyvale via Oakland. It turned out to be a pleasant ride but more populated and industrialized.

The sun was setting as they pulled up to the gate at the base. They stopped at the Gedunk and had some supper, then off to the BOQ for a good night's sleep.

Sunnyvale, California, Next Day

This was going to be a short flying day for all hands. By 7:30 a.m. the crew of the Akron were all over her like ants in a colony. Some on the crew had been working all night on the number 6 engine. It had been losing power periodically and they were trying to fix the problem. All maintenance equipment was pulled away by 8:12 a.m. and Akron was being pushed out onto the launch circle. Duane and Walt manned their airplanes with Walt flying the Sparrowhawk and Duane in the N2Y.

By 8:53a.m. Akron was airborne and within minutes Duane and Walt had assumed their parade position on the Akron. They proceeded towards San Francisco. As they approached the city, Akron ordered the planes to commence trapeze operations. Duane made the first hookup followed by Walt. Two more hookups each followed as Akron reached the Golden Gate Bridge. She made a 90° turn to port and passed over the bridge headed west. After proceeding about a mile, she made a port 90° turn followed by a starboard 270° turn heading directly east and back over the Golden Gate Bridge. At this time, Walt and Duane, who had been flying in a parade position on Akron, were directed to circle the airship. They broke off and joined in a right echelon and commenced flying a circle over the Akron.

She descended into the bay and leveled off at 1500'. The purpose of this section of the flight was to moor the Akron to the Fleet Oiler USS Patoka which was currently anchored approximately one mile northeast of Alcatraz Island. Akron continued to descend, finally spotted Patoka, and descended to 150' as she approached the mooring mast. Lieutenant Scott Peck had boarded Patoka at Fort Mason, on the north shore of the city of San Francisco, and would supervise the mooring operation.

Akron made her approach and came to a stop at one and a half feet. A designated officer attached the mooring cable to the mast and Patoka reeled in Akron until she was snug at the mast. She remained moored for about 15 minutes then the mooring cable was released, and Akron reversed her engines and backed off from the mast. She began to rise, forward motion was realized and altitude gained. Akron's planes were released to proceed to base. Walt and Duane broke off from circling and proceeded to Sunnyvale. Akron arrived shortly thereafter and was rolled into the Hangar.

The month of May was nearly over and the CNO had assigned them one more flag-waving flight to Bellingham, Washington, near the Canadian border to show the citizens of the northwest the airship. At this point, at least, the Hangar deck crew on board Akron, would get some actual training. Walt and Duane took turns after hookup being brought aboard Akron and pushed onto the Hangar deck. Then relaunched for more hookups. By the time the Akron returned to Sunnyvale, the Hangar deck crew could retrieve a plane and be ready for another in less than 10 minutes. This was a real success for all hands.

On May 27th, Akron received orders from Commander Scouting Forces Pacific to proceed to San Diego and participate in the Fleet Exercises currently being held off the coast. At 8:20 a.m. on June 1st, the crew began filling Akrons cells with helium. By 10:30 a.m., her cells were at full capacity and provisions were being stowed aboard.

Duane and Walt were aboard Akron to have a conference with the Commanding Officer. Duane and Walt knocked on his office door and were ushered in.

"Good morning," The Commanding Officer said. "Come in and have a seat. I have just a couple of things to discuss with you."

Duane and Walt took a seat.

"I'll get right to it, gentlemen. The Commander, Scouting Forces Pacific and I have exchanged a few messages. He feels that since the N2Y does not have floatation gear aboard the Sparrowhawk and the N2Y should remain in Sunnyvale during our exercise time with the fleet for safety reasons."

"Skipper, we understand your position. It's difficult to convince a two-star he's wrong. We were looking forward to working with Akron on this scouting mission," Duane said.

"We had also been working on a scouting doctrine for Akron which we wanted to try so we could refine it, but I guess it will have to wait, Skipper," Walt said.

"So just to be clear, you two have been beached until we return to Sunnyvale. You're on your own so just stay out of trouble. I expect we should be back in a week or so," the Commanding Officer said.

"Roger that Skipper. Have a good trip and we'll be here waiting," Duane responded. And with that, they left the Commanding Officer's quarters and the Akron.

By 5:30 pm the Akron was loaded and ready to go. She was pushed out of the Hangar and wassoon on her way south.

Duane and Walt were extremely disappointed with the decision to leave them behind.

They looked at each other, "Well, here we are grounded so to speak. I guess we should work on our plan for the week the Akron is gone?" Walt said.

"Yeah, let's go back to the office and think this thing over. We know we have at least a week to do whatever the hell we want," Duane answered.

They got on their bikes and headed for some dinner.

Next morning

They were in the office early. The crew mustered at 7:30 a.m. and Chief Schoonderwoerd came in and reported all-hands accounted for.

Duane spoke first, "Chief, the Akron won't be back for about a week. I think if your work is done, and the planes are in an up status, you should let the men go on liberty. I'll leave it to your judgment. Give the crew some time off to see the beautiful sights of California."

"Yes, Sir, I can do that. I will have some of the men working on the N2Y, however. We are experiencing some engine trouble on it and I'm not sure of the cause," The Chief said.

"Sounds great, Chief. We may need a test flight later in the week. Just keep me advised of the status of the aircraft. By the way, Mr. Pellman and I may take a couple of days off to see more of this area, but I will keep you advised of our plans. If we coordinate things, you too can get some time off." Duane noted.

Suddenly and without warning the telephone rang. After the first ring, Walt picked up and answered it.

"Lieutenant Pellman." He listened for a minute and then placed the receiver back on the cradle. "That was base communications on the phone. We have some messages which need to be picked up. Chief, can you assign someone to do that?" Walt asked.

"Yes, Sir, I'll get on it right away," The chief replied.

"Chief, we should also have someone on duty when Mr. Pellman and I are not in the office. We'll keep you advised, and you can have someone man the phone here."

"Just keep me advised, Sir," the Chief grabbed a cup of coffee and went back out into the Hangar.

Walt and Duane got out their proposed scouting plan for the Akron planes. It was incomplete and they discussed some of the aspects of the plan that needed work. Walt took notes and when they had completed their discussion, he began writing and filling in some of the missing pieces.

Petty Officer LeBlanc entered the office and gave Lieutenant Harrison the messages from the Comm center. Duane began to look through them. He stopped at about the third message.

"Walt, here's a personal message addressed to you from Admiral McMillin," Duane said.

He passed the message to Walt. It read, *"Lieutenant Pellman, request you visit the facilities of the Stearman-Hammond Aircraft Company's manufacturing plant and give us an evaluation as to their suitability to provide the Navy with drones. I will advise the company of your impending visit. Request your report be sent to BUAER, Attention: Director, RADM McMillin."*

Walt looked up from the message. "I have an assignment from Admiral McMillin to inspect a company for suitability to supply drones to the U.S. Navy. It looks like that's going to eat into our free time this week."

"At least we'll be doing something useful," Duane offered. "It sure beats sitting around here all day and making work. I hope I'm invited to accompany you on this foray?"

"Damn, Duane, you know you are welcome to go with me. The two of us are better than just me going alone. I'll need to do a little research and find out where they are located and possibly set up an appointment for a visit," Walt said.

Later in the day, he found their phone number, and that they are located in Redwood City. He talked with Dean Hammond, Vice-president of the company. Dean said he would be available to talk with them and give them a tour of the facility tomorrow after 10:30. a.m.

Walt told Dean they would see him tomorrow. Turning to Duane, he briefed him on his discussion with Dean Hammond and advised him they would need to wear their dress khakis for this inspection.

Next Day, Sunnyvale, California.

The two Naval Aviators were off on their bikes after breakfast. They headed for Redwood City via the Federal Highway 101. Within 30 minutes they pulled up in front of a huge warehouse at 365 Sierra Heights Boulevard. They put on their dress khaki blouse and headed for the door to the building.

Once inside they found the office and Dean Hammond at his desk.

As they entered, Walt spoke and extended his hand.

"I'm Lieutenant Pellman," he said. "And this is Lieutenant Harrison. Rear Admiral McMillin has directed us to inspect your facilities for suitability in the manufacture of the Y-1S."

"Welcome, gentlemen, to our manufacturing facility. Please have a seat. Would either of you care for a drink or cup of coffee?" Dean asked.

They both answered in the negative for a drink of coffee.

Duane and Walt took a seat facing Dean at his desk.

The conversation continued. "Mr. Hammond, I am certain the Bureau of Aeronautics will furnish you with the specs for the JH-1s and our engineers will coordinate with you on their research with drone technology. Your aircraft code will be "H" and therefore our planes will be designated as the JH-1. Today we are mainly concerned with the suitability of your facilities to manufacture these JH-1s in a safe and timely fashion," Walt said.

"I think we can deliver that," Dean said. "Let's go out on the plant floor and I will show you, our plan."

The trio left the office and proceeded out onto the manufacturing plant's floor. Dean began describing where each facet of the manufacturing and assembly would take place. He showed them where the fabric would be applied and the doping area before painting. Things were in a state of flux as the company was just accumulating materials and machines before hiring staff to man positions needed to complete building of the Y-1S and JH-1. One interesting part of this aircraft was the aluminum construction and the tricycle gear arrangement, quite a difference from the stick and fabric aircraft the Navy was currently flying.

Dean Hammond was quite convincing in his presentation of how and when this new aircraft would take to the skies.

The tour took about an hour, and they finished where they started, in Dean Hammond's office.

"That concludes our tour, gentlemen. Do you have any further questions?" Dean said.

Walt interjected. "I think we have the essence of your plan on the manufacture of this aircraft. I can tell you I will give the Admiral my recommendation to go ahead with plans to grant a contract with your company."

Walt and Duane shook Dean's hand and walked out the door. They changed into their working jacket, cranked up their bikes, and were on their way back to the base.

Once in the office, Walt wrote his observations and opinions on the suitability of the Stearman-Hammond Aircraft Company to manufacture the JH-1s for the Navy. When he finished, he handed it to Duane and solicited changes and comments to the report. Duane had none so Walt typed it up, addressed the envelope, and made it ready for mailing.

It had been a great day and they had done something useful for the United States Navy.

34

"Love Blossoms"

Sunnyvale, California

The Akron had returned from participation in the current fleet exercise with the Scouting Command. She had demonstrated to higher command, she could add to fleet readiness and be a useful partner in scouting for the fleet.

The Chief of Naval Operations had wished for her to return to Lakehurst via the Caribbean to show support for the Atlantic Scouting Command, but her need for maintenance could be handled only at Lakehurst. Therefore, she was ordered to Lakehurst ASAP.

June 11th rolled around and early morning found her crew adding helium, aviation fuel, and other consumables for the flight east. By afternoon her helium and fuel tanks were full, and the airship was ready to depart.

Duane and Walt sold their bikes back to BSA Motorcycles in San Francisco. The return price was $750 so it cost them only $50 to have the bikes while they were in Sunnyvale. The dealer had picked them up on the 10th and Walt could now pay the old man back his loan.

Duane and Walt manned their planes with Duane in the N2Y and Walt in the Sparrowhawk. Duane chose to fly the N2Y since the engine was unreliable and he was the senior officer of the Unit.

Once the Akron was airborne, Duane and Walt did their hookup to the trapeze and were moved to the Hangar bay. Duane reported to the Skipper that the aircraft Unit was aboard. The two of them settled in for an uneventful trip to Lakehurst.

As the Akron approached Phoenix, she needed to be over 6000' in altitude. The sun was setting, and the heat was being dissipated from the helium cells. Also, they were still very heavy because they had burned very little fuel on the trip from Sunnyvale. Coming west had been easy and they had burned plenty of fuel just reaching West Texas, but going east they were extremely heavy. As they approached the mountains east of Phoenix, the airship was still unable to clear the mountain tops. The Skipper turned back to circle Phoenix and dump some fuel. Having done that, the airship was still unable to clear the mountain tops. The Skipper decided to launch the airplanes which would lighten the airship and very likely make it possible to proceed.

Duane and Walt were awakened and told to launch ASAP. They didn't even have time to stop for a cup of coffee. Within twenty minutes after getting out of bed, Duane was on the trapeze starting his engine. Walt followed 10 minutes later. He joined up with Duane and headed for Texas. The Skipper indicated he would rendezvous with them over Pecos, Texas. Walt and Duane landed at the Pecos Municipal Airport and refueled in anticipation of Akron's arrival. There was a boarding house nearby the airport, so they rented a room for the night. It was within walking distance so they hiked to and from the boarding house.

Akron's ETA Pecos was 9:00 a.m. the next morning. Duane and Walt made sure they were ready for takeoff by 8:45. a.m. They manned their aircraft and lifted off exactly at 8:45 a.m. Duane was in the lead in the N2Y, and as soon as Walt joined on his wing, headed west to intercept Akron. He leveled off at 3000' and spotted Akron off in the distance. They closed the distance quickly and Duane called on VHF radio. There was no answer, so Duane circled the Akron and leveled at eye level on the control car. No matter what he tried he could not get an answer from Akron. Walt went below the airship to check if the trapeze would be lowered. No matter what the two of them did, Akron was silent. After twenty minutes of frustration, they joined up and proceeded to Pecos. When they checked with the airport administration to see whether there had been any communication with Akron, the Airport Manager gave them a telegram addressed to them. Akron's message was, *"Proceed to Lakehurst independently".*

This was perfect as far as Walt was concerned. He and Duane talked it over and decided to go via Wichita, Kansas. This way Walt could see his sweetheart Zimmy. The next morning, they manned their aircraft and headed to Wichita. They followed the railroad to Abilene then on to Wichita Falls and finally to Oklahoma City, where they refueled and then flew on to Wichita. They taxied over to the Stearman Aircraft manufacturing facility where the U.S. Navy had a liaison office. The office took care of filing an arrival report with USS Akron.

The office also furnished them a ride downtown where they found a room at the Great Western Hotel. Walt called Zimmy's home phone number. A strange voice answered. She identified herself as Jane Moorhead, Zimmy's roommate. "Oh hi, Jane. This is Walt Pellman. Is Zimmy there?" he asked.

She indicated Zimmy would be home after 7 o'clock tonight, as she was on the afternoon flight from Chicago.

Walt decided to meet Zimny's flight. It was due to arrive at 6:30 p.m. so he took a taxi to the airport and saw that the flight from Chicago would be arriving on time at American Airways Gate 4. He proceeded to the area of Gate 4 and sat on a bench awaiting the flight's arrival.

At 6:30 p.m. the Trimotor pulled into Gate 4 and opened the cabin door. Passengers exited and shortly thereafter the flight crew exited the aircraft.

Zimny was the third of the crew to exit. She spotted Walt standing there in his Naval flight uniform and broke into a dash directly at him. They ran into each other with open arms. He kissed her with great passion before he said, "God, how I really missed you."

She returned with, "Not as much as I missed you."

He swung her around as he breathed in her essence "You still are the most beautiful woman I have ever seen and held in my arms," he said.

Zimmy blushed as he once again pulled her up close and hugged her with great resolve which exuded a sense of sincere passionate love. She returned his feelings which both freely gave to each other.

Finally, she pushed away and said, "I need to check out with the company and then I will be ready to go home."

"Okay," Walt said. "I'll meet you out at the street. I'll get us a taxi."

She kissed him with great passion then broke away and headed for the checkout desk for the airline crew.

As she exited the main entrance, she spied Walt standing next to a taxi. She walked over and brushed against him as she entered, "Hey sailor are you ready for some liberty?" she asked.

"I was born ready," Walt answered. The taxi drove away from the terminal with a lot of hugging and kissing going on.

They arrived at Zimmy's living quarters. She and Jane lived together in a small apartment attached to a beautiful 1920s Arts and Crafts style house both inside and out. It was a one-bedroom apartment with a living room, bathroom, and kitchen.

Jane greeted them as they arrived.

"Hi Jane, great to see you again after all this time." Walt said.

"Great to see you again too Walt," Jane answered.

Walt asked if the ladies had eaten dinner. They answered negatively so Walt made the suggestions that his friend Duane could pick up some food at the hotel and bring it to them at the apartment. They all thought that to be a great idea, so Walt made a call to the hotel and finally got in touch with Duane. He gave Duane the address of the girl's apartment and told him food for four. Walt indicated he would share the cost of dinner.

Within twenty minutes Duane was knocking at the front door. Jane answered.

"Hi, I'm Duane, your friendly delivery man. I have dinner for four, which by the way is getting cold with me standing here so how about you invite me in."

"Oh, please come on. I'm Jane. Sorry, but I was expecting a much younger man," Jane said.

Duane stepped into the apartment. "Are you saying I'm too old? I want you to know I'm all of 25 years old and have never been kissed."

Jane was captivated by the young Naval Aviator. She leaned over and kissed Duane with great gusto. "I never kissed a Naval Aviator before," she said. "Now both our dreams are fulfilled."

Walt and Zimmy came to the door just as Jane was kissing Duane. "I see you've met Duane," Walt said to Jane. "Yes, I did. He needed a warm welcome, so I gave him one," she said.

Walt introduced Zimmy to Duane and they all proceeded to the kitchen. Duane had acquired four dinners at the hotel. Each consisted of baked potato, corn on the cob, and Salisbury steak. The dessert was chocolate pudding. Zimmy had preheated the oven, so she placed the four dinners in it to warm the food.

Jane observed, "We're almost ready for dinner. Wouldn't you guys like to change out of your uniforms?"

Duane responded, "We sure would like to, but we left the airship in such a hurry that this is about all we have to wear."

"I guess it will have to do," Jane said.

The dinner was placed on the table and all four sat down to enjoy the food.

After finishing dinner, Zimmy and Walt moved to the living room while Duane volunteered to help Jane with cleaning up the kitchen. Jane and Duane seemed to hit it off as they were both laughing and enjoying each other's company as they cleaned up the kitchen.

The evening was a hoot with the guys learning more about the gals. After an hour Zimmy, took Walt back into the bedroom for a little more privacy and intimacy. The gals laid down the rules. No sex, but plenty of kissing and hugging. Around midnight the ladies decided they needed some sleep. They determined it was too late to send the boys to the hotel, so the ladies went to the bedroom while the boys were relegated to the living room. Duane flipped a coin with Walt to see who got to sleep on the couch and who got the chair. Walt lost so he was left with the big puffy leather chair with an ottoman.

The sun broke through the blinds about 7:30 a.m., which woke Walt from a sound sleep. He slipped on his pants and went into the bathroom. The noise of flushing the toilet woke the rest of the house and soon everyone was up and dressed.

Walt greeted Zimmy with a good morning kiss and a big hug. Duane and Jane did the same only not quite as passionate.

"How about some bacon and eggs this morning?" Zimmy offered.

They all responded in the affirmative, so everyone set about to make it happen. Jane and Duane set the table while Walt made the coffee and Zimmy had the main task of frying the bacon and eggs. Walt also made toast. Teamwork paid off and they all quickly sat down at the table.

After breakfast, Jane needed to go to the airport for her final class to become a flight stewardess. Duane decided he would go with her and check out the Stearman manufacturing plant.

Walt and Zimmy had the apartment all to themselves, so they decided that they needed to talk and clear up their predicament.

They sat down on the couch and Walt opened the conversation.

"Zimmy, you know that I love you deeply and I want us to get married," he said.

"Did you just propose marriage?" she asked.

"Yes, I did, but I can't make it official until I get you a ring," Walt answered. "So, what is your decision?"

Zimmy started to cry, "That makes me so happy. Yes, I'll marry you," she said. "However, it comes with limitations and a caveat."

They embraced each other and kissed in a long and loving kiss. They continued to embrace for what seemed a long time when Walt finally spoke.

"And tell me the limitations and caveat," he said, Zimmy began, "I want us to be married and live together, but I also need to carry on with my career. Also, Jane is finishing her Flight Stewardess training today. We have been friends for a long time, and I don't want to abandon her until she is firmly engaged in the job. I have figured out a solution, but it will take some time to solve itself. Here is what I think I can maneuver the company to do. Each month we bid on our route to fly the next month. When Jane and I can get a route out of New York or Philadelphia, we can then move close to Lakehurst and then think about getting married."

"I think that's a great plan. Duane and I will be gone a lot and having Jane with you will give you two some feeling of comfort and security," Walt said

"Okay, come over here and give me a hug," Walt said

Zimmy came over and more hugging and kissing occurred.

"We need to go to the store for a few groceries," Zimmy offered.

"I could use a few clothes," Walt responded.

"We can do that too while we out," Zimmy said.

The two of them dressed for the foray and off they went for the day's shopping.

Meanwhile, Duane dropped Jane at the Flight Stewardess school and went over to the Stearman Plant. He found the Naval Liaison office and stopped in. Stearman was presently building the NS-1 trainer for the Navy and had plans to deliver a new trainer, the N2S. The liaison officer arranged a tour of the facility for Duane. It lasted about two hours and he found it very interesting. While he was there, he arranged for the Stearman line crew to refuel the N2Y and XF9C-1.

Walt and Zimmy returned to the apartment at about 4 o'clock. They were followed shortly thereafter by Jane and Duane. Walt and Zimmy had been successful in their grocery shopping, acquiring some macaroni and cheese plus a few vegetables for a salad. Walt bought a couple of pairs of underwear, a few for him and a few for Duane.

Jane had finished her training with flying colors and had graduation tomorrow.

Duane reported to Walt what he had seen and done at Stearman.

They each took a shower and changed their underwear. While they were showering, Zimmy put the dirty clothes in the washing machine. Eventually, they had clean clothes to wear. While all this was going on, Jane began to cook dinner.

Finally, they all sat down for dinner. Zimmy and Walt announced that they were getting married. Jane was excited and she and Duane expressed their congratulations. Of course, the first question was when. Zimmy laid out their plan to Jane and Duane. Both were extremely happy with that as Duane would be able to see Jane more often, so it was a winwin situation for everyone.

The excitement of the ladies moving close to Lakehurst was the topic of discussion for the evening plus a lot of hugging and kissing.

"I need to get to bed and get some sleep," Zimmy announced. "I have a flight at 10:32 a.m. to Chicago with a return to Wichita later in the day."

Jane sounded off, "My graduation is a 10:00 a.m. at the American Airways Fight School, so I should probably get some rest. I need to press my uniform, so I look decent tomorrow."

"Same sleeping arrangements as last night guys, sorry," Zimmy said. "Reveille is at 6:00a.m.

They were all disappointed with no more lovin', but everyone would have a long day tomorrow, so they settled in for the night.

Walt was the first one awake and up. He got partially dressed and went into the bathroom. He had purchased a razor and shaving cream and a toothbrush. He shaved and brushed his teeth then washed up and finished dressing. Duane was next and did the same. Meanwhile, Zimmy was up and started the coffee. They had purchased more eggs and bacon while they were out shopping so that was the menu for breakfast. Jane was next in the bathroom followed by Zimmy. Jane took over the cooking while Zimmy got dressed. When she came out of the bedroom, she looked gorgeous. She was wearing her Flight Stewardess uniform and it looked stunning on her.

Jane, assisted by Duane, put breakfast on the table. They all sat down to eat.

Zimmy commented how great Walt and Duane looked in their Naval Fight Uniforms. Zimmy and Jane were dressed alike. The guys couldn't get enough of these two beautiful women. They all gathered their belongings and were ready and waiting for the taxi they had called to arrive. Walt mentioned they needed to check out of the hotel on the way to the airport.

They reached the airport and said their long goodbyes. Jane went to her graduation, Zimmy checked in for her flight. Walt and Duane filed their flight plan, walked over and cranked up their aircraft and departed Wichita. What a great time they had for two days with the ladies. Now it was back to business.

35

"Disaster Strikes"

Lakehurst, New Jersey

Duane and Walt were back home. The trip from Wichita had been uneventful and they were glad to be home and in familiar surroundings.

Akron had returned safely, but was considered grounded with all her discrepancies, VHF transceiver being one of them. She had a tough time and had to land at Paris Island and spend a couple of days. Her crew was busy fixing all those problems.

The Air Unit was a busy place as well. Two new pilots reported aboard. Bob Fitzwater and Paul Day arrived. They checked in with the Chief Yeoman on the Akron before he sent them over to the Unit's offices. When they arrived, Duane and Walt were in the office doing some mundane work.

Bob first spotted Walt.

He shouted out across the room, "Well, we're here old Buddy. What the hell have you gotten us into?" he asked.

"And a welcome to you too, Bob. Glad to see you," Walt said, as he walked over and shook Bob's hand.

He turned to Paul and shook his hand as he welcomed him aboard. He asked Paul, "What have you been feeding him, Paul, anchovies and pinto beans?"

"Nah it's just his ugly nature finally showing," Paul said.

"And you two can go piss up a rope," Bob answered. "So now let's get serious. We're here to join this ragtag squadron and get some work done."

"First, you guys remember Duane? He was at the christening in Akron. He is our O-in-C, and I am his deputy." Turning to Duane, "you remember Bob?." Walt said.

Bob stepped forward and extended his hand, "Great to see you again, Sir,

"Duane, you remember Paul?" Walt offered.

"Yeah,good to have you aboard, Paul," Duane said. "I hope you boys had a nice trip?"

Paul spoke for both, "We had a spectacular trip, stopped in Washington, and saw some of the great monuments. We even went to a session of the House of Representatives at the Capitol.

"Well, both of you step over here," Duane said.

Bob and Paul stepped over to Duane's desk where he reached for some paperwork.

"Raise your right hand," Duane said.

He then read the oath of office promoting them to the rank of Lieutenant. The look on Bob and Paul's faces said it all. They were completely taken by surprise.

Duane shook their hands. "Congratulations, gentlemen. You are now officially out of uniform, and you may now address me as Duane."

Walt shook each of their hands. "You can thank Admiral McMillin for your promotion. He felt our flight leaders should all be Lieutenants to put us in a better position when we are on board the Akron. They are staffing Akron with higher ranks who are jockeying for positions, and he doesn't want us in a pissing contest with Akron staff."

Duane asked, "Do you have your check-in sheet?"

Bob and Paul acknowledged they did.

"Go ahead and finish your check-in then and get settled at the BOQ. We'll see you later," Duane said.

Bob and Paul departed, and Walt and Duane went back to work.

Walt piped up, "I see we're getting delivery of an F9C-2 this week. It's about time."

"Yeah, it's been at Flight test for acceptance in Anacostia for over a month and NAF for two more weeks to get a skyhook. I had information that our suggestion that the upper wing be raised was incorporated.

Bob and Paul finished their check-in and then checked in to the BOQ. They occupied rooms near Duane and Walt on the first floor. They also joined the Mess so they could eat their meals at the BOQ.

Walt and Duane worked right up to the dinner hour getting the N2Ys all in an up status. The one Duane flew back from the West Coast was found to need an engine change. That was almost complete.

Walt and Duane were joined by Bob and Paul at dinner. It was a great reunion. After dinner, they continued their get-together in the lounge area of the BOQ.

"So, tell me what we're going to be doing?" Bob asked.

"First of all, we are going to check you and Paul out as flight leaders. The first thing we need to do is get you flying the N2Y. It looks like after Akron is in an up status, they will be doing some training in the mission they were designed for, meanwhile, we will be doing hookups on the trapeze to get you guys qualified on hookups and in turn training the Hangar deck crew on the Akron. It's going to be a little while before we get all our F9Cs so the N2Y will be our primary focus, although we are getting another F9C this week which will give us the XF9C-1 and an F9C- 2. We need to get you both checked out in the N2Y ASAP," Walt said.

"Well, tell us what you guys do for excitement when you're not at work," Paul asked.

"We haven't had much relaxation time, Paul. Walt and I have been on the West Coast for about a month although we did have a few days in Wichita," Duane said.

Paul immediately blurted out, "Did you see Zimmy, Walt?"

Walt smiled then said, "Yeah, I saw her and we're going to get married."

"Hey, Buddy, that's great. When's the wedding?" Bob asked.

Paul chimed in with, "Walt, you dirty dog, a married guy in our midst. You want to break up the team, huh."

"We're not getting married for a while. Zimmy has some things to work out with her airline and when that happens, she is moving close to Lakehurst, and then we'll get married," Walt reported.

"Hey, Buddy, we're happy for you. Sounds like a good plan," Bob said.

It was getting late, and Duane said he was tired and going to bed. The other three sat for another hour and recalled old times and wondered about the future. With the F9C in the picture, at least they would be flying fighters. Walt reminded them that only about 20 Naval Aviators would ever do what they were about to do, i.e., fly a plane aboard an airship.

Having exhausted their conversation for the moment, they all decided bed was the best option, so they said goodnight and went to their rooms.

In the morning, after breakfast, Walt and Duane headed for the Hangar while Bob and Paul walked over to the uniform shop. They purchased shoulder boards for their khakis and Lieutenant's bars for their shirts. They didn't have their blues yet so they would have to wait to have them striped with the gold braid.

They were now in the proper uniform and headed for the Hangar. They entered the Unit's office and were greeted by Duane.

"Hey, guys, glad to see you are in proper uniform. Come sit down so we can talk," Duane said.

Bob and Paul pulled up a couple of chairs around Duane's desk.

"We are trying to find a couple of desks and chairs for you so you can have an office," Duane said. "Walt and I discussed your orientation, and we think you should first get a tour of the Airship to familiarize yourselves with her basic nomenclature and specifically the trapeze and Hangar deck operations. When you get back, Walt and I will work with you one- on-one to get you started on N2Y familiarization. After that, we'll send you off into the wild blue to have some fun and log some flight time."

"When the Akron comes out of maintenance, we will fly some hookups to get you qualified on the trapeze and help train the Hangar deck crew at the same time. After you get some hours logged in the N2Y, we will get you qualified in the F9C Sparrowhawk. So how does that sound for a start?" Duane asked.

"Sounds like a busy schedule. I like it," Paul said.

"Yeah, should keep us busy for a day or two," Bob joked and everybody chuckled.

"Okay, then, you two head over to the Akron. Ask for Lieutenant Commander Stoddard. He'll set you up for a tour and indoctrination of the trapeze and hangar deck," Duane directed.

"We're on our way, boss," Paul said.

Paul and Bob headed over to Akron and Duane went back to his paperwork.

The next few days were filled with all kinds of training for the four young Naval Aviators of the Akron's Air Unit. Today Bob and Paul were scheduled to fly their first flight in the N2Y.

They were briefed by Walt on the local operating area, restricted areas, and what they should accomplish on the flight. He suggested that, after they practice their stalls and maybe a few acrobatics they join up and fly a little formation. That way they can recall their hand signals and procedures.

As Paul and Bob were taxing out to the runway, the unit's brand new F9C-2 landed and taxied over to the Hangar. Walt was there to meet the pilot and accept its transfer into the Unit. Chief Schoonderwoerd was also there to inspect the plane and take possession of the logbooks. The plane was in great shape. Flight time since it left the factory was 22.5 hours. The maintenance crew pulled it into the Hangar and began a complete inspection of the plane. Once the plane was inspected and then wiped down, the paint crew took over and painted "USS Akron" near the tail and then painted the squadron insignia, designed by Walt, on each side of the plane just forward of the cockpit. The insignia showed a burly and smiling acrobat in red tights and yellow shirt hanging by his knees from a trapeze, reaching out for a skinny fellow performer who is flying. From this day forward the men of the Heavier-Than-Air unit were known as the "men on the flying trapeze."

Paul and Bob returned from their flight. Then came up to the office where Duane and Walt were busy working on their publications.

"Well, gentlemen, how was your flight?" Duane inquired.

"A piece of cake," Paul said. "It's not a fighter, but it's better than a desk anytime. We did everything but spin it."

"Sounds good, Paul. I think tomorrow you guys should try it one more time before we move into four-man formation flying," Duane said.

"And tomorrow I think you and I should fly the F9s, Duane," Walt said.

"That'll be a hoot, Walt. I can't wait to see the differences from the X-1 model."

"I sat in the cockpit, and it looks like the visibility is better with the upper wing being raised 4"," Walt said.

Duane directed his comments to Bob and Paul.

"You guys can work on developing an open book test for the N2Ys nomenclature. We should all have one in our training jacket."

Things at the unit were going very well. All the pilots were now checked out in the N2Y. Duane and Walt took a flight in the F9Cs with

Duane in the -2 and Walt in the X model. Duane found it to be a better plane than the X, especially with the wing 4" higher and the increased horsepower. He was still not quite convinced, but would make his decision when they got some hookups on the Akron.

A couple of days went by and two new pilots checked into the unit, Lieutenant (JG) Mike Brunner and Lieutenant (JG) Joe Russell. Walt put them on the same training plan as Bob and Paul had when they checked in. These two pilots had come from the training command. They were "Plow Backs" who had earned their wings then remained as instructors for another year. That was an indication they were some of the best, however, they had flown only trainers but no fighters. Within a day these two were scheduled to fly the N2Ys. Walt decided he would fly with them to evaluate their skills. On the flight, he directed their maneuvers. His evaluation was that these two Naval Aviators were very good pilots. When he felt they had completed their formation review, he told them to return to base and he joined up as number three in the parade position. As they came into the break, each kissed off in turn and made their approach and landing. Joe was number two, and as he rolled out, he blew the starboard tire and the plane ground looped. It did no damage, just a little embarrassing. Walt was close behind him on the runway and stopped, pulled up alongside Joe's airplane, and signaled thumbs-up. Joe returned the signal indicating he was okay so Walt continued to taxi back to the Hangar.

Maintenance was out to the airplane quickly with a wheel and tire. They changed it and towed the airplane back to the hanger. The landing gear was inspected just in case there was damage. However, no damage so the plane was in an up status within a couple of hours.

The unit now had its six N2Ys in an up status, so Duane called all his pilots together and briefed them on their next flight. It would be a six-plane formation flight. Duane would lead with Walt and Bob as section leaders. Duane covered the Parade and free cruise positions as well as all the hand signals.

The pilots manned their planes. As they made their take-offs, they made a running rendezvous and joined in step-up right echelon. Duane had them practice gentle turns in right echelon. He then had Walt's section in number 3 and 4 position move to left echelon and take a position so they were then in a "V" formation. His next maneuver was free cruise. He practiced steep turns in right and left echelon then switched to a parade formation in step-down position. From there he practiced carrier breakups and rendezvous.

Duane was pleased by the performance of his pilots, so he headed back to base. He brought them into the break at 800', called the tower, and when cleared, kissed off as did each pilot in turn where six pilots made six beautiful landings.

They all taxied to the Hangar and shut down the aircraft. Duane was pleased with his pilots' performance, and he told them so in the debrief of the flight.

When Duane arrived back at the office, he had a message from the Bureau of Aeronautics directing him to take delivery of the F9C-2s at the Curtis Wright plant and fly them to Lakehurst. He was ecstatic. At last, the unit would have their fighters.

Lakehurst, New Jersey

It was already into July and the Unit's pilots had been unable to make any hookups to Akron. She was ordered on an emergency search for the yacht *Curlew* which was in a race from New London to Bermuda. No N2Ys were on board so search patterns were of the type that had been used for years. The yacht was not found and Akron returned to base. Later the yacht was discovered in port.

The next day Akron was finally scheduled for a training flight. She departed at 7:40 a.m. followed by the unit's six N2Ys. By the end of the day, the Unit's planes had made 54 hookups with all six pilots having qualified.

The pilots returned to Lakehurst in 3 sections, and about 20 miles out, joined in a six-plane step-down parade position. They dressed it up beautifully and looked professional. It was a beautiful break and landing for all six planes. After taxiing off the duty runway, they closed the interval between aircraft and looked sharp taxiing into the chocks. Duane was proud of all his pilots.

On the 20th of July, Admiral McMillin flew to Lakehurst to take a flight on the Akron. Akron launched just before sunset and headed out to sea for training and testing the water separators. The next morning the 6 N2Ys rendezvoused with Akron made some hookups before requiring returning to base due to low fuel state and bad weather. Walt was scheduled to stay aboard and bring Admiral McMillin back to Lakehurst, but the Admiral thought the weather would be too rough enroute to Lakehurst, so he told Walt to proceed back to base with the others.

After Walt left, the weather worsened and thunderstorms appeared in every quadrant. Lightning was everywhere and the Akron's Commanding Officer first headed East but the weather appeared worse in that direction, so he then headed West and the weather was just as bad in that direction, so he headed Southeast. At this point, the rudder operator reported his lower rudder inoperative and the airship was headed nose down. The elevator operator applied up elevator to no avail. The commanding officer ordered emergency release of the forward ballast. 1600 pounds of water were released with still no effect. Lieutenant (JG) McMasters went aft to help the elevator operator. When he arrived, he tried to assist him, but the cable on the elevator snapped, and the turbulence was severe.

At this point, the stern of the airship hit the water and the airship disintegrated. It first broke in half and the control car was swamped with water. The ocean was boiling with high winds and waves. The men of Akron did everything they could but to no avail. Eventually, all but three of the crew were lost at sea.

The next morning a search was conducted for Akron. Bits and pieces along with a few bodies were recovered but the three survivors were rescued.

Word reached the men back at the base. Duane called the unit together for an emergency meeting. He passed the preliminary report of the loss of the Akron with all but three of the crew aboard to his men.

Walt took this loss extremely hard as Admiral McMillin had been a great boss and mentor to his career.

The base was in mourning from the loss of all those crewmen of the Akron. A memorial service was held at the base chapel. It was a solemn occasion with many journalists from around the country attending. The loss of Akron was a huge story in the media and of course, the Heavier-than-Air Unit personnel were the only remaining personnel from the Akron cadre. They were contacted by many news outlets for comments and interviews. Duane and Walt handled all these requests, as they were the most qualified to do this.

There were many repercussions to the loss of Akron. Many of those crewmen lost were slated to man the new dirigible, USS Macon. This put

Unit personnel first in line to be selected to replace them. Everyone was in limbo and would just need to wait out the selection process.

Two weeks after the accident, all hands including the Unit were awarded the Air Medal for their great work on bringing Akron to the point in the development of a flying aircraft carrier.

Duane and Walt were jointly honored as the recipients of the National Air Trophy sponsored by the Cliff Harmon family.

Walt and Duane managed orders to the Stearman Aircraft Facility in Wichita in the Naval Liaison Office where, upon arrival, Walt and Zimmy planned their wedding, while Jane and Duane announced their engagement.

Paul Day received orders to assume command as O-in-C of the Heavier-Than-Air Unit with Bob Fitzwater as his deputy.

Epilogue

The men on the flying trapeze left their mark on Naval Aviation. Only 20 men ever made a hookup to an airship. These men went on to serve their country and add to the annals of Naval Aviation.

Lieutenant Walt Pellman, USN, went on to become the Commanding Officer of Fighter Squadron Five followed by promotion, when WWII started, to Captain where he commanded the aircraft carrier USS Lexington. He married Lisa Zimmerman and had four children.

Lieutenant Duane Harrison, USN, commanded Scouting Squadron 12 and later was promoted to Captain and commanded the aircraft carrier USS Saratoga. He married Jane Moorhead and had three children.

Lieutenant Paul Day, USN, was promoted to Captain and commanded Naval Air Station Ford Island and sadly was killed on December 7th, 1941 when the Japanese attacked Pearl Harbor.

Lieutenant Robert Fitzwater, USN, commanded Fighter Squadron Five Alpha then Commander Carrier Air Group 3, and when WWII started, was promoted to Captain and commanded the aircraft carrier USS Ranger. He married Ethel Martin and had seven children.